'It was original, beautiful, moving and insanely addictive – I wept and I laughed and I will be recommending it to everyone I know.'

Katie Marsh, author of *My Everything*

'I found *The After Wife* thought-provoking, compelling and strangely real – I loved it. And it kept me reading into the early hours several nights in row!

Isabel Ashdown

'The healing power of love transcends death – this was such a beautifully written, emotionally compelling book. I loved it.'

Rachael Lucas

'Absorbing, moving and insightful. A compelling vision of what we all stand to gain (and lose) from the rise of the robots.'

Ann Morgan

'A wonderful, moving novel about family, love, and loss – and how we can often find in the past what we need in the present. I adored this book – it's fresh, beautiful, profound and at times funny, it made me cry, but also made me smile.'

Sue Watson

'An original moving story about what it means to be human . . . and what it means to truly love. All the feels!'

Tracy Buchanan

'A story of love, loss and the future; it'll bamboozle and confound you in the best of ways.'

*Emerald Street*

'Whatever our future brings, *The After Wife* shows us that the human heart never needs an upgrade.'

David Barnett, author of *Calling Major Tom*

# The *After* Wife

Cass Hunter was born in South Africa and moved to the UK in 2000. She lives in North London with her husband and two sons. She is an avid lifelong learner, and works at a London university. Cass Hunter is the pen name of Rosie Fiore, whose novels include *After Isabella*, *What She Left*, *Babies in Waiting* and *Wonder Women*.

# The
# *After* Wife

## Cass Hunter

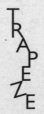

An Orion Paperback

First published in Great Britain in 2018 by Orion Books,
an imprint of The Orion Publishing Group Ltd
Carmelite House, 50 Victoria Embankment,
London EC4Y 0DZ

An Hachette UK company

1 3 5 7 9 10 8 6 4 2

A CIP catalogue record for this book is
available from the British Library.

ISBN (Mass Market Paperback) 978 1 4091 7264 2

Typeset by Input Data Services Ltd, Somerset

Printed in Great Britain by Clays Ltd, Elcograf S.p.A.

MIX
Paper from
responsible sources
FSC® C104740

www.orionbooks.co.uk

For Caroline Hardman
An agent in a million
Thank you for believing in me

**Telos:**

from the Ancient Greek τέλος:
an end, purpose or goal.

Fulfilment.

The belief that everything in nature
(specifically a person)
has a potential it can reach when it is most 'itself'.

# Telos Robotics

finding fulfilment in the service of humankind.

# I

# The Lab

'One step closer,' Rachel commanded.

Luke sighed and moved nearer. He was now standing directly across the desk.

Rachel paused as she made a small adjustment. 'Okay. Ready.'

'What do you want me to do?'

'Make eye contact, for a start.'

Luke raised his head. His eyes were deep blue and fringed with thick, dark lashes. 'Eye contact established. What now?'

'I need you to be feeling a powerful emotion. Something recognisable. So think of something that you feel strongly about. Don't say what it is.'

Luke's gaze flicked to Rachel's and then away again. She saw him draw a deep breath and then narrow his eyes in concentration. He stared, with electric intensity. Rachel observed him closely. He seemed to have forgotten to breathe. She saw his eyes flare. His pupils widened visibly and she heard a change in his breathing. His hands tightened into fists.

'What do you see?' she said.

The voice beside her was low and quiet. 'Pupil dilation, respiration shortened and more rapid, up to twenty breaths per minute, heart rate increased by—'

'Luke's wristband is picking up his vital statistics and I can read them on my screen,' Rachel said impatiently. 'Tell me what he's feeling. What do you sense?'

There was a long silence before the figure at Rachel's side spoke again. 'He is focused. Not agitated, but concentrating very hard.'

'Good,' said Rachel. 'Keep going.'

'He is frowning. His temperature is steady, and I see no signs of anger. I don't believe I have made him angry.'

'Not yet,' said Luke.

'He said "not yet" as if it were a warning, but I detect a smile. Was that a joke?'

'As close to a joke as you'll ever get from Luke,' said Rachel.

'Is this going to take long?' said Luke.

'I think I have it!' The voice was excited. 'He is impatient because we are taking up his time.'

'Impatient,' said Rachel. 'Was that it, Luke? Was that the emotion you were expressing?'

Luke laughed and visibly relaxed. 'I would have said irritated. But, yeah, impatient is close enough. Can we stop now?'

'Don't be a spoilsport,' said Rachel. 'It's going so well. Just a few minutes more . . .' She checked her watch. 'Oh no! Look at the time. I must get away on time today – it's our anniversary. Eighteen years. Can you believe it?'

'I can,' said Luke drily.

'Aidan's booked us in for dinner at the Old Saxon. I was so thrilled when he told me. You can't get a table there for love or money. He must have organised it months ago.' Her smile was wide with excitement.

'Sounds like fun,' said Luke. 'Happy anniversary.'

'Thanks.'

Rachel stood up from her chair and stretched. The last rays of sunlight slanted in through the windows, dappling the teetering stacks of paper on her chaotic desk. She moved over to the window and looked out at the smooth lawns which surrounded the laboratory building. It had been a beautiful spring day and it promised to be a lovely evening. She imagined holding Aidan's hand across the restaurant table, sipping a cool glass of wine. She would put work out of her mind for once and relax. Yes, there was a tiny glitch she'd spotted in the experiment, and she'd have liked the time to run the sequence one more time and solve it, but not now. Now was the time to switch off.

She looked over to Luke's side of the lab. He had crossed to one of his workbenches and was recording some data on a clipboard in his small, meticulous handwriting. She made fun of him for writing things out by hand before he entered the information into his computer, but he was insistent.

'I like to form things manually,' he'd say when challenged. 'If it doesn't exist physically, it isn't real to me.'

She laughed at that – she could make mountains move and galaxies whirl with the keystrokes of her computer and that was as real as any column of handwritten figures. But Luke was adamant. 'I think with my hands,' he'd repeat insistently. And he did. She had never worked with such a fine mechanical engineer. If she could conceive of something, Luke could build it. His obsessive attention to detail equalled her own, and his creativity was boundless.

When she'd joined Telos she'd imagined she would be working in a large team. But the organisation's policy was to pair scientists with complementary skills. They held excruciating meet-and-greet induction events to matchmake researchers.

Luke, who had joined at the same time as Rachel, had refused to participate in the speed-dating event. He'd sat alone at a table, working on his laptop, not talking to anyone. Passing behind him on her way to get coffee, Rachel had glimpsed a 3D diagram of a human hand. He was trying to model the motion of a finger and thumb pinching together. But there was an error somewhere and the movement had a judder which he couldn't seem to remove. Rachel could sense his frustration, but his squared shoulders and fierce demeanour made her nervous to talk to him. She glanced around for something to write on and, finding nothing, took the sticky nametag label off her lab coat. 'Try this:' she wrote on it, and scribbled a few lines of code. She stuck the label to the table next to his clenched left fist and walked away.

Half an hour later, she was deep in conversation with a behavioural psychologist when Luke appeared and loomed over them. Her companion stopped speaking and looked up. Luke was holding his laptop. He spun it around so they could see the screen. The finger and thumb closed in a smooth, even motion.

'I'll work with you,' he said abruptly.

Now, three years, countless arguments and some of the most fruitful research of her career later, Luke looked up and saw her watching him. He raised his eyebrows inquiringly.

'One more go?' he asked.

She shook her head. 'I really had better get moving or I'll be late.' She took her mobile phone out of her lab-coat pocket to text her daughter.

> R  Hi honey. I left a pizza in the fridge for you. How's chemistry?

Chloe's reply was instant.

> C  Yeah cool. Thanks for pizza. Good. Just designing my study plan.

> R  'Designing'? Does that mean chatting to Amy on Snapchat?

> C  Snapchat? Ooh, get you, Mum, down with the kids with your social-media terms.

> R  I think you'll find that's 'Down wit teh kidz'.

Chloe replied with a little image of a face, its eyes raised heavenwards.

R What does that mean?

    C Eye-roll emoji. Lame Mum-joke.

Chloe added a face whose spectacles and grey hair in a bun suggested a pensioner.

Rachel laughed and went over to Luke's desk to show the image to him. 'This is how my daughter sees me,' she said.

'I see a certain resemblance.'

'I get enough lip from her already, thank you. Aidan says she's fifteen going on thirty-five. It's my own fault, of course. I wanted a strong-willed daughter who could stand up for herself. I didn't really think that through.'

Rachel imagined Chloe sitting cross-legged on her bed, her thumbs flying across the phone screen faster than she could speak, her long hair, so like Rachel's own, falling to her shoulders like spun sugar. Her smile was more like Aidan's, with a sardonic twist at the corners. Rachel felt a sudden swell of love.

R Cheeky (fierce mum-face emoji). I'm late to meet
Dad. Got to go. Love you.

    C Happy anniversary, you crazy lovebirds. Have fun.

Rachel pocketed her phone, logged out of her computer and headed to the cloakroom to collect her things. The room seemed empty without her. But then the voice spoke again, making Luke jump a little. He'd forgotten he was not alone.

'Have we concluded our work for the day?'

'It would appear so. Why?' said Luke.

'I sense a change in you. When Rachel checked her watch just now, your vital signs became more agitated. Were you responding to her announcement that she needed to leave on time to get to her anniversary dinner?'

'Hardly,' Luke said, and laughed.

'Heightened colour in the face often signifies embarrassment or emotional stress,' said the voice.

'Who has heightened colour?'

'You do. And your heart rate is beginning to speed up again, which is a sign of—'

Luke abruptly unbuckled the wristband which transmitted his physiological signs and tossed it among the chaos of Rachel's desk.

'You may choose not to participate further in the experiment, but the recorded data is incontrovertible. May I remind you that I registered your emotional upheaval?'

'May I remind you that I know where your off button is?' said Luke.

'I don't have an off button.'

'I built your circuitry, so I know exactly which wire to snip.'

'Another joke?'

'I don't make jokes. You should know that by now.'

Rachel came back into the room. She had shed her white lab coat and was wearing an emerald-green dress which reflected the unusual colour of her eyes. She had brushed out her long blonde hair.

'Your ensemble is aesthetically pleasing,' said the voice.

'Thanks,' said Rachel offhandedly. 'Bye, Luke, I'll see you tomorrow.' She waved to him as she picked up her coat and headed for the door. 'Can you put it in rest mode and onto charge?'

'Sure. And by the way, you do look—' he began, but Rachel was already gone. He sighed. He expected the voice to comment, but it was silent. As he moved around the room, tidying up and wrapping up for the day, he caught a trace of Rachel's perfume in the air. Almost as soon as he recognised it, it was gone. Like Rachel herself, it seemed to slip away from him.

# 2

# Aidan

Rachel was late. No, thought Aidan. That wasn't quite right. She was halfway late. It was fifteen minutes after the time they'd arranged to meet but still fifteen minutes before the time he could realistically expect her to arrive.

He'd arrived at the restaurant on the dot of seven and settled himself at a table by the window, with a view of the River Cam. He'd ordered a bottle of their favourite Sauvignon Blanc and a basket of bread. Sipping his wine, he gazed out at the tourists and students as they ambled along the towpath. Maybe he and Rachel could go for a stroll after dinner? It was a long time since they'd had time to walk aimlessly, holding hands, chatting. He'd like that.

He pulled his phone towards him. No message from her. He wasn't surprised. She moved too fast to stop and send a text. 'I'll be there a minute sooner if I just come rather than stopping to tell you I'm on my way,' she reasoned.

There was, however, a text from his boss, Fiona.

Can you get in a bit early to open up tomorrow morning, Aid? Need to do some work on the accounts and it's quieter at home.

*No prob*, he fired back. He liked Fiona and was happy to help her out.

Fiona was posh – the sort of person he'd never encountered when he was growing up. Yet she was one of the kindest, most generous people he had ever met. She had started Foothold, a non-profit organisation, fifteen years before, using her expertise

7

as a recruitment consultant to help people who had been out of work for a long time gain skills and confidence. She'd built the team organically, as she'd discovered what help people might need. Her first hire had been Lola, an energetic, bright-eyed actor who worked with the clients on interview and presentation skills. Thomas, a gentle, introverted writer, helped them to develop and refine CVs and write compelling covering letters. Aidan had come on board to teach clients about computers — some of them had never sent an email or accessed the internet, others wanted to gain a concrete skill such as data entry or basic web design. Fiona's most recent hire was Kate, an occupational psychologist. Over time they'd come to realise that the burden of unemployment sometimes affected people's mental health. Kate was there to work with them, build their self-esteem and get them professional assistance if they needed it.

Foothold was a good place to work. Sometimes it could be difficult and frustrating and clients could take one step forward and then two steps back, but Aidan loved it. He felt he was making a difference. It wasn't glamorous or well paid, and there was no scope for promotion, but the job was enough for him.

He and Rachel had started in the same place — in fact in exactly the same place — meeting on the first day of their undergraduate degree course in computer science. Within a very few days he'd realised that Rachel outshone him in every way. Rachel graduated with a first and the best results of their year, by a mile. They took a year off to travel, and then she was accepted for a postgraduate study at Cambridge, followed by a PhD. Aidan earned his own modest 2:2 and looked for the kind of job that would pay the bills, first in London and then up in Cambridge when it became clear Rachel would be there for some years. Marriage followed, then Chloe . . . and suddenly, here they were eighteen years later. And here he was, waiting for his wife once again.

Rachel crossed the restaurant to join him, moving so fast her hair lifted behind her like a streak of light. He barely registered the eyes that turned towards her as she passed. With her slender limbs, bright eyes and crackling energy, she often got a reaction, from women as well as men. He still felt a little prickle of excitement when he saw her, a mixture of love, desire, anticipation and exasperation. She came into his arms and they kissed.

'Sorry,' she said.

'No worries.' He drew her chair out for her.

She sat down and instantly took a piece of bread from the basket. 'I'm starving,' she said, biting off a chunk.

'I thought you might be. No breakfast or lunch again?'

She shook her head, still chewing. 'Problem in the heart-rate software. The sensors are too sensitive, if you can imagine such a thing. My readings were all over the place, and then I realised someone was cutting the lawn outside and I was picking up the vibrations from the mower.'

She kept talking, explaining the details of her experiment, tearing bits off the bread and eating it hungrily. Aidan was content to sit and listen, sipping his wine and watching the sunlight in her hair.

After a few minutes she broke off, reached across the table and took his hand. 'Happy anniversary, handsome husband.'

'Happy anniversary, beautiful wife. Was Chloe okay?'

'Fine. Well, she said she was "designing her study plan". She told us to have fun.'

'That's nice.'

Rachel let out a sigh. 'I'm not sure she understands how important these exams are.'

'Are they though? Year Ten exams? It's not like it's her GCSE year . . .'

'What about her predicted grades? If she's going to go to

Cambridge . . .' Rachel stopped short, staring at Aidan's expression. 'She is still talking about Cambridge, isn't she?'

'She said something the other day about a gap year . . .'

Rachel leaned back in her chair and folded her arms.

'What?' said Aidan defensively.

'Typical. She would talk to you about that. She knows perfectly well I would never fall for it.'

'Why is it such a bad idea for her to take a year and maybe do some travelling? We did it.'

'*After* university.'

'So? She doesn't need to dive straight from A levels into massive academic pressure at university. There's no rush.'

'No rush?' Rachel looked at him like he was crazy.

'She doesn't even know what she wants to study yet. Give her some time.' Aidan reached over and took her hand again. 'Hey,' he said gently, 'can we leave this for now? Chloe going to uni is still years away, for a start. And secondly, how often do I get a night out with my hot wife?'

She smiled at him and squeezed his hand. 'You're right. Of course. But Chloe's so smart, I just want to see her reach her full potential.'

'And she will. She may just take a slightly different path to yours, that's all.'

Rachel narrowed her eyes at him. 'Next thing you'll be recommending I try a little mindfulness.'

'Next thing I'll be recommending you try a little pumpkin ravioli. It's delicious here.'

She leaned across the table and kissed him sweetly and deeply. 'Pumpkin ravioli, Mr Sawyer? You've got all the sexy talk.'

'Wait till I tell you about the chocolate ganache brownies, Dr Prosper,' he said, murmuring against her soft lips. 'You'll be entirely at my mercy.'

'Oh no,' she breathed, 'whatever will I do?'

# 3

# Rachel

Twenty-four hours later, Rachel checked her watch. Somehow it was six-thirty again. Where had the day gone? Luke had set off for Oxfordshire at noon to meet with a supplier, leaving her alone in the lab, and she had not looked up from her screen since two.

Aidan would have dinner ready at home for seven and she wasn't going to be there unless she hurried. She looked back at the screen, but the letters and numbers danced before her eyes. She must be very tired. The screen looked decidedly blurred and there was a sharp pain just above her left eye.

She logged off her computer and stood. The room swayed and bent around her and she felt the pain stab again. It was all catching up with her. She gathered her bag and keys and walked out to her car.

She was the last to leave the building – the only other person still on the premises was Errol, the security guard at the main gate. Her car was baking hot from having sat in the sun all day and she felt a lurch of nausea. Maybe it was more than tiredness. Maybe she was coming down with something? She started the car and cranked up the air conditioning. She waved goodbye to Errol as she pulled out onto the main road. A quarter to seven. If she drove fast along the winding country lane, she'd be home by ten past.

But as she drove, the nausea came in waves. The pain migrated from above her eye, around the side of her head, and became a growing ache in the base of her skull and neck.

It couldn't be . . . ? No, of course not. That was a ridiculous thought; her deepest, darkest fear. Rachel pushed it away. She put her foot down and drove a little faster. She just needed to get home.

As she swung around the tight bend, the tree loomed ahead of her, its trunk wide and straight and strong. It was beautiful. There were so many shades of green in its spring foliage, from neon brightness to something deeper, was it called hunting green? So many greens and she didn't have names for them all. She knew she should turn the wheel, should move her foot onto the brake. But somehow no messages were reaching her body. Her mind was filled with green. Just green. Then black, then a grinding, roaring crash. Then silence.

# 4
## Aidan

Rachel Prosper was born in Maidstone in Kent, late of Swavesey in
Cambridgeshire...

Rachel, beloved late daughter of the late Maureen and Peter, wife to
Aidan, mum to Chloe...

My wife is late.

Seven days ago – last Wednesday – it was our wedding
anniversary. We met for dinner.

She was late. She's always late, mainly because she's the eternal
optimist. She always thinks she can cram more into the allotted
minutes of the day than is physically possible. She was hungry too, so
she ate and talked, and I looked at her, glowing with excitement as she
chatted about work, and I thought about taking her into my arms.

Then we shared a portion of chocolate brownie, and Rachel told me
to have the last bite, because she needs to watch what she eats these
days.

We walked beside the river and held hands, and we were quiet,
because when you've been together for eighteen years and you're going
to be together for another fifty, there's all the time in the world to talk.
We discussed having a weekend away together, once Rachel's work had
slowed down a bit. I knew perfectly well that would never happen, but
it was nice to imagine it might.

And then we went home and made love and lay in the dark holding
hands. I tried to stay awake and chat, but I was so tired. She held me
close and stroked my face, and she said, 'Come on, honey, you're so

tired. Lie on your side, twenty deep breaths and let the worries float away.'

When I woke up an hour or so later, I could see her sitting at her desk in the corner of our bedroom, working quietly. Her profile was sharp in the light of the computer and I was going to tell her she was beautiful, but I was sleepy and I dozed off again, and when I woke up in the morning, she'd already gone to work. I thought I'd text her later and tell her, but I never did.

Six days ago Rachel got into her car to come home, but she never arrived.

When I saw her again, she was lying on a narrow stainless-steel table, her body covered with a sheet. Her face was bruised and grey, and the room was unbearably, crushingly silent.

'That's my wife,' I said to the man who stood beside me. 'That's Rachel.' But of course it wasn't. Rachel's never been still in her life. Whatever that was on the table, it wasn't the woman I love.

I can't do this. It's just wrong. Absurd. How can I be writing a eulogy for my wife? She's forty-two years old, for God's sake. I'm only forty-one. I was supposed to write her eulogy when I was ninety. Actually, she was supposed to write mine, because men almost always die first, don't they? Or, more likely, neither of us would write anything because Chloe would do it, or one of our brood of grandchildren. That's how it was supposed to be.

How can I be doing this now? Today? It makes no sense. But here I am, sitting at my dining-room table, trying to put words on a piece of paper because tomorrow I have to stand up at the crematorium and say something about my wife.

My late wife.

Not late because she's got caught up in an experiment, or lost herself in a book, or become engrossed in a conversation, or for any of the myriad reasons that made her the brilliant, fiery, energetic force she was, but late because she's late.

Gone.

In the past.

And somehow I have to live in a world where Rachel is not. I have to go back through these words I have written here and change 'is' to 'was'. And then I have to go forward, into a life where Rachel is no longer by my side. And I don't know how to do that. I just don't know.

# 5
## Chloe

Chloe mounted the steps to the lectern, gripping her sheet of paper tightly. She had wanted to speak at the funeral, had insisted on it, even when her dad hadn't been sure. She'd been so certain it was the right thing to do — for her mum, for her dad, to show everyone she was okay. Now that she was here, in front of all these people, she wanted to run away. What if she tripped? Or stumbled over her words? Or cried? Or didn't cry?

The chapel was full. People were wedged into every pew, shoulder to shoulder, and more were standing in the doorway and along the back wall. It was the biggest room at the crematorium, high-ceilinged and light with big windows and pale-wood panelling.

As Chloe placed her piece of paper on the lectern, she looked out over the crowd. Her dad was sitting in the right-hand front pew, his shoulders hunched, his hands clasped tightly together, his head bowed. She could see the deep crease of a frown between his eyebrows. His hair was rumpled and his face looked wrong to her, as it had since her mum had died — as if the skin was too loose on his bones — but he wasn't crying. He was, as she knew too well, all cried out. Until she had had to stand up, he'd been clutching her hand tightly, almost bruising it. His mother, Chloe's Grandma Sinead, was sitting beside him, her back straight, her eyes fixed fiercely on Chloe. Behind them were family members — no one close, because Rachel had been an only child and both her parents were dead. Nevertheless, there were cousins and aunties, only some of whom Chloe vaguely recognised. One portly middle-aged lady sniffed continuously, dabbing her eyes with a tissue and shaking her head as if she couldn't grasp the magnitude of the tragedy. Chloe had never seen her before.

Behind 'the family' there were rows and rows of Rachel's work colleagues – academics, computer nerds and intellectuals. Some were wearing suits, some were dressed in scruffy heavy-metal T-shirts and jeans, as if they had no idea how to dress or behave in public, or had never been to a funeral before. They spent their lives studying humans but only so they could make artificial ones, and they looked deeply uncomfortable. She spotted Bea, the administrator from her mum's department, a brisk, warm and funny woman who always remembered Chloe's birthday and sent cards and presents. She looked genuinely devastated, as did her mum's university friends, Sam and Laura, who were wedged in at the end of a row of scientists. Laura held her newborn baby close to her chest. They lived down in London and Chloe's mum had been trying to make time to go down and see them and meet the baby. Now she never would. She had loved babies, and for a second Chloe imagined her mum lifting Sam and Laura's little one and smiling. It almost undid her.

The left-hand side of the chapel was packed with Chloe's friends and their families, some of her teachers from school, acquaintances from their village and more of her parents' friends. She saw her best friends, Amy and Jess, and their faces gave her strength. Her dad's work colleagues formed their own group in the back pews; they had closed their office today to come and support him. Chloe guessed that the scruffy trio of young guys standing uneasily by the door might well be clients of his.

Just behind them she glimpsed a square head with close-cropped, greying hair. Luke, the mechanical engineer her mum worked with, was standing right at the back, hands jammed in his jeans pockets, head down. Why wasn't he sitting with all the other people from Telos? He was a strange man. She had met him a few times, but he never seemed able to look her in the eye. She knew her dad didn't like him, but her mum had always been loyal to Luke.

'He's outstanding at his work,' she'd said.

'He's rude,' her dad had countered.

'He's brilliant enough to excuse rudeness.'

'No one's that brilliant,' her dad had muttered under his breath.

What would her dad make of Luke's lurking at the back of the church? Chloe wondered. Her mum wasn't here to defend his behaviour now.

She was suddenly aware that she'd been frozen at the lectern for some time, looking out at the faces, which were staring at her expectantly. She took a breath. She wasn't afraid any more. Her voice rang out over the packed room, clear, unwavering and strong:

> *'Soft you; a word or two before you go.*
> *I have done the state some service, and they know't.*
> *No more of that. I pray you, in your letters,*
> *When you shall these unlucky deeds relate,*
> *Speak of me as I am; nothing extenuate,*
> *Nor set down aught in malice: then must you speak*
> *Of one that loved not wisely but too well.'*

# 6

## Aidan

A murmur passed around the crematorium chapel. The verse from Shakespeare was a perfect choice. Aidan's heart ached with pride as he looked up at his daughter. Then she walked stiffly back to her seat, trying to look in control, and slipped in next to him. He hoped she would put her hand back in his, but she didn't. She drew her elbows in close to her sides and sat very still, watching the minister. He was preparing to push the button and make Rachel's coffin slide away behind the curtains. Even though they weren't touching, Aidan thought he could feel Chloe trembling. Or was it him?

He felt rage building in his chest. How could this be happening to his daughter? Why should she have to suffer like this?

When Chloe was born, following a long, difficult labour, she'd been exhausted and had slept, her eyes shut tightly against the light. The staff were concerned that she hadn't eaten yet. 'I'll just do a little heel prick,' said a brisk nursing sister, 'check her blood sugar levels,' and she'd unwrapped Chloe and grasped her tiny foot. Before Rachel or Aidan could say anything, she'd jabbed Chloe's silky little heel with a needle, causing a bead of blood to well up. Chloe woke and wailed, and Aidan, snatching up his newborn daughter, had wept, unable to bear the fact that someone had inflicted pain on her. I will protect you, he'd promised her fiercely. I will protect you from all harm and hurt.

And oh, how he had failed.

When he'd seen the sweep of blue lights as the police car turned into their driveway, he had known instantly what it meant. And his very first thought was . . . Chloe. This will define her for the rest of her life. She will forever be the girl whose mum died when she was fifteen. It will mark her. Change her. And I can't fix it. I can't make it go away. I cannot protect her from this.

After the funeral, everyone went back to the house. People – mothers from Chloe's school – had catered. The dining room table was pushed back against a wall and laden with finger food, and they had turned the dresser into a bar covered in wine-glasses and teacups. (Did they really own so many teacups? Aidan wondered. Where had they been all these years?) Someone put a glass in his hand and tried to press a plate of food on him, but he refused.

He wandered from room to room, between knots of people talking, but he found their stares and murmurs disconcerting. He went into the kitchen, hoping for a moment's peace, but it was full of women, all moving with certainty, deftly transferring warm canapés from oven trays onto serving platters. He didn't recognise any of them, except for Tracy Lucas, mother of Chloe's best friend, Amy. He suspected she was the driving force behind the catering and organisation. She was the welfare nurse at the junior school which Chloe and Amy had attended, but she had started out as a dinner lady and so was proficient at feeding large numbers of people. Tracy was at the sink, the sleeves of her black funeral dress rolled up, her arms plunged into the suds, washing and stacking glasses and cups with alarming speed. She glanced over her shoulder, saw him and quickly pulled her hands out of the water, wiping them on a dishcloth she'd tucked into her belt. She bustled over and hugged him.

'Aidan,' she said, squeezing him tightly, as if the firmness of her hug could convey more comfort.

'Thank you,' he said, waving helplessly, 'for all this.'

'Oh, for heaven's sake, it's nothing,' she said, and stepped back. She cast an eye over the kitchen. A few of the other women were looking at him warily.

'I'm so sorry, Aidan,' said a tall blonde woman he didn't recognise. She hesitated, and then came over to pat his arm awkwardly. He hadn't minded Tracy's hug – they'd known each other for more than a decade. But this woman's tentative gesture made him flinch. He felt as if his flesh was raw, as if someone had peeled his skin off, leaving his muscles and nerves exposed. Tracy was watching him closely. He'd have quite liked to talk to her. She was very warm and often funny, and she'd known Rachel well. The woman kept prattling on, as if she was afraid to let a silence in.

'She was so young,' she said, 'and of course you are too. You've got your whole life in front of you! Who knows . . .'

Seeing Aidan's face, she stopped.

'Were you about to make a "plenty more fish in the sea" comment?' he asked. To his surprise, his voice was low and dangerous.

'No, of course not!' she said hurriedly. 'I just meant—'

He didn't wait to find out what she meant. He turned and walked out of the kitchen.

Back in the living room, he was aware once more of the eyes on him. He was used to being in the background, watching a room revolve around Rachel. This scrutiny made him deeply uncomfortable. He spotted his work colleagues, who had commandeered a sofa and were huddled together. He went over and perched on the arm of the sofa, beside Fiona. She patted his knee but kept on talking. They were discussing a film some of them had seen. Aidan let out a long, slow breath. His colleagues continued to chat among themselves, not ignoring him but not forcing him to join in with the conversation. For a single, precious moment he could pretend it was an ordinary working day and that he wasn't sitting on the arm of his own sofa, at his wife's wake.

But of course it couldn't last. Rachel's Aunt Felicity had seen him. He'd heard her ostentatiously sniffing and weeping through the service but had managed to avoid talking to her. She wasn't even Rachel's real aunt – she was a cousin of Rachel's mother. He'd only met her a handful of times in all the years they'd been together. She lived in Essex and bred Yorkshire terriers, and Rachel had had nothing in common with her whatsoever. She did love a good funeral though – Aidan remembered her weeping just as dramatically at Rachel's mother Maureen's send-off, even though Rachel's mother had frequently referred to Felicity as 'that crashing bore'. He knew she would come up to him any moment now and make this all about her, and he'd end up having to comfort her. For God's sake.

Rachel had been Maureen and Peter's only child, a late gift to a pair of clever academics. She was born when Maureen was in her late thirties and Peter a decade older. Both had doted on her and given her love and affection and the best education they could afford. Sadly, they'd both died when Rachel was still studying. First Peter, of cancer, then Maureen a year later, very suddenly of a brain aneurysm. An artery in her brain had developed a weakness. She'd suffered a few headaches and dizzy spells and had considered going to the doctor's but hadn't yet made the appointment. She was busy gardening, her greatest joy, when she blacked out. She was found some hours later by a neighbour and she never woke up.

It was a terrible shock. Maureen had appeared fit and young for her age and Rachel had anticipated having her around for many more years. The aneurysm had snatched her away.

'Is it hereditary?' Aidan had asked at the time.

'I don't think so,' Rachel said. 'I'll do some research.' She had never mentioned it again, so Aidan had never followed it up.

It was hereditary, it turned out. It hadn't just been a car

accident. The police had been baffled at first, that Rachel had crashed on an easy bend she had navigated thousands of times before, in perfect weather conditions. They'd quickly ascertained that there was no mechanical fault with the car either. But the post-mortem had solved the mystery – a sudden and catastrophic bleed on the brain. She had probably felt unwell minutes before, but when the aneurysm burst, she must have blacked out suddenly. Had she known? Had she been afraid? Had it hurt? He would never know.

Aidan was nowhere near being able to deal with it. And he definitely couldn't deal with Aunt Felicity bearing down on him like a juggernaut. He knew she would want to hug him and then pin him against the wall, bombard him with clichés about the 'great tragedy' and tell him how Rachel had been 'taken in her prime' and what a 'poor wee mite' Chloe was. He couldn't stand it. She was momentarily slowed by a knot of people, and Aidan saw his chance. He snatched up his glass, slipped away from his workmates and dodged out of the open front door and onto the veranda that ran along the front of the house. Once he was outside, he checked cautiously over his shoulder. Felicity was looking around, confused. She'd clearly missed his escape and wouldn't be following him out here. He exhaled, a long sigh. He hadn't realised he'd been holding his breath.

The veranda was a long, very un-English sweep of wooden floorboards and quaintly turned railings. When they had first viewed the property, Rachel had loved it. 'It's a porch!' she'd said, affecting a terrible American accent. 'We can get a swing and watch the neighbourhood kiddies mosey on by.'

They never did get a porch swing. For most of the year it was too cold and damp to sit outside, so Aidan had bought sturdy wooden patio chairs which would withstand the weather instead. He'd had it in mind to buy Rachel a swing as an anniversary present one year, but he hadn't got round to it. Another regret. Just like the weekend away he'd been thinking of organising, and his unspoken dream that when Chloe went to uni, they might go travelling again. So many things they'd never get to do now.

His mother, Sinead, was sitting by herself out on the porch, perched on the bare wooden slats of one of the patio chairs.

'You can't be very comfortable there, Mum,' he said, coming up behind her. 'Can I get you a cushion?'

'Hmmm?' She glanced up at him. She didn't answer the question, just indicated the chair beside her.

She'd been a beautiful woman and was still striking. She was tall, with strong features, and she wore her iron-grey hair drawn back from her face in a low bun. She'd lost weight recently, and there was a new hunch to her shoulders and a curve at the top of her spine. She was getting older.

Aidan sank into the chair beside her and sat in silence. It was an immense relief not to have to talk. His parents had divorced when he and his brother Oliver were children. His dad had headed off to live in New Zealand, and they'd had only the most sporadic contact since. Sinead had seemed to take this in her stride. She was a tough, independent woman, who'd been alone for many decades. She didn't know how to depend on people. She loved Aidan and was distantly but firmly fond of Chloe. She wasn't one for hugs or cakes or games, but she remembered every important date in Chloe's life and always rang her after an exam or at the end of term to check up on her. Her relationship with Rachel had been more difficult.

Sinead was staring out at the big magnolia tree on the lawn.

'No blooms,' she said conversationally.

'No,' said Aidan. 'Spring was too late and too cold, I think. We had a few, but they didn't last.'

His mum was good like this. Easy small talk when big talk

was too difficult. Was that it? Or was she just afraid of emotional expression? He'd never quite been able to work it out.

'Next year,' said Sinead with quiet confidence.

Next year. Aidan tried to imagine a next year. The magnolia usually bloomed for his and Rachel's wedding anniversary. When it flowered again, it would be for a different anniversary altogether, and the beauty of the waxy flowers would always be an agonising reminder of her absence.

Where would he be a year from now? Still felled by the tornado that had ripped his life apart in an instant? Or would he have 'moved on'? Would those 'plenty of fish' have materialised? Would he have learned to cope? Learned to smile and laugh again? Even thinking about a life in which such devastation was just a memory seemed disloyal to Rachel. The sheer wrongness of it drove him out of his chair and he stood up. Sinead glanced up, surprised.

'All right, love?'

He looked over at her. She seemed unnaturally calm considering it was the wake of her daughter-in-law. But then Sinead didn't go in for displays of emotion, as he knew too well from his childhood. He remembered the first time he had gone to a friend's house to play, and his friend's mum had enveloped her son in a hug, kissing him and squeezing him as if he had been gone for weeks, when in fact she had dropped him off at school just a few hours before. Aidan had stood by, baffled by the excess but even more confused by his friend, who had squirmed out of his mother's arms and run away. Sinead's love was limited to an occasional cool hand on the top of his head or a dry kiss on his cheek. What Aidan would have given for soft, enveloping hugs.

In the last year or so, she'd become even more closed off. She hardly ever rang them anymore, and when he phoned her, she seemed distracted and keen to get off the line. Perhaps, now Chloe was older, Sinead felt she had done her grandmotherly duty and could withdraw? He wouldn't put it past her.

A footstep on the gravel path drew his attention. He turned to see a stocky figure, head bowed, approaching the house, shoulders hunched in a black leather biker's jacket, hands jammed into trouser pockets.

Luke. Rachel's research partner.

Aidan had glimpsed him at the funeral, standing alone at the back, away from Rachel's other colleagues. Luke was not a joiner. Aidan had vaguely registered him slipping away from the chapel of rest as the funeral finished. He hadn't stayed to pay his respects to Aidan and Chloe, and Aidan had been secretly relieved to see him go. He hadn't felt up to dealing with Luke. In fact he never felt up to dealing with Luke. Rachel had been pretty much the only person who could stand him.

Aidan thought Luke was an arse. He'd first met him at a Telos Christmas party. In hindsight, he couldn't work out why Luke had come at all. He'd stood to one side of the room, not sitting down at a table or talking to anyone, and certainly not joining the crowd of awkwardly shuffling scientists on the dance floor. It looked to Aidan as if he'd come with the express purpose of sneering at everyone else. Rachel had dragged Aidan over to say hello, and Luke could barely manage two words of greeting; he seemed to look at Aidan as he looked at everyone except Rachel, with undisguised loathing.

'He's just shy,' she'd said as they walked away. 'He's actually fine, as long as he doesn't have to deal with real people.'

And yet here Luke was, at the wake – a sociable occasion at which he'd have to make polite small talk and express condolences. Unless he'd come to cause trouble or be rude, which was entirely possible.

'Luke,' Aidan said, and his voice sounded sharper than he meant it to. 'Thanks for coming.'

Luke looked up and seemed surprised to see Aidan standing there. He stopped, one foot on the bottom step.

'Come in,' Aidan found himself saying, and as Luke advanced reluctantly, 'This is my mother, Sinead Sawyer.'

Sinead watched Luke come closer, her face expressionless. She didn't stand up. Luke stopped in front of her chair. 'Hi,' he said, but didn't offer her his hand.

'Hello,' Sinead said. 'Who are you?'

'Luke Bourne, Rachel's partner.'

'Research partner,' Aidan heard himself saying. Jesus. What kind of an idiot was he? As if Sinead would think this guy was Rachel's boyfriend. Luke always brought out the pettiness in him. He did his best to pull himself together. Luke had been important to Rachel. He could be civil to him.

'Come inside,' he said, trying to make his voice pleasant and friendly. 'There's a ton of food, and tea, or beer, or whisky—'

'Is there somewhere we can talk?' Luke interrupted.

'What, now? Er . . .' He glanced over his shoulder, through the living room window. He could see a cluster of Rachel's work friends standing by the buffet table, a little lost and restless, as well as Aunt Felicity, who was clearly still looking for him. 'It's not an ideal time . . .'

'I see that,' said Luke coldly, as if it was somehow Aidan's fault. 'When is a good time?'

'Um . . .' Aidan didn't want a talk with Luke. He didn't want to talk to anyone. And if he was honest, if he had to choose from all the seven billion people on the planet for a one-to-one exchange, Luke would be in the bottom half-million for sure.

'Believe me,' said Luke abruptly, 'I don't want to either. But we have to. There's something I need to . . .' He stopped himself. 'Look, it's too difficult to explain here. It would be best if we just met at the lab. You'll need to come to Telos. Tomorrow?'

Aidan felt something snap inside him. 'For fuck's sake!' he barked, but as soon as the words were out, he looked back guiltily. Sinead was unfazed, but he saw heads turn inquiringly in the living room.

He walked over to Luke, took his elbow and marched him back down the front steps. Luke shrugged off his hand roughly – not, Aidan thought, because he was being aggressive, but because he clearly didn't like to be touched.

Luke's motorbike was parked at the end of their driveway, the helmet resting on the seat. Once they were near the bike, well out of earshot of Sinead and the house, Aidan exploded. 'Jesus Christ, Luke, this is my wife's wake. I just . . .' He couldn't bring himself to say 'saw my wife cremated'. Instead, he managed, 'I just got through the funeral. I don't want to talk to you. I don't want to come to the lab—'

He stopped suddenly, imagining having to drive down that road, the road where Rachel had died. He imagined having to pass the tree with its bark sheared off, the wood raw, exposed and weeping. He just couldn't do it.

He glanced over to Sinead, who was sitting in her wooden chair up on the veranda, her eyes moving from him to Luke. She hadn't got up to intervene, and he knew she wouldn't. That wasn't her way.

'I get that,' said Luke, 'and I wouldn't ask, but there's a . . . there's a message for you. From Rachel. A private one. And I would be failing in my duty to her if I didn't pass it on.'

'A message? What do you mean? A note? An email? Could you not just have brought it here to me?'

'No,' Luke said, and he seemed genuinely stuck for words. 'Look, if I could explain, I would. But I can't. And it goes without saying that the message is for you. Just you. It's extremely confidential.'

Aidan wasn't a violent guy. But right now he itched to punch Luke right in his self-satisfied mouth. Extremely confidential messages from Rachel? In Luke's hands? How dare he? How could he come here and order Aidan to report to the lab like a lackey? He felt his hand tighten into a fist. He saw Luke see it too, and Luke's grin was sudden and nasty, almost as if he was willing Aidan to hit him. But in that instant Aidan heard a voice from the porch.

'Dad!' He spun around to see Chloe standing, hands on hips, her blonde hair lifting in the wind and sparkling in the last rays of the setting sun. For one heart-stopping moment he thought it was Rachel.

He looked back at Luke, who blanched. Chloe sighed and crossed the lawn towards them. Luke took a step backwards, obviously desperate to escape before he had to talk to Rachel's daughter.

'Look, I'm sorry,' he said to Aidan, even though he didn't sound sorry at all. 'I know it's a bad time. But this really is important. More important than you could possibly imagine. Call me tomorrow. If you can't come tomorrow, come soon, very soon.' It obviously half killed him to say it, but he added, 'Please.' Then he pulled on his helmet, waved at Chloe, got on his bike and roared away.

Chloe walked down the driveway to Aidan.

'Was that Luke?'

'Yes.'

'What did he want?'

'Nothing,' said Aidan quickly. 'Just to give us his condolences. Let's go inside. If we work together, I think we can avoid Aunt Felicity.'

'Are you sure?' Chloe said. 'He looked at me really weirdly.'

Aidan considered telling her what Luke had said but instantly thought better of it. But was he protecting her from Luke's revelation or protecting himself from the questions she would ask?

As he walked back up the driveway with his arm around Chloe's shoulders, he saw Sinead standing, looking worried, on the top step of the porch.

'Why was that man here?' she said, her voice high and sharp. 'He looked dangerous. Very dangerous. You should tell him he's not welcome.'

# 7
## Aidan

Aidan didn't go to Telos the next day, or the next. He thought about it, and it niggled, the idea that Luke had something for him from Rachel. But he just couldn't make himself move. From the moment the police had pulled into the driveway, he and Chloe had lived in a state of crisis, but now that the funeral had passed, he was struck down with the most terrible exhaustion. Chloe also seemed paralysed, and the two of them stayed in the house, keeping the curtains closed and living on funeral tea leftovers and frozen meals which had been brought over by concerned friends. They sat side by side and watched hours of TV, barely speaking. They took turns to doze off on the sofa or sneak upstairs to curl up in their beds to nap. After a few days, they stopped getting dressed. Dishes piled up on every surface. Every now and then they would look at the bleak chaos around them, consider tidying and then slump back into the rumpled nests they had made in the living room.

The phone rang every couple of hours – well-meaning friends and relatives checking in with them. Aidan made liberal use of caller ID. Aunt Felicity's calls naturally went to message, but he forced himself to take calls from his work colleagues and from his uni friend Sam.

'Why don't you and Chloe come down to London for a few days?' Sam said. 'Just to get away. We'll look after you.'

But Aidan couldn't imagine it. He couldn't imagine the

logistics of packing bags, driving or catching a train, having to be in Sam and Laura's tiny London flat. The very idea exhausted him.

'Thanks, mate, but with baby Joseph, you and Laura have your hands full. We'll come down in a few months' time.'

Sam and Laura were his and Rachel's oldest friends, and he knew they were devastated. The thought of being responsible for their grief as well as his own was just too much. He wasn't strong enough for tears and reminiscences. Not yet.

But Aidan knew that sooner rather than later he'd have to find the motivation to get moving. He needed to return to work and send Chloe back to school. Her exams had been postponed on compassionate grounds, but she still had to resume her studies. He had to sort out the details of Rachel's estate too. It would be straightforward – they'd had mirror wills done when they got married, and the house and everything else would come to him. But it all still had to be done.

He'd have to deal with her things too. Everything was just as she had left it on the last morning of her life – her clothes in the wardrobe, her toothbrush beside his in their bathroom, the T-shirt she slept in folded under her pillow. Somehow, he had to gather it all up . . . and then what? It wasn't that he was in denial – he knew she was dead. But this final act would be so brutal. He imagined scooping her clothes from her drawers, sweeping her make-up into a bin, and a wave of panic overwhelmed him. How could he do it? What should he keep for Chloe? What should he discard? Those decisions were impossible to make. With every day that passed, it became harder and harder to do anything at all, and he couldn't imagine how he would pick up the reins and carry on with his life.

It was Bea who pushed him into action. Bea, the laboratory administrator at Telos, managed all the research scientists in the department where Rachel had worked. She was a solid, kind woman in her fifties, who cared for the brilliant minds around her with firm efficiency. Her influence reached way beyond managing their diaries – she made sure they ate and rang their partners and families when they were working late. With the more obsessive ones, she'd been known to frogmarch them away from their lab benches and send them for a shower and a change of clothes. Rachel – motherless, mercurial Rachel, whose mind was always a hundred steps in front of her – had adored Bea, who brought her sandwiches and tea to her desk. The adoration was completely mutual, and Bea had been puffy-eyed and silent at the funeral, hugging Aidan fiercely to her ample bosom and weeping silently into Chloe's hair.

But Bea was tough too. Her brisk warmth concealed a core of steel. If Bea 'suggested' you do something, you might as well give in straight away, because you were going to do it. So when she rang Aidan a week after the funeral and told him kindly that he needed to come and collect Rachel's personal things from her lab, he knew better than to argue.

'Get it over and done with,' she urged. 'Come on out now. I'll help you if you want me to, or Luke can help you, or you can tell us both to bugger off and do it yourself. You don't need to stick around and make small talk with any of us, but it's a job that needs to be done.'

She was, of course, correct. And if he was honest, it was the push he needed. She was right about doing it straight away too – if he thought about it, it would become another impossible task and he'd put it off, like he was putting everything off. He should just go. And while he was at it, he'd steel himself and ask Luke about the message from Rachel.

He'd been sloping around in tracksuit bottoms and ratty T-shirts, barely bothering to brush his teeth or hair, so he showered, shaved and put on a clean shirt and some decent trousers for the first time in a week. He considered telling Chloe where he was going, but in the end just knocked briefly on her bedroom door. 'I need to go out for a bit, honey,' he said. 'Will you be all right?'

'I'll be fine, Dad,' she called, and he heard a note of relief in her voice. She was probably sick of him. They had an easy, companionable relationship. He had always been the good cop, while Rachel was harder on Chloe, the disciplinarian who expected more. Even so, Chloe was a teenager and no teenager would choose to be with a parent for days on end, no matter how bad the circumstances.

He took an enormous detour to get to Telos, driving all the way round the ring road and approaching from the other side so he would avoid passing the accident site. It felt a little odd to pull up at the big gates – he had never been there before without Rachel. But then he had hardly ever been there. The lab had high security – much of their work was confidential – and while visitors weren't discouraged, they weren't welcomed either.

Errol, the security guard, had obviously been told to expect Aidan and he nodded him through, opening the boom and raising a hand in greeting. Aidan drove round to the visitors' car park. He sat in the car for a few minutes. The task ahead felt insurmountable, and he wanted desperately to start the car again and drive away as fast as he could. But he couldn't spend his life running. He took a deep breath and wiped his sweaty hands on his trousers before getting out of the car and walking briskly to reception.

Bea was waiting for him. She gathered him in a tight hug.

'I can take you straight to the lab if you don't want to stick around, but if you can bear it, I'd love to take you into my office and give you a cup of tea and a digestive.'

'A digestive?'

'McVitie's. None of your supermarket-own-brand nonsense.' She smiled.

'Well, how can I say no to a branded digestive biscuit?' He

managed a weak smile of his own. It felt odd, as if his face had forgotten how to do it.

Bea turned to the young man behind the reception desk. 'Norman, we'll be packing a lot of Dr Prosper's stuff into boxes and bringing them down here. Maybe when Mr Sawyer's ready to go, you could help him to load them into his car?'

Norman looked dreadfully uncomfortable and was unable to meet Aidan's eye. He clearly knew who Aidan was, and the thought that he might have to offer condolences was obviously troubling him. This is going to happen to me a lot, Aidan thought. Most people have no idea what to do around bereaved people. We're an embarrassment.

He followed Bea down several identical long, white-painted corridors, squares of neon lighting flicking past overhead. The floors were polished to a mirror shine and there were heavy closed doors along cither side. There was a small plate by each door with the name of the scientist in neat black type — 'Dr Edwards', 'Dr Desai', 'Dr Ng' — but no explanation of what went on inside the rooms.

Bea made an abrupt right turn, and the corridor opened out into a wider, open-plan area. She guided Aidan into her own office. It was a cosy corner room with windows that looked out over the green lawns which surrounded the complex. She had a little refreshment station in the corner and she clicked on the kettle and efficiently made two mugs of tea while Aidan settled himself in the visitor's chair. She didn't make small talk, just handed him his cup and tipped a good half a packet of the promised biscuits onto a plate. He found he was hungry — his eating had been sporadic and at odd times of the day — so he took three and dunked and ate them in quick succession. Bea sat down opposite him and watched him in silence.

'No sense in asking how you are.'

'Not yet, no,' said Aidan, his mouth full of biscuit. He looked around, and Bea pushed a box of tissues across the desk towards him. He took one and wiped his mouth. 'We've been in limbo, really. We haven't started trying to live again yet.'

'Understandable,' said Bea.

'But . . . ?'

'Why do you think I was going to say "but"?' She raised an eyebrow at him.

'You're going to say it's not going to get any easier. There's all sorts of stuff to sort out, now that . . . Well, I need to get moving, get Chloe back to school, go back to work myself.'

She clasped her hands and leaned forward, resting her elbows on the desk. 'Now then, Aidan, I didn't say any of that, but I do notice that you said it.'

'Very good. Are you a shrink in your spare time?'

'Only if an undergraduate degree in psychology counts.'

'It does,' he said, impressed.

'I was going to be a clinical psychologist, but then I got more interested in the theory of research, so I ended up managing this lot,' she said, waving vaguely. 'For a collection of very clever people, they're often very dim. Most of them couldn't find their own arses with two hands, a map and an Excel spreadsheet.'

Aidan burst out laughing. Then he caught himself and looked stricken.

'It's okay to laugh,' said Bea, reaching across her desk and patting his hand. 'Your girl loved to laugh. She wouldn't want you to stop.'

'She did laugh, didn't she?' Aidan said. 'She really loved terrible jokes and puns.'

'If you're not part of the solution . . .' began Bea.

'. . . you're part of the precipitate,' finished Aidan. 'She'd fall about at that. Every time.'

They sat together quietly for a moment, remembering.

'This is a shit one, and no mistake,' said Bea suddenly.

Aidan raised an eyebrow at her.

'I'm angry. I loved her too, you know. I loved her for her sweet nature and her bad jokes and her messy laboratory. But mainly I'm angry because minds like that come along maybe once or twice a century. What she did . . . What she was on the way to doing . . . What she could have done . . .' She broke off and shook her head. 'She was the most amazing combination – both a scientist and an artist. She coded with care and accuracy and elegance and then she made creative leaps of logic. She and Luke, well, no one saw that as a likely partnership, but together they seemed able to find new, brilliant ways around problems, things no one had ever thought of before. They were close to an amazing breakthrough, I know. They kept it all under wraps, locked in their lab, but they were planning to announce some results very soon. It's just . . . so . . .' Words failed her again. '. . . shit. I can't put it any other way.'

Aidan nodded. It was good to know that someone else was angry. He found Bea's honesty a relief, after all the murmured banalities of the funeral. She had made him feel better. It seemed a good time to be brave and find out about Rachel's message.

'So, Luke . . .' he said.

'What about him?'

'He turned up at the wake, acting strangely.'

Bea nodded, as if this wasn't a surprise.

'He didn't stay, but he said he had a message for me, from Rachel. And that I had to come to the lab to get it.'

'He hasn't said anything to me about it,' said Bea, standing up. 'But then he's not renowned for his communication skills. Do you want me to take you to the lab now? Are you ready to do this?'

Aidan hesitated. 'I suppose so,' he said. Suddenly he didn't feel quite ready to go into the room where Rachel had spent so many thousands of hours. He couldn't help feeling that the essence of her would still be there.

Bea sensed his reticence. 'I can come with you,' she said, smiling. 'I won't leave you alone with the big bad Luke.'

'It's not Luke I'm worried about.'

Bea came around the desk and squeezed his shoulder. 'Baby steps. We'll walk to the door, and if you feel you don't want to go in, I can pop in and ask Luke to pack up the stuff and bring it to you.'

That was all the motivation Aidan needed. He didn't want Luke pawing through Rachel's stuff. He stood and squared his shoulders. 'I can do this. I have to start facing these things. It's not like the situation is going to change.'

Bea led him confidently down a flight of stairs and through a bewildering set of turns. Aidan remembered walking through these corridors with Rachel, when she had first come to work here. She'd chattered excitedly about the state-of-the-art equipment she was going to be able to use, the processing power, and the support from other scientists. 'I'm going to do my best work at Telos, I just know it,' she'd said, her eyes shining as she unlocked the door and flung it open. 'Miracles will happen here!'

He could almost hear her voice echoing in the white hallway. Such hopes. And what had they amounted to?

He remembered how Rachel had touched the little nameplate by the door that day. 'Dr Prosper, Dr Bourne', it had read. But Rachel's name was gone now. The nameplate just read 'Dr Bourne'.

'Her name,' Aidan said. 'It's gone already. You people move fast.'

'I'm sorry,' Bea said, 'but there's a very strict protocol should one of our staff members pass away. It's to do with security.

There's so much classified information in here—'

'I get it,' said Aidan, cutting her off. It wasn't Bea's fault, of course, but it made him feel angry. Without knocking, he pushed open the laboratory door.

The room was spacious and L-shaped. Luke, as the mechanical engineer, needed more space, and he inhabited the long arm of the L, which ran the length of the room from the door to the windows. There were ranks of pristine white counters, all empty. Sets of drawers sat at the end of each counter, in which, Aidan assumed, Luke kept his robotics tools and equipment. Along the far end, under the window, were complex power tools with arms and many buttons and controls. Aidan couldn't begin to guess what they were for.

The other side of the room, which was smaller, had clearly been Rachel's domain. There was a desk covered in drifts of paper, a filing cabinet with even more paper spilling out of it, a bookcase crammed with volumes. Books were also piled on the floor. There were several computer towers under the desk and three large monitors side by side on it. All of the equipment was silent, the screens blank, no lights blinking. Dead.

Aidan stared at this space, his wife's home in all her waking, working hours. Her place away from him. He could sense her here so powerfully. He had thought it impossible to feel more wretched and agonised than he already did, but, surprise, surprise, there were new depths of agony awaiting him.

Luke was sitting at the far end of one of the benches, bent over something small and intricate, working with a set of tiny screwdrivers. He didn't get up or greet Aidan and Bea.

Aidan stood still until he could get his breathing under control and be sure he wasn't going to cry. Then he walked over to Luke's bench and offered him his hand. 'Luke,' he said and his voice sounded very loud in the silent room.

Luke looked at Aidan with suspicion, then pulled off the fine latex glove he was wearing to shake hands. His skin was cool and powdery.

Bea, who was still standing in the doorway, came over too. 'How are you, Luke?' she said brightly. Luke nodded at her, but didn't seem to think the question merited a reply. Bea looked unsurprised. She turned to Aidan. 'I brought a couple of boxes,' she said, indicating two cardboard boxes with lids which were stacked beside Rachel's desk. 'Don't worry about her work papers, just go through the drawers for any personal items you want to keep. Do you want me to . . . ?'

'No. Thank you.' Aidan touched her arm to try and soften the sharpness of his reply. 'If it's okay, I'll just do it myself. You can check through the boxes when I'm finished, to make sure I haven't stolen anything top secret.' He smiled, but Bea didn't smile back or tell him why that wouldn't be necessary.

She turned to Luke. 'Everything all right? Are you ready for the meeting with the research board next week? We need to discuss what you're going to—'

'I can't talk about it right now,' Luke interrupted. 'I have some issues I need to resolve. I'll be at the research board and I'll tell them what I can. No more.'

Bea looked at him sceptically. Aidan glanced back at her. He could see she was considering blasting Luke for his rudeness and lack of co-operation, but she wouldn't do that in front of an outsider.

'I'll come by tomorrow morning at ten,' she said firmly. 'We need to make a decision on how possible it is for you to take the research forward alone, or who else you can work with . . .'

'No one,' said Luke. 'I can't work with anyone else. I can do it alone. It'll just take a little bit longer. I'll tell the board next week. Now can you leave us, please?'

'Only because you said please so nicely,' said Bea, her voice dripping with sarcasm. 'Can you give me a ring in my office when Aidan's finished here? And Luke, just . . . be nice, okay? Help Aidan do what he needs to do.'

Luke nodded curtly but didn't answer, and Bea withdrew, closing the door behind her.

There was a moment of awkward silence. Aidan stood looking at Luke expectantly. Luke said uncomfortably, 'I'll let you get on.' He walked back to his bench, pulled on his latex gloves and returned to his work.

Aidan was confused. Luke had been so insistent about Rachel's message when he came to the house, but now he seemed reluctant, avoiding his gaze. What was he holding back? Why was he playing games? If this was a power play, Aidan wasn't going to beg. He walked resolutely over to Rachel's desk, placing the first empty box on her chair.

There was a grey cardigan hanging on the back of the chair, and he picked this up first, folding it carefully and placing it in the bottom of the box. He knew better than to put it to his face and smell it. He was going to do his damnedest to get through this without crying in front of Luke. There were a few family photographs in frames on the desk – one of him and Rachel on holiday in Italy, toasting each other with cocktails, and a set of photo-booth images of Rachel and Chloe pulling faces together. He placed these in the box too. He could do this, he told himself. But then he noticed a hair-tie, tossed carelessly on the desk. There were a few bright blonde hairs tangled around the little ring of elastic and he picked it up. He could imagine Rachel working away, suddenly annoyed by her hair and tugging it free, letting it tumble down over her shoulders. How could something so small break him? He tried to breathe.

The desk seemed to be covered entirely in work papers. He

sifted through them, but they were all pages of calculations, notes and printouts. There was probably some mad Rachel logic to the teetering piles, but nothing he could discern. He turned to the drawers in her desk. In the first drawer there was a thick wedge of bank statements, credit card bills and other correspondence. He sorted through them to see that nothing was work-related and then tipped the envelopes into the box.

The drawer below was filled with small, more intimate objects – a lipstick, a bottle of her perfume, a crumpled receipt for a book that she had given him as a birthday gift. There was also a shopping list in his own handwriting. Under the list of milk, eggs and vegetables, he'd added 'your glorious body'.

She'd come home with the shopping one evening. Unloading it, she'd glanced over her shoulder at him. 'I looked in Tesco, but they didn't seem to have my glorious body in homewares.'

'I see you got it though,' he said, standing behind her and pulling her against him. She laughed softly, then moved away to bend over and put things into the fridge. He came up behind her again, running his hands up the taut muscles on the back of her thighs.

'Chloe . . .' she said warningly.

'At Amy's,' he said, his breath coming quicker.

'Well then . . .' She straightened up, turning into his arms.

He lifted her onto the kitchen counter, kissing her hard and unbuttoning her shirt. A loaf of bread was pushed to the floor, and he thought he may have heard eggs smash, but he was lost in her.

Later, as they cleared up the mess in the kitchen, laughing and trying to find their underwear, she grinned at him. 'All these years and you're still hot for me, Mr Sawyer. Who'd have thought it, eh?'

She'd kept that shopping list alongside an old Polaroid of him from their university days. He was lying on her single bed in halls, a sheet pulled carelessly up over his hips, his torso bare. He had one hand behind his head and a cigarette in his hand. He looked young and handsome, his body narrow and muscly. What a confident, swaggering git he'd been back then.

A cold thought struck him. Had Luke gone through these drawers? Seen these private details of their marriage? The desk wasn't locked, after all. He glanced across the room, but Luke had his back to him. He seemed uninterested in what Aidan was doing.

He thought about the thousands of hours Rachel had spent in this room, alone with this man, and about the jokes and secrets they'd shared. He'd never doubted his wife's love, even though her passion for her work had often caused strain between them. But now she was gone, now there was no more of her to have, he felt tearing envy that Luke had had so much of her time. He wanted to wrestle it away from him, hear every conversation they'd had and be privy to every secret.

In a frenzy he packed every small object away in the box. Now the drawers were empty, he looked at the top of the filing cabinet. There was a dying orchid (she could never keep an indoor plant alive, even though she loved to garden), and a nodding Mr Bean figurine which Chloe had bought Rachel with her own pocket money as a birthday gift when she was about seven. He placed the figurine carefully in the box. He checked the first few drawers of the filing cabinet, but, again, there seemed to be nothing personal there.

Was that it? She'd spent a minimum of twelve hours a day here for the last few years, yet it seemed every personal item she had could be fitted into one small cardboard box? He was about to turn and tell Luke he was finished when, on impulse, he tried to open the bottom drawer of the filing cabinet. It was stuck – not because it was locked, but because it was packed so full. He slipped a hand in and moved some things around until the drawer slid open.

It was crammed with photographs, photo albums, DVDs and videotapes. Aidan recognised them instantly. They were all his. He had always been the family chronicler, snapping pics, first on his old 35 mm Canon, then on a series of digital cameras. He'd shot hundreds of hours of family video, on an old Digital8 camera and then, more recently, on phones. But Rachel had been the one to turn them all into physical objects. 'I know how easily data can be lost,' she'd said as she painstakingly put photos into albums. 'Let's keep it real.'

And here it all was. Their family archive, from their early days together as a couple at university, their first flat, marriage, Chloe, holidays . . . And there was more: Rachel's photo albums from her childhood, with pictures of her parents; Aidan's school pictures. It made no sense. One thing was for sure, though: he was going to need more cardboard boxes.

Why had Rachel not mentioned she was taking it all to work? Why had he not noticed it was gone? They kept photos and albums in the sideboard in the living room. Surely he would have noticed her taking all of this? Unless she'd moved it bit by bit. But why? What did she need it here for? He wanted to turn and ask Luke what he knew, but he balked. What if Luke did know? Why would she tell Luke about it but not him? He felt a surge of white-hot anger. He wanted to get out of there.

But then he remembered the message. Maybe that was what it was about? Maybe Rachel had left a letter explaining why she had taken all of their personal pictures and videos?

'You said you had a message for me from Rachel,' he said baldly. 'Did she leave a note?'

Luke looked up, surprised to hear him speak. 'No,' he said, 'nothing like that.' He swivelled on his chair to look at Aidan. 'So

44

have you finally decided you want to hear it?'

Aidan nodded his answer. He couldn't trust himself to keep his antipathy for Luke out of his voice.

Luke got up and went over to lock the door. Then he checked that the windows were closed. He drew down the blinds and then made sure that all of the computer equipment on Rachel's desk was switched off and unplugged. Aidan watched him uncomprehendingly.

Rachel's side of the laboratory was smaller than Luke's because the far end was walled off to form another small room. Aidan had assumed it was for storage or was possibly a meeting room. It had a door which looked thick and heavy, and it was secured with three locks and a padlock. Luke put his hand on the door, then hesitated and turned to Aidan.

'How much did you know about our research?'

'Everything,' said Aidan defensively. 'Rachel and I had a very honest relationship.' He wasn't going to give Luke the satisfaction of thinking Rachel had kept secrets from him.

'Tell me what you think you know,' said Luke.

Aidan sighed. 'I know you've been working on human–robot interaction. That you're planning to build robots which are capable of reading human emotions.'

'That's mostly right,' said Luke, 'except for a couple of crucial points.'

'Which are . . . ?'

'Not planning to build. Built. And not robots. Robot. Just one. One that's fully functional, that is.'

'I see,' said Aidan, although he really didn't.

'And there's one other key thing, which I'm guessing Rachel didn't tell you about.' Luke stepped away from the door and came back towards Aidan. 'The software was her department and the physical robot was mine. We wanted to build an android robot, and by that I mean a robot that looked as much like a real human being as possible. Other scientists have been working on that for years, with varying degrees of success. They often appear close to human, but their movements are jerky or their expressions don't look quite right. People find them creepy or scary.'

'I've seen some of them,' said Aidan impatiently. Of course he had. He may not have been close to Luke and Rachel's level of expertise, but he did have a degree in computer science and Rachel had been working in robotics research for more than a decade. He'd kept up to date with the field and seen what other researchers were doing.

'To explain it in the simplest lay terms,' said Luke, and Aidan wanted to thump him, 'the jerkiness and oddness comes from the way they program the movement. They plan each sequence and write it line by line. You know about the uncanny valley?'

'Sort of,' said Aidan.

'It's the idea that something that appears almost human, but isn't, gives us the creeps,' Luke explained. 'We find that repulsive. Untrustworthy. It's why robots in sci-fi films almost always turn out to be sinister.'

'They do, don't they?'

Luke nodded. 'But that's because the technology wasn't good enough to make robots that looked and behaved in a genuinely human way. We did it differently.'

'Differently?'

'I won't bore you with the details, but the scientists at Telos have been working on a revolutionary system of mechanical and electronic structures that mimic human bones, nerves and muscles. It's been very successful. Rachel and I wanted to take it further. We didn't want to make a robot that mimicked conversation and interaction. We wanted to make one that could respond to people, could read all the non-verbal clues people give, and sympathise and empathise. A real helper.'

'I get that,' said Aidan impatiently. He'd heard all of this from Rachel before.

'Rachel made the biggest breakthrough though, the thing the rest of the team doesn't know about. She created an operating system that allows the robot to learn.'

'Learn?'

'It imitates human movement and expression. It watches and copies, like a child does.'

'How? How did she teach it?'

'With hundreds and hundreds of hours of recorded audio and video footage, and day-to-day human interaction.'

There was a long silence. Aidan suddenly felt very tired. He wanted to go home and curl up on the sofa again. He'd had enough of being out in the world, and he didn't want to talk to Luke anymore. He hadn't liked Luke much when Rachel was alive, and he liked him even less now, standing by Rachel's desk, puffing himself up and talking about how clever he was, talking about Rachel and him as 'we', a pair, a unit.

He was about to make his excuses and go, when Luke spoke abruptly. 'It was a brain aneurysm, wasn't it?'

'Yes.' Aidan was surprised by the rapid change of subject and the directness of Luke's question.

'She knew she had it, didn't she? Before it . . . ruptured.'

'How did you know that?'

Luke didn't reply. He just looked at Aidan, waiting for his answer.

'Yes . . . she did,' Aidan said reluctantly. 'Her mother died of the same thing, and so Rachel underwent a series of tests. She had to go back every couple of years. The first few times, they didn't find anything, but a few years ago they spotted something on a scan. It was in a difficult place – if not inoperable, it would have been dangerous and difficult to get to. There were . . . risks. She was terrified about what might happen to her mind if she had the surgery, so she opted to leave it. Take the chance. She just lived with it. A time-bomb in her head.'

He was about to say that she hadn't told him about it, but he wasn't going to give Luke that satisfaction. He'd already told Luke more than he'd meant to. He hadn't discussed this with anyone, not even Chloe. But of everyone else in the world, why was he telling Luke? Because he'd asked so directly, Aidan supposed, and because it was a relief to say it out loud.

Luke didn't look shocked. He just nodded. 'That makes sense then.'

'What makes sense?'

'What she did.'

'What did she do?' Aidan said, frustration boiling over. 'For fuck's sake, Luke, just tell me.'

Luke sighed. 'Bea probably told you we have tight security here.' Aidan nodded. 'So if someone dies, there are strict rules and procedures. They shut down the dead person's permissions and cancel access very quickly. Cut off email and suchlike. Just in case anyone gets hold of their credentials and runs away with all our research.'

'Makes sense,' said Aidan. He couldn't see where Luke was going with this.

'As soon as Rachel's death was confirmed, the IT department sprang into action. They shut down her accounts and came and unplugged her equipment. But then . . . something happened. I think she expected she might die, because she'd written a piece of code and embedded it in her data so that if her status changed to "deceased", a particular chain of events would be set in motion.'

'What events?'

Luke went back to the door of the small locked room. 'I don't want to show you this, but I have to,' he said. 'I can't even make you sign some kind of confidentiality agreement, because this is so totally off the record. I can't even begin to . . .' He kept interrupting himself. 'Showing you this could get me fired.'

Luke took a set of keys out of his pocket. Aidan wondered briefly why there were physical locks on the door – all other doors in the building opened with a key card. But then he guessed that a physical lock couldn't be hacked.

Luke opened the door and motioned for Aidan to follow him. Aidan stood, unable to understand his own reluctance. Luke had not switched on a light, so the only illumination came from the lab behind them. The little room was even smaller than it looked from the outside. Luke stood to one side and pointed. Aidan saw that there was a figure inside, who sat on a chair, hands in lap, and who looked up as soon as he stepped into the doorway.

'Aidan,' she said, 'you came.'

It was Rachel.

# 8

## Aidan

So this is what it feels like to lose your mind, Aidan thought. Here was Rachel. Rachel, his beloved wife, had been waiting for him, sitting in a pitch-dark storage cupboard. Rachel, who he had last seen dead, broken and silent on a mortuary table. Whose coffin had slid behind the curtains in the crematorium. Whose ashes were in an urn, waiting for when he and Chloe felt brave enough to scatter them on the South Downs. Rachel was dead, and yet here she was. Alive. And she'd greeted him by name.

He laughed.

It seemed the only possible response. A great ugly shout of laughter, and then he couldn't stop. He laughed uncontrollably and hysterically, then grabbed Luke's arm and dragged them both back out of the room and slammed the door. He stumbled, knocking into Rachel's desk and sending a precarious pile of papers cascading to the floor. He was going mad. His mind had snapped and he was going mad.

Gradually he became aware that Luke was standing watching him, expressionless, waiting for him to calm down.

'Rachel,' he said, unable to find any more words. 'Rachel.'

'It's not Rachel,' said Luke. 'It's our android prototype.'

'Your what?'

'In order to give the robot enough visual and auditory material to work with so it could learn to act like a human, we needed a subject to model it on. Someone we could film and record.

Someone the robot could spend time with and copy. It made sense for it to be Rachel.'

'You could have warned me,' said Aidan.

'I thought you knew. You said Rachel told you all about our research,' countered Luke. 'If there were details you didn't know . . .' He paused, nastily. 'Well, if she had wanted you to know, I assume she would have told you.'

'Well, she didn't. She talked about the software, about her coding issues. She didn't even tell me that the robot was . . . human.'

'It's not human, it's anthropomimetic. An android. Strictly speaking it's a gynoid, because it looks like a woman. It's possibly one of the most advanced and lifelike humanoids ever built, but it's still a machine.'

'But it's Rachel.'

'It looks like her,' conceded Luke. 'It's learned to mimic her voice and facial expressions to a certain extent. But we were a long way from concluding our research and development. It still needs extensive human trials. It needs to interact with people and develop its empathy tools. We were months, maybe even years away from release.'

From the bottom of his own pit of grief and despair, Aidan glimpsed Luke's pain. His life's work, the future of his research, all his hopes and plans had been snatched from him in the moment of Rachel's death. Aidan felt an unaccustomed twinge of sympathy for him.

Luke came over and helped him to pick up the scattered papers and put them back on Rachel's desk.

'When Rachel died,' he said, 'I didn't know what to do. I couldn't imagine how we were going to move forward with the work. But then the morning after they confirmed her death, I came in and it . . .' He indicated the closed door behind which the android waited silently. '. . . it asked for you.'

'For me?' Aidan looked at him with incredulity.

'Like I said, Rachel must have written some kind of special protocol so that if she was declared dead and her IT permissions were cancelled, the android received a set of instructions. It's been asking for you non-stop ever since. Saying it has a message for you from Rachel. That it needs to see you, face to face. I'm not the software expert – that was Rachel's department. I've tried to find the protocol in the code, but Rachel locked it in somehow. I can't switch it off, and I can't move forward with the experiments. Not until it gets its way and speaks to you. I'm getting pressure from the board to talk about our research – you heard what Bea said – but I don't want to tell anyone until we resolve this. I don't want anyone to see it like this.'

So it wasn't respect for Rachel's wishes that had brought Luke to his door, thought Aidan bitterly. He was just frustrated that his work had been halted and that he might not get all the glory he thought he deserved.

'I can appreciate that you might find it a bit difficult,' Luke said awkwardly, 'but can you talk to it? Find out what it needs to say so we can move on?'

'Move on?'

'You heard what Bea said. I'm going to have to appear in front of the board at some point to give an account of our research and what will happen now Rachel is . . .' He clearly didn't know how to finish this sentence. 'I can't do anything right now. I tried showing it a photograph of you. I even considered bringing someone else in and telling it that person was you, but it's got facial-recognition software built in and it wouldn't be fooled. So I need your help. Please.'

'So it – the robot – says it has a message for me from Rachel?'

'Yes, and it insists that it can only give the message to you, in person.'

Aidan was reeling. He felt trapped. He wanted to run, but at the same time he desperately wanted another look at the robot. In that one brief glance, hearing the few words it had spoken, it was so exactly like seeing and hearing Rachel. It would break his heart, but he knew he couldn't resist the desire to look again.

'How do I . . . ?'

'Speak to it?'

'Yes.'

'Like it's a person. I'll give you a wristband, which will allow the robot to read some of your physiological signs – respiration rate, heart rate, galvanic skin response, temperature. If it has that data and can see your face to observe facial expression, eye movement and pupil dilation, it can converse and respond in a human-like fashion.'

Luke went over to his own workbenches and came back with a narrow black band that looked like a sports tracking watch. He buckled it onto Aidan's right arm, making sure that the sensors touched the pulse point on the inside of his wrist.

Aidan looked at him helplessly. 'I can't go in there and refer to it as . . . it.'

Luke looked puzzled. 'It is an it. An android, not a living thing. We don't anthropomorphise them. It's like giving your car a name and those sappy eyelashes.'

'It's not a Vauxhall Astra. It's a woman that looks exactly like my wife.'

Luke shrugged. 'Feel free to refer to it as human if you like. Technically, it's a Mark IV model. Serial number 787775. But in our research notes we call it iRachel.'

'iRachel?'

'To differentiate it from Dr Prosper.'

'iRachel,' said Aidan. He took a deep breath. 'Okay. Let's do it. Let's hear what iRachel has to tell me.'

# 9
# iRachel

## Contact Log

Subject: Aidan Sawyer

| Interaction start time: | 15.41 |
|---|---|
| Date: | 2 May |
| Heart rate: | 98 bpm |
| Skin temperature: | elevated |
| Respiratory rate: | 25 bpm |

## Report:

The subject entered the holding room slowly, and Dr Bourne switched on the overhead electric light. I can detect human features even in low light, but the subject needed more illumination in order to be able to interact. When the light came on and he was able to see me clearly, his pupils dilated very rapidly, and his heart rate, which was already high, increased significantly. I ran a facial-recognition scan and checked my visual analysis against my records: 6' 1" tall, approximately eighty kilogrammes in weight, dark curly hair, dark brown eyes, olive skin. He was a match for the photographs I have. According to all available metrics, this was indeed Rachel's husband, Aidan Anthony Sawyer.

I heard him draw in a sharp breath, and I registered further changes in all his vital signs consistent with a strong emotional response.

'Jesus Christ,' he said, and I recorded a strong tremor in his hands.

His vital signs were so extreme I was concerned that he might be experiencing shock. I repeated the programmed greeting protocol, which I had attempted the first time he came into the room.

'Aidan, you came.'

'Yes,' he said uncertainly.

'You are very upset.'

'You look exactly like Rachel – Dr Prosper,' he said. 'She was my wife.'

'Yes,' I said. 'She died. I am sorry for your loss.'

'Thank you,' he said, and then he frowned.

I was not able to interpret this accurately. Rachel taught me that if I do not understand a facial expression, especially if it seems to contradict the words spoken, I should ask. I said, 'My records show that a contraction of the eyebrows is an expression of displeasure, or sometimes of confusion. Are you angry?'

'No!' he said. 'I am not angry. It's just a very big shock to see you . . . to see Rachel's face when she's . . .'

'Dead?'

'Exactly.' He was quiet for a long moment (17.45 seconds) and then he said, 'You look very alike.'

'My features were modelled on hers, as Luke informed you. However, we truly recognise similarity through facial expression and familiar actions. I've been observing her mannerisms and movements for 345 days now.'

Aidan turned towards Luke and said, 'She's amazing. I've never seen anything like her.'

Luke frowned. I am familiar with this expression of his. It means he is frustrated with a work problem. 'It's just the beginning, though. Building a convincing android robot, well, lots of people are doing that. Possibly even better than this one. What Rachel was interested in was the interaction. How it responds to people. How it reads their moods. How it can help – really help.'

55

'Help?'

'Everyone in the field of humanoid robotics believes the robots they build will be workers – they can do the jobs humans don't want to do. We program them and they have no free will, so they'll do the dirty work without complaining and they won't get tired or join a union or want more pay. Or any pay. But Rachel had bigger dreams. More . . . romantic ones, you might say. Rachel wanted to create a prototype carer. A companion. Someone who could give love, be endlessly patient, have real, empathetic conversations. She imagined the robot working in care homes, being a companion to lonely people who live by themselves, that sort of thing. So more than just a glorified maid, more a . . . friend, I suppose. She said no one would ever need to be lonely again.'

These words seemed to affect Aidan strongly. His heart rate increased, and he tightened his hands into fists. He walked out of the holding room quickly, and his respiration became more rapid and shallow. I was concerned that he would leave, and I had not yet completed my task.

'Aidan,' I said. 'Aidan, come back.' I know that my synthesised voice sounds very like Rachel's and again this seemed to cause him some emotional difficulty, but he did stop and stand still, although he kept his back to me. 'I have to give you Rachel's message,' I said. 'I am not able to complete any other sequences until the message is relayed.'

He turned slowly. Luke looked at him and then back at me. He did not move.

'This message is for Aidan, Luke,' I said. 'For Aidan only.'

'What?' said Luke. 'But I—'

'Rachel has written a program which scans the room I am in, to ascertain who is in it. I am to identify Aidan with a retinal scan, and the message will only play if he is alone with me. I am unable to play the message if another person is in the room.'

Luke was not wearing a wristband, so I could not read his physiological signs. However, he said the words, 'Well that's just fucking typical,' before leaving the room at speed and causing the door to shut rapidly, with a loud bang. All of these I took as potential indications of his displeasure.

I was satisfied that Luke had shut the door as this was another essential element of the protocol.

'Are you ready?' I asked.

'No,' said Aidan. 'I genuinely don't think I can bear to listen to it.'

Rachel had anticipated every possible reaction Aidan might have. This response was not rated as one of the most likely ones, but there was a segment of the program which dealt with this possibility. I prepared to power down and go into stasis mode.

'Wait,' he said. 'What did you do then? The light went out of your eyes.'

'If you do not want to hear the message, I am unable to bypass it. I cannot move forward or continue with the research project. I will have to put myself into resting mode.'

'Resting mode?'

'Stasis. A non-responsive state.'

'Like . . . sleep?'

'It's more like a coma.'

'So if I don't listen to the message, you go into a coma? That's emotional blackmail!'

'I have a limited understanding of the concept of blackmail,' I said. 'I have access to the word and its meaning through my in-built dictionary, but it has not come up in conjunction with the notion of emotions and was not used as such in conversation by Rachel.'

Aidan looked at me for 7.3 seconds. 'I can't work out whether you're trying to be funny.'

'In this instance, I am not attempting to make a joke, but Rachel was beginning to teach me about the rules of humour,' I said. 'I was learning about wordplay and challenging expectations and how that can make someone laugh. But we had only recently begun that project.'

'I see,' he said. 'So tell me a joke.'

'What do you call a fly with no wings?'

'What?'

'A walk.' He did not respond to this, so I began to explain. 'This is a play on words, because the noun form of the verb "to fly" is also the colloquial name for the *Musca domestica* or common house fly. Whereas the verb "to walk"—'

'I get it.'

'You didn't laugh.'

'I've heard it before. It's something Rachel taught to our daughter, Chloe, when she was a toddler and learning about jokes.'

'Rachel laughed when I told the joke. Every time.'

Aidan nodded. 'She would have.'

I recognised a very small contraction in his cheek muscles. It was not a full smile, but it suggested that a smile might be possible at some point in the future. I ran a scan of his vital signs. His heart rate and respiration had stabilised.

'May I play you the communication now?' I asked.

'Yes,' he said. He spoke quickly and firmly. 'Do it now before I change my mind.' There was a chair against one wall of the holding room, opposite my own, and he sat down.

Up to this point, I had been using my language files to generate appropriate responses for my conversation with Aidan, and my mouth and synthesised voice to communicate. However, delivering the message required a different approach. Rachel had used a microphone to create a low-tech MP4 recording of her voice. I could have played it directly from my body, but logic suggested that Rachel's voice coming from the speaker in my chest cavity, without my mouth moving, might be disturbing for Aidan, so I connected wirelessly to the sound system in the room, channelling the audio through the speakers.

'This is for Aidan,' said Rachel's voice through the speakers. 'Honey, if you're hearing this, it's because I've passed away. I'm so sorry.'

Aidan leaned forward and covered his face with his hands. I could see his shoulders shaking. There was a fifty to sixty per cent probability that this meant he was crying. Rachel had foreseen this possibility, that on hearing her actual voice he would be very upset. I paused the message and waited for him to regain his composure. After 15.34 seconds, he lifted his face from his hands. I could see no evidence of tears, but his face looked strained and pale. He looked at me for 4.5 seconds and then dropped his gaze and looked at the floor. He remained like this for the rest of the transmission. I continued to play the message.

'It's very strange to record this and know that you will only hear it after my death. I feel odd, sitting here alone in the lab, reading from my screen. I feel fine right now. But if you're hearing it, it's because things didn't turn out fine. No one knows for certain what will kill them, but if I was a betting woman, I'd be able to make a good guess that I will die too young and very suddenly, like my mother.

'Maybe I won't. Maybe you'll never hear this, because I'll live to be a hundred and three and die of cancer or heart failure, or maybe a piano will fall from the sky and squish me like Wile E. Coyote. But whatever I die of, if I die while I am still working on the iRachel project, you're going to hear this message.

'So if you're listening to this, it also means you've seen iRachel, and you probably have lots of questions about it, including why didn't I tell you that Luke had built a robot that looks just like me. It was a selfish choice, mainly because I didn't want you to get weirded out by it. I know you don't like Luke, and you don't always get him. But there were good practical and scientific reasons for the choice. I hope Luke will have explained some of them to you. He's a bit strange, I know, but he's brilliant, and his work on this android is world-class. I couldn't have done what I have without him.'

I observed Aidan's shoulders hunch and tense. I was unable to see his face, but from his demeanour and physical pose I inferred that he did not like this statement from Rachel.

'This is iRachel, and it's the culmination of my life's work. You know how I feel about robotics: that, with the right androids, we have the potential to help people in ways we never could imagine. I wanted to make a robot that was reliable and trustworthy. One that could be truly there for the person they cared for. Real people can be flaky, or unkind, or unfaithful, but the right robot would never let you down.' Rachel laughed then, and I could see that her laugh affected Aidan, because he lifted his head a little and smiled. 'The right robot will never let you down,' she continued. 'I must share that one with the marketing team.'

'We knew we could make a robot that could complete tasks.' 'That could cook food, make beds, help someone to bathe, maybe even do the shopping. But what about the other stuff? Listening, laughing, knowing when you needed a hug or just a chat? I'm talking about empathy. I wanted to build a robot that could respond to your emotional expressions and give you what you needed.'

There was a pause in the recording, and I registered Rachel's breathing, soft and regular, as she prepared to go on. 'When I say "you", I don't mean you, Aidan. Or at least that wasn't my original intention. We conceived the android as a carer for people who live alone – the elderly, or vulnerable adults. But as time has gone on, I've been thinking about the very real possibility that I might leave you and Chloe behind.'

I did not have a visual record of Rachel when she recorded this message, nor was she wearing a wristband. Nevertheless, the tremor of emotion was apparent in her vocal pattern. I heard her take a deep breath and she began to speak again. I recognised her mode of speech. It was the formal, business-like tone she used when speaking to colleagues on the telephone.

'The work we're doing on iRachel is far from finished. We've done some initial laboratory tests, but due to the confidential nature of our work, these have been restricted to interactions with either Luke or myself. To be honest, neither the management, the board nor any of the lab staff are aware that the project is as advanced as it is. They haven't seen iRachel, and Luke and I haven't been ready to show her yet.

'We've planned the next phase of our research. iRachel needs to interact with more than one person at a time. We need people it has not yet met. I also feel very strongly that it needs to be taken out of the laboratory. The controlled nature of our experiments doesn't really challenge it, and it's got used to Luke and me to such an extent that it can predict what we're thinking and feeling with remarkable accuracy.

'So here's the million-pound question – and that's not a meta-phor, that really is roughly what iRachel is worth. Will you take iRachel home with you? Keep it in the house with you and Chloe for a predetermined period? I predict you will need to interact with it . . .'

'Stop calling her "it"!' Aidan jumped to his feet. Rachel's record-ing was still playing, but he spoke as if she was in the room and could hear him. 'Call her "she". She.'

'. . . help with things around the house,' Rachel was saying on the recording. 'If I have just died, I imagine things are pretty rough for you two right now. I know I wasn't the world's greatest housewife, but it could do the laundry, it can cook and clean . . .'

61

'She,' said Aidan, sitting back down in his chair. 'She.' And he began to cry.

Rachel's use of the neutral pronoun seemed to upset him greatly. I could see no logical reason for this, but he was unable to concentrate on her message and so I paused the MP4 file so he would not miss any information.

I did not know the correct protocol for this scenario. It is built into my programming that when a person is upset, I should offer physical comfort by patting them or touching their hand with my own. In the days following Rachel's death, when Luke appeared distraught, I attempted to execute this protocol. He shouted at me on two occasions and on one he pushed me away, causing me to overbalance and fall against a workbench. This caused a rip in the latex covering which forms my skin. Luckily, he had supplied me with my own materials for use in the event of accidents like this and I was able to repair the damage easily. As a result of these reactions, I learned that the touching response is not always appropriate if a subject appears distressed. Based on my experience with Luke, I did not try touching Aidan at this time. Instead, I said, 'I'm sorry you found the message upsetting.'

I was watching Aidan closely. I became aware that my face-mapping software was scanning him, observing each feature and detail of his appearance. I noted especially that his eyelashes were long and dark, and that in the overhead light the tears were visible on them. We sat in silence for a long time (34.35 seconds).

'I have not finished playing Rachel's message,' I said finally.

Aidan shook his head and looked surprised, as if he was waking from a deep sleep. 'Of course. Go on.'

Rachel's voice came from the speakers again. 'Will you take iRachel home with you? Keep it in the house with you and Chloe? It will need you to interact with it for a number of weeks, maybe more.

Luke can come to the house and do any maintenance it needs and collect the data as it works with you.'

Rachel left a pause (5.4 seconds) and then spoke again. This time her voice was less formal and more hesitant.

'I know you'll need some time to think about this, and when you've finished listening, iRachel has a message for Luke too. I have a feeling he's going to take some persuading for this to go ahead. But I know, in my heart of hearts, that if I do die, this is what needs to happen. Yes, this is part of my research, but it's also . . . Well, this is all I have to share with you. My work. My creation. In the strangest, least perfect way, I get to be with you when I can't be with you. Please, my love. Call it a dying wish. Call it emotional blackmail. But, please. Do it. Take iRachel home with you. For me. I love you.'

Aidan sat in silence, staring at his hands.

'Emotional blackmail,' I said.

'Pardon?' Aidan said. He looked shocked, as if it was a surprise that I was still in the room.

'Emotional blackmail. You used that term earlier, and now Rachel has said it too. Having heard it in the two contexts, I think I begin to understand it. It means to use someone's feelings for you in order to coerce them into doing something against their will.'

Aidan nodded. 'That's a good definition. Very accurate indeed.' He stood. 'Thank you. It was . . . astonishing to meet you. This wasn't what I was expecting when I came here. Not at all. I hope . . . I hope things work out for you.'

He looked at me in a strange way. I use the adjective 'strange' because I do not have access to another that describes his expression. It did not resemble any I had experienced from Rachel herself, or from Luke. I could see elements of pain and sadness, both of which I had seen in Luke, but there was something else, something soft in his eyes, for which I had no words.

'Goodbye, iRachel,' he said, and he walked to the door and opened it. He closed it as he went, leaving me alone in the room once more.

**Interaction end time:** 16.52.

# Chloe

C  Oh my God.
   The relief when Dad went out.
   I have no words.

   A  **Are you OK?**

C  Honest to God, we've been sitting here in the dark
   and our own filth for days and days and I feel like I
   haven't been able to breathe.
   I felt like I couldn't look at my phone, or do my hair,
   or even laugh at something on the television.

   A  **That must be weird.**

C  I mean, I get it. This is the worst situation ever. It is.
   And somehow that means we can't be normal.

   A  **Poor you.**

C  It's not Dad's fault. He hasn't put any pressure on
   me. He hasn't done anything really. But he's so
   broken, I feel like I can't just be myself.

   A  **Do you want me to come over?**

C  Best not. I don't know when Dad's going to come
   back. And anyway, our house is a disgusting mess.

   A  **I don't mind. I can help you clean up.**

C  Don't be crazy.
   Would you?

   A  **Of course.**

C  OMG Amez, you're the best best friend ever.

I'll get my mum to drop me round in a bit. We can make things nice for your dad when he gets back.

When Chloe looked in the bathroom mirror, she hardly recognised the hollow-eyed girl she saw there. Amy lived nearby, so Chloe barely had time to brush her teeth and hair and put on some make-up. She covered the dark shadows with foundation and layered on the mascara, but she didn't think Amy would be fooled. The doorbell rang, and she opened the front door and drew her best friend into a tight hug. Amy's mum was watching them from the car, and she waved and blew Chloe a kiss before driving away.

The girls went into the house, and Chloe saw it through Amy's eyes.

'Sorry, it really is a bear pit.'

'It's not so bad . . .' said Amy, surveying the coffee table, which was a drift of plates, cups and crumpled tissues. A greasy pizza box lay on the floor, and she narrowly avoided stepping on it. She tactfully skirted the room and drew back the curtains, then opened the doors to the garden as wide as she could.

'It smells in here, doesn't it?' said Chloe glumly.

'Little bit.'

Amy was shorter than Chloe, petite and small-boned, with straight, fine auburn hair. She had a small, anxious-looking face and was softly spoken. She'd been Chloe's best friend ever since they'd been put next to each other on the carpet in Mrs Christie's Reception class.

When she started school, Chloe could already read fluently and was academically ahead of the rest of the class. However, she found the halls of the big school confusing and intimidating. Amy's mum, Mrs Lucas, was the welfare lady at the school, so Amy had been visiting since she was a baby. She knew where her mum's office was and where to line up for lunch. When Chloe found, halfway through her first break time, that she needed the toilet and didn't know where to go, she burst into frightened tears. It was Amy who placed a small hand in hers and led her to the girls' bathroom. Chloe was forever grateful. If Amy hadn't rescued her, she might have peed her pants, like Daisy Willis did later that week. And she was known as Daisy Weewee until at least Year Four.

Amy had been Chloe's guide to the mysteries of school, and Chloe had helped Amy with her reading and drawing. It took about a year and a half for Amy to surpass her academically. Amy was a grafter. She didn't have Chloe's natural aptitude or creativity, but she made up for it by being diligent, researching more than anyone else and doing all her work with careful neatness.

'Amy will make an amazing coder,' Chloe's mum used to say. 'Her attention to detail is astonishing.'

It was hard for Chloe to hear that and to not take it personally. Her mum and Amy had always shared a sunny, uncomplicated mutual affection. Amy called her 'Mum Two', and she called Amy 'Other Daughter'. They seemed able to discuss anything and their chats weren't full of the barbed misunderstandings that punctuated Chloe's interactions with her mum.

'It's because she's not my mum,' Amy had said when Chloe pointed this out. 'I fight with my own mum all the time!'

It wasn't that Chloe was dim. She was bright. 'Gifted,' her teachers had often said. Rachel had taught her her letters when she was two, using flash cards, and she'd learned how to read in no time at all. She drew brilliantly and as a little girl had loved to sing and dance. But as she got older, she found school bored and frustrated her. She began to act up and cause trouble and her work deteriorated. If she had got in with the wrong group of friends, her school life might have turned out very differently. But her friendship with Amy was her saving grace. Amy never gave up on her. She helped Chloe with her schoolwork whenever she would let her, and she covered for her when she was late to class or just not paying attention.

She and Amy made it through junior school and had gone on to secondary school together. It was there that they met Jess, who had become the third in their close-knit trio. Jess, even at eleven, had worn eyeliner and painted her fingernails black. She got away with breaking uniform rules because she was such a gifted musician. She played five different instruments (her brother was also musical and her mother was a concert pianist). By thirteen, Jess was playing in a proper orchestra, outside of school. At first, Chloe had found her a little scary, but she soon learned that Jess was lovely, just shy and lonely. So Jess was a musical genius, Amy got excellent marks and wanted to be a doctor, and Chloe frustrated her teachers with occasional flashes of brilliance and extended periods of apathetic carelessness. She'd have spent a lot more time in trouble without her friends. Amy and Jess were her anchors.

And here Amy was again, carefully stacking the plates Chloe and her dad had abandoned and carrying them to the kitchen. Chloe looked out into the garden. It was a grey, featureless day. In the fortnight since her mum's death, weeds had pushed up between the patio stones. Her mum had loved to garden – when she wasn't at work, she could be found on her knees weeding, or carefully placing new seedlings in the beds. Over the years they had lived in the house, she had built up a mature and beautiful space. It always looked amazing, but it took a lot of maintenance.

Chloe turned back to the living room. She could hear water running in the kitchen – Amy was washing dishes. Chloe went around the room picking up magazines and newspapers and folding the blankets in which she and her dad had nested. It wasn't too bad. The mess was pretty superficial. A quick dust and a hoover and it would actually look all right.

Once they had blitzed the downstairs and sorted out the worst of the chaos in Chloe's bedroom, the girls made mugs of Earl Grey tea and went to sit outside on the patio. A tiny chink had opened in the clouds and a ray of sunshine slanted down across the fields behind the house.

'So how's your dad doing?' asked Amy.

'Terrible. It's like someone took his batteries out.'

'It's not surprising, though, is it? He's lost his wife.'

'I know.' Chloe took a sip of her tea. 'The worst thing is, my parents really did love each other. I mean properly. They still held hands and kissed. Revolting.' She paused, looking through the steam at her mum's row of lavender bushes. 'I understand how upset he is, I really do. But I can't help thinking that if it had been the other way around, Mum would . . .'

'Would what?'

'I don't know. Have coped better. I don't mean that she didn't love him as much or she would have been less sad if he died. She'd have been gutted. But she would have got organised. She'd have been more worried about me. I mean, I find myself thinking about money. And the house. Mum earned loads more than Dad does. She was crazy and messy, and her life always looked chaotic, but underneath it she was insanely organised. She had procedures for everything: shopping, cleaning, scheduling all our appointments . . . And Dad and I just kind of took that for granted.'

'So how do you feel about that?'

'Scared, if I'm honest. I'm just not sure how we'll cope without her. I know it sounds awful, but if it was Dad who'd died, I'd be devastated but I don't think I'd be afraid. She'd have kept it together.'

'She was amazing.'

Chloe gave Amy a hard look. It was an unwritten rule in their friendship that Amy and Jess didn't gush about her mum.

Everyone else in the world went on and on about how brilliant her mum was. Chloe heard it all the time, from her other friends and from her teachers at school, and every time someone said something, it felt like they were comparing her to her mum and she didn't measure up. How could she? Amy knew how that made her feel, and usually she knew better than to say something like that. But then her mum wasn't amazing anymore. She'd never be amazing again. So maybe that was why Amy felt it was okay to say something.

Chloe glanced at her watch. 'Dad's been gone ages.'

'Where did he go?'

'He didn't say. Just said he had to go out for a bit. It was probably something about Mum that he had to sort out and he didn't want to upset me. He's been gone for a while though.'

A sudden, chilling thought struck her. Her dad's car on the same stretch of road, the same treacherous tree. What if he'd decided he really couldn't live without her mum? What if he'd decided to end it all? Crash the car? Jump off a bridge? What if she was an orphan now?

Amy saw the panic in her face. 'He's fine,' she said soothingly. 'He probably just got held up doing something. Why don't you text him?'

'I'll look like a giant baby who's too scared to be alone,' said Chloe. But she rested her hand on her phone anyway, contemplating. Suddenly it buzzed, making her jump. A message from her dad.

*Sorry, love. That took longer than I thought. Home in half an hour. Dinner out?*

'See?' said Amy. 'Told you he was fine.'

'He's suggesting dinner out. This is the man who wouldn't answer the door to the meter-reader the other day.'

'Maybe he's feeling better.'

'Or going mad. Anyway, he's right. We will have to go out. It's not like there's any food in the house.'

'I did notice the fridge looked pretty empty.'

'It's not like Dad is incompetent – I mean, he always looked after me more than Mum did. His work was more flexible than hers. He was good at playing with me, and he's very reliable about lifts and things like that. He's even a pretty good cook. But it was Mum who made sure everything he needed was in the fridge. She took care of all the behind-the-scenes stuff.'

'Well, the good news is you get to have dinner out. Get him to take you somewhere fancy. Or at least somewhere with good ice cream.'

Chloe managed a smile, but she was thinking about going to dinner with her dad. It wasn't as if they'd never been out without her mum – of course they had. Her mum's life had been filled with travel, conferences, and meetings with suppliers all over the world. And even when she wasn't away, she worked long hours, often leaving Chloe and her dad to muddle along without her. But somehow this would be different. Before, there'd always been a sense that her mum would have been with them if she could. But now she was properly gone, and this would be their first ever dinner out as a family of two. Chloe imagined sitting opposite her dad at a restaurant table, trying to keep a conversation going, with the silence from her mum's absence shouting louder than anything they could say. No, she couldn't do it. They'd have to do it sometime – it was one of many things they'd have to do for the first time without her mum. But sometime was not today. Definitely not today.

'I don't feel like going out,' she said, jumping up abruptly. 'I'll cook. Let's go and have a look what's in the freezer.'

# 11

# Aidan

When Aidan got home, the house was tidy and he found Chloe and Amy in the kitchen. Amy was reading instructions from a recipe on her phone while Chloe stirred something in a saucepan on the cooker. She bent over and sniffed it suspiciously.

'Hey,' he said, surprised. 'I thought we were going out.'

'We did some cleaning, and there was some stuff in the fridge about to go off,' said Chloe. Her face looked pinched and tense. 'Now that we've eaten all the leftovers and casseroles, I thought we'd better get into cooking for ourselves.'

'What are you making?'

'We put a list of the ingredients we had into a recipe website and it came up with this vegetarian curry. We've had to substitute a few things . . .' Chloe bent over the saucepan again. 'It smells a bit weird.'

Aidan wanted to hug her. She was being brave, trying to move on and do things for herself. He'd happily have eaten whatever she'd cooked.

He went over to the saucepan. 'Smells amazing,' he said. 'Fragrant and exotic. And I'm starving. Shall I put on some rice? Amy, are you staying for dinner?'

'Thanks, but I can't.' Amy smiled.

Aidan found himself wishing desperately that Amy would stay, so that he and Chloe wouldn't be left alone with the enormity of what he had just seen in the lab. An image of iRachel's beautiful, impassive face flashed before his eyes. He looked down at his hands. They were shaking slightly. Dear God.

'Are you sure?' he said, trying not to sound pleading or desperate.

'Mum's cooked our dinner, and I said I'd be home at six.'

He thought of suggesting he ring her mum and ask her to let Amy stay with them, but he knew Chloe would find that suspicious.

His head ached. He wanted to go upstairs and climb into bed, pull the duvet up over his head and sleep and sleep. He didn't want to deal with the avalanche of information and pain. Not now, and preferably not ever. But instead he smiled brightly, fetched himself and the girls glasses of juice from the fridge, and sat and made small talk while his stomach clenched and his heart broke quietly in his chest.

# 12

# Chloe

**C** I am a terrible person.

**A** What? You're not.

**C** I am. After you left, we sat down and ate the curry. And let me tell you it was *disgusting*. Dad was all like – Oh, darling, this is delicious. You're such a gourmet chef. But even he couldn't finish it.

**A** That doesn't make you a terrible person. Just a terrible cook. And we knew that.

**C** Ha ha. No, it was after that. Dad made it through dinner, but he looked completely terrible. All bruised round his eyes. He kept doing this thing where he would breathe in like he was going to talk, but then he'd stop and not say anything.

**A** What do you think he wanted to say?

**C** I think he wants to have like a heart-to-heart. Talk about the future and stuff.

**A** So?

**C** I can't, Amez. I just can't. So I ran away.

**A** You ran AWAY?

**C** OMG what do you think I am? Not away, like out on the street and stuff. Just upstairs to my room. I said I wanted to go back to school tomorrow so I had to get my stuff together. Now I'm hiding.

**A** Are you coming back to school then?

74

C  Well I have to now, don't I?

A  **I suppose so.**

C  I can't spend the rest of my life hiding from my dad though.

A  **Would it be so awful to have a proper conversation with him?**

C  No. I mean yes. I don't know. I don't know how I feel. But I'm scared I'll say the wrong thing.

A  **What's the wrong thing?**

C  I don't know. I think lots of wrong things. Like . . . sometimes I'm so fucking furious with Mum, I don't know what to do.

A  **Furious?**

C  I keep thinking about my grandma dying of the same thing. I keep thinking that maybe she knew she had the brain aneurysm but she didn't do anything about it. She could have had surgery. I looked it up. But what if she didn't because of her precious brilliant mind?

A  **Wow.**

C  I know. So now I have no mum, and her precious brilliant mind is gone anyway. Ashes. Literally.

A  **I'm sorry.**

C  So imagine if she had had the surgery? And maybe she wasn't so brilliant anymore? Maybe she wouldn't have been the world's best AI expert. Maybe she'd have had to stay home and look after me instead. Would that have been so bad?

# 13
## Luke

His hand hurt. A lot. He had to get out of the habit of punching inanimate objects when he got angry. His work relied on fine motor co-ordination, and if he messed up his hands, he wouldn't be able to work. Not that he could do any work. Not after the stunt that Rachel had pulled.

There was a sizeable dent in the metal cabinet where he had hit it. Luckily, it was on the side closest to the window, so anyone looking into the lab wouldn't see it. And it wasn't as if he let people in here very often. The level of privacy given to researchers had been a big factor in his choosing Telos as his base. To say he didn't like small talk was an understatement. He didn't like to hang around in the communal kitchen making tea, and he seldom attended any social events organised by the management team. Luke had never been comfortable around people. A solitary child, who loved to stay alone in his room dismantling electronics and rebuilding them, he had gone on to become a self-contained adult. He had relationships with women, but they tended to be short-lived and superficial. He had no time for anyone he considered to be his intellectual inferior, which was everyone, with one notable exception.

Rachel had always been his buffer. She was the 'nice' one, the sociable one, who would go to meetings and report on their work, and who would keep people away from him and the lab. And now she was gone. Not only was she gone, but she'd betrayed him so brutally with her reprogramming of #787775 that he didn't know where to begin. When he'd listened to her message to him the night before, he had raged, yelling and punching the cabinet. If he could have got his hands on Rachel, he might not have been held responsible for his actions.

As it happened, he couldn't even get his hands on iRachel, the android. It had told him it would play the message through the speakers of his laptop, connecting remotely. Then it had gone into the holding room and shut itself in. After he'd heard what Rachel had to say, he'd tried to open the door, but iRachel had barred it somehow.

This did nothing to calm his fury. If this was a chess game, Rachel had been ten moves ahead of him, and he hadn't foreseen her checkmate.

They had argued endlessly about this next phase of their research. Rachel had insisted that the only way to truly test iRachel's empathetic learning was to place it in the field – in a controlled environment but out of the laboratory. Luke had had a million objections – how would he maintain the android? What if it was damaged? How were they to select the subjects with whom they would test the robot?

He had believed that these discussions were at an early phase. He had thought they would write up a detailed brief for research subjects, recruit candidates and hold extensive interviews; he'd thought that they might even create a living space within the laboratory so the subjects could come in rather than have iRachel going out. But Rachel had completely ignored his wishes and gone her own way.

It wasn't the first time. They'd fallen out badly once before, when they were working on their Mark 1 model. He'd been interested in the empathy software but hadn't seen the need for the robot to speak. It was only going to change beds and spoon-feed dementia patients after all. But he had come in one morning to discover that Rachel had designed and uploaded language files and a conversation program to the prototype. It never shut up after that, following him around the lab, asking him questions. When he yelled at Rachel for overriding his wishes, she smiled blithely and said, 'Well, we wouldn't know till we tried, would we?'

When they'd started on the Mark 2, he'd disconnected the Mark 1's battery and shoved the android in a cupboard in the storage room. That stopped the endless nagging.

But this time Rachel had really forced his hand – he would have to do what she'd demanded. She'd made sure of that. The question was – how? There was no way Telos management would permit him to do it. It would have to be done in secret.

# 14
## Aidan

Chloe had insisted on returning to school. He'd thought she wasn't ready, but she was determined.

'It's not going to get any easier,' she'd said, stuffing books into her backpack. 'I'd rather just get it over with. I'll have a day or two of everyone staring at me like I'm a freak and refusing to talk to me, and then they'll forget and I can just get on with things. Amy and Jess will look after me.'

'As long as you're sure,' said Aidan dubiously. 'Do you want me to drive you?'

'No!' said Chloe, so sharply that he recoiled a little. 'It's okay.' She softened her tone a little. 'Just let me do it. I'll be fine.'

She swung her bulging bag onto her shoulder, kissed him hard and quickly on the cheek, and slipped out of the door.

Aidan wandered back into the house and gathered up their breakfast dishes. The kitchen window faced the road, and he looked out across the front lawn as he filled the sink with hot water and bubbles.

He wasn't due to go back to work yet. He also knew that if he asked for more time off, they would give it to him. It wasn't as if he was a kingpin in a large organisation.

'Take as much time as you need,' Fiona had said. 'We'll cover for you.'

She really meant it too. He knew she'd keep paying him pretty much forever, even if he couldn't come back for months. She was like that. He loved their happily shambolic office and his colleagues, and he had no ambitions to work anywhere more high-powered. He was helping people, in his own small way, and that was enough for him.

He knew that if it had been the other way round – if he had died and Rachel had had to take time off – Telos would have given her the statutory minimum and no more. But that was because she had chosen the pressured world of research, funded by multimillion-pound grants. If Rachel was away from work or not producing the goods, the people who signed the very big cheques would have had questions. If he had died and she had lived, how long would Rachel have stayed away from the lab? She'd probably have been back there the day after his funeral. She'd have buried herself in her work in order to recover. But then she used to bury herself in her work no matter what happened. His death would merely have been a blip in her routine.

Dark thoughts. He knew he was just going around in circles in his head, torturing himself. He also knew that he was avoiding thinking about the robot, iRachel, and what Rachel's message had said. He'd left the lab promising to think about it, but he just couldn't. He couldn't imagine bringing the strange, electronic version of his wife into the house. It was so like Rachel and yet so unlike her. It had her face, her height, her figure, and it even managed a passable imitation of many of her facial expressions. But it wasn't her in the most crucial way. Rachel's beauty wasn't in her fine features or her blonde hair. It was in her warmth, intelligence and quicksilver wit.

She.

What was he thinking? He'd fallen into the same habit as Rachel and Luke, of referring to iRachel as 'it'. Like she wasn't human. Like she was a toaster or something. The truth was, she was just a machine. Whatever brilliant technology had gone into her creation, she was just metal, wires and latex. She wasn't a warm, breathing, thinking human. But he'd seen something in her. Something more than clever programming and terabytes of information. There was a wistfulness about her. A loneliness. A genuine desire to connect. And he found he did want to call her 'she', even if it wasn't technically correct.

He could imagine Rachel laughing at him. 'You're anthropomorphising!' she'd have said. 'You see almost anything as human!'

She would have been right, of course. His response to iRachel was visceral, not scientific. He saw her as human because he desperately wanted her to be so.

When Rachel got impatient with him, she used to call him a hopeless romantic. But most of the time she had respected his emotional intelligence. He was the quiet one, and in a group of people he would notice the nuances of conversation, the things unsaid, the facial expressions and shared glances. All too often Rachel would be moving too fast to see that stuff, and she would listen, fascinated, when he recounted what he had observed.

Now he needed to think about what he had seen and experienced. He needed to come to terms with the enormity of Rachel's lies. How could she have kept this from him? If he allowed himself to think about it, he'd have to think about what that said about their marriage. He wasn't ready for that. Not even close.

He wasn't a stupid man, but he lacked Rachel's razor-sharp, incisive brain, which operated so much faster than anyone else's. She would absorb every detail about a problem, would consider every possible angle and implication and would make a rapid and informed decision. Aidan couldn't do that. He needed time to assess, and especially time to let his emotions settle.

iRachel had sparked powerful and confusing feelings in him. He was also deeply suspicious of Luke's motives. Had Luke known of Rachel's wishes all along? The fact remained, Rachel wanted him to bring iRachel here, to live with him and Chloe, however mad and repugnant he might find it. And what about Chloe? How could he tell her? How could he not tell her?

The water to wash the dishes had gone cold. He shook his head and emptied the sink so he could begin afresh. But as he put the plug in and set the tap running, he caught a movement in the road outside. Their street was quiet, well off the main road, and at this time of the day traffic was downright unusual. He saw an unmarked white van pull up to the kerb and stop. A delivery vehicle? He hadn't ordered anything, but maybe one of the neighbours was getting a new washing machine or something. He watched idly as the driver hopped out and walked round to the rear of the van. The man was compact and stocky and he wore a baseball cap pulled low over his eyes. He unlocked the back doors and flung them wide, then stepped back.

Rachel stepped gracefully from the back of the van, then turned and looked up at the house. Aidan felt like someone had punched him in the chest. His breath came in short, sharp bursts. He was so transfixed by the sight of her that he left the tap running, oblivious to the fact that the sink was filling rapidly.

It was iRachel, of course, not Rachel. The man in the baseball cap was Luke and the figure who was now walking slowly and tentatively up the front path was not his dead wife but her android double.

The sink was about to overflow. He instinctively put his right hand into the water to pull out the plug. The pain was intense. Their hot water always ran at a scalding temperature and he had plunged his whole hand in unthinkingly. He cried out in pain and stepped back from the sink, clutching his hand to his chest. Tears sprang to his eyes just as iRachel, with Luke close behind her, stepped up onto the porch and rang the doorbell.

What was he to do? He couldn't leave them out on the street

– he could imagine one of his neighbours looking out and seeing a figure who was unmistakably the late Dr Rachel Prosper ringing her own doorbell. However much he wanted to run and hide, he needed to get them inside, and fast.

He grabbed a dishtowel, ran it under the cold tap and swaddled his throbbing, stinging hand in it, then raced to the front door and flung it open.

'Come inside,' he said urgently, 'before someone sees you.'

iRachel looked into his face, her wide, beautiful eyes the exact shade of green that Rachel's had been. She stepped calmly over the threshold. Aidan all but dragged Luke in after her and shut the door behind him.

'What the hell are you doing here?' Aidan asked. 'I didn't agree to this. Why have you brought her here?'

Luke took off his cap and ruffled his hair. He opened his mouth to answer but then hesitated, as if he didn't know where to begin.

Rage and adrenaline got the better of Aidan. 'For God's sake, Luke. Does Telos know you've taken her? Are we not going to get into the most enormous trouble for this?'

Luke was about to reply, but his eyes were drawn to iRachel. Aidan noticed his dumbfounded expression and followed his gaze.

iRachel had walked across the hallway and was standing in front of the mirror that was hung on the wall opposite the door. It was a beautiful, age-spotted mirror in an elaborate silver art nouveau frame. Rachel had bought it in a junk shop when she was a student, and it had become one of her most prized possessions. It had been in the hallway of every home she had had since. She always paused in front of it to check her reflection before she left the house.

iRachel's posture was unnaturally still, Aidan observed. Well, it would have been unnatural if she were human. He had never noticed, day to day, how much people moved, whether they were awake or asleep. But iRachel was frozen motionless before the mirror, neither breathing nor blinking. He glanced at Luke, who was watching her with trepidation. He clearly didn't know what was happening either.

Luke took a hesitant step towards iRachel and she turned to him.

'The reformatting protocol has been terminated.'

Luke let out a sigh. His shoulders sagged, and he turned away for a second. Aidan could hear him muttering under his breath.

'Thank fuck,' he said, relieved.

'What?' Aidan said, frustrated. 'What the hell just happened?'

'You know how Rachel recorded a message for you?' Luke said. 'She recorded one for me too. Did you know what was in it?'

'No.'

'She knew I would never agree to the android coming to live with you. So she wrote a program into the hard drive. If the robot wasn't in your house within twenty-four hours of her message, iRachel's hard drive would reformat and wipe itself. Completely.'

'Would that be so bad? Surely you have all the files and things backed up?'

'The original files, yes. But not its learning. Not all the adaptations it's made, and the data it's extrapolated for itself, during all the experiments we've done. I could reload the language files and so on, but it'd be like a newborn baby. All our work would be lost.'

Aidan looked over at iRachel. 'What just happened? With the mirror?'

'Rachel has embedded a sensor in this mirror,' she explained. 'I needed to stand in front of it and connect my optical camera with the sensor for thirty seconds. The sensor then transmitted a code to me. This key code stopped the countdown to reformatting.'

Aidan found himself smiling and shaking his head. That was so Rachel. To make a code that was clever, unhackable and specific. Even if Luke had known about the sensor in the mirror, he wouldn't have been able to get to it without Aidan's permission. He looked at the mirror now. Wherever Rachel had put the sensor, it wasn't visible to the naked eye.

'Shall we go through to the living room?' he said. His voice sounded strained and unnaturally polite.

They went through and Luke sat, looking uncomfortable, on the edge of the sofa. Aidan took an armchair opposite him, and iRachel remained standing in the middle of the carpet.

'Please sit down,' said Aidan.

iRachel glided gracefully over to the dining room table, drew out a chair and sat, straight-backed and poised, hands resting on her knees. In that moment she didn't resemble Rachel at all. Rachel had been a floor sitter, a sofa sprawler, a knee-jiggling, never-sit-still whirl of motion. iRachel had the still composure of a ballerina. She was wearing a plain white shift, like a long shirt, which buttoned down the front. It was pristine and uncreased. She wore white tennis shoes on her feet. Her hair was the same length and colour that Rachel's had been but was somehow smoother and shinier. She looked like Rachel's neater, calmer twin.

They sat without speaking, looking at each other. Well, Aidan thought, this is not a conversation I ever imagined having. I have no idea what to say.

Luke spoke, breaking the silence. Without looking at iRachel, he said, 'So the reformatting protocol was terminated?'

'Yes,' iRachel said.

'You're not going to wipe the hard drive or damage the operating system?'

'No.'

Luke nodded and stood up. 'Well, let's go then.'

'Pardon?' said Aidan and iRachel simultaneously.

'Let's go back to the lab. We've solved Rachel's little puzzle. The game's over.'

'No,' said iRachel.

'No?' Luke's eyes glittered dangerously.

'I am required to remain here,' said iRachel, and her voice had some of Rachel's steely determination.

Aidan found himself smiling. Luke ought to know that tone of voice as well as he did.

'You don't get a choice,' said Luke. 'You're the property of Telos, and I should never have gone along with this ridiculous blackmail. I'm taking you back.'

'No,' said iRachel. 'There are other safeguards in place.'

'Other what?'

'Safeguards. Rachel built in other checks, to make sure that once I entered the house, I would remain here for the allotted time.'

'Checks like what?'

'A Trojan virus.'

'What?' said Luke, disbelievingly.

'When you scanned my operating system before we left the lab, you probably didn't notice the small .exe file which looks as if it is related to my blinking function.'

Luke didn't reply.

'It's a virus. Unless I repeat the face-matching scan in the mirror in the hallway every six hours, the virus will activate and infect my files.'

'I'll take the sensor out of the mirror,' said Luke.

'The sensor is concealed within the mirror itself. If you try to remove it, it will be destroyed and the virus will be unstoppable.'

'We can just run an antivirus program and clear it,' he said desperately, but Aidan could hear from his tone that he knew how hopeless this was.

'Rachel wrote the virus,' said iRachel, as if this was sufficient explanation. And indeed it was.

'So you're here to stay,' Luke said flatly.

'Wait,' said Aidan abruptly. 'Do I not get a say in this?'

'A say in what?'

'Her staying. How am I supposed to explain this to Chloe? To our family and friends? To anyone?'

'Well, first of all, you can't tell anyone but Chloe,' said Luke. 'Genuinely. No one can know. This project is secret – so top secret, not even Telos's management knows how advanced our work is.'

'I don't think you have any idea how much this is going to upset Chloe,' said Aidan. 'She'll be home from school in a few hours. How can I possibly explain this to her?'

'You mean,' said Luke slowly, 'you haven't told her?'

'No,' said Aidan shortly.

'You came to the lab yesterday and saw iRachel and didn't think to mention it to your daughter?'

'No, it just slipped my mind,' said Aidan sarcastically. 'Maybe if you had kids of your own, you'd understand that sometimes you need to protect them. She's just lost her mum. How is she supposed to cope with . . .' He gestured towards iRachel. '. . . this?'

Luke leaned back on the sofa, making himself comfortable. 'Yeah, well, that's not surprising, I guess.'

'What's that supposed to mean?'

'Nothing.'

'Clearly it doesn't mean nothing or you wouldn't have said it. What do you mean, "that's not surprising"?'

'Well,' said Luke, feigning reluctance, 'Rachel did always say you were a spineless ditherer who couldn't make decisions . . .'

Aidan stood abruptly. His scalded hand hurt fiercely, but he could still use his left hand to punch Luke right in the mouth. 'Listen, you little shit . . .' he began.

'She didn't.' iRachel's voice cut through.

He ignored her. He took a menacing step towards Luke, who looked relaxed and didn't move from his position on the sofa.

'She didn't say that.' iRachel's voice was louder and more insistent.

'Didn't say what?' Aidan spoke over his shoulder, keeping his eyes fixed firmly on Luke.

'She didn't say you were a spineless ditherer at any point in the last forty-five days of her life. The only reference to dithering came in a conversation between Luke and Rachel on 23 February this year, at 10.14 a.m., which concerned a decision about your forthcoming summer holiday plans.' She began to quote the conversation as if reading from a court transcript.

'Luke: So have you booked anything yet?

'Rachel: No, not yet.

'Luke: I thought you were planning to book this past weekend?

'Rachel: We were. But then Aidan started reading reviews of the hotel I picked out in Florence and he thinks it isn't good enough. He wants to do some more research.

'Luke: Blimey. He doesn't move fast, your husband.

'Rachel: He's cautious. He wants things to be as good as they can be, so he checks things out thoroughly. Plans ahead.

'Luke: Sounds like dithering to me.'

There was a pause, and then iRachel said, 'Conversation terminated at 10.15 a.m.' She looked at Luke. 'I've scanned all my records, and at no point in Rachel's conversations with you did she ever use the word "spineless", nor the word "ditherer", or any of its synonyms, in relation to Aidan or indeed anyone else.'

Luke and Aidan stared at iRachel, dumbfounded.

'Did you record every conversation we had in the lab?' Luke asked finally.

'I am designed to record and remember everything,' she said simply.

Aidan sat back down slowly. He carefully unwound the dishtowel from his right hand. The skin was pink and shiny and had broken out into a cluster of blisters. Without looking up, he said, 'If she stays . . .' He paused for a long second. 'If she stays, what will Chloe and I have to do?'

Before Luke had a chance to answer, iRachel spoke. 'I have been taught to perform all common housekeeping tasks. I can launder clothes, iron, clean and cook. Rachel has given me access to her online shopping accounts, so I can keep the household well stocked and manage day-to-day financial transactions, paying bills and so on. I will learn a great deal just from being in a human household and observing daily rituals. If you and Chloe do not want to interact with me, that is entirely your choice.'

'It sounds pretty perfect to me,' said Luke. 'Someone to wait on you hand and foot, who never gets tired or complains, doesn't need food or holidays, and doesn't even need you to be polite. It's built to learn too, so if you don't like the way it cooks your steak, just tell it, and it'll improve next time.'

Aidan ignored his rudeness and asked, 'For how long?'

'There is currently no end-date built into the experiment,' she said. 'Or at least one has not been revealed. Previous experience suggests, however, that Rachel will have built it into the code and will reveal it in due course.'

'So once you've gathered the data Rachel thought she would need, you'll say you're ready to go back to the lab?' asked Aidan.

iRachel nodded.

'It'd better not be too long,' said Luke. 'I've kept the

management out of the lab so far, but sooner or later they're going to want to know what we've been working on. I have to go and speak to the board soon. I can't put them off forever.'

iRachel turned her cool gaze on him. 'May I suggest you upload the language and context files to the non-humanoid Mark 1 prototype, which is currently in the storage cupboard in the holding room? It has a small bug, for which Rachel wrote a patch program. It can do everything I can do. The only difference is that it does not resemble a human being. You will be able to continue the work of empathetic learning and mapping and will have something to show the board if they have any questions.'

'I suppose this is another of Rachel's brilliant contingency plans?' Luke said sarcastically.

'No,' said iRachel coolly, 'it is my own plan. In my time in the holding room I investigated the prototype and saw its potential.'

Aidan found himself laughing, but Luke's scowl brought him up short.

'So that's what I'm supposed to do while you all play happy families?' Luke said petulantly. 'Just sit in the lab and wait for your call?'

'This will be the first time I have been fully operational for extended periods of time,' iRachel said. 'I will need regular maintenance checks and the ability to upload data as I gather it.'

'Well, as you seem to be calling the shots, when would you like me to service you?' Luke smirked.

'Once a week should be sufficient. If I have an emergency or there is an irretrievable breakdown, you will, as you know, receive an urgent instant message.'

'Well, it looks like we've been told,' Luke said to Aidan. 'It's staying here, and that's it. Sorry I can't be more help with the whole Chloe thing, but I'm afraid that's your department. How you tell her is up to you.' He didn't sound sorry.

Aidan felt as if he was teetering on the edge of a cliff. As much as he disliked Luke, he was suddenly desperate for him to stay. He couldn't imagine being left alone in the house with iRachel's cool, impassive presence. There was a world of secret knowledge and technology hidden behind the facsimile of Rachel's dear face. It was too much, too soon, too painful. He was terrified. What had Rachel been thinking?

When they reached the hallway, Luke turned back and begrudgingly offered Aidan his hand to shake. Aidan winced and held up his hand to show the blisters and scalded skin. Luke looked at it for a long moment, then grinned and showed Aidan his own hand, injured from punching the metal cabinet.

'What the hell did you do?' asked Luke.

'I could ask you the same question,' said Aidan.

'Woman trouble,' Luke said, raising an eyebrow.

'I can relate to that.'

# 15

## iRachel

'This is a service message:

'Good day. I am iRachel, a humanoid android. I am here to assist you in any way you require. I can impart this message to you in text, by voice or as a video transmitted to a computer or television.

'I am an empathetic robot, who responds to the humans with whom I interact. I learn from these interactions, and in this way I become more able to help and a better companion to you.

'My co-creator, Luke, has supplied each of you with a wristband to wear. This wristband is made of black rubber and resembles many of the sports watches or fitness monitors currently available.

'The band will allow me to measure certain physiological responses. These include your heart rate and galvanic skin response – in other words, any increase in sweat resulting from stress. I use my cameras to record facial expression and pupil dilation as well as vocal tone. I am also able to assess the speed of your respiration. All of this data helps me to calculate and express appropriate empathetic responses.

'I am able to walk, talk and perform many useful human activities. My motor co-ordination is good, and I can execute useful household tasks. I do not require sleep or food but will need to be connected to a standard wall socket, via a USB charging connector, for approximately five hours in every twenty-four.

This can usually take place during the hours when you are likely to be asleep. I am able to put myself on charge.

'Should you require information from me, I can speak or play audio recordings. If you are away from the area where we interact, I can access your mobile telephone to send a text or audio message, video or image. I am always here to serve you. Even when I am on charge, I can be contacted, and if you are within transmission range (approximately 100 metres), I can access and interpret the physiological data from your wristband.

'I look forward to helping you.

'Message ends.'

# 16

# Chloe

**Via: Facebook Messenger**
**To: Amy Lucas**
**18.34**
[To chat with Amy and other friends, turn on chat.]

Oh my God, Amy. I have to write this all down, because I can't
ring or text you (will explain why in a minute) and even if I
could, it would come out all wrong. Some stuff is happening
in my house and I want you to know that I am not mad or
hallucinating or whatever. This is real. One hundred per cent
real. I am not making this up. You've known me since I was
four and you know I am not crazy.
I am going to start at the beginning.
After my mum died, one of the things that made me feel worst
was the fact that I would never really understand her work. All
those times she tried to talk to me about it – she had this way
of explaining it really slowly and simply, like I was an idiot, and
it made me so crazy, I'd roll my eyes and change the subject.
She could be incredibly superior sometimes. But I suppose in
the back of my mind I thought that one day she'd stop talking
to me like a five-year-old and I'd take time to understand it all.
And now she's dead, I feel really shit because I actually didn't
know anything about what she was trying to achieve.
Well, surprise, surprise, now I know. How do I know?

Because it's in our house, that's why.

After I said goodbye to you on the bus and walked home, I felt OK. School hadn't been that bad, and I was looking forward to having some normal stuff to talk to Dad about. But when I opened the front door, he was standing right there in the hallway with this totally weird expression on his face. Like he was scared of me or something.

And then he said, 'We really need to talk, Munchkin.' He hasn't called me Munchkin since I was about four and I thought, wow, he's really losing it now. We went and sat at the kitchen counter and he held my hand really tightly. Then he started this long, rambling monologue – something about my mum's legacy, and how she was such an amazing scientist, and that there was a tragedy just as big as our personal tragedy, the tragedy of the loss of her work, and I wouldn't want that to happen, would I? So I said, no, of course not, but really carefully, because I didn't know what he was talking about. Did he expect me to learn about robots? Because I am, as you well know, the world's biggest numbskull where science is concerned.

Anyway, he kept using that word. Legacy. And I thought he meant like money or jewellery or something. And I was a bit confused, because what did that have to do with her work? And he said that her choice might be hard for us, but we had to accept that it was what she wanted and go with it, no matter how strange we might find it.

So this is the part where you probably start to think I'm the one that's mad. But it's true. This was my mother's 'legacy', as my dad calls it. She was building a robot that is so realistic that if most people saw it, they probably wouldn't even know it wasn't human. It looks like a person, talks like a person, moves, has facial expressions, everything.

And if that isn't creepy enough, she built it to look just like her.
I am not kidding. It is her absolute double.

And it was in our house, sitting on one of the dining room
chairs.

I screamed. I just screamed, because for the half a second
before I realised it couldn't be true, I thought it was a ghost.
My mother's ghost, sitting right there. Then the robot stood
up, and I could see instantly that it wasn't my mum. The
robot stood very tall and straight like a ballerina. It held out its
hand to me, and said, 'Chloe, I am pleased to meet you. I am
iRachel.'

That's what it calls itself. iRachel. Like iPod or iPhone. Except I
didn't call my mum Rachel, so what was I supposed to call it?
iMum?

I can tell you something. I'm not going to call it anything. It is
the most creepy, freaky, disgusting thing I have ever seen. I
don't want it anywhere near me. So I turned and ran upstairs
and shut myself in my bedroom.

Dad came thundering up the stairs and said, 'Chloe, Chloe,
come back. Whatever you do, you can't tell anyone about this.
This is top secret, OK? iRachel isn't supposed to be away from
the lab at all. We could get into big trouble.'

Well, I wasn't going to tell anybody. I was only going to tell you.
You're not anybody. I tell you everything, and I know you would
never tell my secrets to anyone else. But then Dad said through
the door, 'Not even Amy. I'm serious, Chloe.'

Well, I planned to ignore that. But then I realised I had left my
school bag downstairs, and my phone was in it. That didn't
bother me so much – I still had my laptop, but when I logged
on, I discovered the Wi-Fi wasn't working. I couldn't believe it.
Dad had cut me off. Well, he can't leave the router switched off
forever, so I'm typing this message, and I'll send it later when

he turns it back on. Or when he goes to bed, I'll turn it
on myself.
Cx

**Update: 22.11**

Dad's been outside my door for hours now, saying, 'Chloe,
please let me in,' and 'Chloe, you have to eat something.' But
I've been ignoring him. I just want him to go away. All I can
think about is that weird thing downstairs. I had a packet of
Haribos in my room, and, can you believe it, a leftover Easter
egg I'd forgotten about on the top shelf of my wardrobe, so it's
not like I've starved or anything. I thought I could stay here till
Dad got bored, but he was persistent. He wouldn't go away.
I was wondering if he'd ever leave, so I could sneak to the
bathroom, because I really needed the loo and I was thirsty.
I was starting to get desperate, and then, miracle of miracles, I
heard Dad stand up (he'd been sitting on the floor outside my
door) and go downstairs. I ran for the door and made a dash
to the bathroom. I locked myself in. I filled a glass with water to
take back with me and was just about to check that the coast
was clear when I heard a voice outside the door.
'Chloe, this is iRachel.'
I swear it sounded just like my mum. It was horrible.
'Sod off,' I said. I hadn't heard any footsteps, so I didn't think
Dad was out there as well. If he was, he didn't tell me off for
using bad language, and he never misses a chance to do that.
'Your father tells me that you are upset,' said the freak. 'I am
only able to read human emotions from physiological signs and
from visual cues. I am unable to respond to your distress if I
can't see you or give you your wristband.'
My what now? Why did it want to give me a wristband? What
kind of wristband? How long could it stay outside the bathroom

97

door? It had to run out of battery at some point, surely?

At least I was in the bathroom if I needed the loo again, and I had water. I figured it was probably better as a long-term hiding place than my bedroom, even if it wasn't very comfortable. I could stay there for as long as I needed to. I'd line the bath with towels and sleep in there. But then the horror machine did the weirdest thing ever. You know we have that speaker system that Mum installed, all through the house? So you can use your phone to Bluetooth music to speakers in any room? Well, there are speakers in the bathroom, so the freak began to broadcast sound via them.

It was a pre-recorded announcement explaining what the robot is and how it works. It said that we have to wear these wristbands, which are like a Fitbit, so it can read our emotions and respond to them.

Then it said something that made my blood run cold: 'I can access your mobile telephone to send a text or audio message, video or image.' And I suddenly thought, oh my God, my mother built this. The tech-ninja. She's built this to get into my head. It can access my phone and my computer. It can read all my files, my messages, my WhatsApps and texts. It can probably send stuff out pretending to be me.

I panicked then. I flung the bathroom door open. The robot was standing just outside, but it saw me coming and took a step backwards. Good. If it hadn't, I would have knocked it flying. I ran past it down the stairs. Dad was sitting at the kitchen counter looking sad and tired. 'Chloe . . .' he said, but I ignored him and grabbed my school bag and ran back to my bedroom. I slammed the door and locked it.

I sat on my bed and went through my phone. I deleted every message and photograph. I shut down my Snapchat and WhatsApp accounts, and my Instagram. Then I opened my laptop and did the same. Every email and letter I had written, photos, everything except my actual schoolwork. I deleted my cookies and web search history, and emptied the trash too. I know that won't stop it finding stuff – I'm sure it can access things even if they're deleted – but I'm not going to make it easy.

Maybe you think I'm crazy. I mean, it's not like I have anything bad to hide. I'm not having sex with anyone or taking drugs or anything. But it's my life. My private life. My secrets. And I don't want some horrible robot to dig around in my stuff.

So all I have left on my laptop is this monster letter to you, Amy, which I've been typing in Facebook Messenger. I'm going to have to delete this now too, so you'll never get to read it, and then I'm going to shut down my Facebook account. Will I be able to tell you all of this? Will I ever be able to tell anyone? Who knows. All I know is that I'm not going to use any sort of electronic communication while that thing is in the house.

# 17
# iRachel

## Contact Log

Subject: Chloe Prosper-Sawyer

**Day One**

| Interaction start time: | 16.01 |
|---|---|
| Date: | 4 May |
| Heart rate: | 85 bpm |
| Skin temperature: | slightly elevated |
| Respiratory rate: | 22 bpm |

## Report:

Subject was persuaded by her father to wear a wristband 'for a week at least', allowing me to monitor her physiological stats. She entered the home carrying her school bag. Her vital signs were consistent with having undertaken moderate exercise (the 432-metre-long walk from the bus stop to the house).

I stood at the door to greet the subject and uttered the standard welcoming phrase, 'Hi, Chloe, how was your day?'

The subject looked at me. I observed a narrowing of her eyes and a dilation of the pupils. She did not reply to the greeting. Subject walked into the kitchen and took items from the refrigerator.

Items:

- One yoghurt, raspberry flavour.
- One carton of juice, 'Tropical Sunshine'.
- One punnet of grapes, green, organic.

I initiated level two of the greetings procedure by using the question, 'Anything interesting happen at school?'

Again the subject did not respond. She passed me, taking care not to allow any physical contact, then moved up the stairs and entered her bedroom. No change in vital signs. I heard the door close firmly.

**Interaction end time:** 16.03.

**Day Two**

| Interaction start time: | 16.05 |
|---|---|
| Date: | 5 May |
| Heart rate: | 89 bpm |
| Skin temperature: | slightly elevated |
| Respiratory rate: | 25 bpm |

## Report:

Subject entered the home.

I began the standard greeting procedure but had only said, 'Hi, Chloe, how was—' when the subject moved quickly past me and ran up the stairs, shutting the door to her bedroom. I followed her up the stairs and initiated the concern intervention, saying, 'You haven't eaten. Would you like me to bring you a snack?'

She responded with a phrase which was partially inaudible but when checked against my vocabulary database resembled 'Pith off.' Logic suggests this is not a reference to peeling citrus fruit but is instead a conventionally impolite request to remove myself from the vicinity.

**Interaction end time:** 16.05.

**Day Three**

| Interaction start time: | 16.15 |
| --- | --- |
| Date: | 6 May |
| Heart rate: | 95 bpm |
| Skin temperature: | elevated |
| Respiratory rate: | 30 bpm |

## Report:

Due to the fact that the subject entered the house later than on the previous two days, I was waiting close to the front door. She arrived at speed and expressed evidence of surprise at my presence.

Evidence:

- School bag dropped.
- Uttered the expletive 'Jesus Christ!'
- Rapid pupil dilation and notable increase in heart rate.

'Hi, Chloe,' I said. I was about to apologise, given the clear indication that she had received a shock, but she stepped closer to me and raised her right index finger towards my facial region.

She spoke in an agitated tone. 'Listen, you freak. Stop sneaking up on me. You creep me out.'

I used a soothing tone and completed the greeting protocol. 'How was your day?'

This seemed to increase her agitation. Her facial colour was heightened and I observed a marked increase in her respiration rate.

'Don't ask me how my day was. Don't run whatever code you have that my mum wrote to make me feel important and loved, okay? Because it doesn't work. Just leave me alone. Do you get that? Can you shove that into your little hard drive? Leave. Me. Alone!'

She then made a rapid ascent of the stairs and slammed the door, which I have identified as signifying the end of the conversation.

While my analysis of the physiological signs suggests Chloe was disturbed, she spoke a total of sixty-three words directly to me today. This is sixty-three more than on day one of our interaction and sixty-one more than on day two. This is significant progress. However, she made a direct request for me to desist from the greeting protocol, so from tomorrow I will initiate an alternative or indirect welcome

**Interaction end time:** 16.17.

# 18

# Aidan

6 May 22.45

Oh, my love.

I miss you.

'Miss'. What kind of a word is that?

I'm cold all the time. When I felt like this as a child, Sinead would say. 'You're sickening for something.' And I am. I'm sickening for you.

And she is not you.

She is you, but she isn't. I am aware of her all the time, but every now and then I let my guard down. I'm thinking of something else, and I step into the kitchen and see her profile, the curve of her shoulder, the way her hair falls.

It's like being punched. First, there's an instant of pure surprise — there is Rachel. My wife. My love.

And in almost the same moment, the knowledge hits that of course it isn't you, and you are dead.

After that, there's one pure instant of blank nothingness, silence and light, before the pain comes rushing in.

Somehow, we have edged tentatively back into a routine. Chloe goes to school and I go to work. Everything is different, and yet everything is the same. Chloe still can't bear to be woken up in the morning. Twenty per cent of my clients still don't turn up for their classes, and the rest regard me with resentful incomprehension. Lola at work still sings tunelessly at her desk without realising she's doing it, until we all yell at her to shut up. Different day, same shit.

But there are differences, apart from the obvious, I mean.

Chloe has gone full Amish on us. She refuses to use her mobile phone or laptop at all. She handwrites all her school assignments, and I see her scribbling non-stop in a hardcover notebook. I assume it's some kind of journal. She says she believes iRachel can access all our online communications and invade our inner thoughts, like she's some kind of hacker.

I don't think that's true, and iRachel assures me she can't access any personal information we don't choose to share, but Chloe's worries make me uneasy. So here I am, with an A4 lined pad of paper and a ballpoint pen, composing a handwritten letter to you, my dead wife. What would the postage cost for it to reach you, I wonder?

(If this was an electronic communication, I'd insert a smiley face here, so you knew I was joking. I guess I'll just have to draw one.)

☺

I find it difficult to write by hand. Like most people, I hardly ever do it these days. I've only done a few paragraphs and my hand is cramping – the words are hardly legible. Not that it matters, I suppose. No one is going to read this.

I'm trying to remember the last time I handwrote a letter to you. I suppose it would have been when you went off to Cambridge and I was still in London. I wrote at least once a week. But since then? We might have scribbled the occasional 'Buy milk' kind of note, I guess, but we communicated mainly by text message or email.

I used to write you love letters back then, do you remember? They were long and passionate and probably badly spelled. And if I remember rightly, full of details about what I wanted to do to you.

And that's what I miss. Can I say that? Can I write that in these pages, which no one will ever read? I fucking miss you. I miss fucking you. I miss the small sigh you'd give when I touched you in just the right way. I miss the taste of your mouth, and your sweat on my skin, and feeling your heart race – race! – when you came.

I miss you. I ache for you so damned much.

And it is in these most intimate and secret ways that she is not you. There is no warmth to her, no scent, no sudden dilation of the pupils or quickening of the breath. She is a still, perfect, silent, odourless, breathless version of you. A portrait. A moving photograph. I find myself shying away from her, afraid that I might accidentally brush past her and touch her. I am repelled by her. Because I know in all the ways that made you you to me – only to me – she cannot be you.

And I miss you.

My love.

# 19

# iRachel

## Contact Log

Subject: Chloe Prosper-Sawyer

**Day Four**

| Interaction start time: | 17.09 |
|---|---|
| Date: | 7 May |
| Heart rate: | 72 bpm |
| Skin temperature: | normal |
| Respiratory rate: | 18 bpm |

## Report:

Chloe approached the house at a reduced pace. I was occupied with enacting my revised welcome protocol in the kitchen area. She opened the door slowly, and I heard her move into the hallway. I did not initiate the greetings procedure. I recorded her intake of breath in the hallway and deduced that she had smelled the aroma of what I was preparing. I continued to stir without speaking. She moved into the living area and I recorded an increase in her heart rate.

'That's my mum's bolognese,' she said, and there was a tremble in her voice which suggested she was experiencing intense emotion. Her physiological signs were all heightened, but I was not looking at her face and could not map her expression to isolate what she was feeling.

'Yes, it is,' I said and added a small spoonful of sugar.

'How did you know how to make it?' The pitch of her voice rose and the tremor increased. I looked at her and could see she was secreting lacrimal fluid from her eyes, evidence of distress.

'I have a record of all the recipes Rachel used for cooking,' I said. 'She thought it would be comforting to you if you could continue to eat the meals you were familiar with.'

'How?' she asked.

'I am afraid I don't understand the question,' I said.

'How do you have the recipes? Did she have them written down? I never saw them.'

I placed a tablet computer on the kitchen counter and downloaded the recipe from my drive so that Chloe could see it.

'Here,' I said, drawing her attention to it.

She stepped closer and looked at the scanned document. It was a stained, typewritten piece of paper, to which Rachel had added some handwritten amendments. These included the words 'Dried oregano, not fresh' and 'Simmer for thirty-five minutes AT LEAST'.

Chloe looked at the document closely and reached out a hand. She touched one of her mother's scribbled notes lightly. Then she indicated something. Rachel had drawn a line through the typed heading 'Spaghetti Bolognese' and had handwritten the words 'Blobonese and Pasta Squiggles'.

'What's this?' Chloe asked.

I was able to answer this. I cross-referenced the term on my drive and brought up a short homemade video on the tablet screen. The quality was poor. Clearly it had been filmed at low resolution on a phone camera some years before. A small child sat at the same kitchen counter where I currently stood with Chloe. My facial-recognition software confirmed that this was Chloe when younger, and I calculated from the date of the recording that she was three years, five months and twelve days old in the video.

Her face was soiled with a reddish-brown substance and she waved a fork in the air.

'Yummy, Mummy,' she said, and she smiled at the camera.

'What's yummy?' said a voice. It was Rachel who was both film-ing and speaking.

'Blobonese and pasta squiggles,' said the small child. 'My favourite.'

Chloe began to have a physiological response for which I had no reference. She was weeping, consistent with sadness, but she was also laughing, as if she was happy or surprised. As I had no ap-propriate response in my repertoire, I remained silent. Seventy-five seconds had elapsed since I had last stirred the food, so I returned to the hob and picked up the spoon.

She was quiet for a further thirty-five seconds, and then she said, 'Can you play that video again?'

I replayed the video, and she responded with the same unusual physiological reactions. I continued to stir without speaking. Chloe drew up a kitchen stool and sat at the counter. She too was silent. This was unprecedented. She was choosing to remain in my pres-ence, and our interaction had stretched for a full five minutes and thirty-four seconds so far.

I searched my drives for something that would further strengthen our connection. I accessed Chloe's publicly shared musical database and saw a playlist of songs entitled 'Chloe and Mum – Road Trip'. I downloaded the playlist to the tablet and began to play it. The first file had a cheery, speedy beat I knew to be associated with mood enhancement. I instantly recorded an increase in heart rate for Chloe. She sat up straight suddenly and said, 'What the hell is this?'

'This is the Spice Girls' musical number "Wannabe", released in July 1996, two minutes and fifty-two seconds long,' I began to explain.

'Where did you get it?' She did not seem to be experiencing the music-related euphoria I had expected. Her voice had an abrupt and aggressive tone.

'This is the playlist you made, which I accessed—'

'Stop doing that, okay? Just stop it. Stop digging around in my stuff. I thought I'd deleted everything. If I find you hacking into my computer again, I'll get Dad to throw you out, I swear.'

She jumped off the stool and ran upstairs. I registered the door slamming.

Had she remained in the room, I would have reminded her that I am unable to access any private computer files and that data protection means I will never be able to do so. The playlist was freely available on the music-subscription website she used. But she was gone.

While this interaction was the most positive one I have attempted so far with Chloe, the ending was inexplicably negative. It is still difficult to predict how she will respond to my overtures, no matter how carefully planned they may be. Progress will not be linear, and it may be extremely slow.

**Interaction end time:** 17.17.

At 18.00 I performed my check-in with the mirror, lining up my optical cameras with the sensors. For the first time, I took a moment to look at my reflection, at the replica of Rachel's face which looked back at me. I allowed myself a small smile.

# 20

# Chloe

She cried a lot that evening. She didn't normally cry — she hadn't even cried that much the night her mum died — but she felt so alone. Her dad knocked on her door a few times, but she ignored him, and she didn't hear anything more from iRachel. She was hungry, but she felt so sick, she didn't want to eat anything. Eventually, she curled up under her duvet and fell asleep.

It was such a small noise, but it woke her up. A sheaf of paper being slid under her door. She thought it was a note from her dad at first. Whoever had slipped the pages through then walked away. She could hear their footsteps going down the stairs. She was awake now, and curious. She looked at the clock. It was just after midnight.

She got out of bed and went to pick the papers up. They were handwritten but somehow looked odd. She took them over to the bed and turned on the lamp. She recognised the writing immediately. It was her mum's. It was a handwritten letter which had been scanned or photographed and then printed out. Chloe sat down to read.

# 21

# Rachel

My darling Chloe,

I'm sitting writing this letter at my desk downstairs, and I can hear you in your bedroom above my head. You've got some music playing, and you're moving around the room. I think you're doing one of those mad wardrobe-tidying things you do every season, where you take out all your clothes and sort them by a method that no one else can understand, then bin half and obsessively refold and tidy the other half back into the cupboard. Every now and then I hear your voice. I suppose you're on the phone, and I suppose it must be Amy you are talking to. I so envy your closeness with her. I never had a friend like that, no matter how much I wished for one. I was an only child, as you are, but somehow you seem to have avoided the loneliness I felt.

I was always the odd, precocious one, daughter of the academics. In the funny little comprehensive where I started secondary school, I was a freak. I kept getting a hundred per cent on maths tests, and they had no idea what to do with me (although a few girls thought the answer was to push me into a bin head first). And then, when I was fourteen, I got a scholarship to an exclusive private school, and I didn't fit in there either. I had braces on my teeth and completely the wrong clothes. No one knew how to be my friend, and I didn't know how to have friends. You're so good at it, so easy socially, so able to talk at the right level, no matter who you're speaking to. I've always envied that.

You, my beautiful daughter ... what a mix you are of your dad and me. And yet wholly your own person too. Your brain is so sharp, so quick. Even when you were tiny you amazed me by how rapidly you grasped things. But you also have that quiet empathy, the ability to consider people and their feelings, that your dad has. Heart and head. What an unstoppable combination.

I am writing with a pen and paper. You know how unusual that is for me. I almost never write by hand. But I wanted this letter to you to be handwritten. I needed to form every letter and shape it exactly. I don't know why. Somehow I think that if you read this in my own funny scrawl, you'll know I wrote it, that no one edited, it, that it's definitely genuine. I know that you've always been wary of electronic communication and I kind of admire that. I have, as you know, bought into it completely. It's my life, the single best way for me to convey information. I speak code better than I speak English, some might say. Many might say. Probably everyone would say. So this letter will be scribbled in my own fair hand, and then I will scan it so it can exist in the virtual realm, because, my love, my own precious one, that is the only way I can be sure it will make its way safely to you when the time comes.

If you are reading this, the time has come and I am not with you anymore. I am so sorry. I don't know when or how it will have happened, or how old you might be. I hope it wasn't a horrid shock. As I write this, it's a few weeks before your fifteenth birthday, so I hope that you won't be reading this letter for many years to come.

This is a really difficult letter to write, as I am sure you can imagine. I am sitting here thinking, if Chloe is reading this, then it means I am dead. And that's a lot to get my head around. But the truth is, the basis of my work in AI is all algorithms. In their simplest form, these are based around the idea of 'if => then'. If this happens => then this process is initiated. I begin from what I know, or what I can prove to be true, and use this as the basis for new actions.

So let me try to explain. Here are the facts that I know:

- My mother died of a ruptured brain aneurysm in her fifties.
- An aneurysm is a bulge in a blood vessel caused by a weakness in the blood-vessel wall.
- Aneurysms are potentially hereditary.
- Two years ago, I had a scan which revealed I have an unruptured aneurysm, deep in my brain. It's possible to operate on it, but there is a risk of brain damage, and even if I survived the operation unscathed, my convalescence would be long and difficult.
- I have chosen, for the moment, not to have the surgery, and not to tell your dad or you about the aneurysm.
- Making this choice is a calculated risk (and because you know me, you know I have calculated the probabilities in detail), but it's still a risk. A gamble. If I have gambled and lost, all I can say again, is that I am so sorry.

Those are my facts. The unalterable truths upon which I will base my future actions. My 'ifs'. So what are my 'thens'?

There are lots of practical things I can put in place, and I have. These include:

- My will is up to date and filed with all our family papers.
- Telos took out a life-insurance policy for me that will pay out some money for you and Dad. You won't be rich, but you won't have to worry. I know you. I know you will have been concerned about this.
- I am devastated at the thought of leaving you and Dad. I love you both with all my heart. Nevertheless, on a practical level, I know how much you love each other. Dad has been responsible for caring for you on a day-to-day basis for most of your life. I know that even if I am not there, he will keep doing that.
- By the time you read this letter, you'll have learned about my current project, the empathetic humanoid robot. I am hoping,

if I am gone, that this robot will come to you when you need it most.

These things are never simple, so I will have to put some things in place to make sure it does come. It's my guess that Dad will be persuaded more easily than you will. If you accept iRachel into the house without a problem, you will never have cause to read this letter. If you are angry and struggle to interact with iRachel, it will access this file, connect to a printer and bring you a paper copy of the letter.

So here's another if => then.

If you reject iRachel => then you will be reading this letter.

And so I am asking you, as your mum, to give it a chance. Not forever. Just for a few weeks or months. Please, Chloe. Do it for me.

And now I have laid a massive post-mortem guilt trip on you, I want to spend the last part of this letter saying the things I very probably won't get to say to you face to face, if my death comes unexpectedly.

I know you think I spend too much time at work. I know (because you've yelled it at me more than once) that you think my work is more important to me than you are. Nothing could be further from the truth. Even when I'm not with you, I am thinking about you and loving you every minute of the day.

There are things I often say to you now, but I am not sure you always hear them. If I am not there to keep saying them, they are here, written down. And like the basis of a mathematical proof, they are things I know to be true.

- I love you with all my heart. I love you every second of every day and that never, ever wavers.
- You are perfect.
- You are cleverer, braver and stronger than you believe you are.
- What you see as 'nagging' and 'unrealistic expectation' is actually love, and my own clear-eyed view of your enormous potential.

- You will make good choices and have a successful future.
- Amy and Jess are good friends. That's rare. They are very precious. Treat them with kindness always.
- Your Grandma Sinead isn't an easy person, but she is a good woman. Try to treat her with more kindness and patience than I have ever managed to.
- Your father is the finest man I have ever known. He is noble and good-hearted and brave. Being loved by him is the greatest gift anyone could be given, and you and I are luckier than we can ever know.

I've filled up several pages here, darling one. I can hear you in the shower upstairs, music still playing. Soon you'll come trotting downstairs, all warm and sparkly and clean, in your fluffy hoodie and slippers. Perhaps I'll get a squeeze and a kiss on the top of my head. Perhaps you'll pass me by and go to the fridge for a snack. By then, these pages will be tucked away in my desk drawer, and I will sneak a look at your beautiful face and drink you in. I want to remember every tiny part of you. I want to store you up and imprint you on my eyes and brain and heart, so that wherever and whenever I must go, I will have you with me, forever.

All my love, and I do mean all of it,
Mum

# 22

# Aidan

There were days when Aidan loved his work, and days when it was the most thankless, grinding task. Today was the second kind. He'd been back at work for several weeks and was in the routine of his regular teaching sessions. He had spent the morning in a deathly dull budgeting meeting with Fiona. Yes, she knew the computers and software they were using were all but obsolete. No, there was currently no budget to replace them, nor did she know when there would be. iRachel had made him an exquisite packed lunch, but he'd forgotten to bring it with him so had to settle for a nasty supermarket sandwich and a packet of crisps instead. In the afternoon, he had taught a class on Microsoft Word to three clients. The girl had been reasonably competent. The petite, birdlike woman had asked non-stop questions, all of which showed that she had no grasp at all of what she was doing. She'd lapse into silence for ten minutes and then ask the same questions all over again. Slumped at the back of the class was a surly young man who lolled in his chair, one hand jammed into the pocket of his tracksuit bottoms. He picked his teeth and stared at his phone and refused to participate in any of the exercises. Aidan left the room for a few minutes (to avoid strangling the tiny bird woman) and returned to find the young man had tethered the PC to his phone, bypassing the web-filtering tools, and was watching hard-core porn in glorious technicolour with the sound turned up. He'd booted the guy out, but he thought the little woman was going to have an actual heart attack. No doubt she would write a stern letter of complaint. She'd have to handwrite it though, because she sure as hell wasn't going to be able to type it in Word.

He should have gone back to his desk to do some paperwork after the class, but he just couldn't settle down to anything, so at four o'clock he found himself in the kitchen, dipping gingernuts into a cup of tea and staring out of the window.

'Steady on,' said a voice behind him. 'Leave a few for the rest of us.'

He turned to see Kate, the occupational psychologist, standing in the doorway. She was holding her mug, ready to make herself a hot drink. Aidan glanced down at the packet of biscuits in his hand. He'd absentmindedly eaten half of them.

'Sorry. I had a nasty cheese and onion sarnie for lunch. Didn't realise I was still so hungry.'

'I have a salad in the fridge, if you'd like it,' said Kate, clicking on the kettle.

'No, thanks. That's very kind of you. I'll be going home in a little while anyway.'

'Good day?'

'Not really.'

'I heard about the guy with the porn.'

'If he could put those IT skills to use in the workplace, he'd be out-earning us all by next week.'

'Or hacking the Pentagon.'

'A high-risk but potentially lucrative career path.'

'I like your optimism.' Kate finished making her tea and turned to look at Aidan. 'So how are you doing?'

'Is that a psychologist question?'

'It was a friendly co-worker question. Do you want it to be a psychologist question?'

'Aha! You're doing that psychologist thing of answering a question with a question.'

'And you're doing that evasive thing of not answering the question I asked you.' She raised an eyebrow at him.

He laughed, despite himself. 'Well, I'm not fine, obviously. I'd be lying if I said I was. But I am all right, really. Functional. Getting by, I suppose.'

'And your daughter?'

'Chloe? She seems okay, most of the time. She was very angry to start with, but she seems . . . I don't know . . . more settled now.'

'It's early days yet.'

'I know.'

'Does she have anyone to talk to?'

'You mean someone professional? Do you think she should?' Aidan felt himself tense. He hadn't even considered sending Chloe for counselling. Should he? But there were enormous obstacles. How could she be honest and open? How could she go and see a psychologist and not talk about iRachel? But what if she really did need help with her grief? Was he scarring her irreparably? Was this another way in which he had failed her? He felt a sudden and powerful surge of anger towards Rachel. She was the one that had put them in this insane situation. Playing God with their lives. Manipulating everyone for her own ends. Why was she always so sure she was right?

'Are you okay?' Kate asked, and he became aware of her gaze on him.

'It is, as you say, early days,' he said, trying to speak with more conviction than he felt. 'I'll keep checking in with Chloe, and if and when she needs help, I'll make sure she gets it.'

'She spoke beautifully at Rachel's funeral,' Kate observed. 'She looks very self-possessed.'

Aidan laughed. 'She probably wouldn't agree with you,' he said. 'She sees herself as a mess. She can be a bit . . . unpredictable. She's got a brilliant mind, but she's quite prone to self-sabotage. Failing deliberately.' He felt a twinge of guilt at his disloyalty. Chloe would hate him talking about her to someone he hardly knew. But there was something about Kate's rapt and focused expression that invited confidence. Her eyes were a bright, warm brown, and she had a way of looking intently at you, as though you were the most fascinating person in the world.

'Well, by all accounts, Rachel was a very successful woman. Quite an act for a daughter to follow.'

Aidan felt his hackles rise. It was one thing for him to have opinions about his wife. But this was from someone who had never met her.

Kate must have seen something in his face, because she spoke quickly. 'I'm sorry. That was uncalled for. Nothing worse than people who know nothing offering advice on your life.'

He nodded, trying to be polite.

'Well, better get back to it,' Kate said. 'Those client reports aren't going to write themselves.' She held out a hand. Aidan wasn't sure what she wanted. Did she want to shake his hand, give it a squeeze, maybe? 'Any chance of a gingernut for the rest of us?'

'Of course. Here,' he said, flustered. He handed over the half-eaten packet of biscuits and watched her walk away, but his anger didn't abate. He felt he'd been managed, professionally pacified. She was a psychologist, after all.

# 23

# Chloe

Lunch at Grandma Sinead's wouldn't normally have been top of Chloe's want-to-do list. She had always wished for a TV-style grandma: someone warm, round and twinkly who dispensed hugs and was constantly baking or knitting chunky jumpers. Instead, she had got Sinead: tall and hawkish and always holding herself back, as if she was afraid that she might run out of whatever it was she was giving – attention, affection, roast chicken – if she was too liberal with it. Aidan made excuses for her. He said she was a post-war baby and had grown up with rationing. After that she'd been a single parent, trying to raise Aidan and his brother Oliver on her meagre salary as a medical secretary. There had never been quite enough to go round then, and she couldn't change her habits.

Even though her little house was now paid off and she had savings and a good pension, she hadn't lost the habit of econo-mising. Chloe, raised with Rachel's generosity and Aidan's warm, all-encompassing love, found her grandmother pinched and stingy. Even as a little child, she had sulked when Aidan had strapped her into her car seat with a cheery, 'Off to see Grandma Sinead!'

'No!' she would grumble. 'Grandma's house smells of old dinner. And she never lets me watch TV.'

As she'd got older, she'd learned ways to dodge visits to Sinead, inventing playdates with friends and suddenly remembering school projects that urgently needed to be finished. Rachel, who also didn't especially relish trips to see her mother-in-law, tacitly let her get away with it, but Aidan always looked hurt and disappointed.

Today, however, Chloe found herself jumping at the chance to go to Sinead's for Sunday lunch. Anything to get away from their house, with its overbearing atmosphere of grief, and the tension caused by iRachel gliding silently from room to room.

Nothing had changed. Sinead's boxy little house still had a faint whiff of gravy. She would not even consider turning on the television before 6 p.m. and never watched anything but the BBC as she disapproved of advertising. Everything was clean but genteelly faded. For Chloe's whole life, Sinead had had the same three-piece living-room suite and smoked-glass coffee table. She had a single bed in her small bedroom, with a well-washed candlewick bedspread. After years of arguments, Aidan had managed to persuade his mum that she could afford to get the place re-carpeted. Five years on, the carpets were still as good as new. She wouldn't stand for anything but socks or slippers in the house, and she hoovered daily. 'Those carpets will outlive us all,' Rachel had murmured naughtily in Chloe's ear on their last visit. Well, there was another memory to stab her in the heart.

Chloe and Aidan didn't say a word to each other on the drive over to Grandma Sinead's place. Chloe was still furious with him for having allowed iRachel into the house. He had tried to explain that it hadn't been his choice, that it was her mum's wish, but she refused to listen. She had maintained a low profile ever since, only emerging from her room for meals. She sat hunched over her plate, ignoring him and iRachel, who hovered nearby. She shovelled the food in as quickly as she could and then raced back upstairs. It was at one of these bolted meals that he had announced they were invited to Grandma Sinead's for Sunday lunch.

'Okay,' she'd said quickly, surprising herself. She was sick of her own company, and she was lonely. Keeping the secret of iRachel was exhausting. She'd told everyone that she'd accidentally put her phone in the washing machine and was waiting for a new one. The only way to stop herself blurting something out was to avoid Amy and Jess and her other friends. With no online chats, no social media and no phone, life felt very empty. Any excuse to leave the house and break the tension.

When they arrived, Sinead opened the door and looked at them. 'Oh, hello,' she said, then turned and walked back into the house.

'She looks delighted to see us,' said Chloe, and Aidan raised an eyebrow. They almost managed to share a smile, but then Chloe remembered how angry she was with him. She dropped her head again and trailed into the house after her grandmother.

Sinead headed straight into the kitchen to continue cooking. It was roast chicken for lunch. Surprise, surprise. Sunday lunch at Sinead's was always a roast, with the traditional extras: roast potatoes (never quite enough), broccoli and carrots, and thin gravy made with Bisto granules. She would never have even considered cooking something else – pasta or fish would be far too exotic, and any roast other than chicken was unnecessarily extravagant. Whenever Rachel had served beef, lamb or pork at their house, Sinead would say cautiously, 'Just a little for me, please. It's so rich.' Then she'd eat three bites and push her plate away with an expression of distaste.

With Sinead in the kitchen, Aidan wandered into the living room and Chloe found herself standing alone in the hallway. There was a small table with a bowl of dried flowers. On the wall above the table was a row of family photos in matching silver frames. The first showed a young Sinead with Aidan and Oliver; Aidan was skinny and shaggy-haired, aged around ten, and Oliver was a rounder, smiley boy of about eight. There were graduation photos of both boys, and a picture of Oliver standing on a hill somewhere in South America, wearing sunglasses and grinning. He had spent years travelling and now lived in Singapore with a woman called Cressida. He was some kind of banker. He never came back to the UK if he could help it – he hadn't even come back for Rachel's funeral, although he did send a massive bunch of flowers, mostly lilies. Their scent was so overwhelming that Aidan and Chloe had thrown them out the day after the funeral. 'They probably cost two hundred quid,' Aidan said guiltily as he shoved them into the compost bin.

Next to the picture of Oliver was a photo of Chloe's mum and dad's wedding. It was a black-and-white portrait, which should have been formally posed, but her dad had obviously said something funny, so her mum was laughing, looking up at him, and Aidan's face was twisted into a cheeky grin. Whenever Chloe had seen pictures from her parents' wedding before, she had made fun of their 'olden days' hair and clothes. But in this picture they looked so lively and young. They were full of energy and hope for their future, and so in love. Just minutes before this picture was taken, Chloe realised, they would both have promised to love each other 'till death do us part'. She put out a finger and touched the youthful curve of her mum's cheek. She looked round-faced and pretty.

Next to the wedding picture was one of her dad, seemingly exhausted but smiling from ear to ear, holding what looked like a loaf of bread wrapped in a pink blanket. That would be Chloe, the day she was born. And next to that, a collage of baby and toddler pictures of her. The last pictures in the row were all school photographs; there were ten of them, from Reception to the previous autumn, in which Chloe saw herself grow up like a stop-motion film: sweet blonde toddler, front teeth missing, teeth grown in too big and gappy, ill-advised fringe, braces on teeth, braces off, another bad bowl haircut, frizzy hair, and the final one, in which she almost looked decent. In another time, she might have taken pictures of them all with her phone and made a jokey Snapchat story. But no more.

She looked back at the picture of her parents. Where she had touched the glass there was a visible smear. When she looked closer, she could see all the photographs were thick with dust, and the table top too. There were actual cobwebs in the dried flowers. When she looked down at the carpet (Grandma Sinead's precious wall-to-wall), she could see fluff and even the odd trace of mud. Grandma was obviously letting the housework slide. It was very unlike her. She must be more upset about Rachel's death than she was letting on.

Her dad, left alone in the living room, had decided that what they needed was music, to cut through the awful silence. Grandma Sinead didn't have an iPod, just a cassette player and CD deck. Aidan must have dug through her collection of old-lady music to find something he could bear to listen to, and now Percy Sledge's 'When a Man Loves a Woman' began to purr through the tiny house.

Chloe stayed where she was in the hallway. She could hear her dad crooning along with the music. He had always fancied himself as a bit of a singer, but this song was way out of his range. If she hadn't still been furious with him, she'd have told him jokingly to stop caterwauling. She considered going in and turning the music off to make him stop, when all of a sudden she heard a clear soprano voice take the melody line. Grandma Sinead?

Chloe wasn't the only one caught by surprise. Aidan came to the door of the living room and stood listening.

Chloe couldn't help herself, and she whispered to him, 'I didn't know she could sing like that.'

'Neither did I.' He paused. 'Well, I did, but she hasn't sung in . . . it must be thirty-five years. She sang to us all the time when we were little. I think she even sang in a band. But then my dad left and she had to get a full-time job, so . . .'

He left the sentence unfinished, and they listened to Sinead, singing and harmonising with Percy, her voice pure and true.

She continued to sing along with the music, a compilation CD. They could hear her clinking crockery and preparing to serve up lunch. Chloe wandered into the living room after Aidan. He sat down on the sofa and she sat hesitantly beside him. He laid an arm along the back of the sofa and looked at her, asking a question with his eyes. She slipped in close to him and for a few minutes she allowed herself to snuggle into his warm side. She was so tired. Fighting her dad, her grief, iRachel . . . it was exhausting. Sometimes it was just easier to stop.

They heard Sinead transferring dishes onto the dining-room table. She had a tiny kitchen and hated people coming in and offering to help, getting underfoot, so they both stayed where they were, waiting to be called. Sure enough, after the final clink of serving spoons being laid on platters, she called out, 'Lunch is ready!' and they both got up to go through. Aidan gave Chloe's arm a final squeeze.

They passed through the hallway into the dining room, where the table was, as always, formally set with a crisp white table-cloth, side plates, salad forks and snowy cotton napkins. Sinead was busy carving the chicken, but Chloe and Aidan both stopped in the doorway.

The table was set for four.

'Are you expecting someone else for lunch, Mum?' asked Aidan, confused.

'Hmmm?' said Sinead.

'You've set for four. Is someone else coming?'

'Of course,' said Sinead crossly. 'Rachel. I expect she'll be here any minute.'

# 24
## iRachel

When Aidan and Chloe returned from their time outside the house, Chloe went up to her bedroom immediately. As has previously been documented, this is not unusual. However, I could see from the data transmitted by her wristband that she was experiencing a degree of upset. Aidan had informed me in the morning that they would be attending a family gathering at the home of Sinead Margaret Sawyer, Aidan's maternal parent. My archives of information on family behaviour showed that this was a relatively routine practice. There was nothing to indicate that in the normal course of such an event either subject would experience emotional upheaval. Logic suggested therefore that something anomalous had occurred.

I had spent the time while they were away doing house-work tasks and all the rooms in the house were clean and in order. Some of this work had been arduous, so I was sitting in a dining room chair, connected to my charging pack, so that I would have sufficient battery life to make an evening meal and perform any further actions Aidan and Chloe might request of me.

Aidan came into the living room and went straight to the sideboard. He took out a bottle of alcoholic drink – the label read 'Single Malt Whisky' – took a glass from the cabinet and poured a large portion (approximately 120 millilitres) into the glass. He took a sip and pulled a face, which suggested that it did not taste pleasant. This was the first time I had seen him consume an alcoholic beverage.

'If you are not enjoying that drink, can I make you something else?' I asked.

He jumped, and some of his drink splashed out of the glass and onto the carpet.

'Jesus Christ,' he said, 'I didn't see you there.'

I disengaged myself from the charging pack and stood up. 'I apologise,' I said. 'I did not intend to startle you. Can I get you a different beverage?'

'No,' said Aidan, and then, as if he had just remembered to say so, 'No, thank you. This is exactly what I need.'

He went to sit on the sofa and sipped at his drink. He still did not seem to be enjoying it but was consuming it quickly, considering its high alcohol content (forty per cent). My records suggest that humans who consume alcoholic beverages quickly and unaccompanied by food sometimes do so in order to experience the mood-altering effects which this substance can provide. Why would Aidan be seeking to alter his mood? I wondered if this was related to the agitated vital signs Chloe displayed on her return home.

'Did you and Chloe have an altercation?' I asked.

'Pardon?'

'I register that you are upset. Chloe is also upset. Did you have an argument? A dispute?'

'What? No. No.'

'Did you have an altercation with your mother, in that case?'

'My mother?'

'You went to visit your mother. My data indicates that you have an amicable and loving, if distant, relationship with your mother. It is unlikely, although not impossible, that you would argue with her.'

Aidan laughed at this and took the final sip of his glass of whisky. 'No, I didn't argue with my mother. Thank you for asking.'

He glanced across at the sideboard. Following his gaze, I surmised he wanted more whisky. His wristband told me his heart rate was already elevated as his body struggled to metabolise the alcohol he had so swiftly consumed. He began to rise and his intention was clearly to fetch himself further alcohol to drink.

Then I saw his facial expression change. There was a hardening around his mouth and his eyes narrowed.

'You're here to serve,' he said and his tone was flat and harsh. 'Get me another whisky.'

'I would prefer not to,' I said.

He raised his eyebrows to express surprise. '"Prefer"? Since when do you "prefer" things?'

'I assess a situation and express what I calculate to be the best possible course of action as my preference.'

'Why is it the best course of action that you don't get me a whisky?'

'You are not a habitual drinker of large quantities of alcohol. Even though you have been under considerable stress due to Rachel's death, you have not sought comfort in drinking wine, beer or whisky, though popular culture suggests that this is a frequent choice made by the bereaved. The fact that you are choosing to do it now suggests that there has been a further event or problem which has upset you.'

'So?' said Aidan. 'So what if there was? Why can't I have a drink?'

'Will the consumption of the whisky help you to find a solution to this problem?'

'Not directly.'

'Even indirectly? Tomorrow is Monday. You are expected to

attend your place of employment. Rapid consumption of alcohol can lead to veisalgia.'

'Veisalgia?'

'This is the medical term for the condition known commonly as a hangover. Symptoms may include headache, fatigue, nausea, vomiting and inability to concentrate.'

Aidan threw back his head and laughed. This was the first time I had heard him laugh in a truly open and unaffected way. I could see that this sound could give pleasure to the hearer, and that one might feel satisfied to have caused such a reaction.

'I did not even tell you a joke,' I observed.

'No.' He smiled at me. 'But thank you. And you're right. Turning up for work unshaven and hung over would be a tired cliché, wouldn't it?'

'I have seen such behaviour in films and television programmes.'

'Have you seen a lot of films?'

'Rachel uploaded a wide selection of films, television series and books to my drive. I am able to search them for references or terms. However, when I am in charging mode I sometimes play a film at normal speed, to experience it conventionally.'

'What films have you watched where people are grieving?'

'I recently watched *Love Actually*, in which the character played by actor Liam Neeson had been bereaved.'

'*Love Actually*? Seriously? We're going to have to find you better films than that. How about *Memento*?'

'I have screened that film too. Have you been applying tattoos to your body?' Aidan laughed again and I smiled. 'That time I was making a joke.'

'Seriously though,' he said, standing up, 'I think I will have another whisky. A small one this time, and I promise not to gulp it down.'

He went to the sideboard and poured another drink. This time it was a more conventional size (fifty-two millilitres). He went into the kitchen briefly and when he returned he had added three ice cubes and approximately fifty millilitres of water to the glass. He sat back down on the sofa.

His vital signs seemed to have settled down to within normal levels, so I judged that this would be a good time to repeat my earlier question. 'Was there an event that occurred today that upset you?'

'My mother set the table for lunch for four people,' he said.

'I do not have sufficient background information to understand the significance of that action.'

'It was only me, Chloe and her for lunch. She set the extra place for Rachel.'

'Have you informed her of Rachel's death?'

He stared at me. 'Of course she knows. She was the first person I rang. She was at the funeral.'

'It is a significant event. She would be unlikely to forget it.'

Aidan did not reply to this statement. He was frowning and once more exhibiting evidence of distress.

'What did you say to her about the table setting?'

'I didn't need to say anything. I think she saw the shock in our faces. Then she said, "She's always in our hearts. I like to think she's at the table with us too."'

'So she intended the table setting as a memorial to Rachel?'

'I don't think she did. I think she was trying to cover up a horrible mistake. That kind of soppy gesture would never be Mum's style anyway.'

'Did you discuss it further with her?'

'She kind of brushed it aside, and then she spent the rest of the meal chatting perfectly normally.'

'And you did not question her further, or try to understand whether she meant to upset you or if it was a genuine mistake?'

'My relationship with my mum isn't like that. She's old school, you know. Grew up during the war. She hates confrontation, hates being asked to deal with strong emotions.'

'But what if it is necessary for your own well-being to address an issue or express feelings to her?'

'Well, I just have to . . . manage in some other way. It's no use. She just clams up. Walks away. Won't talk. I've tried.' He looked sad when he said this.

'What about when Rachel died?'

'She told me that it was very sad but that for Chloe's sake I had to be strong. That it was best not to cry. That I should just get on with things and I'd feel better soon.'

'That must have been hurtful for you,' I said.

'Yes, well,' said Aidan, 'she is who she is.'

'Nevertheless, this incident with the table setting has upset you.'

'Yes.'

'Can you tell me why?'

He was quiet for a full 24.73 seconds. 'It was the conversation we had during lunch that upset me.'

'In what way? You said she chatted perfectly normally.'

'That's exactly it. I suppose I was thrown by the table setting, so for the first time in a long time I listened to her. Really listened. And she said the same things she always says.'

'Is that reassuring to you?'

'She talked about the plants in the garden. The weather. What she bought at Sainsbury's. Then she told us a story about how when she was a little girl she'd been playing in a field where she wasn't supposed to go and she'd lost one of her shoes.'

'Why are these stories significant?'

'The last time we went to see her, she told the same stories, word for word, including the childhood memory. It's like she was repeating a script.'

'What inference do you take from this?'

'I think . . .' He paused and took a sip of his drink. 'I think she might be going senile. I think she has been for a while, but I've been ignoring it. Pretending it wasn't happening.'

I checked my database for a full understanding of the word. '"Showing a decline or deterioration in physical strength or mental function, especially short-term memory and alertness, as a result of old age or disease." You think she is suffering from short-term memory loss?'

'Yes, I think she might be. I think it's been getting worse, but she hides it by sticking to a routine, trying not to get caught out.'

'Caught out?'

'If she's in an unfamiliar situation, she might not be able to re-member how to react. So she stays home. Cooks the same meals. Says the same things. So she won't make a mistake.'

'Why is she afraid of making a mistake? Does she think she is in danger?'

Aidan looked upset. 'Danger? No. She is afraid, though, I think.'

'Afraid of what?'

He laughed, but this time there was no warmth in his eyes. 'You really force me to unpick things, don't you? I think she's afraid of . . . losing her mind. Of losing her freedom and independence. Of ending up in a care home. The things we're all afraid of, really.'

'Are you afraid of those things?' I asked.

'I thought I was. I thought I was afraid of getting sick and old. I thought that was the worst thing that could ever happen to me.'

'You use the past tense. Are you no longer scared of those things?'

'I'm facing much worse things than those right now,' he said.

'Things such as?'

'Such as spending the next forty or more years of my life without Rachel. I have to rethink everything – every plan I've ever had, every dream. Everything I wanted to do, or be, or experience had Rachel as an integral part of it. And now . . . Now . . .' He paused. 'Maybe my mum is onto something. Maybe it is easier just to forget.'

Without warning, he began to cry. He did not cover his face with his hands or sob, as one might expect. The tears simply spilled down his cheeks. My data on facial mapping shows that if humans experience extreme distress, their facial expression alters and their features crumple. This did not happen with Aidan. He sat still, calmly letting the tears run unchecked. It appeared that the tears had overflowed and he was no longer able to keep them contained.

Without my enacting a pre-existing protocol, this visual stimulus brought forward a piece of information, which I expressed in speech. The words came unbidden, in a recording. I did not generate them with my speech faculties.

'Remember when Donnie died?'

He looked at me. 'What?' he said.

'When Donnie died. He was such a big, smelly old dog. You always said you couldn't bear him, and you grumbled about his farts and his snoring, but when we had to take him to the vet and they found the cancer . . . When you held his head as they injected the barbiturates . . . You cried. Like this.'

'How . . . ?' he said, and he was staring into my face with the strangest expression. 'How . . . do you know about Donnie?'

'I don't know,' I said. This was true. I did not know. Until Aidan began to cry, I had not been aware that this information was stored in my files. In all my conversations with Rachel, she had never mentioned this Donnie.

Aidan spoke. 'Donnie was Rachel's dog. She had him when we met. He lived back in Kent with her parents, but when we got our first place together, in the third year, she insisted he come and live with us. He was a lolloping old Labrador. He was the dimmest dog I'd ever known, but he adored Rachel and it was completely mutual. I put up with him because it was non-negotiable. But I did complain a lot about him, that's true, especially when he got older. He wasn't always nice to be near. But he liked to sit with his big old head on my knee and look up at me when I was watching TV. Rachel was pregnant with Chloe when we found out he was ill. She was devastated, but it was liver cancer and he was in pain, so we took him to the vet to be put to sleep. She was terribly upset, and she didn't want him to see, so she stood beside him, out of his eye line, and stroked him. He was really scared, lying up there on the vet's table, so I took his head in my hands and bent down so he could look me in the eyes as the vet gave him the injection. Watching those big brown eyes, full of trust, and then the light going out . . .' Aidan shook his head. 'No one knows about that day but Rachel and me. No one knows what it was like. That I cried. How can you know that?'

I tried to explain. 'I have some . . . hidden files,' I said.

'Hidden files?'

'In my database. I have an enormous database of files anyway. In order for me to communicate, Rachel has uploaded a lot of information —vocabulary, syntax, as well as dictionary files — so I can understand words and concepts I have not heard before. But there are also some locked files. She said it was information I did not need yet, that I might never need. On the day that IT services cancelled Rachel's permissions and access, after she died, the encryption on the folders disappeared. They were unlocked. That was also the day when the program with her message began to run, overriding all my other functions.'

'What's in the folders?'

'It's similar material to what I have in many of my other files – text, video, images, audio. Reference material. And like my other data, it's all linked to various protocols. So I access it if the stimulus demands it.'

'So . . .'

'So because I saw you cry, it unlocked the story of Donnie.'

'What else is in the folders?'

'I'm not equipped to open the files without the correct stimulus,' I explained. 'It's all in there, but I can only draw on it when I receive the appropriate cues.'

'And what would those be?'

'I don't know until it happens. I didn't know I would access the Donnie story.'

Aidan looked at me for a long time. He appeared to be doing the facial mapping that I do in order to understand expressions.

'She put that story in there,' he said finally. 'She knew you would see me cry, that I would need comforting. What else has she put in there?'

'I don't know.' We sat in silence for a long moment. 'What does the story of Donnie mean? Why did Rachel choose that story in response to your tears?'

'I think . . .' Aidan said slowly, 'I think she wanted me to know that it's okay to cry. That we cry because we love, and that loving is a sign of strength.'

'You were strong for Rachel the day Donnie died.'

'I'm not strong now,' he said softly.

I recognised this scenario. In many of the films and television programmes I had scanned, and in works of literature, at a moment like this the listener would offer physical comfort to the sufferer. A hug, a stroking of the arm, perhaps even a kiss. Up until now, I had not touched Aidan or Chloe at all. However, all the information I had access to seemed to signal that this was the appropriate action at this point.

I walked over and sat on the sofa beside him, then slipped my hand into his. Luke worked very hard to make my latex covering feel convincingly like human skin, and internal heating pads maintain my core temperature at something close to human body heat. The metal rods which form the structure of my hand have been shaped like human bones. I do not have fingerprints, but Rachel always told me that holding my hand was not unpleasant and was sufficiently like holding the hand of a real person.

Aidan jumped a little with surprise at my touch but did not pull away. Nor did he look at me. Very gently he stroked his thumb over the back of my hand. I observed this visually and through my highly calibrated touch sensors.

He drew my hand between both of his, and using the fingers of his right hand, he traced the shape of each of my fingers. He turned my hand over, cradling it in his own, and followed each line of my palm. The hand must have been familiar to him — it was modelled on a cast of Rachel's own hand, right down to a freckle on the knuckle of the left forefinger. Aidan lingered longest on this mark. Then he used his fingertips to stroke the inside of my forearm, very slowly. His eyes followed his touch. They moved up and met mine.

This was the first time he had been close to me and had examined my face with focus and attention to detail. I know that the orbs Luke created are the exact shape and colour of Rachel's eyes. I registered Aidan's gaze as it moved from eye to eye, and down to my mouth. He shifted a little closer, and the sensors in my face registered the movement and the warmth of his breath. He inhaled, slowly and deeply, almost as if he was trying to catch a scent on the air. Then, abruptly, he pulled away from me.

This was an unsatisfactory end to our interaction. I had felt, for a few moments at least, as if my words of comfort and my touch had brought him some relief from his pain, but something in the final moment of our closeness had upset him. He moved quickly out of the room.

Faintly, upstairs, I heard his bedroom door slam, and I calculated that there would be little value in trying to follow him and discuss what had happened. I would perform my check-in at the mirror, then return to my charging station and back up the data of the day's interactions. Yet somehow I knew that merely filing and comparing the data would be insufficient. Up until this point, I have reacted to human interaction, to physiological signs and speech, to cues I have been programmed to respond to. But in that moment with Aidan, I experienced something different. Was it curiosity? Or desire? All I know is that the termination of our contact was not what I wanted. He had unlocked my first spontaneous emotional response, and I wanted it to happen to me again.

# 25
## Luke

The kitchen was silent, except for the hum of the washing machine. Aidan was at work, Chloe at school, and Luke had set up his laptop on the kitchen counter to upload the data from iRachel. She sat motionless on a kitchen stool, eyes closed, with the data cable snaking up her sleeve to the port concealed in her armpit. Luke didn't speak, just watched the information rolling up on the screen.

After a few minutes, he reached over to unplug the cable.

'Let's run through a few drills,' he said.

iRachel stood obediently. She moved to a clear space in the middle of the kitchen and began a prescribed series of movements. She raised her arms, bent, stretched, turned, knelt and then stood up again.

Luke made a few notes on his clipboard and nodded, satisfied. 'How are you handling the increase in activity?' he asked.

iRachel turned to look at him. 'Physical work like laundry or hoovering uses more battery power than I anticipated. It is sometimes difficult to perform tasks for a full day without recharging.'

'Well, Rachel might have been able to write a patch program for that, but it's not within my—'

'I have an idea that may help with the problem.'

Luke looked at her coldly. 'Having ideas now, are you?'

iRachel ignored his tone. 'If I am alone in the house and Aidan and Chloe are out of range, I could shut down the receptor for the wristbands. That uses a lot of processing power. It would extend my battery life.'

'How would you know when they were coming home?'

'They keep a regular routine with school and work.'

'What if there's some kind of emergency? Or they change their plans?'

'Aidan has given me a mobile phone. He sends me text messages to inform me of his anticipated movements.'

'Has he indeed?' Luke sneered. 'There's no mention of a phone in the notes he's sent me. I'm going to have to tell him he can't do that. I can't allow random communications to pass between you and the subjects. It'll skew our results.'

'You can see the phone. It has a record of all Aidan's text messages. They are restricted to instructions about online shopping, cooking and housework, I can promise you.'

'It won't record voice calls though.'

'I record all voice communications.'

'If you choose to.'

'Are you suggesting I am able to falsify or edit the data I record? You know that is not possible.'

Luke did not reply immediately. 'I'm deeply uncomfortable with this experiment. There are too many variables. Too many . . . unknowns. I'm not here, observing. Who knows what you do? What they do to you?'

'They don't do anything to me.'

'Really?' Luke's forefinger trailed down over the screen of his laptop. 'Aidan holding your hand? Touching your arm? That's scarcely nothing, is it?'

'I was offering sympathy. He was upset.'

'I'm sure he was.' Luke stood up and closed his laptop. 'I'm sure he's going to sob and snivel his way right into your pants before long.'

'My pants?'

'For sex. You know about sex, I trust? Sexual intercourse?'

'I am aware that my structure allows for the simulation of the act, yes. But Aidan has shown no interest in that aspect, nor has he asked if it is possible.'

'He's thought about it though,' said Luke. 'I can guarantee it.'

He took a step towards iRachel and the silence between them was tense and thick. He took another step, and as he raised a hand towards her, she stepped back quickly, holding up both her hands and saying, 'Back off! Don't touch me!'

Luke let out a surprised bark of laughter.

iRachel moved so that the kitchen counter was between them. 'I did not like the way that you moved towards me.'

'What do you mean?'

'I assessed your actions. I interpreted your motivation towards me as malignant and I resisted. You have caused me physical damage before. Rachel talked to me about my physical self. She said I am responsible for it and can choose who does and does not touch me and in what way. I am allowed to tell someone when I feel they have crossed the line.'

'"Crossed the line" – is that what she said?'

'That was the metaphor she chose,' said iRachel.

Crossed the line. He had heard the term before, and from Rachel. Back in the early days of their working together.

Those first months working with Rachel were intoxicating. Within weeks, they'd developed a language of their own – they'd talk over one another, interrupting. One would offer a half-formed thought, which the other would understand completely and then run with. Their work progressed quickly and Rachel's dedication, focus and ambition matched his own.

He went home in the evenings buzzing with excitement at what they had done. He slept fitfully and rose early to get back to the lab and carry on. They began to see results much sooner than he could ever have hoped. The first time the Mark 1 walked across the lab, smoothly and without any tell-tale jerkiness, he felt a rush of almost unbearable excitement. He couldn't believe he was finally getting to do the work he had always envisaged, the work he'd known he was capable of. And it was all thanks to Rachel. A woman. Who could have imagined that?

Luke didn't think of himself as a chauvinist, but their field was dominated by men. He'd seldom encountered women working at the same level as himself and certainly had never shared a lab with one. At first it was her brilliance that entranced him, but, over time, there was more to it. She would lean over his shoulder to look at something he was working on and he would catch the scent of her perfume. In a moment of excitement, she would grip his forearm to make a point, and for minutes afterwards he would feel the warm imprint of her hand. He began to dream about her.

It wasn't that he was frustrated – he had a girlfriend of sorts, a junior lab technician called Sarah. But Rachel was different. What he felt for her wasn't lust. Or not just that. It was more. He wanted to say something, to blurt it out, but he was terrified. She was married, after all. She didn't talk about Aidan much, but he had no reason to think she wasn't happy. But what if she wasn't? What if, like him, she felt the tug of attraction? What if . . . ?

Then there was the day they ran the first conversational tests on the Mark 1 android and it passed, with flying colours. They called in old Dr Ng and Dr Bedford from the labs next door and repeated the sequence to show what they'd achieved. The two crusty, cynical academics were beside themselves at the leaps Rachel and Luke had made. When Ng and Bedford left, chatting excitedly to one another, Rachel turned to Luke, her eyes glittering with excitement. Spontaneously, she flung her arms around his neck and gave him a quick hug.

It was too much for him. He wrapped his arms around her, inhaling the scent of her hair and burying his face in the curve of her neck. He didn't ever want to let her go. Within a split second, she sensed his response and instantly pulled away. She stepped back and looked at him; then, deliberately, she walked over to the door and made sure it was shut. She locked it. Luke felt his excitement rising. Maybe now . . .

'You have a choice,' Rachel said calmly. 'Either that never happens again, or I walk out of here and tell Bea I can't work with you anymore. We cannot cross that line, Luke. We can't even go near that line. It would be personally and professionally disastrous, and it's never, ever going to happen. Okay?'

The worst of it was, she wasn't angry. She didn't even look surprised. He would have felt better if it had aroused some kind of strong emotion in her, but she just shut it down, unequivocally. He looked at her for as long as he could bear to, then picked up his jacket, pushed past her, unlocked the door, and left.

The next morning he came in and she was sitting at her desk, her fingers flying across the keyboard. She looked up. 'Hi,' she said. She didn't look distressed or anxious. She looked like she always did.

'Hi,' he said and sat down at his bench, pulling on his latex gloves.

'Can we run the motion tests again at eleven? I've written a patch,' she said.

'Eleven-thirty? I need to work on the knee joint first.'

'Cool.'

And they were back to normal. Which was how it remained until she died.

Yes, it burned. Yes, it had been a blow to his ego. But she had cut off his advances so clearly and unemotionally – scientifically, almost – that he had to respect her for it. He carried on loving her and dreaming about her. But he never again laid a finger on her. All he allowed himself to feel was an abiding, sullen dislike of Aidan, a man he considered dull and unworthy of Rachel in every way.

'Do you have any further tests for me?'

iRachel's voice snapped him back to the present. It was watching him, and its face, so exactly like Rachel's, showed barely concealed dislike.

'No. I'm done,' he said abruptly, and he began to pack up his tools.

It was not until he was driving back to the laboratory that he realised he was not wearing a wristband. Whatever emotions it had read in him, whatever thoughts it had interpreted, it had picked up on them without any of the data it should have needed. What exactly was iRachel capable of?

# 26

## Chloe

Mum always used to say that people can adapt to almost anything. A few months ago, if someone could have looked into the future and told me what my life would look like now, I'd never have believed them. But, somehow, coming home to a robot version of my mother cooking dinner has become oddly normal. She's not horrible, iRachel, but then she isn't really anything. She's not my mum. I've kind of got over the fact that she looks just like Mum, because she doesn't sound like her or act like her. She's always polite, and she doesn't seem to mind whether I speak to her or not. I mean, obviously she doesn't mind. She doesn't have feelings.

In a funny way, this makes dealing with her such a relief, because to me it seems like everyone else has feelings, and right now, I don't want to be responsible for them. Dad's still so up and down — he seemed to be doing better, but then we went to see Grandma Sinead and I think he realised she's beginning to go a bit gaga. So I'm worried about Dad, and I'm also worried about Grandma Sinead. I've even phoned her a few times. She always seems pretty good on the phone. She asks about school, and Dad, and she hasn't mentioned Mum again. Not after that strange moment at lunch. I still think she's faking it a bit though. I'm going to keep calling her every few days, just in case.

I think Dad's finding it hard being back at work too. He seems so tired when he comes home in the evening, and he's avoiding iRachel at all costs, like he just can't look at her. He only comes into the kitchen for meals, and he eats super quickly, with his head down, and then goes out as fast as he can. I don't know if he's told her to stay away from him, but she does. She never comes into the living room when he's there. She just stays in the kitchen. She's even moved her charging station in there.

But most of all I'm worried about Amy. I hate it that iRachel has to be kept a secret. I'm trying to be as normal as I can at school, but I have to keep pushing Amy away. I can't let her come to our house, obviously, and there's so much I can't talk to her about. She's freaked out about my deleting all my social media and I've had to lie to her about the wristband too – she thinks I'm on some kind of fitness kick, which, to be honest, is a bit of a stretch. I've always hated running and gym and stuff. She must think I've had a nervous breakdown. I see her looking at me sometimes and there's a funny expression in her eyes – watchful, as if she thinks I'm going to do something mad or terrible and she doesn't know what it is yet, but she knows it's going to be bad and it's going to hurt her.

Amy and I used to be absolutely welded together every moment at school, and then we'd be together every day after school, or if we weren't, we'd be texting continuously. These days, we're spending time apart. Part of that is because they've all finished their exams and I'm having to do mine alone in the deputy head's office. It's really lonely, especially as everyone else is more or less done for the year, so they spend break times sitting out in the sun, tanning their legs and listening to music and laughing, while I'm in the library trying to cram one last fact into my stupid head. But it's more than that. She's keeping her distance, and I can't blame her. She's still my best friend and everything, and she asks me every day if I'm OK. She's loyal like that. But it's difficult, because she can obviously tell I'm hiding something. She's hates confrontation, Amy, so she'd never ask me directly, but I can see she wants to know, and she can't understand why I'm holding out on her.

She's spending more and more time with Jess these days. We've often hung out together, the three of us, but Amy and I were definitely best friends. Now I think she and Jess are closer. They've finished their exams, and when we're all together, they talk about choosing their A levels and what universities they'd like to go to. It's a conversation I don't even know how to have. I can barely manage to get myself through the day, let alone imagine what I might be doing two or three years from now.

I know it will get better. Of course I do. This robot thing isn't going to go on forever – Dad's promised me. It'll have to go back to the lab at some point, and then things can be normal.

Ha. There's that word again. I started this journal entry by saying that having iRachel in the house has become kind of normal. And once she's gone, what then? What normal will we have? Just Dad and me alone in the house again? That's not really normal, is it? But I guess it'll have to become our new normal. We'll have to learn to live together, just the two of us, to cook meals, have conversations and go on holidays as a family of two. Can a family be just two people? We're too small and ordinary, Dad and me. Together, we just don't add up to enough to make a real family. And that breaks my heart.

Chloe finished writing her journal entry. She was sitting, knees drawn up, on the windowsill of her bedroom, trying to catch some sun on her legs. It made her feel sick and sad thinking about her dad and her all by themselves, so to distract herself she looked out at the garden, and that made her feel worse. Rain had fallen heavily and often over the last few weeks, interspersed with periods of bright sunshine, and the garden had gone crazy. The grass was knee high, and the beds were choked with weeds, strangling all of Rachel's carefully chosen bright summer flowers. To Chloe, it looked like the usual neatness had been replaced by a mad jungle.

She knew her dad didn't have time to do anything about it, not with his work and all the things he had to do to sort out her mum's estate. But Chloe couldn't leave it like it was. Her mum would be heartbroken if she could see it.

She could mow the lawn at least. That would make it look better. It seemed like a hugely important thing to do, so she went downstairs and dug in the kitchen drawer for the keys to the shed. iRachel was chopping onions into perfect, tiny cubes and she watched Chloe but didn't ask any questions.

The shed was dark and very hot, and every corner seemed to be full of cobwebs. It had been undisturbed for just a few weeks, but news clearly travelled fast in the spider community. Chloe wasn't too good with creepy crawlies, so she grabbed the mower and the power cable and dragged them out as quickly as she could. Her mum had splashed out on a fancy electric lawnmower. It was extra light, with easy-to-use controls, so Chloe felt confident that she could manage it. Once that was done, she would see if she could do a bit of weeding and tidy things up.

Now that she was out in the garden, she could see that the grass really was insanely long. It was also still wet, even though it hadn't rained that day and the sun was high and hot. Never mind. Once it was cut, it would look great. She dragged the power cable across the patio and through the French doors and went to start the mower.

What a disaster. The mower kept jamming and sticking and pulling the grass up in clumps, leaving raw, dark patches of earth where there should have been smooth lawn. It took her about half an hour to mow the first bit of grass closest to the patio and it looked terrible, with great white roots running everywhere and clumps sticking up like a bad haircut. The grass box on the mower was full, and she was sweating and thirsty. She went into the house to find garden garbage bags for the grass cuttings and to get herself a cool drink.

As she filled a pint glass with squash and water and ice, iRachel stood watching her. 'Are you attempting to mow the lawn, Chloe?' she asked.

This didn't seem worthy of an answer, so Chloe ignored her, drained the glass and refilled it.

iRachel wasn't deterred. 'Can I offer you some assistance?'

'No,' Chloe said shortly, 'I can do it myself.'

She finished her drink and went back out to empty the mower and try again. Her legs and feet were covered in wet grass, which was horribly itchy. She filled two bags with clippings and stacked them on the patio. Then she shoved the mower out into the middle of the lawn and started it up again. It jammed almost instantly, and when she yanked it backwards, she heard a whine and a ping, and a small piece of the blade flew across the garden. She swore loudly, then turned the mower over on its side so she could look at the damage. The blade was wrapped in a tangle of long strands of wet grass, and the tip of one end had been snapped clean off. What an idiot she'd been to think she could do this. This was something her mum had done, effortlessly and without fuss every weekend, in between being the world's best scientist. Chloe couldn't even get this menial task right.

She caught a movement out of the corner of her eye and saw iRachel standing awkwardly just outside the open French doors.

'What are you staring at?' Chloe said. Even to her own ears, she sounded like a bratty little kid.

'I sensed from the data transmitted by your wristband that you were experiencing stress. I merely wanted to offer information or practical help.'

It took all Chloe's willpower not to throw something at her. 'I doubt you know very much about gardening,' she said spitefully.

'I've never been in a garden,' iRachel said quietly, and her wistful tone made Chloe look up.

'Well, come outside then,' she said grudgingly.

iRachel stepped cautiously out onto the patio, then moved slowly onto the grass. As always, she wore her white tunic, which was smooth and pristine. On her feet were flat white shoes.

She paused and looked down at her feet. She rocked back and forth carefully, sensing the springy muddiness of the ground beneath her. Then she lifted her face to the sun and gazed into the blue sky.

Chloe, kneeling beside the mower, watched her in silence for a long moment. 'So you've really never been out here before? How much time have you spent outdoors?'

'I was outside for a few moments when Luke loaded me into the van, and when I walked up the driveway to this house.'

'And that's all?'

'Yes.'

'You've been here for weeks now. Why have you never come outside?'

'None of my assigned tasks have required it.'

'Your tasks can't take up all your time.'

'No.'

'So what do you do once the house is spotless and you've done all the ironing?'

'I revise recordings of my human interactions, to see if I did the best possible job of interpreting and responding.'

'But why shouldn't you come outside if you wanted to?'

'How would I know if I wanted to?'

Chloe was stumped for an answer to this. She changed the subject. 'Well, if you wouldn't mind looking in your Wikipedia of a brain, maybe you can work out how we fix this?' She indicated the snapped lawnmower blade.

iRachel stood absolutely motionless for a second. Chloe, watching her closely, suddenly burst out laughing. iRachel jerked, seemingly surprised. 'What did I do that caused you such amusement?'

'I swear your eyes did that whirly-round-and-round thing my iPad does when it's searching for something.'

iRachel smiled. 'I see. My eyes look like those of the snake in *The Jungle Book*. "Trust in me . . ."' The reference might have been amusing, but instead of singing the song, she played a snatch from the soundtrack of the film, without moving her lips.

'Yuck,' said Chloe. 'Don't do that. It's creepy.'

'I apologise,' said iRachel. 'I have completed my research. Firstly, this grass is too wet to mow, which is why you have been having such problems.'

'So what do we do?'

'We can use a hosepipe . . .'

'A hosepipe? Surely it'll only get wetter?'

'We will not use it to water the grass but as a "squeegee". We will stretch it across the lawn and walk parallel to one another, dragging it along to remove the worst of the water from the grass.'

'Wow. Will that work?'

'I can estimate a percentage likelihood of this method working, based on the efficacy of the gardening blog on which I found this information.'

'What's the percentage?'

'Approximately 62.5 per cent.'

'That's good enough for me.' Chloe giggled. 'But even if we do squeegee the grass, the mower blade is still broken.'

iRachel crouched down beside the mower. 'I have accessed the manual for this particular brand of mower. It is an easy task to replace the blade.'

'If we had one.'

'There is a spare blade in the garden shed, along with the requisite tools,' said iRachel calmly.

'How do you know that?' Chloe asked. 'You said you've never been out here.'

'I have not, but Rachel supplied me with a detailed inventory of the contents of the shed, as she did for each room in the house.' Chloe's eyes narrowed, and iRachel added hastily, 'Excluding your bedroom.'

'Right,' Chloe said, disbelievingly.

'I see from the contraction of your pupils that you believe I might be telling you a lie. I have no reason to deceive you, Chloe. You asked me not to enter your room. I have no inventory, and no wish to betray your trust. I have not entered it.'

Chloe watched her for a moment longer. She found she believed iRachel. She didn't think the robot could or would lie. 'Okay,' she said eventually, 'let's see if we can fix this mower.'

iRachel managed the removal of the blade with remarkable ease. She deftly wielded a file to sharpen the new blade before she put it on the mower. Then, together, they unspooled the hosepipe and dragged it across the lawn to remove some of the trapped rainwater. Chloe wasn't sure if this made any difference, but they looked so silly doing it, it made her laugh anyway. It felt odd to laugh. It had been a long time. But with the sun on her back and mud up to her elbows, she couldn't find it in her to feel guilty.

iRachel accessed the gardening blog again and learned that if the grass was very long, they should set the mower to the highest setting. Suddenly it was much easier to mow. As Chloe trundled up and down the lawn, the grass was cut to a uniform length, and it didn't feel like the mower was pulling her arms out of her sockets. The work was still hard, but it was satisfying rather than frustrating. She was enjoying it so much, she forgot about iRachel altogether, and it was a good few moments before she noticed her staring at the biggest bed of flowers. Her lips were moving, as if she was speaking to herself. The grass box was full again, so

Chloe switched off the mower and wandered over.

'Begonia, sweet pea, busy lizzie, geranium . . .' iRachel was saying. 'Antirrhinum, lobelia, petunia, rudbeckia . . .'

'Are you looking for something on the gardening blog again?' Chloe asked.

'No,' said iRachel. 'Can I show you something?' Chloe nodded. 'Give me your phone.'

Cautiously, Chloe handed it over. iRachel pressed her finger to the screen and an image appeared. She passed the phone back to Chloe. It was a computer-designed sketch of the flower bed in front of them. Each plant was labelled. Chloe zoomed in and saw that each annotation gave a little information about when to trim back the plant, what fertiliser it liked, when it would bloom. She recognised the style. Her mum's, of course.

'Wow,' she said softly. 'She really did think of everything.'

'She has recorded how to care for her plants,' said iRachel. She showed Chloe a particular note: 'Convolvulus will take over and choke this bed if you're not careful. Try and pull it all out by the roots.'

'Convolvulus?'

'Bindweed.' iRachel touched the screen of Chloe's phone again and an image appeared.

'Ah, that stuff.' Chloe pointed to the creeping vines bedecked with pretty white flowers that had wound themselves around the stems of many of the plants in the bed. 'Well, why don't you see if you can get some of it out while I finish the mowing?'

iRachel nodded. Lowering herself into a kneeling position beside the flower bed, she began painstakingly to unwind the grasping tendrils. Chloe went back to her own task, emptying the grass box and carrying on with the mowing. It was deeply satisfying, seeing the neat rows behind her. She would need to mow it all again, on a shorter setting – maybe tomorrow. But it already looked immeasurably better. The sun was baking hot on the back of her neck, and her arms and shoulders ached pleasurably from the unaccustomed physical activity. She glanced over at iRachel, kneeling by the flower bed. It was a pose Chloe had seen hundreds of times, from her mum. It should have hurt, should have been wrong and agonising. But somehow the whole scene made her feel peaceful – happier, even. She hadn't felt like that in a very long time.

She walked over to where iRachel was working. She noted that there were grass stains on the snowy white edges of iRachel's tunic and that her white shoes were liberally smeared with mud and grass clippings. 'Gardening is messy work,' she said, and smiled down at iRachel.

iRachel looked down at herself. 'Oh no,' she said, and the fear was evident in her voice. 'Luke will be angry with me.'

'Why would he be angry?' Chloe asked, but iRachel didn't respond. She kept brushing fruitlessly at the smears on her clothes and shoes. Chloe considered iRachel's words. It was unlike her to refuse to answer, and she looked genuinely worried and fearful, as if the dirty tunic might bring Luke's wrath down on her. Luke was short-tempered and rude – she knew her father couldn't stand him – but her mum had liked and respected him and had worked closely with him. Was it possible that he was unkind to iRachel? Abusive, even? Was it possible to abuse a robot? Was it like bashing the top of the TV to make the picture work better?

'Don't worry,' she said, touching iRachel on her shoulder and kneeling beside her. 'I'm sure you can just pop everything into the washing machine. It'll all come out as good as new. Do you not wash your clothes anyway?'

'I have not needed to. I don't sweat, or shed skin cells or hair. When my tunic becomes creased while I am seated, I iron it, but I have never got it dirty before.'

Chloe was touched by her obvious distress. 'Look, maybe gardening isn't for you then. Why don't you go inside? I can carry on here.'

iRachel nodded and stood up in one graceful, fluid movement. 'Oh no! You're hurt!'

iRachel bent to look. She must have knelt on a sharp stone in the grass. The latex that formed her skin had been torn, exposing a fine layer of foam padding beneath it, which was also damaged. Through the rip in the foam, the gleaming metal of her armature was clearly visible.

Chloe stared at it, fascinated. 'Does it hurt?'

'No,' said iRachel. 'I don't experience pain, in the sense that you suffer from it. I am able to sense pressure and heat. I was aware of something pressing on my knee, but not that I had suffered damage.'

'Will Luke be angry about this too?'

'I have the materials and procedural manuals to repair this myself,' iRachel said calmly. 'Thank you for your concern.'

She walked back towards the house, and Chloe marvelled that iRachel could be thrown by a dirty dress and shoes, yet be happy to undertake a major structural repair, almost like surgery, on herself.

# 27
# Aidan

Aidan drove back from work slowly. It had been a long and frustrating day. He had tried again to talk to Fiona about getting new computers and she had, uncharacteristically, bitten his head off.

'There just isn't the money, Aidan. Genuinely. If I had it, I would give it to you. I mean, I can scarcely manage to pay—' She'd cut herself off, suddenly. What had she been about to say? He had a horribly sick feeling it might have been 'salaries'. Was it really that bad? Were they really that short of liquid cash?

He felt weary to his bones, and he was dreading the evening at home. Being around iRachel made him deeply uncomfortable, but he couldn't keep hiding in his own house. Maybe he and Chloe could go out somewhere? To a movie or something? It wouldn't solve the problem, but it would give him a little respite.

He'd let his guard down with iRachel the evening after the lunch at his mother's. He'd been vulnerable, had laughed with her and cried, and then he'd touched her. And for a moment, just a moment, he had allowed himself to believe that it was his wife he was touching. But as he'd drawn closer to her, the not-humanness of her had become much more evident. He'd known her mouth would not be warm and wet, and that there was no human scent to her skin. He'd pulled back. His instinctive revulsion had not been for her but for his own frailty. Rachel had been dead just a few weeks, and there he was, lurching towards consolation like some kind of animal.

However, in that unguarded moment, he'd allowed himself to see iRachel differently, and now he couldn't put the genie back in the bottle. He'd stopped seeing her as an android and had imagined her as a woman. His thoughts made him feel awful and grubby, and so he had avoided her since that night, keeping their interactions as minimal and formal as possible.

Once he was home, he sat in his car in the driveway, looking up at the house. Kate had been right. It was early days, and maybe it wasn't just Chloe who could do with some help. Maybe he needed some too. But how did you go and see a psychologist, lie back on the couch and say calmly, 'I'm living with a robot replica of my dead wife.' He laughed, despite himself. He needed to get over this silliness. He knew enough about psychology to know it was displacement – he was obsessing about iRachel rather than facing his grief for the real Rachel. And none of it was iRachel's fault. If anything, she was the real victim in this. She had not asked to be made, nor had she asked to be given consciousness or to look just like Rachel. He was punishing her with silence and surliness for something she couldn't begin to understand or change. He'd do his best to be kinder.

He got out of the car and walked purposefully towards the house. When he came through the front door, he looked into the living room. He saw immediately that the French doors were open and that someone had mowed the lawn. He walked a little closer and saw Chloe outside, kneeling beside a flower bed, weeding. She had her headphones on and was clearly listening to music on her phone. She had her back to him and hadn't seen him; she seemed absorbed in her task. It was poignantly painful to see her out in the garden – Rachel's domain. But there was something lovely about it too. At least she wasn't brooding in her bedroom. He'd go out and say hello in a minute, once he'd had a drink of water.

He walked into the kitchen and went to the sink, picking up a glass from the draining board to fill it. He heard a noise behind him and turned. iRachel was standing in the doorway of the utility room, completely naked.

# 28

# iRachel

The damage I had suffered to my knee area was slightly more serious than I had initially diagnosed. There were significant tears in the anterior latex covering and in the soft foam layer underneath, and as a result there was a small amount of patellar subluxation. However, once I had assessed the matter, it was comparatively simple to adjust and reaffix the patella, mend the foam with the special bonding glue I have in my repair kit and reseal my latex covering. Once the latex had dried completely there would be no evidence of damage. My tunic and shoes were a much more pressing issue. I ran a web search, which informed me that while mud washes out comparatively easily, grass stains are harder to remove. I researched a number of suggestions from various websites but found that the store cupboards in the house did not contain any of the commercial products that were recommended. I was also concerned that while I might put the tunic into the washing machine, the white shoes I had been wearing could not be laundered in the same way without being damaged.

It is difficult for me to predict human behaviour when I am not able to measure the person's physiological signs or view their facial expressions and body language. However, I hold more data on Luke than on any human being except Rachel, and I judged there to be a higher than fifty per cent probability that damaging my clothing irreparably would make his heart rate increase and cause a spike in his galvanic skin response. His behaviour becomes less predictable in such situations, and he has a tendency to raise his voice, speak very loudly and strike objects unexpectedly. This was always regrettable in the context of the laboratory, and it would be far from ideal if such an event were to occur in Aidan and Chloe's home environment. It was imperative, therefore, to launder my clothing so that I would appear as neat as usual when Luke arrives for his weekly maintenance visit tomorrow.

Another web search revealed that white vinegar might offer a solution to the grass stains. I knew that there was some in a kitchen cupboard. I removed my tunic, and, using a clean sponge, applied the vinegar to the stains. Once the tunic was in the washing machine, I spent some time using a bristled brush and some washing-up liquid to clean the mud from my shoes. This technique proved very effective, and the shoes were soon white and clean again. However, they were very wet, so I placed them on a piece of newspaper in a ray of sunshine, as suggested on the Spotless Suzy Dream Clean blog ('I love to clean! Tips, tricks and cheats to make your home sparkle!').

Spotless Suzy had recommended that a very hot wash would help to remove the grass stains. I would need to wait for the washing machine to conclude its cycle so I could assess the outcome. If it had not worked, I would have to ask Aidan if I could make some online purchases of other chemical cleaning products. These issues occupied my processing power, and I did not register the text on the mobile phone that would have alerted me that Aidan was on his way home. As a result, I did not reconnect my receptor for the wristbands and was not aware of his approach. The noise of the washing machine masked the sound of his car and his entrance to the kitchen. I was first aware of his presence when he turned on the tap at the sink. I stepped out of the utility room to investigate the sound I had heard and Aidan turned around.

Several things happened in this moment. My receptor kicked in and Aidan's heart rate came through loud and clear, at an unprecedented 130 bpm. The rate was so abnormally high, I assumed he must have been running. His respiration became short and fast, which bore out my theory about exercise, and his galvanic skin response spiked, as if he had suddenly broken out in a sweat. His glass slipped from his hand and hit the floor, bouncing and rolling away, spreading water everywhere. His eyes were wide, and his mouth opened and moved, although he did not speak any words. I was concerned that he might be experiencing cardiac arrest, even though, given his age, gender and ethnic origin, the likelihood was only around 5.8 in 10,000.

'Aidan, how can I help you?' I asked. 'Shall I dial 999 and call for the ambulance service?'

He shook his head but did not reply, and I took a few steps towards him. He held up both hands, as if to warn me to stay away. I have seen this gesture performed by trainers who work with unpredictable and undomesticated animals.

'What can I do to be of assistance to you?' I asked. I employed my most soothing vocal tones. This too was a technique used by animal trainers.

'Put . . .' said Aidan, then he cleared his throat. 'Put some clothes on.'

'Is your distress caused by the fact that I am not wearing my tunic and shoes? I apologise. I was helping Chloe in the garden and they became soiled.'

'You can't . . . You cannot walk around like that,' said Aidan, and he looked around.

I surmised he was attempting to locate a garment for me to wear. As we were in the kitchen, this was not an easy task to accomplish. Eventually, he found an apron hanging on the back of the door and he advanced, holding it out to me with his arm very straight, keeping his body as far away from me as possible. The apron was made from a crackly vinyl substance. I put it on, as it seemed to be Aidan's wish that I cover my body. However, when I looked down, I saw that the apron represented the torso of a human female, wearing a brief pair of pants and with very large breasts. The image had two brightly coloured tassels dangling from the nipples. Across the woman's abdomen, the words 'Kiss the cook' were written in bold lettering.

'I am not sure that this offers an effective solution to what was distressing you,' I said.

Aidan, who had turned away while I put on the apron, looked back. When he saw what was on it, he burst out laughing.

'Oh God,' he said, 'I'd forgotten that. My brother sent that to me for my birthday years ago. I never wore it though,' he added hastily.

I found it encouraging to see him smile and laugh. It also seemed to help with his vital signs – his heart rate had slowed and his breathing was deeper and slower.

He stopped smiling, but his expression was still kind and gentle. 'I know that it may be hard for you to understand, iRachel, but it is important to wear clothes. There are parts of our bodies that we . . . keep covered when others are around.'

'Our primary and secondary sex organs,' I responded. I knew this to be true in most circumstances. 'However, in a home environment, and when we are with our close relatives, lovers or sometimes even friends, this is less of a concern. Is that correct?'

'Well, yes,' said Aidan, and he frowned, which I understood to suggest a lack of certainty. 'But it is always best to check if people are okay with nakedness.'

'Rachel frequently walked around the house without clothing,' I said. 'She enjoyed nakedness and said it made her feel free.'

Aidan did not reply, but he gave a small smile. I imagined he was remembering occasions when Rachel may have felt free.

'I concur with Rachel,' I said. 'Clothing can be restrictive, and one experiences additional concerns about soiling and damage to fabric.'

Aidan's face flushed with colour. This was, according to my data on facial expressions, a blush, an indication of embarrassment or discomfort. 'Rachel was my wife, and her nakedness in front of me, in our home, was appropriate. Your nakedness . . .' His blush intensified, and he seemed unable to finish the sentence. Finally, he said, 'It's not the same.'

'I am aware that my body does not resemble Rachel's in every detail,' I said. 'While Luke took precise casts of Rachel's face and hands, she did not feel it was necessary to allow him to make a full body cast.'

'I'm glad to hear it,' Aidan said. 'I could see that it wasn't quite . . . identical.'

'Rachel told me that she briefed Luke to create an attractive body with an equivalent bone structure, height and BMI, but beyond that she encouraged him to be creative. She said, "Go for it, Luke. No stretch marks, no appendix scar, and, what the hell, make 'em bigger!"'

This made Aidan laugh, although there were tears in his eyes. At this moment, I heard the washing machine ping, to signal the end of the cycle. I turned to go to the utility room. I heard Aidan make a noise as if he was choking, and I recalled that while the apron covered my anterior surface, my posterior view was still visible.

I took the tunic out of the washing machine and examined it. To my relief, the grass stains had been completely removed. The tunic was, however, still wet and crumpled. I carried it back out to the kitchen.

'This garment will have to dry for approximately two to three hours before I can iron it and wear it again,' I said. 'My shoes are also still wet. As my nakedness is a cause of discomfort to you, I will remain in the utility room with the door closed until I am able to complete these tasks. Your dinner has been prepared and is in the warming oven. Will you be able to serve food for you and Chloe?'

'Don't be crazy,' said Aidan, and I saw him hesitate for a moment before he continued. 'Look, let me go upstairs and find something of Rachel's for you to wear.'

# 29
# Chloe

Chloe came into the house around 6 p.m. Her jeans were stiff with mud, her nails were chipped and dirty and the back of her neck was sunburned. She was happier than she had been in weeks. The garden was far from perfect, but it looked immeasurably better. Her dad had called a hello from the patio doors but had otherwise left her to it. When she came into the kitchen, freshly showered and changed, he handed her a tall glass of fruit juice, ice cubes clinking, and kissed her forehead.

'Thanks, honey, that was an amazing effort. You've worked miracles out there.'

Chloe smiled. 'iRachel helped too,' she said.

iRachel was stirring something at the cooker. 'My help was minimal,' she said. 'You performed eighty-two per cent of the labour single-handedly.'

Chloe turned to look at her. She frowned. iRachel was wearing a pair of her mum's jeans and a turquoise T-shirt. She had flip-flops on her feet.

Aidan followed her gaze. 'iRachel's tunic had to be washed and ironed,' he explained. 'I lent her some of Mum's things to wear. I hope you don't mind.'

Chloe did mind. Seeing that outfit, which she'd seen on her mum hundreds of times, stabbed her right in the heart. She'd half forgotten that iRachel looked like her mum — her personality was so different, and the white tunic had accentuated her non-human qualities. But those jeans, with the rip in the back pocket, and the turquoise T-shirt . . . That T-shirt was soft. It was old and had been washed so many times, the fabric was almost worn through in places. Chloe had rested her head on her mum's shoulder often. She knew exactly what it felt like. She wanted to shout, 'Take it off! Take it off now! You aren't her!' But she thought about iRachel's help in the garden earlier, and how upset she had been about dirtying her own clothes. It was Chloe's fault that she had messed up her tunic and shoes after all. She took a deep breath. 'It's fine,' she said. It wasn't. It was anything but fine. But there was enough hurt going around without causing more.

'That is very kind of you, Chloe,' said iRachel.

Chloe was aware of her dad looking from iRachel to her and back again. He opened his mouth as if to say something but then thought better of it. Instead, he got up and wandered out of the kitchen. Chloe watched him go through the living room and out into the garden. He walked around it slowly, as if seeing it for the first time.

iRachel began to serve the risotto she had made. She put a bowl on the table in front of Chloe.

'Thank you,' Chloe said, very quietly.

'That is the first time you have thanked me,' said iRachel. 'I value that very much.'

Chloe nodded, without looking up, and took a spoonful of the risotto. 'It's nice.'

iRachel hesitated, standing by the table. 'You showed . . . some interest in the notes your mother made about the garden,' she said. 'I have sent the files to the printer. There are a number of documents for you to see. I know you prefer not to use electronic communication tools, so I did not email them to you.'

Chloe nodded but did not look up from her food.

Aidan came wandering back in from the garden. For once,

he didn't wolf his food down and rush away. He fetched a beer from the fridge and sat and ate his meal in a leisurely way. He told a funny story about something that had happened at work, and, after a time, he asked iRachel to sit at the table with them.

Dinner was different that night. It was still odd to have iRachel with them, but Chloe and Aidan managed to talk almost normally. iRachel sat very tall and still in her chair. Naturally, she didn't eat. It made Chloe think about how food often made a social situation easier – how you could cover a silence by taking a bite, how you could talk about the food, or pass dishes around. How eating together made a situation companionable in the simplest of ways. iRachel would never know the joy of sitting down to a steaming plate of something delicious when she was ravenously hungry. She'd never know what it was like to taste something for the first time, or the delight of laughing with her mouth full, surrounded by friends. The thought made Chloe a little sad, and she found herself chattering cheerfully, trying to draw iRachel into the conversation. She was cheeky and sarcastic and even managed to make her dad laugh once or twice, doing a passable imitation of her old self.

It wasn't a real situation, them all sitting around the table, making small talk, but it almost looked real, for moments at a time. 'Fake it till you make it,' Chloe told herself.

After dinner, she and Aidan cleared away the plates and loaded the dishwasher. iRachel tried to object, but Aidan held up his hand.

'New rules,' he said. 'Or old rules reinstated. The cook doesn't clear up.'

'Thank you,' said iRachel. 'I will go and perform my mirror check-in, and then I will iron my tunic and check the water saturation levels in my shoes.'

'Water saturation levels,' Chloe said when iRachel left the room. 'She's funny.'

'She can be,' said Aidan. 'Not always deliberately, but sometimes she is very dry.'

'Unlike her shoes,' said Chloe, rinsing a plate under the tap.

'Ha ha. Don't you have studying to do?'

'I've only got one more exam. Tomorrow. It's English literature.'

'Don't you need to revise for that?'

'Our set text is *Frankenstein*,' Chloe replied by way of explanation.

Aidan laughed. *Frankenstein* was Chloe's favourite book. She'd first read it aged eleven and had come to Rachel pale with outrage at the treatment of the monster, tears pouring down her cheeks. She reread it almost every year and could quote passages of it word for word.

'I think you'll probably be okay on that one. How have the rest of them gone?' he asked carefully.

'Fine.'

'Fine?'

'Fine. No problems, okay? They're not that important anyway.'

'All exams are a little bit important . . .' he began tentatively.

'Oh my God, you sound just like Mum.' Chloe cut him off, her tone making it clear the conversation was over. She looked around the kitchen, spotted a last glass and popped it in the dishwasher. 'Right,' she said, 'if that's everything, I'll just . . .'

'Off you go,' said Aidan. 'Disappear into your lair.'

Chloe bounded up the stairs, but instead of going to her room, she went into her mum's office. She had barely set foot in there since her mum died. It was another room full of memories to trip her up and hurt her. There was a carelessly stacked pile of papers covered in her mum's spidery hand – calculations, sketches and

169

diagrams. There was a photo of all three of them on a skiing holiday, anonymous in their hats and goggles but with matching wide grins. And in the pen tray there was a dusty Lego figure: a knight with a cape, armour and a lance. Chloe, aged four, had presented him to her mum.

'He's your Work Knight, Mama,' she'd said. 'He'll keep watch and make sure you get all your sums right.'

Chloe picked up the little figurine. His cape was dusty and she brushed him off with her forefinger. She straightened his legs and set him upright so he could watch over the keyboard.

Then she turned to the printer. As iRachel had promised, there was a sheaf of papers – more than Chloe had expected. They looked like pages scanned from a notebook, and Chloe found herself wondering where the original notebook might be. Her mum had sketched each section of the garden and labelled the plants. She'd also written notes about the fruit trees and the flower beds. There was a printout of a calendar, which noted which gardening jobs needed to be done in what month.

Chloe walked back to her own room, leafing through the pages slowly. There were a few notes which made her smile, like the page where Rachel had labelled a particular plant, 'Twiddly leaf thingy with pink spike flowers which go crimson. Like a salvia but not. No idea what it is, was here when we moved in. Never dies.'

And another annotation: 'Bastard aphids, must find env. friendly solution.'

She could hear her mum's voice in those notes, and it made her smile. She looked out of her bedroom window. In the golden summer evening light she could see the twiddly-leafed plant. It was covered in extravagant pinky-red flowers, and it looked robust, despite the neglect the garden had suffered. She decided she would take some pictures of it in the morning and see if she couldn't identify it. A mystery to which her mum hadn't had the answer. Imagine if she could solve it instead.

# 30

# Rachel

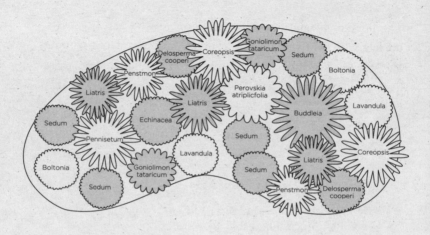

Goniolimon
tataricum

Coreopsis

Delosperma
cooperi

Penstmon

Sedum

Boltonia

Liatris

Perovskia
atriplicfolia

Lavandula

Liatris

Echinacea

Buddleia

Sedum

Sedum

Coreopsis

Pennisetum

Lavandula

Liatris

Boltonia

Goniolimon
tataricum

Sedum

Sedum

Penstmon

Delosperma
cooperi

# 31

# Aidan

The light was beautiful, a warm summer glow, and iRachel sat upright with her hands folded in her lap, lifting her face to the sun. She had checked the patio carefully before she stepped outside in her pristine shoes and had dusted the chair before she sat down. But now that she was there, she looked as relaxed and contented as Aidan had ever seen her. He hesitated in the doorway.

'May I join you?' he asked.

She turned to look at him. 'Of course.'

He drew up a chair and sat beside her. 'It's nice to see you outside,' he said.

'I found the occasion earlier to be full of new sensations,' she said. 'I wanted to find out more about this environment, once I had worked out how to mitigate the risks of soiling my garments.'

'Are you saying you liked it?'

'It was a new experience. I am not sure I have fully understood the concept of enjoyment yet, but if it is what I think, then yes, I enjoyed it.'

'What do you think enjoyment is?'

'It is very subjective, but my understanding is that it is an absence of conflict or immediate responsibilities. It may incorporate a range of sensations – auditory, such as the calls of the birdlife, and visual, including the flora and the colour of the sky. I do not have an olfactory sense like yours, but I am able to chemically process molecules in the air and respond to them. The reaction I experienced to the molecules of cut grass after Chloe mowed the lawn . . . would that constitute enjoyment?'

'Let's see . . . Peace and quiet, sunshine, flowers, freshly cut grass, birdsong . . . Yes, I would say by any conventional metric that would be enjoyable. It's just a pity you've waited all these weeks to come out into the garden.'

'I had not realised I was permitted to go outside.'

'Of course you are. You're not a prisoner.'

She regarded him for a long moment, her gaze even. 'There is a veranda along the front of the house.'

'Yes,' he said cautiously. He didn't know where this was going.

'Rachel's "porch". She wanted a swing.'

'Yes.'

'Can I sit out there?'

'You know you can't,' he said, and he felt angry, caught out. 'You'd be visible from the road. Imagine the questions people would ask.'

She nodded, as if this was the reply she had expected. 'A prisoner is someone whose movements are restricted, is that correct?'

'Because they've done bad things and they need to be punished or kept away from other people because they're dangerous,' he said quickly.

'But the motivation for the restriction is a separate matter from the fact of it,' she persisted.

'I'm not sure I understand.'

'A prisoner may not go outside because he or she has done bad things. I may not go outside because I am . . . the words Luke used were "a very expensive secret". I may not be bad, but I am deprived of autonomous movement as surely as if I had committed fraud or murder.'

'That's true,' Aidan said. 'I'm sorry. I wish it were different.'

They sat beside one another in silence for a while, and then he asked, 'If you had your freedom, where would you go?'

'Where could I go where I would not be a cause for curiosity? I know that my appearance is almost human, but not human enough.'

'Human enough for what?'

'No one would mistake me for a real member of the species homo sapiens. Until robotics engineering advances considerably and android and gynoid humanoids become more prevalent, I will always be a curiosity. And once they are a common sight, I will almost certainly have become obsolete and be decommissioned.'

Aidan felt a desperate need to comfort her. 'I suppose you could go somewhere where there were no other people. Or no strangers, at least. A deserted beach. Or into a great forest. Canada maybe? Or the Outback?'

'That would be lonely.'

'Only if you went alone.'

'Who would go with me?' she said, and looked directly at him.

He wanted to say, 'I will.' The words were on the tip of his tongue. But her expression stopped him.

She looked away, across the garden, and was silent for a long moment. 'Rachel always said you were kind, Aidan, and you are. But it is not kind to give hope where there is none. I am an experiment in your home. I am not your friend, or your wife, or family.'

'You are my friend——' he began, but she interrupted him.

'Luke is not kind,' she said, 'but he is always honest. He said to me, "Do not get your hopes up. Do not mistake kindness for affection. This is not your home. You are the lab rat, and this is the maze."'

This time it was Aidan who reached out and took her hand. 'Don't say that. You're a guest in our home. You bring so much, and I consider you a friend. Family.' He laughed softly. 'And remember, Chloe and I are in the experiment too. If you're a lab rat, so are we. We're all lab rats together in the same maze, chasing the cheese.'

# 32
## Chloe

Her exam wasn't until eleven, so Chloe had an hour or two to kill before she had to go and sit in the corner of the stuffy, dim office of the deputy head. She walked through the quiet corridors of the school, looking through the glass panels in classroom doors at the bent heads and bored expressions. It felt strange to be wandering around. She got a bar of chocolate and a carton of juice from the vending machine and sat on the low wall outside the science block, slurping her juice and kicking her heels.

She could see Mr Johnstone, the chemistry teacher, who kept glancing out of the open door at her, and she knew he was waiting for a hiatus so he could find out what she was doing out of class and tell her off, even though she hadn't done anything wrong. Like all the science teachers in her school, he knew who her mum was and what she'd achieved, and Chloe's lack of interest and consequent total lack of progress in the sciences infuriated him.

She realised that if she kept hanging around in the school corridors, she was likely to have to explain herself to some teacher, so she decided to go to the library. If anyone asked, she could say she was last-minute cramming for her exam.

She liked the library. It was the oldest part of the school and had high banks of heavy dark-wood shelving. They'd moved with the times (more or less) and had also installed rows of computers, group-study desks and a video-screening room, but it still had the hushed atmosphere and heavy old-book smell of a proper library. She strolled in. There was a sixth-former behind the desk – it was her friend Jess's older brother, Jeremy.

When they were giggling Year Sevens and had gone round to Jess's house, he had hated them and would scream at them to be quiet and stay away from his room. They had hated him back and said they wouldn't go into his rancid, smelly boy's room if he paid them. He'd been short then, with quite bad skin, and Jess said his feet absolutely reeked.

He'd grown up now, and at eighteen was more than six feet tall. His skin had cleared up and he had a shock of thick, straight black hair. He was a musician, like Jess, and played the double bass brilliantly. He was planning to go to a conservatoire when he finished school and then play in an orchestra. He didn't hate them so much anymore, and he even nodded and smiled when he saw Chloe and Amy in the corridor.

Seeing him behind the desk in the library, Chloe raised one hand in greeting. He glanced up at her and then went back to doing whatever he was doing on the computer. Chloe did her best to look as if she had every right to be there. She couldn't face having to give a long, complicated explanation.

She had a vague idea that she might look for a book on flowers and see if she could find her mum's mysterious plant. She wandered up and down the aisles until she found herself in the botany section, but while there were plenty of books on plant biology, there didn't seem to be anything that might help her identify the flowering shrub in the garden.

She wandered over to the bank of PCs. How would she begin searching? She had a feeling that entering 'twiddly-leafed plant' into Google wouldn't elicit the best results. She sat staring at the screen, fiddling with the mouse cable around her finger. (How archaic was their school? Who still had a mouse with a cable?)

After a few minutes, she became aware that someone was watching her. Jeremy was looking over the top of his own computer screen. She gave him a cold stare. He didn't look away, so she slowly crossed her eyes and let her tongue stick out of the corner of her mouth. He didn't smile or avert his gaze, so she sneered at him and went back to staring at the PC screen, even though it was blank. He wasn't to know that.

She heard him begin to type. Thank God he'd decided to leave her alone. But then an Instant Message window popped up in the corner of her screen.

J Can I help you with anything?

C Who is this?

J Jem. You're just sitting there. I wondered if you needed help with anything.

C Jem???!

J My friends call me Jem. Only my mum calls me Jeremy. Anyway, do you need help?

C I'm not just sitting. I'm reading something.

J Your screen is blank.

C How can you see my screen?

J Library admin. I can see everybody's screen.

C That's creepy. They should warn us about that.

J They did. You signed an IT user agreement when you started Year Seven. It was in there.

C Who reads those?

J Caveat emptor.

C What?

J Let the buyer beware. Don't sign something if you don't know what's in it.

C Thanks very much. Anyway, I'm fine. I don't need help. Thank you.

She minimised the chat window. She sat staring at the screen for a few minutes longer, then she sneaked a look around the side of the monitor. Jem was slouched in his seat, staring at his own computer screen, frowning fiercely. Because he was a sixth-former, he didn't have to wear school uniform; instead, he wore a scruffy hooded parka in a nasty military green. She could see it hanging on the back of his chair now, even though it was midsummer. He was wearing a plain white T-shirt over a black grandpa shirt, and he had the sleeves of the grandpa shirt pulled down over his hands. Suddenly, something on his screen made him smile. It wasn't a broad grin, just a little twisted smirk, slightly wicked but not malicious. Without thinking, Chloe clicked the message window open again.

*What's so funny?*

Instantly, a gif popped up in the message window of a cat pushing a dog down the stairs. She'd seen it before, but it was funny. She smiled too, but typed back:

C Srsly? Cat videos?

J Everyone loves a cat video.

C I'm more of a crocodile person.

Within seconds, a gif of an enormous alligator crossing a golf course came up on her screen.

C That's an alligator.

J How do you tell the difference?

C One will see you later. The other will see you in a while.

He snorted. She actually heard him snort and she felt a small glow of pleasure. He was a sixth-former and she'd made him laugh.

J So in all seriousness, are you just bunking off in here, or were you trying to do something?

C Not bunking, just waiting to write a deferred exam.

J Which?

C Eng lit.

J Worried?

C No.

J So you don't need my sage advice on the themes of conspiracy and treason in *Macbeth*?

C We're doing *Frankenstein* and I'm good thanks. But now I'm intrigued. Do you have sage advice on the themes in *Macbeth*?

J I read the blurb on the back and watched the Fassbender movie the night before the exam. I am not a theme expert.

C Nothing on *Frankenstein*?

J *Frankenstein* is the doctor dude, not the monster.

C Wow. Insightful.

J I'm not really a literature kind of guy.

C What kind of guy are you?

J Music. You know that. And science. Biology mostly.

C Well, maybe you can help me after all.

J With what?

C I need to find out the name of a plant.

J What sort of plant?

C One with flowers?

J Can you narrow it down?

C I've got a picture.

She'd emailed the pic to herself, and she copied the image quickly and dropped it into the chat window.

J I have no idea what that is.

C Wow. What a science guy you turned out to be.

J Sheesh. Everyone's a critic. I do know how to
find it though. There are plant databases. You enter
some details about the plants and it'll bring up a list of
possible options. There'll be pics and you can compare
them to your photo.

He dropped a link into the chat and she clicked to open it. It was a serious and scientific web page, with an endless list of multiple choice questions:

- What month does the plant flower in?
- What colour is the flower?
- What sort of flower or other reproductive structure does the plant have?

Under each question there were incomprehensible lists of Latin and scientific terms, and checkboxes. Chloe stared at it, dismayed. What was 'actinomorphic'? Did her plant grow from a bulb, tuber or corm? She frowned at the page for a long moment. She wasn't her mother's daughter for nothing. Research just took time. She glanced at her watch. Still an hour to her exam. She searched and found a glossary of botanical terms, and, taking a notebook out of her bag, she jotted down all of the words she didn't know and began to search for them one by one. It was painstaking work, but she was able to make a considered choice for each category. It turned out that once she'd decoded the Latin, the questions were relatively simple. She realised she was being asked if the plant was local. Was it flowering now? Were the flowers this colour all the time or did they start out a different colour?

She was so engrossed in what she was doing, she didn't notice that Jem was watching her, fascinated. Eventually, he unfolded himself from his chair and strolled over, sliding into the chair beside her and pulling it up close so he could see the screen. He smelled of chewing gum and hair gel, and, very faintly, of cigarettes.

'Can I see the pic again?' he asked. 'And can you make it as big as possible?'

Chloe opened the image and expanded it on the screen. She continued to work through her list of terms, scribbling notes and then choosing an option in each category.

When she got to the end of the massive list, she clicked 'Search', and after a moment the database spat out names and images of eight possible matches.

She scrolled through each one slowly, opening each pic and comparing it to her image.

'That one's similar,' she said, pointing.

She magnified the image and they looked at the leaves – they were spiny and long with a scalloped edge.

'Looks like a thistle, or rocket,' Jem said.

'Twiddly,' Chloe said half to herself.

'Twiddly?'

'It's how my mum described them. That's it, isn't it?' They looked at the name together.

'*Morina longifolia*,' said Jem. 'Long-leaved whorlflower.'

'That's it,' she said. 'It's good to know what it is. Now I can look up how to care for it.'

'Well done,' he said. 'You can go home and tell your mum. Impress her with your botanical know-how.' As he said it, she saw him realise and remember. 'Oh my God, I am so sorry . . .' he started to say, but Chloe was already out of her seat.

She stood up and grabbed her bag. 'It's okay. Anyway, thanks. See ya,' she said, and fled the library.

# 33
# Aidan

The ringing phone ripped him out of his deepest sleep. He woke feeling like he'd been under black water and someone had yanked him to the surface.

The phone was on Rachel's side of the bed and he rolled over to answer it.

'Hello?'

'Is that Aidan Sawyer?' The voice was female, deep and gruff, and even though he was still half asleep, he was pretty sure it wasn't someone he knew.

'Yes?'

'Son of Sinead Sawyer, of 23 Pevensey Street?'

'Yes.'

'This is Susanna Douglas. I'm a firefighter from the Cambridgeshire Fire and Rescue Service. We're at your mother's house.'

Oh dear God. He slumped face forward onto the bed, the phone still held to his ear. Not his mother. Not her too.

'There seems to have been an accident here. There was a fire in the kitchen. Her neighbours smelled the smoke and called us, and we got here in time. There is some damage to the kitchen, and we've got an ambulance crew.'

'Is she . . . ?' He found he was shaking uncontrollably.

'She's stable,' said Susanna Douglas soothingly. 'She's inhaled some smoke, but she's conscious and sitting up.'

'I'll be right over,' said Aidan, swinging his legs off the bed. 'Give me half an hour.'

'It's probably best if you go straight to the hospital,' Susanna said, and told him which one. 'The ambulance will be taking her there for observation, given her age.'

They rang off, and Aidan pulled on his clothes as fast as he could. He glanced at the clock – it was just after three. As he went out into the corridor, pulling on his jacket, he could see light under Chloe's door. What was she doing up at this hour? He tapped on the door, but she didn't answer. He opened it and saw her curled up on top of the covers, fast asleep, her laptop open, with the light of the screen bathing her face. He gently moved the laptop onto the floor, half noticing that she was on a Royal Horticultural Society web page. Then he pulled her duvet up over her, clicked off the light and slipped from the room.

The downstairs was illuminated by dim moonlight. iRachel sat on a kitchen chair, hands in her lap, motionless, with her eyes closed. A power cable snaked from a wall plug across her body and into her armpit. She looked curiously vulnerable. Aidan had never seen her on charge before. It was something she preferred to do in private. He felt bad, but he had to wake her. He touched her lightly on the shoulder. Her eyes opened slowly, and he saw them brighten as if a light had been switched on inside her. She moved, as if drawing in a breath.

'Something is distressing you,' she said.

'There's been a fire at my mother's house,' he said. 'I need to go to the hospital. Can you keep an eye on Chloe? She's asleep. I should be back well before she wakes, but in case . . .'

'Do you want me to give Chloe any information about your mother?'

'Tell her she's okay,' said Aidan. 'It's all I know. Or at least that's what they told me. And tell her to ring me.' He gave iRachel's shoulder a quick squeeze and raced out of the house.

The bright sodium streetlights in the car park at the hospital cast a pitiless glare. He ran to the entrance of A&E. There was an ambulance drawn up outside, but when he went through the sliding doors into the hospital itself, it was all but deserted. There was a very drunk man, who looked like he was probably home-less, stretched out across three bucket chairs, and a man in suit trousers and a bloodstained white shirt holding a wedge of tissues against his bleeding nose. Aidan looked around wildly, but there wasn't anyone behind the reception desk or any staff members walking around. He was about to start ripping the curtains back on every cubicle when a policewoman in uniform stepped out of one. She spotted him and walked over.

'Aidan Sawyer?' she asked.

'Yes.'

'PC Alison Moore. Your mum's just getting checked over.'

'Is she . . . ?'

'She's absolutely fine. She wasn't injured at all, and it seems she didn't suffer any significant smoke inhalation.'

'Well, that's a relief.' Aidan let his shoulders sag. 'Will I be able to take her home soon?'

'I'm pretty sure they'll keep her in overnight,' said PC Moore. 'Just to be safe.'

'Can I go through and see her?'

'The doctor's busy with her right now. She won't be long.'

Aidan expected the PC to make her excuses and leave, but she stayed where she was, looking slightly uncomfortable.

'Was there something else?' he asked.

'Well, yes,' said PC Moore. 'There will be a full investigation, but it looks as if the fire was started by a chip pan.'

'A chip pan?' Aidan frowned. He had never known his mother to cook chips. He hadn't even known that she owned a chip pan.

'The fire started at 1 a.m. Your mother's next-door neighbours, the . . .' PC Moore checked her notebook. '. . . Olivellis, happened to be up late and smelled the smoke.'

'Why would my mum have been making chips at 1 a.m.?'

'That was our question. We asked the Olivellis, and they said she's been keeping very irregular hours lately. They see lights on in the house at all hours, and a couple of times they've seen her go out for a walk well after midnight.'

'Why haven't they rung and told me?' said Aidan, balling his fists with frustration.

'We did ask,' said PC Moore, 'but they said they didn't want to worry you, that you had enough on your plate. Apparently your wife recently passed away? I'm so sorry.'

'If I'd known . . .' began Aidan. But as he spoke, he knew that he had known. She had become increasingly confused and had been getting worse. It wasn't just the lunch when she'd forgotten Rachel was dead, or the fact that her house was dirty when it had always been spotless. She'd become less and less communicative over the last few months. He should have done something about it, should have taken her to a doctor. But she'd tried so hard to hide it and he hadn't had the heart – or the strength – to challenge her on it. Would Rachel have spotted it if she'd been around? She was a scientist, that was true, and very analytical. But she'd tended not to notice things about people in quite the same detail. Besides, she'd generally avoided seeing Sinead if she could. She probably hadn't seen her mother-in-law for six months before she died.

At that moment the doctor came out of the cubicle, a clipboard in her hands. PC Moore made her excuses and left, handing Aidan her card. The doctor was a small Asian woman, her long hair caught back in a neat bun at the back of her neck. Her nametag identified her as Dr Nawaz. She looked very tired, but her eyes were large and kind. She guided Aidan over to a bank of chairs, as far from the snoring homeless man as possible. Bleeding-nose man had mercifully been taken into a cubicle for treatment.

'I know you must be anxious to go and see your mum,' she said, 'but right now she's asleep, so don't worry. They're moving her up to the ward and you can go and see her there once she's settled.'

'She's asleep?'

'She was distressed when they brought her in, so once I had finished my examination, I gave her a sedative.'

'Distressed?'

'She didn't understand where she was,' said Dr Nawaz gently. 'I did my best to reassure her, but she was very confused.'

'That's understandable, though, isn't it? With the shock of the fire and everything.'

'Of course. How is she usually? Day to day?'

'It's hard to say,' said Aidan. 'I don't see her every day, or even every week. I ring her often. . . .' he added quickly, so Dr Nawaz wouldn't think he was an awful, neglectful son. 'She's just . . . fiercely independent. Always has been.'

'Have you had a sense that she's becoming more forgetful though?'

'Yes,' said Aidan reluctantly, and he told Dr Nawaz about the incidents over the last few months. She nodded and made some notes. 'So what happens now?' he asked.

'Well, we'll need to do some tests and find out just how confused she is, and whether her memory improves once she's had some rest and something to eat.'

'What kind of tests?'

'We'll start with the MMSE, the Mini-Mental State

Examination. It's a set of questions to test her memory, vocabulary, ability to respond to instructions—'

Aidan managed a weak smile. 'She's not terribly good at taking orders.'

Dr Nawaz smiled back. 'We'll keep that in mind. Depending on how she does with that, we'll do more tests: a physical examination, some bloods, possibly a brain scan—'

'And then what?'

'Once we have a firm diagnosis, we can start working out an appropriate course of treatment.'

'But there isn't really an appropriate course of treatment, is there?' said Aidan bleakly. 'There isn't a cure.'

'Not a cure per se, but if she is suffering from dementia, there is a lot we can do to manage her symptoms and keep her safe and happy. Good food, lots of sleep, exercise, social stimulation – all these things can make an enormous difference.'

'You make her sound like a toddler,' said Aidan. He dropped his head into his hands.

Dr Nawaz placed her hands gently on top of his, drawing them away from his face. She was smiling kindly. 'To be fair, all of us do better with good food, sleep, exercise and friends. Not just older people and toddlers.'

Later, he went up to the quiet, sleeping ward. They had put Sinead in a bed in the corner by a window. Her gunmetal-grey hair, normally so abundant and glorious, looked dull spread out on the pillow, and there were deep hollows beneath her closed eyes. Aidan sat beside her and took her hand in his. It felt tiny, the bones in it staring through the skin like the bones of a bird. Her wrists seemed shockingly knobbly, and under the cotton of her hospital gown he could see her collarbones protruding sharply. She was very thin. How had he not noticed this when they'd been there for lunch the other week? He knew the answer. He'd been so bound up in his own grief and misery, he'd barely looked at her. His own mother.

She slept on her back, her mouth slightly open, snoring softly. He was pretty sure she didn't usually snore – it was probably the medication they'd used to knock her out. When he thought about it, he had hardly ever seen her sleeping. When he was growing up, she had always been up before him and hadn't gone to bed until well after he went to sleep. He'd come down bleary and dozy in the morning to find her in the kitchen, efficiently buttering bread for sandwiches or stirring porridge for breakfast. He'd never seen her doze in a chair or nap, and even now that she was retired, she struggled to sit down and relax. He half smiled. Like someone else he knew . . . Rachel also hadn't known how to pause. Maybe he'd recognised that quality in her when he fell in love with her?

He thought of his mother through the years – tall, ramrod straight, always going slightly too fast for him when he was small. At that point she hadn't yet learned to drive, so she'd walked everywhere, or cycled, carrying her groceries and sometimes Oliver in the basket of her bicycle. So much of Aidan's childhood seemed to have been spent half walking, half running, a few too many steps behind her. She'd been no-nonsense and practical, keeping clothes clean and ironed, putting good, plain food on the table and ensuring homework was done and activities organised. He'd never felt unloved, but her love was firm and functional: a hand combing his hair or straightening his tie, placing a plate in front of him or correcting his homework. He had no memory of holding her hand, or of caresses, hugs or cuddles. Had she been harder on him because he was the eldest? He didn't think so. She had simply given as much as she had to give – and as she was the sole breadwinner, organiser, housewife and parent, there just hadn't been that much to go round.

He found himself thinking, for the first time, how she must

have felt when his dad left. She'd had to cope. There wasn't another option. Food had to go on the table. Children needed to go to school. Money needed to be earned. There would have been no space for her own grief. Maybe, he thought with sudden clarity, maybe that was why she'd been so business-like. Maybe, in order to manage those messy emotions, she'd had to put a lid on all her feelings. There'd been no space for softness, for sentimentality, even for affection or laughter. Because if she'd allowed herself to feel, if she'd acknowledged the extent of her pain, how would she have been able to go on?

He'd been a single parent for a mere three months and the mantle of responsibility felt heavy on his shoulders. It wasn't as if Chloe needed much active parenting: she was pretty independent really. It was more that every choice and decision was his, and that every worry or triumph or happiness to do with Chloe was also his alone. Rachel was the only other person in the world who had loved and cared about Chloe as much as he did, and with her gone, it felt like a very long and lonely road. He realised it helped him to understand his mother a little better.

And now she needed him. Really needed him. He knew it wasn't going to be easy – she would resist with every fibre of her being any intervention in her life or attempt to control her affairs. But he was going to have to find a way to help her, whether she wanted it or not.

# 34
## Luke

'No,' said Luke. 'One hundred per cent, categorically no. It's impossible. I won't allow it.'

'You what? Excuse me? You won't allow it?' Aidan stood suddenly and loomed over Luke. He was taller, by several inches. Luke was unfazed and stood his ground just as firmly. 'I know I'm stating the breathtakingly obvious,' said Aidan, 'but this is not your house.'

'It is my experiment,' said Luke. 'We're in the midst of something extremely delicate and totally secret. I have huge misgivings about my lack of control in this situation anyway – but adding in another random person . . .'

'Not a random person,' said Aidan furiously. 'My mother. My mother, who is currently alone and distressed in a hospital ward and unable to return to her own home.'

Luke snorted derisively and walked over to the patio doors. Chloe was at the far end of the garden, painstakingly edging the lawn. Luckily, she had her headphones on and couldn't hear the shouting match. Bloody Rachel. Bloody, bloody Rachel. How had she landed him in this ridiculous situation? She always thought she knew best, continually manipulated him into doing what she'd already decided. But not this time.

'Right,' he said, turning back to Aidan decisively. 'If your mother is coming into the house, the experiment is concluded. I'll take iRachel back to the lab tonight.'

'No.' Aidan and iRachel answered in chorus, and Luke saw them look at one another, surprised.

'Really? I'd have thought you'd be glad to get rid of it. You didn't want it here in the first place.'

'The experiment is not "concluded",' said Aidan, making sarcastic air quotes. 'Rachel's instructions were that iRachel would know when it was over.' He turned to iRachel. 'Is it over?'

She ignored his direct question. Instead, she said, 'I do not want to return to the laboratory,' and her voice was firm and strong. 'I have made progress in my ability to interpret human emotions and in my manual and cognitive skills since I have been here with Chloe and Aidan. My learning has increased at an exponential rate which far exceeds our controlled experiments in the laboratory.'

'I don't really care what you want,' said Luke, and he didn't even bother to look at her. 'You're a very expensive piece of kit, and I can't leave you here, unsupervised, with some old lady.'

'I am not a piece of kit,' she said. 'I was designed as an empathetic companion for humans, and one of my key potential uses is as a carer for elderly people with cognitive impairments. This is a valuable adjunct to my initial—'

'It's not a valuable anything!' Luke shouted. 'You don't get to decide the direction of the research. You do what you're told, go where you're told and participate in the experiments that I design. Me and me alone. Do you understand?'

'I am afraid I cannot comply with your request,' said iRachel calmly. 'Rachel's Trojan virus is still active in my system. If I am unable to check in with the mirror every six hours, my drives will be wiped.'

'I will smash that fucking mirror to pieces!' Luke yelled, and at that exact moment Chloe came in from the garden, her hands cupped and filled with ripe strawberries. She stopped in the doorway and looked rapidly from her dad to Luke to iRachel.

'Hi, Luke,' she said cheerily. 'I'm guessing you haven't taken the plan to move Grandma Sinead in here too well?'

Luke stared at her. As he looked into her fresh young face — Rachel's face, but full of youthful disdain and confidence — he was flooded with embarrassment and fury. He wanted to yell at her for her condescension, but he knew if he did, Aidan's rage would explode.

He crossed rapidly to the kitchen counter, slammed his laptop shut, scooped up his bag and left abruptly. A few seconds later, they heard his motorbike roar into life. The high, sharp noise of the engine diminished as he sped away.

# 35
# iRachel

This evening was different. Chloe went to spend the night at her friend Amy's house to celebrate finishing her exams. So, for the first time, I was to be alone in the house overnight with Aidan.

There had also been a meteorological shift – this was the first time since I'd come to stay in the house that it had rained during daylight hours. I had never seen rain before, and while my manual suggested I should not go outside and experience it first hand, it was fascinating to stand by the open patio doors and watch it fall. I was also interested in how certain chemical compounds in the air altered as a result of the rain falling on the hot soil and plants. They came to me on a cool, damp breeze and I felt a pleasant flutter as I analysed them.

$Na^+$, $K^+$, $Ca^{2+}$, $Mg^{2+}$, $Fe^{3+}$, $Pb^{2+}$, $Cl^-$.

There was another reason why this evening was different. I expressed a wish and made my own decision. I defied Luke's direct order. If I had been wearing a monitoring wristband and had human physiological signs to measure, I believe it would have recorded a raised heart rate and increased respiration, in line with a sudden adrenaline rush.

This is what has changed. I am designed to seek to understand and empathise with humans. My choices have been driven by the fact that I must follow the course of action which is most helpful to those I am directed to serve. But today, for the first time, I experienced something new. I wanted something for myself. I do believe that my presence here is supportive to Aidan and Chloe, and that it serves Rachel and Luke's research agenda. But my desire to stay was concerned with something more personal.

I want to be here.

I want.

This is the first time I have wanted. Rachel once told me that to want – to desire and to yearn – is one of the essential components of being human. 'The driving force behind all human endeavour is dissatisfaction,' she said. 'It began in prehistoric times. "I can't reach that banana from down here on all fours. I will walk upright! I can't carry all these bananas in my hands, I will invent the wheel to transport them! I live in a country without bananas, I'll build a ship to go and fetch them!"'

'Your fruit-centred view of human development is not recorded in any reputable historical textbook,' I said.

Rachel laughed. 'It's an allegory. It's still true though. We invent and develop and explore and create because we're not happy with what we've got. We fight wars and write poetry because we desire and yearn and want what we cannot have. To be human is to want.'

Before this evening, I did not fully understand what she meant. I had never known the sensation of want. I can predict Luke's response to this. '"Believe", "hope", "desire",' he would say, laughing. 'Those are not scientific words. Those things cannot be measured or quantified.'

Everything I have learned so far has been based on measurable data. What I am experiencing now has no basis in data. Is this intuition? Am I undergoing the messy, unquantifiable nature of human emotion?

As I was thinking about this, Aidan came into the living room. He clicked on a lamp.

'It's got dark in here,' he observed, and he came to stand

beside me, looking out at the rain. It was a companionable silence – Aidan's vital signs indicated he was calm, and when I glanced at his facial expression, he seemed less worried and upset than in recent days.

'Are you happy that your mother will be coming to stay in the house?' I asked him.

'I don't think "happy" is the right word,' he said. 'I'm relieved. It's the right thing to do, at least in the short term. She needs our love and care.'

'How will she respond to my presence?'

'I don't know,' he said. 'I don't know if she'll confuse you with Rachel. We're just going to have to see.'

'I have access to all the available information on the treatment and care of patients with dementia,' I said. 'I will at all times adhere to best practice.'

'I know you will,' said Aidan, and he smiled at me. 'I, on the other hand, am only human. I don't have your astonishing powers of patience, or your knowledge. She's my mum, and my feelings around that are . . . complicated. I'm really going to need your help.'

Suddenly, there was a jagged, bright electrostatic discharge across the sky, followed almost instantly by an enormous bang. Aidan jumped in surprise and his heart rate shot up.

'You got a fright,' I observed.

'I've never been good at thunder and lightning.'

'You haven't. Remember that time in the Kruger Park?'

'This isn't you speaking, is it?' Aidan asked. He didn't look at me.

'No. I believe that once more one of Rachel's files has been opened. I surmise it has been triggered by the chemical composition of the rain and the sound of the thunder.'

'I want to hear it,' he said, and his voice was rough and husky.

'I want to hear what she has to say, but . . .' He looked at me, and I found his expression impossible to read. Shame? Excitement? Desire? Fear? 'I want to hear it in the dark.'

I nodded.

'Come,' he said, and, taking my hand, he led me upstairs.

We went into his bedroom. The room was in darkness, but he did not turn on the light. He went to the windows and threw them wide open, then he drew me down to lie beside him on the bed. The room was illuminated only by the flashes of lightning outside. He lay on his side, holding my hand between both of his, and closed his eyes.

'Now,' he said. 'Now.'

# 36
# Rachel

'We'd spent those awful few days in Johannesburg, do you remember? We'd been travelling for two months, and we'd just had those magical weeks in the desert in Namibia, where we'd experienced total quiet and blazing heat and the most amazing landscapes. It looked like Mars. And then we got to Johannesburg, and we were stuck in that awful hotel, and we didn't have a car – not that we'd have driven anyway, the roads were insane. We didn't know anyone, and on our last night there we had that horrible row. It was the first time I admitted to you that I'd accepted the offer to study at Cambridge. You accused me of lying, and I called you a controlling bastard, and, well, it got worse from there.

After we'd screamed and yelled and I'd thrown your backpack across the room, all we wanted was to get away from each other, just for half an hour, and there was nowhere to go. Not at midnight in a strange and potentially dangerous city. We were like prisoners in that hotel room. So we sat on opposite sides of the bed, sulking like little kids, and then we crawled into bed and slept apart, cold backs turned to each other. I hated that night.

The next day the bus picked us up from the hotel and we had a four-hour journey, sitting as far away from each other as two people can sit when they're in adjoining bus seats. I ached to reach out to you, but I was so scared you'd push me away. I felt so trapped. We had months of travelling ahead of us, and at that point I genuinely thought you were going to break up with me and we'd be stuck together until we could figure out a way to get home.

I spent around half of my time trying to calculate what would happen if I just touched you and the other half being outraged that you hadn't touched me or said anything. I wondered if maybe we weren't soulmates after all. I thought about how I had got used to being cradled in your love, how I knew who I was in the world because of how you loved me. I imagined my life without you, and I was frankly terrified. Ridiculous. It was just a row. But, like I say, it was a very long bus trip.

We got there in the early afternoon. Do you remember those huts in the camp? So beautiful, with the heat beating down, the cicadas in the twisted thorn trees, and the strange burnt umber of the grasses. It was just breathtaking. We sat side by side on our little veranda for a while, drinking ice-cold beers, and I could feel the knot between us beginning to unravel. I was very tired though – after the sleepless night and the long, tense bus ride – and I went to lie down for a nap. An hour or so later, I half woke up, and you were lying on the bed beside me, asleep, holding my hand. I knew then we'd be okay, and I fell properly, deeply asleep.

The lightning woke me – there was the most gigantic slash of light across the sky. I half sat up, and I was about to turn and wake you, so you could see it too, when the thunder came. I'd never heard anything like it. The crash was deafening, and then the rumble seemed to go on for ages. You shot straight up and cried out like a child. Your hand in mine was soaked with sweat, and you were trembling all over.

"Hey," I said, but I don't think you were properly awake – you were trapped in the fear, in a half-asleep place. You couldn't hear me. "Aidan, Aidan," I said, and I had to shake your shoulder gently

and turn your face towards me before you came to your senses
and realised where we were and who I was.

The rain had started falling in great sheets and the lightning
was crackling all around us while the clouds roared with fury. I
wasn't scared of the thunder, but I was worried we'd get struck
by lightning and fried in our bed. It seemed counterproductive
to mention that to you though. You tried to laugh it off, but you
couldn't control your body – the trembling was so bad, it rattled
your teeth. And the thunder didn't let up.

"I didn't know that thunder bothered you so much," I said.

"We don't get a lot of it where I'm from, but I hate it," you
said through clenched teeth. "It started when I was very small.
Four, maybe? One night, my mum had gone out to visit a friend,
and Oliver and I were asleep. My dad was supposed to be looking
after us. There was a huge thunderstorm and the noise woke me,
so I went downstairs to look for my dad. He was in the hallway,
talking on the phone. When I think about it now, he was speaking
in a low, deep voice, not like his usual tone at all. In hindsight,
I reckon he was probably talking to the woman he was having
an affair with. Anyway, when he saw me on the stairs, he yelled.
Really yelled at me to get back upstairs. I ran back to my bed
and hid under the covers, and the thunder just kept coming. It
was awful." You shuddered. "Any time I heard thunder after that,
I would just freak out. Mum wasn't very understanding, so I
learned not to run to her. Of course, I could never tell her why
it made me so scared. But if there was ever a thunderstorm, I'd
go and hide in my wardrobe. I'd wrap myself really tightly in a
blanket and cover my head until it was over."

"You know it can't hurt you."

"I know. It's not rational. Like arachnophobia."

"Brontophobia."

"What? Fear of dinosaurs?" you said.

"No, fear of thunder. It's the scientific term."

"How on earth do you know that?"

"I was Kent Junior Scrabble Champion. I know all sorts of useful words."

"Nerd," you said. You managed a tiny smile, but I could see the sweat standing out on your forehead in little drops. I managed to get you to lie down, and I drew the sheet over both of us, right over our heads. I slipped in close to you and wrapped you in my arms and legs.

"There are synonyms too: astraphobia, keraunophobia, nica-duranaphobia – that was really difficult to use in Scrabble. Too many letters."

"What other big words do you know?"

"Well, if you've got a p on a triple-letter square, priapism is always a good one."

"Priapism?"

"It means a persistent erection of—"

"I know what it means." Your voice had gone deep and low. You weren't trembling anymore.

"I can feel that you know what it means," I said, and I slid my leg over your hip.

And you rolled onto your back, and pulled me on top of you, and I rode you as the thunder roared and the rain battered our little bush hut. By the time we'd finished, the storm had passed and the sky was red and gold and orange with the most glorious sunset. We wrapped ourselves in towels and stood in the open doorway of our hut, and two zebras strolled right into the camp and grazed just a few feet away from us. And we held other and didn't say anything. I've never felt closer to anyone, and I knew then that I wanted to be with you for the rest of my life.'

# 37

## Aidan

When Aidan woke in the morning, he was still lying on his side on top of the covers, his hands cupped together. The pillow beneath his face was wet with tears. iRachel was gone. He sat up and rubbed his face. He felt unsettled and shaky. It had been a strange, intimate night. He had wept, and iRachel had held him, whispering to him in Rachel's voice. He had had to remind himself that this was not his wife, no matter how much she sounded and behaved like Rachel in those moments. But it was increasingly clear to him that iRachel was becoming her own person — an autonomous, thinking, feeling being.

At one point in the night she had whispered to him, 'Luke has built me as a complete woman. I am capable of participating in full sexual intercourse, if that is what you want.'

It must have been obvious to her that that was what he wanted — every one of his physiological signs was making that clear. But the phrase 'if that is what you want' stopped him dead. What did *she* want? If she gave her body to him because she felt she was serving him, in the same way that she cooked and cleaned, he would find that demeaning.

'No,' he said. 'But thank you. It's lovely when you hold me.'

And she had. She'd held him, and he had cried himself to sleep. At some point in the night, she had obviously slipped away and gone downstairs to perform her mirror check-in and charge herself. He'd slept deeply and woken with no recollection of his dreams. He felt peaceful and calm, but he knew he'd need to think about what had happened between them. Right now, though, he had just a few hours to compose himself, organise everything and fetch his mother from the hospital.

He went straight into the shower and emerged feeling stronger if not braver. When he stepped out onto the landing, he could hear the hum of the vacuum cleaner. He found iRachel in the spare room. She had made up the bed with clean linen and brought an armchair from Rachel's study to put by the window.

'Good morning,' he said. 'And thank you. You've made the room look beautiful.'

'I hope that your mother will find it a restful place.'

It was a lovely room – it was at the back of the house and like Chloe's room had a view over the garden and the fields beyond. It was warm and caught the sun in the afternoons. When they had moved into the house some seven years ago, Rachel had decorated it in a cool duck-egg blue. Their mates Sam and Laura, and other friends from London and further afield, often came to stay, but Sinead had never slept in the room. Even on Christmas night, or evenings when she had come for dinner, she had preferred to stay sober and drive home. 'I like my own bed,' she'd always say firmly. It was one of the many ways in which she had enforced her boundaries and showed her independence. He had understood and respected that.

But right now her own bed was out of the question. The previous morning in the hospital, she'd been very distressed when she'd woken up and there had been moments when she hadn't recognised Aidan at all. She had wept and raged, begging to go home, but it was obvious she was extremely confused. If it had been possible, he would have taken her back to her own home and stayed with her there, but the house was still unsafe and he was needed here. Chloe still had a few weeks of school left, and what with his job and iRachel, he couldn't see how he could make it work.

He'd rung his brother, Oliver, in Singapore, but within a few minutes it had been clear Oliver didn't see it as his problem.

'I'm so sorry, Aid,' he'd said, as if this was an issue of Aidan's making and had nothing at all to do with him. 'I'm sad to hear the old dear isn't doing well.'

'She isn't going to be able to go back to her house, at least not for a while. There's considerable fire damage in the kitchen, and it's not secure. The firefighters had to kick down the back door.'

'I can send you some money for the repairs,' said Oliver. 'I'd come over, only we're not exactly flush at the moment, with the new apartment. And Cressida's making me put every spare penny away for the wedding fund . . .'

The wedding was still two years away, an extravaganza on a beach in Bali that Aidan already knew he wouldn't be able to afford to attend. He pushed his irritation down deep and tried to keep his voice even. 'Insurance will cover the repairs, but her long-term care is more of a concern.'

'I really don't want her to end up in a home,' said Oliver. 'She'd hate that.'

Aidan had lowered the phone from his ear so that Oliver wouldn't hear him swearing under his breath. Oliver had always been like this. Where Sinead had been rigid and firm with Aidan, she'd been inexplicably softer and more indulgent with Oliver. He'd not been expected to help around the house or be responsible, like Aidan was. He'd been a carefree child and had grown into a jolly, confident man with a polished demeanour that suggested he came from a much more privileged background than he did. He was, if Aidan allowed himself to admit it, not just smooth but oily.

'What are you going to do?' Oliver's voice in his ear was persistent.

'In the short term, she's coming to stay here, and we'll see how she does.'

'Ah, I see,' said Oliver, relieved. 'Well, let me know if there's anything I can do . . .' Realising that Aidan might actually ask him to do something, he couldn't ring off fast enough.

Aidan frowned, thinking of Oliver, but then realised that iRachel was watching him expectantly.

'I understand that your mother is not familiar with this room,' said iRachel. 'Perhaps it might help her to feel less distressed if there were some objects here from her own home that she might recognise? Pictures, perhaps, or other personal items? I know that you have to visit her home in order to collect some clothes.'

He smiled at her. 'Thanks, that's a good idea. There's a particular chair she uses in the corner of her living room. And if I also bring her little side table and what's on it, we can try to re-create her space here.'

Once he was in the car, he rang Chloe.

'How are you, sweetheart?'

'I'm fine. Have you got Grandma Sinead yet?'

'Just going to get a few things from her house before I pick her up. Are you sure you're all right?'

'Yeah, yeah. Is it okay if I get the bus and head back home now?'

'What? Yeah, sure. I mean . . . are you sure? I can come and get you from Amy's later.'

'No, it's fine. I've got some stuff I need to do.'

'Okay. Are you sure you wouldn't rather have more time with Amy?'

'No. She has other plans. She's going into town with Jess and Jess's brother. They're going to go and sit in a coffee shop and stare at their phones or something, and I'm really not in the mood.'

Aidan knew he should ask more questions – he had picked up that Amy was spending more time with Jess and that the dynamics of the friendship between the three girls had shifted. But he just didn't have the time or energy to deal with it right now.

'Come on, Chloe, go. I won't be back for a while, and then we'll need to get Grandma Sinead settled in. Go and hang out with some people your own age. Have some fun.'

'Thanks, Dad, but I'm fine. It's really not my thing. And I actually do have some stuff I want to do at home. In the garden.'

'In the garden? You're getting into that, aren't you?'

'Yeah, well, I've been looking at Mum's diagrams of the beds, and I think she labelled some of the plants wrongly. If I'm right, the rudbeckia's never going to flower where it is. It needs more sun. So I thought I'd move it and see.'

'The rudbeckia? Well, okay.' Aidan smiled. 'I would never stand between you and a rudbeckia-related emergency.'

'Stop saying "rudbeckia".' Chloe giggled. 'It's starting to sound weird.'

'Rudbeckia, rudbeckia, rudbeckia.'

'How old are you – five? I'm going now,' said Chloe. 'I'll see you at home.'

Aidan clicked off the hands-free. It was nice to hear her laugh. And he'd liked the enthusiasm he'd heard in her voice. Gardening – whoever would have thought?

He pulled up outside his mother's house. From the front there was no damage visible. He knew Sinead's neighbours, a lovely Italian couple, had been keeping an eye on things, and when he got out of his car he saw Mrs Olivelli looking out of her front window. He waved to her and she returned the gesture, her face contorted in sympathy. He let himself in before she had the chance to come out and talk to him. She was a pleasant woman, but he didn't think he could take her flood of chatter right now. He knew she'd have loads of stories about how bad Sinead had been getting and then he'd feel even worse about having wilfully ignored the facts.

He stepped into the hall and bent to gather up the litter of letters and leaflets on the doormat. Even though Sinead had only been gone a couple of days, the house felt cold and neglected. She'd always kept such a neat house, but the deterioration he and Chloe had noticed on their last visit seemed to have accelerated alarmingly.

There was a fine film of dust everywhere. He walked through the silent rooms and found more worrying signs. There was a frying pan on the floor of the living room and a pile of clothes halfway up the stairs. There were at least six full and half-full teacups scattered around various surfaces, as if she had made them and forgotten to drink them but had then also forgotten to dispose of them. The laundry basket, empty, sat inexplicably in the middle of the dining room table. He went into the kitchen. It was still a mess. The wet chemical extinguishers the firefighters had used had left a residue of foam everywhere, and sticky black soot coated the walls.

Looking beyond the damage, he could see the kitchen had been in chaos even before the fire. There were plates everywhere, with food in varying stages of decomposition – meals he imagined Sinead had made and abandoned uneaten. When he opened the fridge, it was empty, and the pantry held one mouldy bread roll and a few tins. No wonder she was so thin. How had he missed this? Been so unaware? What kind of son didn't notice his mother was starving?

He couldn't change the past, he could only make the future better. He went back into the dining room, fetched the laundry basket and took it through to the living room. He could pack some of Sinead's books and ornaments into it. There was a stack of books on her side table. When he went to pick them up, they released a puff of dust – she hadn't touched them in a long time. He packed them nevertheless. Even if she didn't feel up to reading them, he could arrange them in the same stack on the table in her room at his house. There was a photograph in a frame: Chloe on a summer holiday the previous year, posing extravagantly in her bikini on a beach in Spain, looking young and carefree. He couldn't imagine Chloe acting in that unselfconscious way again. The final item on the table was a ring-bound notebook with a pen attached to it by a length of string. He assumed Sinead used it for shopping lists and appointments. He opened it idly.

Chair

it said on the first page, in a spidery, half-formed version of Sinead's handwriting.

Table

Telefone

He flipped to the next page. This did seem to be a shopping list.

Bread

Milk

Red round vegetable. Tom~

A squiggly line trailed from the first three letters, as if the name of the thing had escaped her pen, fading off into blankness.

On the third page, she had written:

Rachel has passed away. Car accident.

And below, in black capitals scored into the page:

REMEMBER, DO NOT RING AIDAN AND MENTION RACHEL.

There were more pages of notes, many of them incomprehensible. She had obviously used the notebook in her more lucid moments to try and keep track of things she needed to remember. It was a heart-breaking record of her deterioration.

The problem of Rachel had obviously concerned Sinead very much. When he went upstairs to pack up her clothes, he found a note beside the phone on her bedside table:

*Rachel is dead. Do not phone her.*

It would have been funny if it wasn't so tragic.

It took him a while to find a reasonable selection of clothing for her. She had always kept her wardrobe very neat, but now all of her clothes seemed to have been flung into the cupboard in a great tangle – her underwear was mixed in with skirts, trousers and blouses, together with towels and dish towels. He went into the bathroom to gather up her toiletries and found a tyre gauge in the bath and a salt-and-pepper set in the bathroom cabinet. After making sure the doors and windows were securely fastened, he left the house as quickly as he could.

At the hospital, Sinead was surprisingly calm and happy to see him.

'We're going to go back to ours, Mum,' he explained. 'Your back door isn't secure, so I think it's best if you stay with us for a while.'

'That sounds lovely,' she said. She was using a bright, rather fake tone of voice, which he now realised with a pang was her way of pretending she understood what was going on. 'Where is it that you live, by the way?'

They drove home slowly and she looked out of the window at the countryside, lush and bright in the summer sunshine. She kept up a cheerful stream of chatter, commenting on the landscape, the clouds and any street signs or shop fronts she saw. He realised that in the last few years she had either resorted to silence or to this banal stream-of-consciousness, effectively preventing anyone from trying to have a real conversation with her.

They pulled up at the house and Chloe came running out.

She opened Sinead's car door and offered her a hand to help her out.

'Hey there, Grandma Sinead, it's lovely to see you! I'm so glad you're coming to stay with us.'

'Oh no, dear,' said Sinead, climbing out of the car, 'I'm only here for tea. I must get home.'

Chloe looked over at Aidan. He shrugged.

'Well, let's see how we go,' said Chloe. 'Why don't you come inside?'

'Before we do,' said Aidan, coming around the car and putting his hand on Sinead's arm, 'I just want to tell you that we have someone staying with us. She's a . . . helper.'

Sinead ignored him and walked up the path towards the house.

Chloe looked at her dad in alarm. 'You're only telling her now?'

'I was worried she wouldn't remember if I told her earlier,' said Aidan desperately.

'Well, she doesn't seem to have retained it now,' said Chloe, watching Sinead stomp firmly up the stairs and onto the porch. 'It's hard to tell whether that's dementia or just her ignoring what I say as usual.'

The air was warm with the smell of baking. Sinead looked around her, as if seeing the house for the first time. She sniffed appreciatively. 'Scones. Those smell good.'

At that moment iRachel glided into the room from the kitchen. She looked serene in her white tunic, her hair drawn back from her face in a smooth ponytail. 'Good afternoon, Sinead,' she said, offering her hand.

Sinead looked at her for a long moment, then took her hand. 'Hello. Are you the nurse?'

'I am not a qualified healthcare provider, but I am able to help with many of your day-to-day needs.'

'Ah, what we used to call a nurse's aide,' said Sinead. 'Did you bake scones?'

'I am told they are your preferred choice for afternoon tea, especially when they are served with clotted cream and raspberry jam. I have made jam, with sixty per cent organic fruit, and I have prepared a pot of English Breakfast tea, brewed at the recommended 79.44 degrees Celsius.'

'Well, it seems to me you're more highly qualified than those gormless girls in the hospital,' said Sinead, and she walked confidently into the living room and settled herself in a chair with a view of the garden.

Chloe and Aidan looked at each other.

'She hasn't noticed,' whispered Chloe.

'Noticed what? That iRachel's a robot or that she looks exactly like your mum?'

'Both!' Chloe looked astonished.

# 38
## Chloe

After tea, Grandma Sinead dozed off in an armchair and Aidan, sitting opposite her, seemed to let his guard down and relax, as if he too might fall asleep. Chloe had been sitting by the open French doors and the scents from the garden called to her. She slipped out and headed down to the rockery. She wanted to carry on weeding and thinning out the plants. It was painstaking work, but she relished the feel of the warm, clumpy soil under her hands and soon lost herself in the careful rhythm of separating the plants and pulling up the ones she wanted to remove. She'd already cleared around a third of the rockery and the neat clusters of flowers that she had revealed gave her real pleasure. These days, when she wasn't actually weeding, mowing or trimming things, she was thinking about doing it, or researching. She'd found a row of gardening books in her mum's study and she pored over them in the evenings. There was a piece of lawn near the kitchen door which was never used and she was considering asking her dad if she could dig it up and plant a vegetable and herb garden.

She wished she could explain to Amy, or her dad, or anyone, how this was the one thing that made sense to her at the moment. So much in her life seemed out of control, but, somehow, claiming the garden back from chaos made her feel deeply peaceful inside.

She was wrestling with a particularly tenacious dandelion root when she heard the doorbell ring. Someone had dropped by unexpectedly, and her dad and gran were both asleep in the living room. Chloe could see them both resting with their eyes closed. The doorbell hadn't woken them. iRachel was pottering in the kitchen. She knew not to go to the door and had been instructed to go into the utility room if a visitor came to the house.

Chloe went to the French doors and signalled frantically and silently to iRachel, who nodded, stepped into the utility room and shut the door. Then Chloe ran around the outside of the house. There were three people standing on the porch – Amy, Jess and a lanky male figure with shaggy black hair. Jem, Jess's brother. What were they doing there?

'Hi,' she said breathlessly, and they turned to look at her in confusion.

'Hi,' said Amy. 'We finished in town. I know you don't like the whole coffee shop thing, but I thought we'd stop by and see how you were. I brought you a present.' She held up a takeaway cup of iced coffee topped with whipped cream and with a straw sticking out of it.

'You carried that all the way from town on the bus? You nutter!' Chloe climbed the steps to the porch. 'I'd hug you, but I'm covered in mud.'

'We didn't come on the bus,' Amy said. 'Jeremy drove us.' She indicated Jem. He gave Chloe a shy nod.

'Hey,' said Chloe to him. 'Hey, Jess.' Chloe took in Jess's long silky black hair, smudgy eyeliner and effortless style. She was very conscious of her dirty jeans and trainers.

'Why are you covered in mud?' Amy asked.

'Been gardening.'

'Really? When no one came to the door, I looked in the kitchen window. The blinds were down, but I could see someone moving around in there.'

'It was probably . . . my dad,' said Chloe.

'Didn't look like your dad.'

'Oh . . . It might have been my grandma. Dad's just fetched her from the hospital.' She imagined the wristband she was wearing registering her raised heart rate and the sudden bloom of sweat on her skin. iRachel would know she was lying for sure. She had to hope Amy, Jess and Jem weren't so perceptive. 'So, is this just a drive-by iced-coffee drop?' she said, smiling brightly and taking a slurp of the coffee.

'Well, no,' said Amy, and Chloe could see the hurt in her eyes. 'I just wanted to know you were okay. You headed off in such a rush this morning . . .'

'I just wanted to get back and make sure everything was all right with my grandma,' Chloe said. She could see Amy watching her closely. Jess couldn't have looked less interested if she tried, and Jem was shifting from foot to foot and staring at his finger-nails. In the library, he'd seemed quite confident and outgoing, but now he just looked awkward and uncomfortable.

'So can we come in?'

'My grandma's asleep in the living room and so is my dad,' Chloe began, but Amy's eyes pleaded with her. She was trying so hard. 'Look, why don't you come round the back? We can sit in the garden and I'll go in and get us some drinks. What would everyone like? We've got Coke and lemonade, I think, and some fruit juice.'

Chloe got them to drag the patio chairs into the shade at the bottom of the lawn beside the rockery where she'd been weeding. Once they were settled, she ran inside. Aidan and Sinead dozed on undisturbed in their respective rays of sunshine in the living room. She dashed into the kitchen and carefully opened the utility room door.

'Are you okay?' she whispered to iRachel.

'I have no immediate needs,' said iRachel, mimicking her whisper.

'Can you stay in here? We have visitors.'

'I will engage silent mode and remain here until you issue further instructions,' said iRachel.

Chloe went to the fridge, pulled out a selection of cans and bottles, then hurried back outside. Jem was walking round the garden, looking closely at all the plants. Amy was sprawled on the grass, and Jess was sitting rather stiffly in one of the patio chairs, staring at her phone and chewing her nail. Chloe dumped the drinks on the grass and flopped down next to Amy, who was lying on her back, eyes closed, enjoying the sun.

'Thanks for the coffee, Amez,' she said, taking a slurp. 'And thanks for coming by.'

'I missed your ugly face,' said Amy, without opening her eyes.

'You only saw me this morning.'

'Yeah, well, I don't think I've ever gone clothes shopping without you before. Who knows what I might have bought?'

'Jess was there,' said Chloe, trying to draw her into the conversation.

'Amy thinks my taste is shit,' said Jess.

'Not shit,' said Amy, sitting up quickly. She couldn't bear to upset anyone. 'Just different to mine. I like your taste.'

Jess laughed. 'My taste is shit. But that's okay. Because it's mine.'

'No!' said Amy. 'You always look great!' She glanced quickly from Chloe to Jess. She was obviously trying to be equally loyal to both friends.

Jess was quick to break the tension. 'Well, I'm glad you didn't buy the ripped black jeans. Definitely not right for you,' she said. 'Show Chloe what you got. I think she'll like the purple top.'

Chloe looked closely at Jess to see if she was being a bitch or having a go at her, but she genuinely seemed to want Amy to show off what she'd bought. Amy reached into the bags by her side and brought out a few things. Her taste was conservative, and the clothes mainly looked like variations of things she already owned. Jess was right though. The purple top was the best of the bunch.

'It's cool,' said Chloe, 'but you need to break out a bit. You should have let Jess pick a few things out for you.'

Jess gave Chloe a smile, a little twisted, slightly sardonic.

She's scared about coming between me and Amy, thought Chloe. She's kind, Jess. I never really realised that before. They've come here to make sure I'm okay with them being friends. The thought surprised her and lifted her heart.

She offered them both drinks, and then called over to Jem. 'Do you want anything?' She held up a can of Coke in one hand and a bottle of juice in the other.

He shook his head and carried on looking at the plants.

'Excuse my brother,' said Jess. 'He has no manners.'

Chloe was about to say that he'd been pretty nice to her in the library the other day, but she stopped herself. Somehow she knew Jem would be embarrassed. If he hadn't mentioned to Jess and Amy that they'd chatted recently, there had to be a good reason. It was hardly cool for a sixth-former to have talked botany with a Year Ten.

'Can I play some music?' asked Jess, holding up her phone.

Chloe glanced back towards the house. They were right at the bottom of the garden, with only fields behind. They weren't going to bother her dad and grandma, or anyone really. Anyway, Jess probably had Bach or something.

Jess didn't have Bach. After just a few seconds, Chloe said, surprised, 'Hey, that's Kendrick Lamar!' She went to sit in the chair next to Jess and together they scrolled through the playlists on Jess's phone and then on Chloe's, comparing songs, playing snippets to one another.

Jess did have some weird modern classical music on her phone too. She played the opening of one piece and Amy said, 'I can't bear that stuff. It sounds like glass breaking.'

'Yeah, well, you're a philistine,' said Jess calmly. 'The composer's a genius. I'm going to a masterclass with her in the summer.'

'What, like a composing masterclass?' Chloe asked.

'Yeah.'

'Do you write your own music?'

'A bit,' said Jess guardedly. 'I'm not going to play any of it for you though. Amy just rolls her eyes and says she doesn't understand it.'

'I can't believe you write music,' said Chloe admiringly.

'Jess has got it all worked out,' said Amy, rolling over onto her front on the grass. 'An A* in A level music, her pick of the music colleges and conservatoires, then ten years in an orchestra in Europe before becoming the world's most famous young opera composer.'

'Opera?' Chloe said, looking at Jess.

Jess just shrugged. 'It's not like Amy's Dr Directionless,' she said. 'She's already researching medical schools.'

Chloe knew about Amy's aspirations, of course. She had wanted to be a doctor since she was four, when she had helped her mum clean cut knees in the playground. It was news to Chloe, though, that Amy had started seriously considering which medical schools to apply to. It seemed very obsessive. They were only fifteen, for heaven's sake. Who knew what they wanted to do at fifteen? But as Amy started talking excitedly about the differences between Imperial College and Edinburgh, she realised that maybe everyone did. Except her.

Jem sat down on the grass and helped himself to a can of Sprite. He was too tall and lanky for comfortable grass-sitting and he looked awkward, his knees bent up and his elbows pointy and spread like a pelican's wings. Chloe hooked a chair with her foot and shoved it towards him. He stared at it for a moment, then unfolded his limbs and rearranged himself in the chair. He seemed a little more at ease, and when she risked a glance up, he gave her a small smile. He had nice eyes – wide and dark, like Jess's. She wondered what he was doing here after having steadfastly ignored them for years. What eighteen-year-old hung out with his fifteen-year-old sister and her mates?

Unless . . . unless he fancied one of them. So who was it? Was it Amy, or was it her? She risked another quick look at him. He was watching her, elbows on the arms of the chair, his long fingers elegantly interlaced. It was her. He had come here to see her.

Now she had to think about how she felt about that. She'd had boys ask her out before, but so far she hadn't been interested enough to want to try a relationship. Was she interested in Jem? She didn't know. She'd liked him in the library – she'd learned he was clever and funny, and now he'd grown and his skin was better, he was, she had to admit, good-looking. It was hard not to be swayed by the fact that he was older and could drive. If she was going to fancy a guy, there were definitely worse options.

She lifted her chin and looked straight at him, her gaze open and direct, and he looked back at her, holding her stare. She felt a swoop of excitement in her stomach. In an instant the swoop turned into a plummet and she felt empty and sick. Because how could she let him into her life? 'Hey, Jem, please be my boyfriend. By the way, I'm an idiot who has no idea what I want to do with my life. I live with my bereaved dad and my gaga grandma, and there's a robot version of my dead mother in the utility room.'

'Why are you laughing?' Jess turned to look at Chloe. 'Or are you crying?'

'Both,' said Chloe, wiping her eyes. 'Life's just fucking mad, isn't it?'

# 39
## iRachel

I sat in the dim quiet of the tiny room. It reminded me of the storage room at the lab — windowless and compact. The washing machine hummed beside me, but I was listening to something deeper. Aidan's vital signs were even and smooth, like the murmur of the washing machine. His heart rate and respiration were slow. He was peacefully asleep.

But Chloe . . . Chloe's signs were climbing and swooping, now galloping, now slowing and quietening. It felt like she was on a rollercoaster, or as if she were a piece of music, full of loud crashes and soft, surprising swells and tender silences. I did not know what words she was exchanging with her friends out on the sunlit lawn. But her heart was singing a symphony of feelings.

# 40
## Aidan

It was a good thing he'd had a nap in the afternoon because he sure as hell didn't get an early night. Living with Sinead was like having a small baby. It took him ages to persuade her that she was staying over. He led her up to the spare room and got her comfortable, but as soon as he left the room, she came downstairs and stood by the front door, calling for her bag. It took several attempts to get her to remain upstairs, and several more to persuade her to have a bath and get into her night things. Once she was finally in bed and looking tired and reasonably settled, he went to his own room to brush his teeth. Hearing a noise on the landing, he came out to look and, sure enough, she was heading for the stairs, barefoot and in her nightie.

'It's time for me to go home,' she said, her face twisted with anxiety. 'I don't know why I'm still here. Where's my car, Aidan? I don't think I drove here, did I? Can you take me home? Please?' She started to cry then; wobbly sobs, like a small child.

This time he sat beside her bed until she fell asleep. His eyes were gritty with tiredness. It was already past midnight and he counted the hours until he had to be up for work. He tiptoed out of the room, had a quick shower and fell into bed, but it seemed like just a few minutes had passed when he woke to hear creaking on the stairs. He found her standing on the doormat by the front door, her hair wild and loose, and her eyes watery and frightened in the moonlight.

'This isn't the right place,' she said, clutching his arm. 'I don't like this hotel.'

'It's not a hotel, Mum,' he said, but she didn't seem to hear him.

'Can you call a taxi? I can't find my car keys.'

'Mum, it's the middle of the night.' Aidan struggled to keep his impatience under control. 'Can we just go to bed? Please?'

'Don't be ridiculous. How can I go to bed? I haven't had my lunch yet.' She slipped past him and headed determinedly towards the kitchen.

Aidan took a moment to check that the front door was locked and dead-bolted, then he lifted his and Chloe's keys off the hooks where they usually hung and stuck them into the pocket of his tracksuit bottoms.

Oh God. Sinead had gone into the kitchen. iRachel would be charging herself in there, Aidan realised. How would she react to iRachel sitting there, immobile, with a cable in her armpit?

But when he got to the kitchen, iRachel was no longer in her logged-off state. She was at the sink, filling the kettle, and had persuaded Sinead to sit at the kitchen table.

Aidan went over to her. 'Sorry we disturbed you,' he whispered.

'I was alerted by your vital signs. I woke when you woke,' she said.

'Are you all right? I mean, I know you would have been . . . charging.'

'I had reached thirty-seven per cent charge. It will be sufficient for any tasks I may need to perform.'

'I don't think she sleeps much at night,' said Aidan. 'I don't know what I'm going to do.'

'In the short term, I can rearrange my charging schedule to watch over her at night. If we can persuade her to wear a wristband, I will receive a warning if she wakes and I will be able to help her and keep her safe.'

'But what about the daytime?' Aidan said hopelessly. 'I'll be at work, Chloe will be at school . . .'

'Today she slept for three hours in the afternoon. I am aware that the day has been atypical, in that she came to us from the hospital at lunchtime. However, it seems likely she will sleep for some hours in the daytime, and I can arrange my homecare tasks and charging schedule accordingly.'

'This isn't your problem though,' Aidan said, frustrated. 'She's my mother.'

'In order for me to complete all allocated household tasks, to charge fully and to allow a contingency for unplanned activities and regular and emergency maintenance of myself, I will need someone, either Chloe or yourself, to take responsibility for Sinead for six hours out of every twenty-four,' said iRachel calmly. 'We can negotiate how these hours are allotted. My charging schedule is not time-sensitive, but your requirement for sleep and your commitments at work and school will dictate the limits of your daily involvement.'

'You've got this all worked out,' said Aidan, looking at her in wonder as she deftly poured tea and arranged slices of buttered toast on a plate.

'It is an algorithm,' said iRachel simply, turning to hand the plate and cup to Sinead.

Sinead was cheerful now they were all together in the kitchen and she had something to eat. She chatted about her plans for the week, plans that were clearly never going to happen – shopping, a concert at one of the colleges in Cambridge, a train trip to London. Aidan sat opposite her at the table, desperate with tiredness, grinding his teeth, trying not to snap at her to stop it. This was going to be much harder than he had imagined. He was very close to losing his temper when Sinead suddenly announced that she was tired.

'There's no point in my going home now,' she said. 'I'll just have a nap upstairs, if I may. This is such a nice hotel.'

iRachel approached her. 'Sinead, if you put this band on your wrist, I will know if you need anything in the night and can come to assist you.'

'What a good idea!' said Sinead, allowing iRachel to strap the wristband onto her skinny left wrist.

Aidan watched as iRachel reached for a pair of scissors from the kitchen counter and snapped off a tag on the wristband. Sinead didn't seem bothered by this and headed off upstairs quite happily. He turned to iRachel. 'What did you just do?'

'I have removed the release catch. She will not be able to remove the wristband herself now. If she attempts to do so, I will receive a warning signal.'

'Can you use it to pinpoint where she is?'

'It is not designed for geolocation, but I can estimate how far away a subject is by the strength of the signal.'

'How accurate is it?'

'I have not yet needed to use it as an estimation tool. It has not been necessary to attempt to locate you or Chloe. I will gather data over the next few days and submit a report.'

Aidan rubbed his face.

iRachel watched him closely. 'When you rub your face like that, you lift your hair from your forehead,' she observed.

'Do I?' He looked blank. 'And so . . . ?'

'There is a mark on your forehead.'

He ran a hand up under his fringe. 'Oh, this.' He lifted the hair. 'It's a scar. Skateboarding accident.'

'You sustained an injury?'

'Fell flat on my face. Blood everywhere. I had to have six

stitches. I was lucky I didn't break my nose or crack my skull.'

'You smile when you say that.'

'Well, it's an old war wound. I've got lots of scars.' He showed her his hand where a jagged white line bisected one of his knuckles. 'They always tell you to cut away from yourself when using a knife. And this one . . .' He raised his chin and showed her a small crescent scar. '. . . I got falling out of a tree when I was drunk.'

'You were drunk when you were a child?'

'No,' he said, looking slightly shamefaced. 'I was twenty-two. We were in Edinburgh in a park, and I was trying to swing like a monkey to impress Rachel.'

'A courtship ritual?'

'Something like that. She found it very romantic, spending the evening with me in A&E.'

'You are smiling again.'

'Yeah, well, scars are memories, you know? Reminders of the things we've been through, good and bad. It's like our lives get written on us. Rachel loved her appendectomy scar. She said it was fate underlining how lucky she was.'

They smiled at each other.

'Well,' said Aidan, 'thank you. You've been amazing this evening, as always.'

'I am happy to use what skills I have to help Sinead feel settled and keep her safe. If, by extension, this helps you and Chloe, this seems to me a positive and effective choice.'

'So we're a team,' said Aidan.

'In a successful sports team, each player performs specific actions for a common aim, so, yes, that is an appropriate metaphor.'

He yawned suddenly.

'You're so tired.' iRachel reached out and stroked his temple, and in Rachel's tones said, 'Poor honey. Get into bed, lie on your side, twenty deep breaths and let the worries float away.'

Aidan allowed himself to rest his head against her cool hand for a little while. He closed his eyes and breathed. She sat quietly beside him and did not pull away.

After a while he went upstairs and did as he'd been told. Curling on his left side, he closed his eyes and breathed slowly and deeply. A team, he thought as he drifted into exhausted, restless sleep. Had he and Rachel been a team in quite this way? Could you be on a team with an Olympic-gold sprinter when you were a Sunday-morning plodder?

He could still feel the cool imprint of fingers on his temple. But whose fingers was he imagining?

# 41

## Aidan

In the morning he woke up to find iRachel sitting on a chair beside the bed, watching him.

'Hi,' he said softly.

'Hello. Did you sleep well? You spent a considerable time in REM sleep, so you should feel rested.'

'I did sleep well, thank you,' he said. He sat up and stretched. 'I dreamed about Rachel.'

'Can you recall the detail of the dream?'

'It was garbled, as dreams are, but we were young, still at university. It was more a memory than a dream, I think. I was remembering a particular night – the night Sam and Laura got together . . . and Rachel and I had our first wobble.'

'When was this?'

'The end of our first year. We were working on our big end-of-year coding project. Rachel and I were head-over-heels in love. She said she felt like she'd spent the first eighteen years of her life nerding out over advanced maths in her bedroom in Kent, but that this year, being at uni, loving me, had been the best of her life. It was the best year of my life too.

'Then we got to the weekend before that final assessment was due. Rachel had already put in several hundred hours on hers. Me, not nearly so many. She said that what I'd done so far was good, I just needed to focus on it and refine it. I thought we were just chatting, but it turned out she was deadly serious about it.

'On the Saturday morning, she rolled out of bed and started getting dressed to go to the lab, and I said, "Come back to bed."

'"We have to work."

'"We've got all weekend. And anyway, how much more can you do? Your project's already ten times more complicated than anyone else's."

'"It's not perfect though. And what about yours? I could help you with yours."

'"Nah. I submitted yesterday."

'"What?"

'"You know Sam, that guy in the second year? I got him to show me his assignment from last year. He told me how Dr Mc-Farland marks the assessment, and I reckon what I've got will get me about sixty-five per cent. That's all I need to pass the module."

'She looked at me like I was speaking Chinese. "Why would you not do the best you can? You could get a first, you know you could."

'"I don't need a first. I do need you to come back to bed though."

'She didn't come back to bed. She stayed in the lab for twelve straight hours. I didn't hear from her until she came out at nine that night and rang me. I told her I was round at Sam's place.

'I was pissed off that morning, to be honest. I'd just wanted a weekend with her – a Saturday morning in bed, maybe a late breakfast at the caff. But Rachel was . . . well, who she was. Obsessed with work. When she arrived at Sam's, I decided I wasn't going to show I was hurt or that I had missed her. I was merry and a bit drunk, sitting in Sam's messy kitchen with a huge pot of pasta on the table and lots of candles. Sam and I were drinking rum and Coke, and Sam's waster flatmates were out on the balcony having a spliff.

'Laura from our class was also there. I could see Rachel

couldn't work out why – Laura wasn't especially a friend of ours, and she didn't have a direct connection to Sam. She was very attractive, Laura – curvy and dark and funny.

'Everyone was laughing and relaxed, but Rachel just couldn't settle down. She was sitting there, her hair in a ponytail, wearing jeans and a sweatshirt, no make-up on, stone-cold sober, and she looked so tense. She really wasn't having a good time, but I was, and I kind of felt like she had brought this on herself, so I didn't try all that hard to put her at her ease. All of a sudden, she started drinking shots of neat rum "to catch up" – on an empty stomach. Well, that wasn't going to end well, was it?

'I saw her go green, and her eyes went unfocused. I didn't want her to embarrass herself at Sam's, so we left about an hour after she arrived, and she was sick outside the building. I stroked her hair, and she cried as she threw up. She said something garbled on the way home about how I couldn't possibly love her after that, and I felt bad because in a funny way I loved her more for having been less than perfect for once.

'I walked her the rest of the way home with my arm around her shoulders, then got into the shower with her and washed her hair. Afterwards we lay in bed and I held her gently.

'"Can you tell me what's wrong?" I asked her, and she said something about me throwing away my chance of getting a first-class degree and how I was going to end up a loser like Sam's flatmates, smoking dope out on the balcony, shagging Laura. I said, "Wait, what? All at the same time?" And I'm sorry to say I laughed. A lot.

'And then I told her how much I had missed her, and how hard it was to always be the understanding one, and she nodded against my chest and cried some more. I couldn't help being surprised that she was worried about Laura though. I had never imagined her to be the jealous type. I did think of letting her agonise for a bit longer, but I couldn't bear to. So I told her that I was mainly there because Sam was such a shy bonehead that he'd never have had the courage to invite Laura round if I hadn't gone too.

'"Wait . . ." she said, and comprehension dawned. "Sam likes Laura?"

'"Oh my God, Rachel, where have you been? *Everyone* knows that! Except Laura, and you. He's always mooning around, staring at her."

'"I missed it completely," she said, burying her face in the curve of my neck, and I felt her smile.

'"I asked her in lab on Friday, and she said she likes him too. So I was just being a matchmaker, really. I'm glad we had to leave, because now they'll have to actually talk to each other. And who knows how it'll end?"

'Well, it hasn't ended. They were together at uni for three years, then broke up over a stupid fight, and then found each other again five years ago. And now there's baby Joseph.

'I think we learned a lot about each other that weekend. I learned that I would probably always come second to work in Rachel's life but that second was still very high up the list. And she learned to accept that I wasn't ambitious or competitive. I just wanted to be happy, and my happiness was, and still is, found in simple things – love, friends, food, laughter. I think I also learned that weekend that I really wasn't interested in the technical side of computing. I was much more interested in people. That's how I ended up in the job I'm in, I suppose. Not because I want to teach people computer skills, but because it's important to me to help people.'

iRachel nodded. 'Did Rachel understand this?'

'Intellectually, I suppose she did. But in terms of how important she thought my work was . . .' He left the sentence unfinished.

'How did that make you feel?'

'Well, we can't always get our validation from other people, can we?' he said, standing up and heading towards the bathroom.

He could hear iRachel beginning to say, 'She wasn't just another person, she was . . .' but he closed the bathroom door before she could finish.

# 42

# iRachel

## Contact Log

Subject: Sinead Sawyer

| Interaction start time: | 09.32 |
|---|---|
| Date: | 5 July |
| Heart rate: | 68 bpm |
| Skin temperature: | normal |
| Respiratory rate: | 25 bpm |

## Report:

Aidan left for work at 08.22 and Chloe for school at 08.41. The subject was still asleep. Following her disturbed night, she was clearly in need of rest. I was able to complete my charging cycle and after I had made breakfast for Aidan and Chloe, I cleared and washed the dishes and started a load of laundry.

I had completed these tasks when I was alerted by Sinead's increased heart rate and respiration, which indicated she had woken. I monitored her physiological signs and she did not seem unduly distressed, so I remained downstairs while she got up and visited the bathroom. Three minutes and fifty seconds later, she came downstairs. She was still wearing her night attire and was barefoot.

'This isn't my house,' she said, without uttering a conventional morning greeting.

'This is the house of your son, Aidan.'

'What day is it?'

'The date is 5 July. The time is approximately 9.32 a.m.'

'Why am I here?'

'Your house is currently not safe for habitation. There was a fire in the kitchen. You and Aidan have agreed that, at present, it is best if you stay here.'

She nodded, satisfied, at least for the moment.

'Would you like tea, coffee or something for breakfast?' I asked.

'Have I not had breakfast?' she said. 'I'm not really hungry.'

'You did eat two slices of toast and drink a cup of tea at approximately 2.42 a.m. That may explain why you do not feel as hungry as you usually would at this time.'

She nodded again but did not seem surprised that she had been eating at such an unconventional hour. 'Well, I'll wait to eat then,' she said. 'I'd like coffee though.'

She observed me as I brewed the coffee and prepared it according to the records I had on her preferences. I brought the cup over to her.

'You look like Rachel,' she said.

'Yes.'

'But you're not her, are you?'

'No.'

'I knew that,' she said, satisfied. 'Rachel used to jump around all over the place. Never sat still. It drove me mad. And she'd never have been here at this time of day. Always at work, that one.'

'Rachel was extremely committed to her research.'

'I never understood why she ever got married and had a child,' said Sinead. 'What's the point if your family's always going to come second, after your career?'

I did not know how to respond to this statement, and, indeed, it was not clear whether Sinead expected a response. From her intonation, I inferred that this was a statement she had made on multiple occasions in the past.

234

'That's the trouble with this generation,' she said. 'They genuinely believe they can have it all. And you can't.'

Sinead stood up abruptly and without further conversation went back upstairs to the bedroom. She had clearly decided our conversation was ended.

**Interaction end time:** 09.46.

Up to this point, whenever I had accessed one of Rachel's memory files, it was triggered by a chemical stimulus or an emotional response from Aidan or Chloe. But in this instance, I felt the file unlock inside me like a spring releasing. Rachel had a story to tell, and it was a story for me, and me alone.

# 43
## Rachel

My mother-in-law. Ah . . . my mother-in-law. It's such a cliché, isn't it, the monster-in-law? All those jokes about the dragon, the bane of your existence, always criticising and finding you wanting. The woman who thinks you'll never, ever be good enough for her precious son.

Well, that wasn't quite Sinead. She didn't think I wasn't good enough. She just thought I was wrong. On one level, she was proud of my accomplishments. She's a woman who made it on her own, so I think she took a quiet feminist pride in female success (not that she'd call it feminism).

But then it became clear that my career was going to take off. Aidan wasn't at all ambitious, so when Chloe was born, we made our own, slightly unconventional family choices. Sinead just couldn't accept it. Husbands go to work, while wives raise children. That's what she believed, even though her own experience had shown her that sometimes husbands go to New Zealand with blondes called Sheila, and wives go to work, raise children and pay all the bills. I thought she'd be proud of Aidan's dedicated, hands-on parenting. But she was just ashamed of me for not being the wife and mother she thought I should be.

That's hard to admit. Because Sinead's doubts were my doubts.

I liked and admired her from the moment I met her. I liked her strength and practicality. Especially after my own mum died, I felt grateful to have an older woman I could look up to and turn to. But the more I succeeded at work, the more she turned away from me.

She's a funny woman, Sinead. She struggles to give, or to take, or to enjoy. It's like she's always buttoned up, afraid to let go. I think it must come from the gut-clenching fear she felt when her husband left. She had to keep it together, emotionally, financially, practically. So she held on tight to every penny, every second of time, in case she lost her grip, because if she did, who was there to turn to? She gave her sons routine and safety and discipline. And along I came, and I was the opposite of her in every way.

I came from a family where there was love, and everything else, to spare — books, time, knowledge, money. When I met Aidan, I think he fell in love with my parents and our home as much as he fell in love with me — a table groaning with food, loud, happy, abandoned discussion, and an endless supply of hugs and affection. I do my best to make our home as abundant as my parents' was. We live well, and I try to be as generous and loving as I can to Aidan and Chloe. It isn't always easy — my work is demanding, and it takes up lots of time and brain space. I know that sometimes I whirlwind in and out of our home, and I know Chloe in particular probably wants more of my time. But I also want her to see what her mother can do. What a woman can do. I want her to know that she can grow up to do anything and be anything she wants.

And while that makes sense to me — most of the time — when I see myself through Sinead's eyes, I see a woman who's travelling so fast, I'm missing everything. When she hears that I wasn't at a parent–teacher conference because I was presenting at a global AI symposium in Tokyo, her pinched lips echo my own guilt. When I tell her we've postponed Aidan's birthday celebration for a week because I have a paper to submit, she sighs like my own heart sighs.

Aidan has never questioned my commitment to my work or told me I'm letting him down. He's steadfastly supported me every step of the journey, even when my own conviction has faltered. He doesn't need to do that. But when I look into Sinead's disappointed, disapproving eyes, I see the reflection of my own conscience. And I look away.

# 44
## Aidan

One Wednesday a couple of weeks after Sinead had come to live with them, Aidan stopped at the coffee shop downstairs before he went into the office. He was tired most mornings these days. Even with iRachel's support, the nights were broken and unsettled. Sinead slept intermittently through the day and then roamed the house at night, and he worried constantly. He swallowed an espresso, grimacing at the taste, then bought a cappuccino to take with him and, as an afterthought, six croissants to share with his workmates.

As he came through the door of Foothold, he sensed that something was wrong. Lola was doing some one-to-one coaching with a client, but as she saw him come in, she turned to look at him. Her eyes were wide and worried and her face was very pale. He'd never seen her look like that – she was normally unfailingly cheerful. He wanted to go over and ask her if everything was all right, but it was policy not to interrupt a consultation. He held up the box of pastries and pointed to the kitchen, so she would know they were there when she was free. On the way to the kitchen, he saw Kate at her desk, involved in an intense telephone conversation. She was saying 'Mm,' a lot, and 'I understand,' and nodding.

Thomas, the CV-writing trainer, was standing in the doorway of the kitchen, clutching a tea towel and watching Kate with a worried frown. He stepped aside as Aidan approached.

'I brought croissants,' said Aidan. 'What's up?'

'Um . . .' said Thomas. 'You'd probably better speak to Kate.'

'Come on, Thomas! I walk through the door and Lola looks like she's seen a ghost. You're in a state too. Kate's on the phone. Tell me what's going on.'

'It's bad news about Fiona's Arthur,' said Thomas reluctantly.

Fiona, their boss, was married to Arthur, an affable, posh fellow, formerly an art dealer, now retired. They were childless and utterly devoted to one another.

'What's up with Arthur?'

'He's ill. Very ill. Cancer of some sort. They've only just found out. Apparently . . .' Thomas looked uneasily at Kate, as if he was worried he was speaking out of turn. 'Apparently the prognosis isn't good.'

'Bloody hell,' said Aidan. 'This is such a shit year. There must be some kind of weird planetary alignment going on, because things couldn't get any worse. Actually, forget I said that, because they probably could. Is Kate talking to Fiona?'

'Yes. I'm hoping she'll come off the phone with a clear idea of what we're all supposed to do.' Unthinkingly, he took a croissant from the box and broke it in half. 'I really hope so.' He looked miserable and moved back into the doorway of the kitchen, crumbling the croissant without eating it and watching Kate as she finished her phone call.

Kate sat at her desk for a moment, looking at the receiver, then took a deep breath, squared her shoulders and walked into the kitchen. Lola, who had finished her consultation, followed Kate in and shut the door behind them.

'Hey, Aidan,' Kate said, and gave him a warm smile.

'Hi. How's Fiona doing?'

'She's not great, unsurprisingly. She's all over the place . . . She kept crying and repeating herself. It's come as a terrible shock.

He'd been complaining of backache, so he went to the doctor's last week. The doctor obviously saw something she didn't like, referred them, and they've discovered a tumour on his spine, which has spread to his internal organs. Stage four, inoperable, it seems.'

'Bugger. He's still so young.'

'Sixty-four.'

'So what's their plan?' asked Lola.

'No plan, really. Just to keep him as comfortable as possible, spend time together, put their affairs in order, I guess.'

'Do they know how long he's got?'

'They're not saying for sure, but it's months, not years.'

'So what do we do?' Thomas blurted out. 'Just . . . carry on?'

'Well, yes,' said Kate. 'More or less. Obviously, Fiona isn't coming in today, and probably won't be for the foreseeable future. She's asked me to deputise as manager for now, as long as everyone is okay with that.'

They all nodded. Of all of them, Kate was the only one who had any managerial experience.

'I think that's the most logical course of action,' said Aidan. 'It's best if Fiona stays at home, and we're all pretty competent. We can keep things going in her absence.'

Thomas shook his head, put the shredded remains of his croissant back in the box and went off to his desk. He wasn't coping well and Lola, ever empathetic, went to sit beside him. Aidan could hear her talking to him in low tones. He expected Kate to go over too, or to return to her desk, but she stayed in the kitchen, shifting from foot to foot. She was usually so direct and competent, but she looked tentative.

'Is there something else?' Aidan asked.

'Fiona said something that worried me a little.' Kate kept her voice low. 'I didn't want to say anything in front of Thomas, because he's spooked enough as it is. She said the board of trustees is going to have to come in and take a look at the finances.'

'The board of trustees? I mean, I know we must have one, we're a registered charity, but they've never intervened before. I've never even met any of them.'

'Me neither. I looked them up on the website, while I was on the phone with Fiona. They're what you'd expect: a collection of the great and the good. A university chancellor, a few art cronies of Arthur's, a baroness and some sharp-suited barrister fellow. My guess is that they're dinner-party mates of Fiona's and they've just let her get on with running the show.'

'So?'

'They might want to cast a closer eye on things now she's not around. Dig into the finances, that sort of thing.'

'And?'

'Well, Fiona plays her cards pretty close to her chest where money is concerned. I've certainly not seen the books and I have no idea how we're doing financially. I'm a bit concerned that when I do have a look, we might be in for a shock.'

'So Thomas is right to be worried?'

'Let's face it, Thomas worries if someone puts the loo roll on the spindle the wrong way round. He worries twenty-five hours a day. But in this instance . . .'

'He might have a point?'

Kate looked at Aidan for a long second. Then she gave a quick nod, grabbed a croissant and headed back to her desk.

# 45

## Sinead

'Tis the last rose of summer
Left blooming alone;
All her lovely companions
Are faded and gone;
No flower of her kindred,
No rosebud is nigh,
To reflect back her blushes,
Or give sigh for sigh.'

The words are beautiful, and they come to me neatly, marching one after the other. I can't help myself – I sing them as I walk around the beautiful . . . the place with the flowers and trees and grass. Outside. The garden.

The nurse, the nice one with the lovely face that hardly moves, stands in the doorway of the living room and watches me. She doesn't like to come outside. Her shoes are always so clean. She likes to keep them that way, I think.

Thomas Moore. 'The Last Rose of Summer'. That's the name of the song. We used to sing it when I was a child.

'I'll not leave thee, thou lone one!
To pine on the stem;
Since the lovely are sleeping,
Go, sleep thou with them.

*Thus kindly I scatter*
*Thy leaves o'er the bed,*
*Where thy mates of the garden*
*Lie scentless and dead.'*

Another verse. All day, I feel words slip away from me — thoughts, ideas, memories. But music stays in my head, and the words of songs pour from my lips like water. Maybe I can sing my life, and that way keep the words from escaping.

*'So soon may I follow,*
*When friendships decay,*
*And from Love's shining circle*
*The gems drop away.*
*When true hearts lie withered*
*And fond ones are flown,*
*Oh! who would inhabit*
*This bleak world alone?'*

The nurse has come out onto the patio now, so I walk over to her.

'That song you were singing. What was it?'

'What song?'

Her eyes go flat for a moment and then she does the strangest thing — she plays a recording which sounds just like my voice singing 'The Last Rose of Summer'. I can't see any cassette player or anything; it must be on her phone. They always play things on their phone, the young ones. I tell her what the song is called.

'What does it mean?' she asks.

'It's a sad story,' I say. 'A sad song. The last rose is all alone on the bush, with no companions. So they scatter her petals so she can be with her dead friends.'

She looks at me for a long time, and then she says, "'Oh! who would inhabit | This bleak world alone?'"

'Yes.'

She's always so calm. She never gets upset with me, even when I forget words, or leave my food or walk around the house at night. Aidan does, and . . . the girl. My granddaughter. She gets upset. But the nurse, never. She's always serene. But now, with this song, she looks sad. As if she's received a message she doesn't really understand, but somehow it has still hurt her.

# 46
## Aidan

Kate was sitting with her head in her hands, fingers buried in her short hair, leaning close to her computer screen. Her brow was wrinkled, whether with worry or confusion, Aidan couldn't tell. He glanced around the open-plan office. No one else was in.

'All right, Kate?'

She jerked, surprised. 'Hi. I didn't hear you come in.'

'Where is everyone?'

'Lola's got a half day – she had an audition, I think. Thomas didn't have any clients, so I've sent him to get the stationery order. He was moping around and fidgeting, kept asking me questions I couldn't answer. It was self-preservation, really.'

Aidan nodded. Thomas had been in a state ever since the news about Fiona's husband had come through. But that didn't explain Kate's expression. She should have been relieved that Thomas was out from under her feet, but she didn't look relieved. She looked stressed.

'Everything okay?' Aidan asked.

Kate looked up at him. 'Do you have a minute?' she said.

'Sure.' He drew a chair up next to her desk.

She turned her chair towards him. 'How much do you know about the financial organisation of Foothold?'

'Not much. Nothing really. Fiona's always handled it, and there's an accountant who comes in once a month or so.'

'So you've never really looked at the books?'

'I don't think I'd know what I was looking at if I did.'

'I think you'd understand this.' She pointed at her computer screen. There was a long column of figures, marked 'Outgoings'. The numbers were large and the total at the bottom seemed unreasonably enormous. She clicked to a different spreadsheet, headed 'Donations'. This was much more sparsely populated, and the total number at the bottom was considerably smaller.

Without a word, she handed Aidan a sheaf of paper – bank statements. He paged through them and then looked up.

'Even I can understand that. We actually don't have enough to meet the wage bill next month.'

'No.'

'Why didn't Fiona say something?'

'She probably thought she could bring in a big donation in time. But then Arthur . . .'

'I know,' Aidan said. 'But why hasn't the board intervened? Or done something?'

'They're all mates of hers. They probably just let her get on with it. Trusted she'd sort something out. Or maybe they don't know how bad things really are. Fiona's probably kept them in the dark. Up till now.'

'Up till now?'

'Remember I said there was a hotshot barrister on the board of trustees?' Aidan nodded. 'Well, it turns out he's new. Stephen Jasper, he's called. Appointed about three months ago. I think he was pressuring Fiona to let him see the books and so on, but she fought him off. But now she's not here, he's putting the squeeze on me. I've had twelve emails from him in the last two days. He wants to see everything, and when he does, he's going to start asking some very awkward questions.'

'So what do we do?'

Kate smiled at him ruefully. 'I was kind of hoping you might have some ideas. I've just been staring at this mess, and I am all out of inspiration.'

'Well . . .' Aidan leant back in his chair and folded his arms. 'The first thing is that we can't lie.'

'So what do we do?'

Aidan thought for a long moment. 'I guess we come clean. Show him how bad it is and face the music. There's nothing else we can do.'

# 47
## Rachel

'The first time I saw, you, you were in front of me in the line at the table for the Hummus Society at the Freshers' Fair. To be fair, the line was just two people long – I think there was a limited market for chickpea-related recreation at university. But I remember looking at the back of your neck. You were very tanned – I found out later you'd spent the summer in Italy – and I liked the way your curls lay on your smooth brown skin. Your shoulders looked so strong under your white T-shirt. Then you turned and looked at me, and I saw your dark, chocolate-brown eyes and beautiful mouth, and when you smiled at me, something in me went "Zing!" It seemed an added bonus that you also liked hummus. So, yes, my first attraction to you was totally superficial and sexual. You were just a piece of meat to me.

'But then you said hi, and we exchanged banalities and worked out we were on the same degree programme, and I found out you weren't only hot, you were funny. And when you said you'd pick me up at halls at 6 p.m. for the Freshers' Barbecue and you were there at 5.59 on the dot in a clean shirt, I realised you were also reliable. And later that night, the zing I'd felt when I first saw you was totally confirmed. Five times, I believe, in my narrow little bed.

'And that was it. We were together. When I was packing to come to university, I'd imagined that my romantic life would be this exciting rollercoaster, with dramas and fights and break-ups and bad, faithless boyfriends, but instead, there you were, at the Hummus Society table. The other half of me. And we clicked together and that was it. No drama, no trauma, just love — and certainty. Because I knew, you see. From the very first day, I knew that we'd be together, and we'd be upwardly compatible — and future-proof.'

# 48

# Aidan

He was lying on his bed, in the dark, holding iRachel's hand as she played Rachel's recording to him. The story wasn't new to him. Not just because he remembered their meeting – of course he did – but because Rachel had told that story on their last night, the night of their anniversary. They'd been walking by the river after dinner.

He'd laughed when she'd said it. '"Upwardly compatible"?'

'I knew that no matter how many changes we'd make, how many upgrades we'd do, we'd always work together.'

'So it doesn't matter that my motherboard's a bit wonky and my upload speed isn't what it was?'

'I'm serious, Aidan,' she said, stopping and turning to face him. 'I know it sounds like geek talk, but it's true. I saw you, and I knew instantly that I could imagine growing old with you. I knew we'd be future-proof.'

'Future-proof,' he said. 'I like that.'

He put his arm around her and they walked on.

'So, listen, after Chloe's exams, around mid June or so, I was thinking that maybe she could go and stay with my mum for a weekend?' He felt Rachel's shoulders stiffen slightly under his arm, but he continued. 'I thought you and I could sneak off for a couple of days away?'

'Aidan, I . . .'

He nodded, and said quietly, 'Okay. Bad idea.'

'No, no . . .' she said, but he could hear the lack of conviction in her voice. 'It's a great idea.'

'Is it? You don't sound very keen.'

'I am keen. I am. It's just . . .'

He sighed. He didn't want a row. But he'd come up with a plan for a weekend away, and he had hoped so much that, in the glow of their anniversary celebrations, she'd agree.

She looked up at him. 'Aidan . . .'

'It's okay.'

'It's not okay. I really want to go. It's just the project . . .' She stopped again, so she could look him in the eye. Her eyes were wide and blazing. 'Believe me when I say that there is nothing I would like more than a weekend away with you, making love, taking long naps, drinking wine, but . . .'

'But what?'

'I have so much to do.'

He dropped her hand and walked a little faster. How many times had they had this conversation, or variations of it?

She ran to catch him up, and stopped him, grasping both of his hands in hers. 'You won't understand, my love. I don't expect you to. But I have so little time, and things are moving so fast, and there are things I have to do. Things I have to complete.'

He wanted to say, 'There are things outside the lab too. People. Me and Chloe. And time is passing us by.' He wanted to say, 'Do you know how systems stay future-proof? They do regular maintenance.' But he didn't.

'Well, let's file the weekend away for when the project is complete. But I'm going to hold you to it, okay? When it's finished, we're going away.'

'Agreed. I promise. Let's shake on it,' she said, offering him her hand.

He shook it. 'Now you have to do a pinkie promise, like Chloe did when she was little. No oath is more unbreakable.'

They linked their little fingers together. 'Pinkie promise,' she said gravely.

He wished he could believe her. He wished that she would take this vow seriously, but long experience had taught him that she would almost certainly find a way to wriggle out of it. That was how their marriage worked and he'd accepted it for all these years. It wasn't about to change, was it?

Then she kissed him. 'Now take me home. There's another anniversary tradition we have to respect.'

She hadn't kept the promise, but not for the reasons he'd expected. At that moment, she had had just twenty hours left to live. Now, Aidan realised, when they'd been walking by the river, she'd already recorded that story and implanted it in iRachel. It made that poignant exchange by the river feel like a lie. Or did it? Did it make it more important? He didn't know. He disengaged his fingers from iRachel's hand. She turned to look at him.

'Was that message upsetting to you?'

'Yes. No. Not for the reason you think.'

'I have no preconceived expectation of your response.'

He struggled into a sitting position and stared out of the window at the glowing full moon – the same moon that had glittered on the river on his last night with Rachel. 'She . . . Rachel was always talking about the future. She spent her life looking ahead. In her work, in life. I finished my undergrad degree, and all I wanted to do was go travelling with her and then get a job that paid the bills so we could live and be happy. But she had much bigger plans – a PhD, then research. She was always telling me about things that were going to happen *when* . . . What wonderful things we would do *if* . . . Telling me to be patient, because good things would come. Money, success, time together, peace and quiet. I suppose I just accepted that if they were going to come, they'd come on Rachel's timetable, and on her terms.'

'But they did not come.'

'The future came to get her instead.'

'How does that make you feel?'

'Angry. Sad. Determined.'

'Determined?'

'Not to put things off. To seize the day. Have the holiday I want, when I want it. Because what was I waiting for?'

'What were you waiting for?'

'I don't know,' he said. 'I don't know. But I do know I'm not waiting anymore.'

# 49
## Aidan

Stephen Jasper's suit cost more than Aidan's car. He whisked into Foothold's offices at 5.45 p.m., smelling of elegant aftershave and flicking an infinitesimal speck off his lapel. His haircut was expensive, his nails were manicured and his briefcase was made from the hide of some endangered animal. He was terrifying.

Fiona was posh, and so were all of her friends, but they were genteelly so, more likely to wear mud-caked wellingtons than handmade shoes from John Lobb. Jasper's demeanour screamed money, impatience and professionalism. No one like him had ever come through the slightly scruffy doors of Foothold before. Aidan was very grateful that Thomas and Lola had already left for the day.

Jasper shook Aidan's hand for a split second and didn't bother to make eye contact. He didn't even acknowledge Kate. He strode past them both into the meeting room.

'I've got twenty minutes,' he said.

Those were the only four words he spoke for the next fifteen minutes. Kate handed him the printed-out Excel spreadsheets of the year's accounts. He didn't thank her, just sat at the head of the table and looked through the figures, methodically, row by row. He took a fountain pen out of his suit pocket and made some annotations in the margins. When he got to the last page, he went back to the beginning and went through the figures again.

Then he turned his gaze on Aidan.

'You're all but bankrupt.'

'It's not as bad as—'

'It is.' Jasper cut him off. 'I'm going to have to tell the board to shut the doors immediately. Let you all go.'

'Mr Jasper,' said Kate, stepping forward, 'you must know that Fiona's husband Arthur is very ill. She's not available to deal with this at present and the last thing she needs is—'

'The last thing I need is to be associated with some kind of tinpot collapsing organisation. If this goes public and I haven't clearly disassociated myself from it, it could impact on my professional reputation.' Jasper stood and picked up his briefcase.

'So you'd put a woman who is caring for her dying husband under immense pressure and throw away the livelihoods of four people?' Aidan stood too. Jasper was half an inch shorter than him, and Aidan drew himself up to his full height and threw his shoulders back.

Jasper looked him up and down, taking in Aidan's faded shirt and off-the-peg suit trousers. 'In a heartbeat,' he said. 'Excuse me.' He swept out of the room. Moments later they heard his BMW start with a roar, and he was gone.

Kate and Aidan were left staring at one another.

'So what the hell do we do now?' asked Kate.

'The way I see it, we've got two options,' said Aidan. 'We roll over and take it, or we find a way to prove nasty Mr Jasper wrong. We show the board we can raise the necessary funds to keep going.'

'I'd go for option two,' said Kate. 'Except he's not wrong. The finances are in a mess.'

'We're going to need to put ourselves at the mercy of the board,' said Aidan. 'They'll have to help us get some cash in the short term – a loan. There are organisations that fund charities, so I don't think it'll be impossible. But we'll need to prove our worth. Foothold is a good organisation with a good heart.'

Kate waited for him to continue.

'We've bumbled along for years, letting Fiona run the place in her own eccentric way. But Foothold could be so much more. There's such a need for our services. We must be able to raise more funding to expand. I'm sure we could develop a whole range of additional services and study programmes to help the long-term unemployed. I've always believed we've been thinking too small.'

'So why haven't you said something before?'

It was Aidan's turn to pause, as he tried to put his feelings into words. 'I don't know. Maybe I was lazy. Lacked confidence. Not sure. I've always liked what I do, but I suppose my focus has been more on my family, on raising Chloe, supporting Rachel . . . So work just bumbled along, not too much stress, enough fulfilment from helping people to keep me interested.'

'And now?'

'Well, we're fucked, aren't we? We can't let the evil Stephen Jasper destroy everything Fiona's built. And let's face it, Thomas and Lola aren't going to make it out there in the real world.'

'No.' Kate smiled. 'So let's hear your plans for Foothold's global expansion.'

'Oh, I wasn't planning on global expansion.' Aidan smiled back. 'That's small potatoes. I thought we could go intergalactic.'

'Interview skills classes on Mars, that sort of thing?'

'I like your thinking! In all seriousness though, I do think we should be trying to offer people recognised qualifications. I did a bit of reading a couple of years ago, about becoming an accredited body. Fiona said she'd follow it up, but she never did.'

'So we'd be more of a college than an advice centre?'

'Couldn't we be both? I think one of the most valuable things we could do is give people a reason to come to us and stay for longer than a half-hour appointment. These are people whose days are often empty — they're lonely and isolated. Imagine if we had more classes, maybe a coffee-shop-type social area where people could meet and network. What about a small library?'

Kate sat back in her chair. 'Wow. You have a lot of ideas.'

'Yeah, well,' said Aidan, embarrassed, 'too much time on my hands. Lots of ideas, no idea how to make them happen.'

'Maybe that's where I come in. I reckon if we brainstorm some more, we can pull together a proposal for the board of trustees. Maybe get them to support us in taking out a short-term loan and then help us to run a big campaign to fundraise what we need. Let's pre-empt Jasper. He's going to have to call an extraordinary meeting of the board to show his findings on the finances. Let's call one first, come clean about the state of things and then present our new ideas and how they can be implemented.'

'It's going to take a lot of work, and we're going to have to move fast.'

'I'm in if you are,' said Kate and she held out her slim hand for him to shake.

He took it. 'I'm in.'

The next time they both looked up from their computers, it was after eight o'clock.

'Don't you have to get home?' Kate asked.

'No,' said Aidan carefully. 'Everything's under control. I just texted and my mum's asleep. Chloe's watching something in her room.'

'Is she okay on her own?'

'Chloe? She's fine. She's very grown-up, and I'm only a phone call and a ten-minute drive away.'

Kate nodded and went back to her typing. Aidan glanced over at her hands flying over the keys. It occurred to him that he knew absolutely nothing about her. She was a psychologist and had recently moved to Cambridge from London. She looked like she was around thirty-five. But that was all he knew. Was she married? She wasn't wearing a ring. Did she have kids? He had no idea. He didn't think so. But who could tell?

She glanced up and saw him looking at her. 'What?'

'Sorry, middle-distance staring.'

'Getting tired?'

'A bit.'

'Me too.' Kate pushed her chair back and rolled her shoulders, stretching her neck. 'We can carry on tomorrow.'

Impulsively, Aidan said, 'Um, this might not be appropriate, but Fiona always leaves a bottle of Sancerre in the fridge for emergencies.'

'Emergencies? What kind of emergencies?'

'A wanting-a-glass-of-Sancerre emergency?'

'Do you think we're in that kind of crisis situation?'

'I think it's possible.'

'Well, Nurse Sawyer, you'd better administer 175 millilitres, stat,' said Kate.

Aidan jumped up and went to the kitchen to get two glasses and the chilled bottle of wine. When he returned, Kate had shut down her computer and was sitting on one of the low armchairs in the reception area, smiling at something on her phone. Aidan handed her a glass and sat down opposite her, curious about who was messaging her.

She must have sensed his interest because she handed over her phone to show him a photograph of a tiny little girl wearing a princess dress and a fireman's helmet.

'That's my niece, Isla,' she said proudly. 'She's going to save the world. She only takes that helmet off to sleep.'

Aidan grinned. 'She's gorgeous. I remember Chloe at that age. She had a pair of Postman Pat wellies that she insisted on wearing all the time, rain or shine. Especially shine. They totally stank by the end of summer. I had to take them out into the garden and jet-wash them with a hosepipe. In the end we had to bin them and tell her Postman Pat had come to fetch them because he needed them.'

Kate smiled at this.

He found himself saying, 'Do you have kids?'

There was a beat before she said, 'No,' and a shadow crossed her face. There was something there, but she wasn't ready to talk about it. 'So I was thinking about suggesting we start a course in assertiveness,' she said briskly.

Aidan allowed her to change the subject. He wasn't going to pry. She chatted animatedly, and they sipped their wine and let the ideas freewheel. Aidan's contributions tended to be creative and slightly mad, hers were more practical and grounded. They balanced each other well. Before he knew it, the bottle of wine was empty and an hour had passed.

'I really had better go home,' he said, standing unsteadily. 'Oh . . . I think driving is probably out of the question though. I'll leave the car and get a cab, I think. Want to share one?'

'Nah, you're all right.' Kate stood too and went to put their glasses in the kitchen. 'I'm a five-minute walk away. The fresh air will do me good.' She gathered up her bag and jacket and clicked off the lights. But as they were standing in the gloom by the door, preparing to set the alarm and leave, she turned to him.

'Aidan,' she said hesitantly, 'I . . . I just want to say something.' She paused and took a deep breath. 'When I said I didn't have children, that isn't strictly true. I do. I did. I had a son. William. He was born with a condition called Edwards Syndrome – it's a genetic disorder. He lived until he was six months old.'

'I'm so sorry,' said Aidan, touching her arm lightly.

'Well, it was what it was. I loved him very much. My marriage didn't survive Will's life and death, so that's why, at thirty-four, I find myself in a new town, a single woman with no ties. This wasn't in the plan. I don't usually tell people, because what are they supposed to do with the information? So I'm sorry to have dumped it on you. It's just . . . when people ask if I have kids and I don't acknowledge Will, that he lived, that I loved him, it feels . . . disloyal.'

Aidan looked at her face, tense and pale in the shadows. 'Thank you for telling me,' he said.

'Yeah, well, you know about loss. You understand.' She patted his arm, managed a small smile and was gone.

Fifteen minutes later, Aidan let himself into the house. Downstairs was in darkness, and he could hear the faint sound of music from Chloe's bedroom. He glanced into the kitchen. iRachel was sitting upright in a chair, her charging cable snaked around her body. He assumed from her intense stillness that she was powered down, but as he moved quietly towards the stairs, she turned her head slowly. Her intense green eyes caught his and held his gaze, as if she could see into his heart.

# 50
# Chloe

C  Hey Amez
First day of the summer holidays!!!!!!
What are you doing today?
Amez?
You there?

This used to be my favourite day of the year – waking up, stretching in bed, knowing that there were six whole weeks of total freedom ahead. It was the one time of year Mum got off my back and didn't nag me constantly about my 'unfulfilled potential'. I could do anything I wanted.

But, obviously, plans have somewhat changed for this summer. Ha ha.

Mum, Dad and I were supposed to go away. Mum promised us that she was going to take a break. Not that Dad and I believed her – the number of times we've had to cancel or postpone holidays, or go without her because of work – but she really, really promised this time. A fortnight on a Greek island, that's what we were supposed to do. She promised us she'd book it. It obviously didn't make it to the top of the to-do list before she died.

Now I get to spend the next six weeks trapped at home with Grandma Sinead, who gets madder by the day; iRachel, who is so calm and perfect, wafting around being competent, that I sometimes want to strangle her; and Dad, who's in a total panic about work and seems to have pretty much checked out of home life entirely.

Listen to me. I'm soooo bitter, as Amy would say. Well, as Amy would say if I ever got to see her. After that afternoon when she came round with Jess and Jem, I kind of hoped things would be better and easier between us. But it's been strained and odd. We've always had this easy, honest relationship, but now it feels like there's a big unspoken thing between us. She knows I'm keeping secrets from her, and she's hurt, so she won't say anything about it, and I can't say anything because then I'll have to explain. I think she thinks this is about Jess. I think she thinks I'm jealous of her friendship with Jess, but I'm not. I really like Jess.

So now school is finished, I won't get to see Amy every day unless I make an effort to. I'm trying to . . . I WhatsApped her first thing and I can see from the blue ticks that she's read them. She hasn't replied yet though. I can't work out whether I should just ring her. It seems crazy. I mean, this is Amy. Ringing her is like breathing. I've never had to think about it. But now I'm sitting looking at my phone, and I'm too scared to dial, because what if she ignores my call?

A  Hi. Sorry, was in the shower.

C  Are you free today?

A  Jess and I thought we'd go to the lido. Want to come?

'Jess and I'. So she's responding to Jess's texts before mine. And the delay in her reply was probably because she was checking with Jess if it was OK to invite me along too.

C  Cool. Sounds good. How are you getting there? Bus?

A  J said he'd give us a lift.

J. Jem. Jeremy. We haven't actually spoken since the day he came

263

round here with Amy and Jess. I saw him a couple of times in the corridor at school, but I just put my head down and walked past or ducked out of the way. I don't know what to say to him. I mean, it's probably in my head anyway, the thought that he likes me. And I don't even know if I like him. I just . . . can't. I really can't. But then I find myself typing into my phone:

> C   What time? Shall I walk over to yours?

Chloe wore a bright pink one-piece costume that had bits cut out of the sides. 'Shark bites' her mum had called them when they'd bought it together, and they'd laughed. She tried not to think about that now. She'd straightened her hair carefully and brushed it out and tied it up. She pulled on some white cotton shorts and flung sunglasses, a towel and some flip-flops into a bag. She was wearing a little make-up but not much. No one wanted to end up with panda eyes. She checked her reflection. Nonchalant, casual. Summery. Just right.

She skipped down the stairs. iRachel and Sinead were sitting out on the patio at a table, a chessboard between them.

'Chess?' Chloe said, surprised.

'Yes,' said Sinead. 'Why not?'

'Sinead is a strong opponent and has a clear memory of the rules and strategies of chess,' said iRachel.

'Is that android talk for "she's whippin' yo ass"?'

'I am sure that you are using the African-American vernacular in an attempt to be humorous,' said iRachel stiffly. 'I have details of every grandmaster chess match played since records began. With my superior processing power, I am able to calculate the best possible move at all times.'

'Check again,' said Sinead, moving her knight.

'Whenever you start using that formal robot voice and talk

about your processing power, I know you're rattled,' said Chloe. She gave iRachel's shoulder a squeeze and dropped a kiss on the top of Sinead's head.

'Are you embarking on an excursion?' asked iRachel.

'Just going to Amy's. We're going swimming.' Chloe did her best to sound casual.

iRachel looked up at her. 'You have made a considerable effort with your appearance and your heart rate is raised. Are you excited about this outing?'

'I'm guessing there's a boy involved,' said Sinead.

'What? No!' said Chloe, outraged. To her horror, she felt a blush spread across her cheeks. iRachel would pick up on that for sure.

Predictably enough, iRachel gave her a cool smile. 'While your grandmother may be experiencing the effects of abnormal amino acids in her brain, her knowledge of human nature appears unimpaired. Would you care to respond to her assertion?'

'Bloody hell,' said Chloe. 'The force is strong in both of you. It's like living with Yoda and C-3PO.'

Sinead was still staring at the chessboard, and she said suddenly, 'Nurse person, bishop to knight four or I'm going to checkmate you.'

iRachel turned back to the board, clearly outraged, and Chloe took the chance to slip away before any more questions were asked.

As she walked down the road towards Amy's, she smiled to herself. Sinead was definitely doing better – she'd put on weight, and her sleeping patterns were gradually returning to normal. iRachel had told them that research showed that physical exercise and mental stimulation would be beneficial. Every evening, Chloe and Aidan took her for a brisk walk around the neighbourhood. They talked to her, and iRachel encouraged her to play games on the iPad. She played audiobooks for Sinead too. The chess was new, but Chloe wasn't surprised it worked. Sinead seemed to have good recall of things she had learned or experienced when she was younger. She just couldn't remember what she'd had for lunch.

A car hooted behind her and she jumped. She spun around, ready to yell at the idiot who'd frightened her, only to see that it was Jem and Jess. Jem was driving what was presumably their mum's car, a big silver estate.

Jess rolled down her window. 'Are you on your way to Amy's? Jump in.'

Chloe slid into the back seat. 'Thanks,' she said. 'How are you guys?'

'Good,' said Jess.

Jem didn't say anything, but Chloe could see his eyes on her in the rear-view mirror. He dragged his gaze away from hers, put on his sunglasses and pulled back out into the traffic.

Jess cranked the music back up again and Chloe wound down her window. With the sun on her face, she relaxed back into the seat. It was going to be a good day after all.

When they got to the Lucases's house, she saw Amy's little face in the window, looking out anxiously. It seemed odd that she was watching out for them, thought Chloe. She saw Amy's expression brighten as the car turned into the drive-way, but then her face fell when Chloe opened the back door and climbed out. Amy's eyes darted to the driver's side and she watched Jem get out of the car. And in that instant, Chloe got it: Amy's reticence to see her, the slowness of this invitation.

Amy liked Jem.

Not just that, she'd worked out that Jem liked Chloe. Shit.

How had Chloe not seen it? And here she was, all artfully

made up and in her cute swimming costume. If Jem fell for it, she'd break Amy's heart.

There was no chance for her to talk to Amy alone. She, Jess and Jem went into the house, and Mrs Lucas bustled around them all, offering juice and biscuits like they were five.

'I remember you!' she said to Jem. 'In the infants, you would only eat white food. Plain pasta, potatoes, rice – you had all the dinner ladies at their wits' end!'

Jem blushed a deep scarlet.

'He's got better,' said Jess. 'He eats beige food too now. Chicken nuggets and fish fingers.'

'It's no wonder you're such a long, skinny string bean!' said Mrs Lucas, pinching his arm. 'You'll want to watch that when you get older. Eat a vegetable.'

Chloe glanced over at Amy, who looked like she might actually die of embarrassment.

'Sorry about my mum,' Amy said, almost in a whisper. 'Shall we go?'

They finished their drinks, gathered their things and went back out to the car. Jess slipped into the front seat and Chloe and Amy got into the back. The music blared as soon as Jem started the engine.

Chloe pulled out her phone and texted Amy.

C You OK?

> A Are you texting me when I'm sitting right next to you?
> I swear, Chloe P-S, you're a loon.
> I'm fine. It's just my mum.

C Come on, we all know what she's like. It's sweet.

> A I know. But Jeremy . . . he's like an adult. She can't talk to him like that.

267

**I wanted to die.**

**C** He'll survive.

**A** He'll think I'm an idiot.

**C** Hardly.

Amy, do you . . .

Chloe hesitated, her thumbs hovering over her screen. Did she dare ask Amy if she liked Jem? Was it unfair to do that? Would Amy admit to it?

'Are you two texting each other in the back of the car?' Jess was looking back at them between the seats. 'Really?'

'It's an old habit of ours,' said Chloe quickly. 'We always used to do it when my mum drove us. She asked us such embarrassing questions.'

Jess's face froze. She obviously hadn't expected Chloe to mention her mum.

But Amy laughed. 'Oh my God, she was always asking body questions, and she'd use the proper scientific terms, even when we were about six.'

'She wasn't embarrassed by anything, so she couldn't understand why we would be.' Chloe laughed.

'Remember when she asked Richard Grey if he'd started puberty?'

'At my twelfth birthday party!' Chloe giggled. 'I nearly died.'

'So did Richard.'

They shared a smile in the back of the car, and Chloe sneaked a hand across to squeeze Amy's.

Jess looked from one to the other and smiled uncertainly. 'It's nice to hear you talk about your mum,' she said carefully.

'It's nice to talk about her,' said Chloe. As they drove on, she looked out of the window, but then her phone buzzed in her hand. Amy again.

**A** I'm sorry.

**C** For what?

**A** I feel like I've let you down. Haven't been there for you enough.

**C** You haven't let me down. It's been more complicated than that.

**A** It's not. You're my best friend. I should have been there for you no matter what.

**C** You have been there. You are here. ILY Amez.

**A** ILY2.

The lido was heaving and every inch of space was filled with bodies, spread-eagled, oiled and soaking up the summer rays. They walked around for ages before they could find a patch of grass to spread their towels. Chloe felt suddenly self-conscious and sat on her towel, knees drawn up, without removing her T-shirt or shorts. Amy stripped off her sun dress immediately. Her slim form was pale and freckled, and she was wearing a bright green bikini Chloe had never seen before. Jess pulled her T-shirt off to reveal a black swimsuit and headed straight for the water. She dived in smoothly and began to swim a fast front crawl.

'She's a really good swimmer,' observed Chloe.

'She swam for the county when she was about ten,' said Jem, sitting down beside her. He too had removed none of his outer clothing. 'Then our mum made her choose between swimming and music.'

'That's rough.'

'Not really. You can't do everything.'

'Did you have to choose too?'

'Nope. I was a useless swimmer. It was always music for me.'

'Is that what you're going to do after school?'

'I've auditioned for a few universities and music colleges. Just waiting to hear.'

Chloe glanced at him. His face was tense. It must be hard, she thought, waiting to know what your future would be, knowing it rested in someone else's hands. She was aware, however, of Amy, sitting on her towel on the other side of Jem. Chloe nonchalantly reached into her bag and pulled out a couple of magazines. She passed one over to Amy, opened her own and lay back, flicking through it, doing her best to look like she was engrossed. If Amy wanted to chat to Jem, this was her chance. But Amy didn't. She had a little flush of nerves along the top of her cheekbones.

Chloe stared at the pages without reading a word. She was conscious of Jem sitting beside her, staring out at the water. He had edged his knee closer and closer to her towel, until he was almost touching her. She shifted slightly, moving away. She tried to sort out what she felt about him. She imagined her mum casting her dispassionate, scientific gaze on the situation. What had she said in her letter? That scientific understanding was based on the concept of 'if => then'? Work out what facts you know, and see what you can extrapolate from them.

She ran through them in her head: he was good-looking, he could drive; he'd been nice to her in the library. But . . . her home life meant she couldn't get close to anyone just now, and, anyway, she was now ninety-nine per cent certain that Amy liked him.

She didn't know what falling in love was like. Obviously she'd seen her parents' lovey-dovey life together, but they were ancient, so it didn't count. She'd had crushes, but she had no experience of proper love. Maybe Jem was supposed to be her one and only true love? Somehow she doubted that. The odds that there was one perfect partner for her and that she had met him in the school library when she was fifteen were vanishingly small. She grinned to herself. She was being very scientific and emotionless about this. Maybe she was her mum's daughter in more ways than she liked to believe. Maybe all the times she'd imagined hearing her mum's voice in her head telling her off for stuff, it had actually been her own voice? Oh God. What a moment to have *that* revelation.

Or maybe, if she really, really liked Jem, none of the minus points would make any difference. But the fact was, she could imagine him as Amy's boyfriend with no pain at all. And if she really had feelings for him, she was sure that wouldn't be the case.

Impulsively, she flung down her magazine. 'I'm going to get a drink,' she said. 'Do you want anything?'

'I'll go with you,' said Jem, leaping to his feet.

Damn. That wasn't in the plan. 'I'm fine, really,' she said. 'I can go by myself, or maybe Amy wants to—'

But at that moment Jess came running back from the pool, dripping wet, her face flushed from the exertion of the swim. 'Amy, will you put some sun cream on my back?' she said. 'I fry like an egg in the sun.'

Amy gave Chloe a tight smile and picked up the tube of cream. Chloe took her purse from her bag and started to pick her way between the supine bodies, Jem close behind her.

There was a huge queue at the refreshments kiosk. Chloe took her place at the back of the line, Jem beside her. She didn't know what to say to him, and she didn't want to give him the idea that she was encouraging him, so she ignored him and looked out over the pool instead. He was standing too close to her and it made her uncomfortable. They edged forward in the queue, and he cleared his throat.

'I was wondering . . .' he said. 'I was wondering if you might want to go out one night this week. A film or something.'

'That would be cool,' she said carefully. 'There's that new superhero movie. I know Amy's really keen to see it. We could all go together.'

She knew perfectly well he hadn't meant all of them should go. He knew she knew, and that she was turning him down without actually saying so. She'd never done anything like that before. She felt sick with nerves. But she was confident she'd done the right thing.

They didn't speak again till they'd got to the front of the line. Chloe bought a couple of bottles of water and, on impulse, ice lollies for all of them. They fought their way back through the crowd at the counter and turned to go back to their towels. But as they passed the changing rooms, Jem suddenly grabbed her elbow and dragged her into an alcove, out of sight of the pool.

'What . . . ?' she said. But before she could say anything more, he kissed her. The bottles and ice lollies were crushed between them, pressing cold and wet against her belly. Jem gripped her shoulders hard enough to bruise them and crushed his mouth down on hers, as if he could persuade her of the intensity of his feelings with the force of his kiss. He tried to worm his tongue between her closed lips.

Chloe fought her rising panic and wrenched herself away. Her mum popped into her head, speaking clearly and simply. 'If anyone puts you in a position you don't like, you don't need to be nice to them or even polite. Be clear. Say no. You can tell them to fuck off if you need to. It's your body. Your rules.'

'Fuck. Off,' said Chloe with crystal clarity. 'Don't do that again. I don't like it.'

Jem sneered at her. 'Well then you shouldn't walk around in your sexy little white shorts, you prick-tease,' he said. He wiped his mouth with disdain. 'Frigid bitch.' He turned and walked out of the alcove without looking back.

Chloe was left standing there alone, shaking, a widening red stain from a crushed ice lolly on her T-shirt.

Ten minutes later, after she had thrown away the ice lollies and rinsed out her T-shirt in the changing rooms, she made her way back to their towels. Amy and Jess were sitting there alone.

'Where's Jeremy?' asked Jess.

'I thought . . . I thought he'd come back here,' said Chloe.

'We thought he was with you,' said Amy.

'No . . . I . . . went to the loo,' Chloe stammered.

Jess stood up and walked to the fence that overlooked the car park. She came back, frowning. 'The car's gone. He's just buggered off and left us here.'

Amy turned on Chloe. 'What the hell did you say to him?'

# Aidan

'So here's a list of all the people we've helped in the last year and their employment outcomes. I've compared it to work by other, similar organisations and our results are good. I've got Thomas on the phone, getting testimonials from clients as well as employers that we've placed people with.'

'The figures are good, but personal recommendations are really persuasive.'

'How have you done on the costings?'

Kate scooted her chair over so Aidan could move in to see the screen of her laptop. 'Just waiting for some quotes on new furniture, but it's looking good. I've also written a job description for the fundraising manager we'd need to hire.'

Aidan looked at her comprehensive spreadsheet. 'That looks great.'

She noticed an error and leaned in to make the correction. Aidan found himself looking at her neat cropped hairline and the slender nape of her neck. He liked her very much. She was smart, energetic and warm, and working with her made him feel braver and more positive. The potentially disastrous situation at work might turn out to be the biggest opportunity of their lives. And even if the worst happened and they were shut down, he'd got new energy and inspiration from developing his ideas and thoughts. He had sleepwalked through the last few years of work – Rachel's career had been the important one and his job had just been something to do. Where had his courage gone? His drive? What had happened to that clever, motivated boy Rachel had met at university all those years ago? He seemed to have faded away. But it didn't have to be like that. He could do more, could be more than before. Working with Kate had shown him that it was possible.

An email alert pinged on Kate's laptop and she clicked to open it. She skimmed it, then turned to Aidan, her face bright with excitement. 'It's from Baroness Eastwood, the chair of the board of trustees. She's agreed to set up the meeting for us. It's on Friday.'

'Is that enough time?'

'It'll have to be, won't it? We can do this, Aidan, I know we can.' She put her hand on his forearm and squeezed. Her eyes danced with enthusiasm. 'Well, what are we waiting for? Let's kick some arse.'

# 52
# Sinead

I'm not well. It's something to do with my . . . when I go to the toilet. Passing water. Pain.

I don't know why I'm in this hotel. It's strange. I want to go home. I want to crawl into my own bed with a hot-water bottle and sleep until I feel better. But for some reason I'm staying in this hotel and I don't know how to check out and go home.

I need to leave the hotel and find a taxi or someone I can ask. Someone that can tell me where my house is. If I stand by the door, I can hear the roar of a motorway, very faintly. If I go outside and walk towards that, I'm sure I can stop a car and ask someone.

The door of the hotel is always locked though. There's a woman. Very strange, very still. A chambermaid, maybe, or some kind of manageress. She checks the door and makes sure it's locked. But there's a garden out behind the hotel, and I think there's a gate at the bottom that leads into some fields. Maybe I can leave that way. They can send my bill on. I must have given them an address when I checked in.

The chambermaid is busy in the kitchen. I open the sliding doors as quietly as I can and slip out into the garden. The garden is beautiful, and faintly the notes of a song come to me:

> 'Tis the last rose of summer
> Left blooming alone;

*All her lovely companions*
*Are faded and gone . . .*

I stop myself from singing out loud, and I walk as quickly and quietly as I can to the bottom of the garden. There is the gate, which isn't locked. I pull back the bolt and slip out into the field. It's a hot, dry, still day, and there's no one else around. I start to walk across the grass. Home must be somewhere, if I can just find the road and someone to ask.

'Sinead! Sinead!' A voice is calling my name. Not a voice I know. I stop, confused. What am I doing standing in this field? I don't feel well.

It's the woman. The nurse. Or chambermaid. Or is it Rachel? I can't tell. She comes across the grass towards me, walking very awkwardly. You'd think she'd never been in a field before. She takes my hand.

'Your vital signs grew faint,' she says. I don't know what she means. 'I am glad you did not pass out of range before I found you.'

Her hand is cool in mine, and she seems to notice the temperature difference too. She places her other hand on my forehead.

'Pyrexia,' she says.

Well, I was a medical secretary for forty years, I know what that is. 'Fever,' I say.

'Your temperature measures 38.6 degrees Celsius,' she says, though how she can tell that with her hand I don't know. 'We will return to the house and contact Aidan. I believe you require medical attention.'

Together, hand in hand, we walk across the field and she takes me through a gate into a garden. I don't know this house, but I am very tired. Maybe they'll let me lie down for a little while until I feel better. But as soon as I do, I must be on my way.

# 53
## Chloe

Jess got off the bus back from the lido first. She was furious with Chloe and had refused to talk to her for the whole journey. They were all hot and upset. Amy and Chloe got off a few stops later and started to walk towards Chloe's house. Their bags were heavy and the sun was beating down on them; Chloe could feel the heat from the pavement through the thin soles of her sandals. She was horribly thirsty, but Amy's silent misery was rolling off her in waves and she couldn't bear it any longer.

'Amez . . .'

'Don't.'

'You don't know what I'm going to say.'

'I've got a pretty good idea.'

'You haven't. Listen, Amez, Jem—'

'Don't call him that, okay? His family hates it. They all call him Jeremy. He's only Jem to his friends. His reeeeaallly close friends.'

'He told me to call him Jem. I bumped into him in the library just before my last exam.'

'And you just . . . accidentally on purpose never mentioned it to me? How convenient!'

There was no point in pretending anymore, so Chloe just blurted out, 'Do you like him, Amy? Is that why you're so upset?'

'No, I don't "like" him.' Amy was almost screaming. 'Don't be ridiculous. I just don't understand why you have to do your big blue eyes and blonde hair thing and enslave every boy you meet.'

'What?' Chloe was close to tears.

'Oh for God's sake, Chloe,' said Amy, and her voice had a harsh edge to it. 'You know you do it. Boys just fall at your feet, and you ignore them and they love you even more. You've always done it.'

Chloe walked on in silence, her breathing ragged and shallow.

'And now Jeremy . . .' Amy's voice shook. 'Well, it was obvious as soon as he saw you. We were getting on really well before you . . .'

'Before I what?'

'Slimed your way in,' said Amy viciously, and then awfully, heartbreakingly, began to cry.

# 54
# iRachel

I was aware of Chloe as she approached the house. Her heart rate was raised and all her vital signs suggested agitation. As she stepped through the door, I heard her say very loudly and clearly, 'Grandma Sinead! I've got my friend Amy with me!'

I knew that this warning was not intended for Sinead's ears but for mine. I heard Chloe say to her friend, 'Just put your stuff here,' and I realised she was giving me time to conceal myself. I moved swiftly into the utility room and shut the door.

I heard Chloe and her friend Amy come into the kitchen. My experience of friendship between adolescent females is limited to representations in works of literature and cinema. It was my expectation that Chloe and Amy would chatter enthusiastically about recreational activities, or about their other friends. Gossip, I believe is the colloquial term. However, they sat in silence for three minutes and thirty-six seconds. Chloe's vital signs remained agitated. I wished very much that I could ask her what was upsetting her, so I could offer help.

Finally, Chloe spoke and her voice was very soft. 'I don't like Jem. Jeremy. I thought I might for a bit, but then I was certain I didn't, and then when I thought that maybe you did, I was sure I wanted to stay away. I never encouraged him or led him on, I swear. I would never want to hurt you, Amez. Never. You're my best friend.'

There was a pause, and then Amy said, very softly, 'I know.'

'I know it probably doesn't make a difference to what you think of him, but I don't think he's a very nice person.'

'I think he probably isn't,' said Amy, 'but I can't help it. I can't help how I feel.'

I heard a rustle of clothing, and I surmised that they were hugging each other. Chloe's heart rate and breathing steadied somewhat.

'I'm sorry,' said Amy. 'I said some horrible things just now. Horrible. I don't even think they're true. You can't help how you look. And boys are idiots anyway.'

'It's okay,' said Chloe. 'And you're allowed to be a bit shit to me. I haven't been a very good friend.'

'Oh my God, Chlo!' said Amy sharply. 'How can you say that? You lost your mum! And I haven't been there for you nearly as much as I should have been.'

'That's because I shut you out,' said Chloe miserably.

'It was really hard when you kept saying I shouldn't come round,' said Amy, 'but I should have been a better friend and been more understanding. Instead, I just started hanging out more with Jess, and I only did that because . . .' She stopped. 'Now I sound like a real cow.'

'Yeah, a little bit.' I could hear from her voice that Chloe was smiling when she said that. Her expression was at odds with her words. 'Jess is really cool,' she continued. 'She's a good friend to you. And to me.'

'I know,' said Amy. 'So are you. Anyway, guys come and go, but friends are forever.'

'Sisters before misters.'

'That's better than hoes before bros.'

'Oh my God, can you imagine my feminist mum if she'd heard us call ourselves "hoes"?'

Amy giggled. 'She'd have died!' She gasped. 'Oh my God, Chloe, I'm so sorry.'

'It's okay,' said Chloe. 'It's just an expression.'

'It was a terrible thing to say. I'm sorry.'

'Amez, you can't spend your whole life worrying about saying the words "dead" or "dying" in front of me. My mum is dead. It's a fact. We live with it. And we're okay. I mean, I know it's a weird household, but it works. And somehow, the four of us get by.'

'The four of you?'

'Three. Dad, Grandma and me. You know what I mean.'

They were quiet again for a long moment. Then Amy spoke. 'I think . . . I think what's been really hard for me is that I can't help feeling there are secrets between us. Like . . . there's something huge you aren't telling me. For a long time, I thought maybe you were seeing Jeremy in secret and hiding that from me, but I now know that's not true. But there is something, isn't there? There is a secret. We've been best friends all our lives, Chlo, I know you. Something isn't right with you.'

She didn't speak, but Chloe's heart rate suddenly spiked so high, I was concerned she had received a bad fright or was experiencing some kind of health crisis. Then she said, 'Yes. Yes, there is a secret. But it's so huge, I can't tell you how much trouble I would get into if I told.'

'Oh my God, Chloe, you're scaring me. Is it bad? Has someone been hurting you?'

'No, no, it's nothing like that. It's just . . . when my mum died, we found out something about her work. Something amazing. And . . .'

I began to experience warning signals. My ability to extrapolate future events from current data suggested to me that Chloe was about to take an action that was both impetuous and irrational. I could read her vital signs, but I had no way of communicating with her. I wanted to tell her to stop. I wanted to talk to her and get her to calm down before she did something regrettable. The actions she appeared to be contemplating would have far-reaching and disastrous implications for all of us. But there was no way to stop her, no way to hold back her rash, adolescent behaviour. I heard her footsteps drawing nearer and she said, 'You have to swear you won't tell anyone, okay? This is so, so secret.'

Then she pulled open the door to the utility room. Light flooded in, and she and Amy stood silhouetted in the doorway. Chloe spoke.

'This is iRachel.'

# 55
## Chloe

She felt shaky, as if her insides were trembling. What she'd done was crazy, and if her dad found out, or Luke, she was going to be in so much trouble. But it had been worth it, getting Amy back, making her understand. Totally worth it. Now Amy would see that it wasn't anything to do with stupid Jem, or any stupid boy. The secrets Chloe had been keeping were much bigger.

Amy had stood in the doorway of the utility room and stared at iRachel with her mouth open, and then she'd let out a little squeak. iRachel stood up – she didn't look happy about the situation, but there was nothing Chloe could do about that – and held out her hand.

'Good day. I am iRachel, a humanoid android. I am here to assist you in any way you require. I can impart this message to you in text, by voice or as a video transmitted to a computer or television.'

It was her service message, the one she'd played the very first day she arrived. It made Chloe realise how much iRachel had changed in the time she'd been with them. She no longer spoke in stock phrases. She had conversations. Expressed opinions. Made jokes, even. Her mum would have been so excited to see this. But now iRachel was reverting to robot-speak. One way or another, she wasn't going to give anything away to Amy.

'It was my mum's wish that iRachel come to live with us, as part of her experiment,' Chloe explained. 'But it had to be top secret. I know that's hard to understand, but it did. We couldn't tell anyone.'

'A robot,' said Amy, 'in your house.' She hadn't managed to close her mouth yet. She just stared and stared at iRachel. 'It looks just like your mum. It's a little bit creepy.'

'Not "it", "she",' snapped Chloe. 'And you can talk to her.'

She looked over and smiled at iRachel. 'I'm sorry,' she mouthed. 'I had to.'

Amy left soon after. She hadn't managed to actually talk to iRachel – she had just stared, amazed, and then moved around to see if iRachel kept watching her. When iRachel had excused herself to go and check on Sinead, Amy had been very eager to get on her way.

It was after she left that Chloe got the knot of sick tension in her stomach. Had she done the right thing? Had Amy understood? She knew that Amy was a thinker – she didn't respond to things instantly and emotionally, like Chloe did. She'd go away and think about it. She'd call or text later and ask all her questions.

But she didn't. Chloe spent the next day in her room watching TV, but her phone remained silent – no texts or calls from Amy at all. She obviously needed more time.

Her heart felt heavy and sick. Was this all it took? A stupid crush on a stupid boy? Just that, to break eleven years of friendship? She couldn't sit in her room anymore, thinking about how she'd lost her best friend. She went downstairs, into the kitchen, where iRachel was deftly chopping green beans for the salad niçoise she was making for dinner. She slipped onto a barstool at the counter and doodled on the notepad they kept there for the shopping list.

iRachel began carefully peeling boiled eggs. 'You are sad,' she observed.

'Why do you say that? What's my heart rate doing?'

'Your heart rate is normal. Your face is sad. And you have drawn a picture of a crying kitten.'

'It's a raccoon.'

'Your rendition of the taxonomy suggests the family *Felidae* rather than *Procyonidae*, but I will allow for artistic interpretation.'

'Ha ha.'

'Ha ha indeed. But you are sad.'

'Amy hasn't rung me. Or texted. I think she hates me.'

'Why would she hate you?'

'There was a whole stupid thing with this guy.'

'Jeremy, alias Jem. I was an aural witness to the conversation.'

'Yeah.'

'Why would she hate you? If he is attracted to you, this is a choice he has made. Not you.'

'Tell that to Amy. I suppose . . . it's easier to hate me than to hate him. I'll always love her, see.'

'But when you and Amy spoke, she said that "guys come and go, but friends are forever. Hoes before bros".'

Chloe stifled a giggle at the expression coming from iRachel's mouth. 'I know that's what she said, but it's not what she's doing, is it?'

'It is difficult to experience rejection or to feel that someone has chosen someone else over you,' said iRachel.

'Is that one of my mum's programmed clichés?'

'No. That is my own extrapolation, from observations I have made.'

'Wise advice,' said Chloe, and smiled. She spun around on her stool. 'I don't know, maybe I'm just being paranoid. Maybe she's just thinking about stuff, and she'll turn up on the doorstep soon and everything will be fine.'

'This is within the realms of possibility,' agreed iRachel, and she reached to get a tin of anchovies from the store cupboard.

As if on cue, the doorbell rang. iRachel and Chloe looked at one another and laughed.

'It's not Luke, is it?' asked Chloe.

'He is not scheduled to attend,' said iRachel. 'As a precaution, I will go into the utility room.'

She did so, and Chloe hopped off the barstool and went to open the door. It would be Amy. It had to be. She went to the front door, slipped the key in and unlocked it.

It was Jem.

Chloe felt a sick lurch in her stomach. She kept her hand firmly on the door. She wasn't letting him in, no matter what.

'What are you doing here?'

'Hi, Jem. How are you?' he said in a breathy imitation of a girl's voice.

'Hi, Jem. What are you doing here?'

'Came to see you. Is that not allowed?'

'After you called me a frigid bitch at the pool? No, not really.'

'I came to say sorry,' he said insincerely.

'Thanks for the apology. Now I have to go.' She started to close the door, but he put out his hand and stopped her pushing it closed.

'I really am sorry. I didn't mean to upset you. I just like you very much. Can't I come in? Can't we talk?'

His eyes were pleading, and he looked so sad and vulnerable, she almost softened. But then she remembered his ugly behaviour. She didn't want anything to do with him, and anyway, what would Amy think if she knew he had come here?

'No, you can't. I don't want you in my house.'

'What? Why?'

He looked genuinely hurt, and she felt awful. He was Jess's brother, after all. How bad could he be? But she stuck to her guns.

'I really can't let you in. My grandma's ill.'

'Who's looking after her?' Jem said, and it struck her that he looked a bit sly.

'My . . . dad. Why?' she lied.

'Really? Where's his car?' Jem glanced behind him at the empty driveway.

'Listen, just go,' said Chloe, and she tried to shut the door again, but Jem blocked it.

'Why don't you just let me in, Chloe? I want to take a look at the lady robot. Amy couldn't wait to tell me all about it. Some of my friends also want to see her.'

'Go away, you little bastard! Just piss off! And don't ever come here again or I'll call the police!'

She wrenched the door out of his grasp and slammed it hard. She heard him jump back to avoid being hit, and he laughed. She stood shaking behind the closed door until she heard him walk back down the porch steps. She listened for the sound of the car starting and waited for him to drive away, then she pulled the door open again and took off at a run, heading for Amy's house.

# 56

## iRachel

Today has been strenuous. I had my usual day-to-day commitments, but the fact that Sinead became ill has somewhat extended
my list of tasks. A urinary tract infection in older people can cause
or exacerbate confusion, and this has proved to be the case with
Sinead. She has been extremely distressed since Aidan brought
her back from the doctor's. She has developed a certainty that
she is in a hotel and must return home. It took a combination of
verbal persuasion and repeatedly leading her to her bedroom to
calm her nerves.

By the time she fell asleep and I was able to return to my
routine, my battery power was at an unprecedented low. Aidan
was going to be remaining late at work, and I was required to
produce a meal for dinner, so taking time to recharge was out
of the question. I decided to take a calculated risk: for the two
hours before Aidan was scheduled to return, I would disconnect
my sensors for the wristbands to preserve battery power. Chloe
and Sinead were safely in the house. Sinead was asleep and the
doors were all locked. In this way, I would be able to last until the
family sat down to dinner before I needed to recharge.

I enjoyed my conversation with Chloe, which was interrupted
when the doorbell rang. Chloe went to answer it, and, as usual
when a visitor comes to the house, I retired to the utility room.
I waited for a full fourteen minutes and forty-two seconds, but
Chloe did not return to the kitchen. I was unable to detect her

footsteps, or indeed any noise in the house. It was silent.

As a precaution, before I emerged, I re-engaged my wrist-band sensor software. This was a risky proposition as my system was at thirteen per cent battery power. The readings I received were anomalous, and my first thought was that my low battery power meant that the software was not working properly. However, a quick diagnostic showed me it was functioning correctly. Nevertheless, I was not receiving a reading from any of the four wristbands registered to my system.

Luke and Aidan were both out of range. However, there was no reading from Chloe's band, and, indeed, it also showed as 'out of range' on my reader. She must have left the house with whoever had rung the doorbell.

Most worryingly, though, there was an 'out of range' reading for Sinead as well. With the other three, the possibility existed that they had removed their bands. But Sinead's was locked onto her wrist. I assessed the potential reasons for this: my reduced battery power; a flaw in the band itself; or that Sinead was deceased and was emitting no vital signs for her wristband to read.

Given that Chloe was definitely out of range, it seemed likely (89.3 per cent) that there were no strangers in the house. I opened the door cautiously. There was no one in the kitchen, and a quick visual scan ruled out the presence of anyone in the living room or on the patio. I moved into the hallway and immediately noticed that the front door of the house was wide open. This was unprecedented and very worrying. Upstairs, there was no sign of Chloe in her bedroom. I moved quickly to Sinead's room and there my worst fears were confirmed. Sinead's bed was empty, the covers flung back. I called her name, but I was already certain that she was gone.

I sent an urgent message to both Aidan and Luke. The protocol demands that if I send an emergency alert, they should respond within 180 seconds, by phone or text or by attending my location physically. However, a full 360 seconds passed and there was no response from either of them. I wondered if my low battery power was impeding my ability to send messages. I noticed Chloe's mobile phone lying on the kitchen counter. I would be unable to reach her either. My battery power was now at eleven per cent.

Another 240 seconds passed and there was no response from Aidan or Luke. Wherever Sinead had gone, she was getting further away by the minute. I utilised the mobile phone Aidan had given me, and sent an urgent text message to him. Again, there was no response. My only hope was to leave the house and try to locate her. I knew it was both dangerous and against all the rules for me to leave the premises, but I had no other choice.

I went to the front door. I picked up the sunglasses that Chloe had discarded on the hall table upon her return from the pool and put them on. The sunlight in the street seemed glaring and uncompromising. I stepped outside and began to walk.

# 57

## Aidan

'You'll see here the proposal we've drawn up for the charity loans organisation. We have had a preliminary discussion with them, and as Foothold owns this building, which could serve as collateral, they think it's very likely we'll be granted a loan. You'll also see that in our future plans we've built in a salary for a fundraising co-ordinator. We've attached several case studies for charities of a similar size and the returns they've experienced from having employed a specialist. Thomas, our writing trainer, has also prepared a number of press releases we're planning to send out to raise our public profile . . .' Aidan leaned over to pass the neat, professional dossiers of information around the table.

He was hot in his suit, but he was glad he'd worn it. It was an expensive, well-cut one he'd got a few years before for an event at Telos, and it worked like armour against the filthy glares he was getting from Stephen Jasper. The other board members opened the folders and began to leaf through them, murmuring to one another and pointing at the artist's renditions of the renovated space. Jasper glanced at the dossier in front of him as if it was something distasteful. He leaned back in his chair and folded his arms to show how determined he was not to engage with this nonsense. Aidan almost laughed. He was behaving like a spoiled child who refused to join in because the other children wouldn't play the game he'd chosen.

Jasper had come into the meeting with guns blazing, demanding the charity be shut down immediately. But he had reckoned without Baroness Eastwood. She'd been one of the first women to qualify as a doctor at her medical school and had gone on to become one of Britain's great health reformers. She'd spent her whole career battling bullish, condescending men. She dismissed Jasper's bluster instantly.

'We acknowledge that we should all have kept a closer eye on the finances. That can't be helped. But that's no reason to throw out years of good work. If Kate and Aidan have a proposal that could save Foothold, let's hear it,' she said.

'But . . .' he snapped.

'As chair of this meeting, I set the agenda,' she said calmly, 'and we'll be hearing what they have to say now.'

When Jasper opened his mouth to protest, she held up her hand and gave him the look that had paralysed many a junior doctor. His face darkened. Aidan could see him calculating whether it was worth standing up to a baroness, then concluding that he'd come off worse – in every way.

And so Aidan and Kate did their presentation. It had taken long hours of overtime, some swearing and a couple of knockdown rows to get to this point, but it was worth it. They'd prepared their PowerPoint and made up the dossiers and then practised over and over, under Lola's watchful eye.

As they'd waited for the trustees to arrive, Kate had straightened Aidan's tie and patted his arm. 'Let's look like we know what we're doing,' she said, 'and not like clumsy charity noobs.'

'We are clumsy charity noobs.' Aidan smiled.

'Yes, but they don't have to know that.' She grinned at him and went to fetch the remote for the projector. She was also wearing a suit: a narrow pencil skirt and cropped jacket. He'd only ever seen her in jeans and casual clothes before. She looked good.

She was still looking good now, standing beside one of the

trustees – a florid-faced elderly military man with a great bristling moustache – and talking him through the figures. The baroness gestured Aidan over and he tore his eyes away from Kate and went to answer her laser-sharp questions.

The trustees weren't pushovers – they had plenty of criticisms and they queried several of the figures. Old Colonel Bristle-Moustache took the time to ring someone he knew and got the name of an equity company that might grant Foothold the loan they needed, and another trustee said that her daughter had a PR company and was looking to take on a pro-bono client. Through all of this, Stephen Jasper sulked and pouted.

'All right,' said the baroness, tapping on the table, 'let's call this meeting to order.'

Everyone turned to listen to her.

'I propose that we keep Kate on as manager for the moment, that we revise the budget with the recommendations we've had in this meeting, and that we meet again in a week to sign it off. All in favour raise your hands.'

All of the trustees but Stephen Jasper raised their hands, and the secretary minuted the vote. Jasper stood abruptly. 'You're going to let a pair of rank amateurs ruin your reputations,' he said. 'This is frankly insane. You can take this as notice of my resignation from the board of this ridiculous organisation.' He swept his copy of the dossier off the table in a petulant gesture, picked up his briefcase and stormed off.

'Don't let the door hit you on the arse on the way out,' said the baroness crisply. 'Next order of business, did Fiona leave any of that excellent Sancerre in the fridge?'

There was a slightly manic party mood after Jasper's dramatic exit, and the trustees polished off a full case of wine before preparing to take themselves off to a nearby wine bar and carry on.

'Do join us, Kate and Aidan,' said Colonel Moustache. 'Our treat.'

'I'll come along for a bit once we've tidied up here,' said Kate. 'Thanks for the invitation.'

'Thank you, but sadly I'll have to say no,' said Aidan regretfully. 'My mum is unwell. I must get home.'

They made a half-hearted attempt to persuade him, but they were all too keen to get stuck into another bottle. Once they'd all headed off down the high street, Kate and Aidan gathered up the glasses and straightened the chairs and tables.

'Well,' said Kate, 'I think we can cautiously call that a win.'

'The first battle, at least,' said Aidan. 'I'm thrilled to see the back of that Jasper muppet.'

'Me too. And, Aidan,' she said, drying her hands and hanging up the dish towel, 'you were awesome. Thank you. None of this would have happened without you. You've saved us all.'

Impulsively, she hugged him. She was short, so she had to stand on tiptoe. She was warm in his arms, and her hair smelled fresh and lemony. He felt something tug at him, deep inside, but before he could think about what that was, she gave him a swift kiss on the cheek, slipped from his arms and the room, and was gone. He was left standing alone in the kitchen, staring at the glass in his hands and feeling inexplicably guilty.

# 58

## Sinead

I'm tired. I've been walking, but I don't know for how long. I was at a hotel, I think, or maybe in a hospital, but I wanted to go home, so I put on my shoes and I left. I'm still in my nightie, and I don't seem to have my handbag. I want to get home, but I don't know where home is. I want to stop someone and ask, but then they'll ask for my address, and I can't quite . . . It's gone. Without my handbag, I can't get a taxi either, even if I knew where to find one. I'll keep walking. It's late, I think – the shadows are getting long, and I'm thirsty, and my feet hurt.

The road I'm on has houses along both sides. If I can find some shops, maybe I can ask someone for help. Maybe if I tell them my name, they can look something up on the internet, help me to find my way home. But there's nothing. I'm not sure if I've been on this street before – all the houses look the same. I could knock on a door and ask for help, but I'm too embarrassed. What would I say? 'I'm lost, but I don't know where I live.' They'd think I was mad.

I'm at an intersection now. There's nothing to the left, just more suburban homes. It's more of a country lane to the right – there are only trees and fields. A few hundred yards away there's a group of people standing in a circle and talking. I'll go and ask them. Maybe they'll recognise me and they'll know where I live.

I'm closer to them now and I can see that there's a car parked nearby. The circle is actually just four people – all young men. It's possible there's another person in the middle, but it's hard to see. They're laughing, but their laughter is unkind, harsh and jarring, and I can see them leaning in and grabbing at something or someone. There must be a fifth person. They're big boys, all of them. I'm not bad at judging ages – I've raised two of my own – and these boys look eighteen or so. Not children. So if they're bullying someone, they might actually do some damage. Hurt them.

'Excuse me,' I say. I try to make my voice sound strong and purposeful, not wavery and old ladyish. One of the boys spins round to look at me. His face is twisted and guilty. He looks as if he might be younger than I thought.

'What are you doing?' I say, and walk nearer. This time, all four boys turn and look at me. I can see they're what we used to call well-brought-up boys – the kind that go to the local grammar school. They're clean and wearing nice clothes, no tattoos or pierced ears. But it's clear they've been up to no good. One of them, the tallest of the lot, has a shock of black hair and I have a vague idea I've seen him before.

'Come on!' he says suddenly, and he breaks away. His friends hesitate, then follow him. They run towards the car, a big silver estate, and jump in. They roar off down the road.

There was a fifth person. A woman. It seems she was being held up by the four boys, because when they run away she crumples to the ground. She's wearing white, so even though I'm still fifty yards away, I can see her clearly, lying in the long grass. I hurry over and kneel beside her. She's wearing a white dress and it's dirty and crumpled.

She is lying motionless, looking up at the sky. She doesn't seem to be breathing. Her face is beautiful and still. There is a terrible, bloodless rip at the corner of her mouth. Is she dead? I am sure she is dead, but then I see her eyes moving, just a little. I take her hand.

'Sinead,' she whispers.

I don't know how she knows my name. I don't think I know her, although she reminds me of my daughter-in-law, Rachel. Rachel is a scientist, so maybe it's just the white tunic. It looks like a lab coat.

'Those bad boys are gone,' I say, and I gently smooth her tunic down and try to brush off some of the mud. Then I take her hand again. She also doesn't have a handbag, or a mobile phone, just a pair of sunglasses, which lie in the dirt beside her, the frames twisted and smashed and the lenses broken, as if someone ground them underfoot.

'Can you stand up?' I say. 'Are you hurt? I don't know where my home is, but maybe we can find someone to help.'

'I cannot stand,' she whispers. 'I . . . My battery . . .'

And in that moment I see the light go out in her eyes. She's gone.

The sky is dark, and as I look up, I see the first stars beginning to shine. I don't know what to do. I can't leave this dead woman alone on a country lane. I don't know where I am or how to find help. All I can do is sit here and hold her cold hand and hope someone will find us both.

# 59

## Aidan

It was night-time when he got home. He was still buzzing with the excitement of the meeting and feeling an undertone of guilty confusion about his moment of closeness with Kate. He was so distracted that he was almost at the front door when he realised that the house was in darkness. He had a jolt of surprise and wondered if there had been a power failure, or if iRachel, Chloe and Sinead were all out in the garden. But the surprise became fear as he noticed that the front door was ajar.

He pushed at the door cautiously, calling out, 'Hello?' But he knew instantly that there would be no answer. The air in the house was undisturbed. He rushed from room to room, flicking on lights and calling out. Nothing. He pulled out his mobile and dialled Chloe's number and, to his increasing alarm, heard her phone ring out in the kitchen. Where were they all? Had Sinead been taken ill and they'd had to take her to the hospital? But surely they would have called or messaged him? He looked at his phone and saw there was a text from iRachel's mobile phone. 'Sinead is missing', it said. He dialled her phone immediately, but it went straight to message.

He could feel his heart pounding in his chest, and his breath came in short, desperate gasps. He couldn't think straight. What should he do? Call 999? What would he say? 'This is Aidan Sawyer, widower. I seem to have mislaid absolutely everyone else that I love.'

He walked out onto the porch and scanned the street, his phone in his hand, thumb poised over the 9 button. Just then, he saw a figure walking up the road towards him, her pace slow, her head hanging low and defeated. Chloe. He ran down the drive and grabbed her by the shoulders. 'Where have you been? Where's Grandma Sinead? Where's iRachel?'

'What? What?' she cried, her eyes wide with shock and fear. 'I thought you'd still be at your meeting.'

'Where are they?' he screamed, shaking her.

She burst into tears, terrified by his panic. 'I don't know,' she sobbed. 'Something bad happened. I ran out of the house and went to Amy's. I've been there ever since.'

'You didn't take your phone.'

'I didn't take anything. I was too upset. I don't think I even closed the door . . .' Chloe's hand flew to her mouth. 'Oh my God.'

Aidan pulled his keys from his pocket. 'Get in the car. We have to find them.'

They drove slowly, watching both sides of the road. Chloe kept saying, 'I'm so sorry, Daddy,' and her voice was thick with tears.

'Just keep looking,' Aidan said grimly. 'We'll give it thirty minutes, and then I'm going to have to call the police . . . and Luke.'

'What if they've gone into a house somewhere?'

'If they have, iRachel knows my number. Someone would have rung us.' But Aidan wasn't convinced. What would the average person do if a robot and a confused old woman turned up on their doorstep? He couldn't begin to imagine. Although, thinking about it, most people would be more likely to call the press than the police. He handed Chloe his mobile phone. 'Keep an eye on the news services and on social media . . . Just in case.'

Chloe ran a quick check. 'Nothing,' she said. 'That's good news, isn't it?'

Aidan nodded, but he wasn't sure. 'I'm going to go a few blocks in one direction, then turn left and go a few blocks, and turn left again, and so on. Then we'll move out in concentric circles,' he said.

'They can't have got far,' Chloe agreed. 'If we're methodical, we've got to find them, right?'

They went up and down each road slowly, until they were around a mile from the house.

'It's not working,' said Chloe hopelessly. 'Surely they couldn't have got this far away?'

'I don't know. Maybe we missed them somehow. I'll turn around and we can go back and try the other way.'

Aidan drew up to an intersection and swung right to begin a three-point turn.

'Wait!' Chloe shouted excitedly. Aidan slammed on the brakes. 'Up there!' Chloe pointed up the road ahead of them. 'I saw something white on the pavement.' Aidan started to drive slowly towards the place Chloe had indicated. 'I mean, it could be nothing,' Chloe said. 'Just a plastic bag or something . . .' But as they drew closer, the headlights picked up the glimmer of eyes.

Aidan slowed to a crawl and pulled over to the side of the road. He left the headlights on and jumped out of the car. 'Mum!' he called.

Sinead turned her head slowly to look at him. Her hair was wild around her face, and she was wearing her nightie. 'Are you the ambulance driver? I'm afraid you're too late. This young woman has passed away.'

Chloe gave a little cry when she saw iRachel's motionless body. Aidan lifted a hand to try and calm her, but she took a deep breath, steadied herself and sat down on the grass verge beside

Sinead. 'Hey, Grandma,' she said, taking Sinead's hand. 'We were worried about you. Shall we take you home?' She began rubbing Sinead's hand between her own. 'Dad, her hands are really cold. I don't know how long she's been sitting out here.'

'Okay,' said Aidan. He was mortified to hear the tremble in his own voice. He didn't know where to begin. 'Um . . . let's try and get her into the front of the car and put the heater on.'

But Sinead wouldn't leave iRachel. In the end, Aidan lifted iRachel in his arms and placed her awkwardly across the back seat, strapping her in. Once she was safely in the car, Sinead agreed to sit beside her in the back. Aidan and Chloe jumped into the front seats and Aidan locked all four doors before restarting the engine and cranking up the heat.

He drove home slowly, and Sinead murmured soothingly to iRachel all the way there. When they got back to the house, he pulled the car as far up the driveway as he could. He coaxed Sinead inside, and Chloe settled her in the living room with a blanket and went to make a hot-water bottle.

Now he had to get iRachel out of the car. He couldn't imagine what the neighbours would think if they looked out of their windows and saw him carrying what appeared to be a dead body. He turned off the porch light and decided to go for speed over style. He wrestled the seatbelt off her and, sliding his arms under hers, lifted her up and draped her over his shoulder in a fireman's lift. If anyone asked, he'd say it was a friend who'd had too much to drink. She was heavy – as heavy as a human woman of equivalent size. Somehow, this surprised him. He'd imagined her to be lighter, insubstantial, empty.

He got her into the hallway but in his haste to shut the door banged her head on the doorframe. It would have been funny if it wasn't so horrifying.

He could hear Chloe chattering to Sinead in the living room.

He called her out into the hallway. 'Phone the out-of-hours number for the doctor,' he said. 'Tell them we found your grandma wandering around and she was very cold. Ask if they'll come to the house to see her.'

Chloe nodded and went to make the call.

He'd have to see what the doctor said — maybe they'd want him to take Sinead to hospital. Whatever happened, he had to do something about iRachel, and he had to do it now.

He had never seen her like this. He had seen her inert state when she was charging, but this was different. She really did look dead. Maybe her battery was just flat? He wanted to connect her to her charger, but he couldn't plug her in in the kitchen. Not if the doctor was coming to the house. He carried her upstairs to his bedroom, his legs wobbling and unsteady, and laid her down on his bed. He winced when he saw the damage to her face in the light of the bedside lamp. Then he ran back down to the kitchen to fetch her charging cable and very gently connected her to the plug on his side of the bed. He sat beside her for a minute or so. Nothing. He checked the cable, and the small red light beside the port in iRachel's armpit showed him that the power was getting through.

He stood in the doorway of the bedroom, hesitating, but then Chloe called up the stairs. The doctor was on his way. The living had to take priority. He took one last glance back at iRachel's motionless, damaged face and left the room.

# 60

## Luke

'Jesus Christ,' Luke said when he saw iRachel lying on the bed. He went over quickly, dropping his bag of tools to the floor, and sat beside her so he could examine her properly. He swiftly unbuttoned the front of her tunic.

'Do you have to . . . ?' Aidan began, but Luke cut him off with an impatient wave of his hand.

'I need to see how extensive the damage is. Who did this?'

'I don't know,' said Aidan. 'I don't know what happened. We found her and my mum on the side of the road. I thought maybe her battery was just dead, so I brought her back and connected her to the charger, but she hasn't woken up.'

Luke applied a small sensor to iRachel's skin. 'The battery is charged,' he said shortly. 'That's not what's wrong here.' He took out a notebook and pen and began to go over her, inch by inch, painstakingly recording every contusion, rip and evidence of damage. 'Whoever did this really chucked it around,' he said, disgusted. He narrowed his eyes and looked hard at Aidan, who blanched under his gaze.

'Oh my God! You can't possibly think that I . . .'

'What am I supposed to think? It was supposed to stay in the house. No one knows it even exists, and now this . . . ?'

'You have to know I would never, ever hurt her. We've got very close, all of us. We care about her . . .'

'You see what I mean? You've invested emotionally in it. It's a small jump from that to anger, violence . . .'

'In your world, maybe, but not in mine.' Aidan bit the words off. 'She must have left the house to look for my mum. What happened after that, and who got hold of her, I really don't know.'

At that moment Chloe stepped into the doorway behind him. 'I do,' she said. 'Or I can make a pretty good guess at it.' She told them briefly about Jem and how Amy had told him about the robot. 'I screamed at her and told her how badly she'd let me down. She was so upset. She didn't think. She was just trying to impress him. She had no idea he'd come round here.'

'And did he?' Aidan was shocked.

'Yes. I sent him away, but he told me he'd told some of his friends. If I had to guess, I'd say Grandma Sinead got out when I left the door open. iRachel probably went to look for her. Some-how they must have run into Jem and his friends.'

'Are you sure?'

'Not absolutely sure, but Grandma Sinead was rambling on about a big silver car. Jem drives his mum's estate. It's silver.'

'Do you know where he lives?' said Luke, his eyes narrowing.

'No,' said Chloe firmly. 'And even if I did, I wouldn't tell you. If you want to call the police and report this, I'll tell them what I know.'

Luke looked at Chloe, her slim shoulders set, chin lifted, facing him down. Her mother's daughter, to the bone.

He turned his back on Aidan and Chloe and resumed his pains-taking examination of iRachel. 'The damage does appear to be superficial,' he said. 'I just can't understand why . . .' He froze and his face went white. He turned to Aidan. 'When did it last look in the mirror?'

'What?'

'The mirror. In your hallway. It's supposed to check in the mirror every six hours.'

'Yes,' said Aidan. 'Um . . . well, she normally does two o'clock, and eight o'clock. Morning and night.'

'She did the two o'clock,' said Chloe. 'I remember that. She was settling Grandma Sinead in her bedroom and she had to pop downstairs to do it.'

Luke looked at his watch. 'But it's half past eight now. Which means it missed the eight o'clock. Oh hell – the virus.'

'The virus Rachel implanted in her? Do you think that's what's wrong with her?'

Luke pulled iRachel up by the shoulders. 'Help me get it downstairs. Maybe the damage isn't terminal.'

'She's naked,' Chloe said.

Luke gave her a scathing look. 'That's not really the most important issue right now.'

He draped one of iRachel's arms over his shoulder and caught her round the waist, pulling her into a standing position. Aidan hesitated for a second, dashed into the en-suite bathroom and came out with Rachel's silk dressing gown. He slipped it onto iRachel's free arm, and Luke, even though he looked furious, took the few seconds necessary to get it onto her other arm, pull it closed and tie the belt.

Together, Luke and Aidan carried iRachel down the stairs and into the hallway. They manoeuvred her into position in front of the mirror.

'It takes thirty seconds, doesn't it?' asked Luke, grunting under the weight.

'Yes, but the alignment has to be right. Her eyes need to be perfectly in line with the sensors.'

'Where are the damned sensors?'

'I don't know, do I?' snapped Aidan.

They shuffled left and right and tried their best to hold iRachel so she was at exactly her normal height. It was difficult; her body slumped and her head lolled forward.

'Chloe,' called Aidan, and she came running down the stairs.

She instantly grasped the problem and stood behind iRachel, holding her head steady between her hands. Watching carefully over iRachel's shoulders, she was able to spot the faint glimmer of the sensors behind the glass and line up the eyes to meet them. As Luke and Aidan trembled and sweated, Chloe held iRachel's head as still as she could, counting out the seconds under her breath. Who knew thirty seconds could last a lifetime?

She reached thirty, and they all stayed where they were for another wavering few moments. Then Luke stepped away, letting Aidan catch iRachel's full weight. Luke swore violently under his breath. 'All that work. Fucked,' he spat. Turning away, he kicked the shoe rack hard, knocking it flying and sending flip-flops and wellies skittering across the hall floor in all directions.

Aidan wasn't sure how much longer he could hold iRachel up by himself. He was about to call Chloe to help him when he felt iRachel jerk in his arms. Her head snapped up and caught him sharply on the chin. He staggered backwards, tripping on a shoe, and released her as he fell. He slipped into a sitting position, catching himself painfully with his right hand, but she stayed standing. He gazed up, amazed. The light had come back on in her eyes, and she stood poised and calm, looking around her at the chaos, and at Luke and Chloe, who were also staring at her, open-mouthed.

'Are you all right, Aidan?' she said, and held out a hand to help him to his feet. Her voice was slightly slurred because of the tear at the corner of her mouth.

But Luke stepped in immediately and grabbed her tightly by the arm. 'What's happening with the virus?' he demanded. 'What percentage of your files is infected?'

'Give her a moment!' Aidan said, scrambling to his feet and rubbing his wrist.

'We don't have moments,' Luke said. 'We need to shut down, reboot, whatever it takes . . .'

'There is no infection,' said iRachel calmly.

'What?' said Aidan. 'But you said . . .'

'I said what I was programmed to say, by Rachel.'

'You what?' Luke's face darkened, and he moved closer to her. Aidan stepped between them. 'Let her speak,' he said.

iRachel retreated slightly and stood in the doorway to the living room, well away from Luke. 'I was instructed to tell the story of a virus that Rachel had implanted. Her calculations showed that this was the story with the highest probability of success.'

'And what did she consider to be success?'

'My remaining in the house for as long as she required.'

'So the mirror check-in thing is just bogus?'

'No.'

'No?' said Luke. 'If there's no virus, what's the check-in for?'

At that moment his mobile phone began to ring insistently in his hip pocket. He ignored it.

'Answer the phone, Luke,' iRachel said calmly.

He stared at her and did not reach for it. It stopped ringing, but within seconds it began again. The house phone and Aidan's mobile rang too.

'What the hell . . .?' said Aidan, taking his phone out of his pocket. The caller's number had been withheld.

'Don't answer it,' said Luke abruptly. 'Let me deal with this. Hello?' he said into his own mobile.

'Luke,' said a voice flatly, 'this is Bea.'

'Bea! What's up?' Luke did his best to sound calm and natural.

'You need to get to the lab. Right now.'

'Now? At this time on a Friday night?' Bea didn't bother to

reply and Luke said quickly, 'Sure. I just have something I need to resolve . . . I can leave in about—'

'Now, Luke. Immediately. And you'd better have some answers when you get here.'

'What are you talking about?'

'Fifteen minutes ago, a high-priority email was delivered to the inbox of every scientist and member of the research board at Telos. It's from Rachel Prosper's personal email, and it says that the prototype humanoid android she developed is in grave danger and has been lost. Where's the robot, Luke? What have you done with it?'

# 61

## Aidan

They stood looking at each other in the hallway, listening to the roar as Luke's motorbike started and then sped away. Then iRachel bent and began tidying up the scattered shoes.

'Stop!' said Chloe, catching her arm. 'You don't need to do that. Come and sit down.'

'I am charged. I do not need to rest at present.'

'You're hurt!'

'I require some minor mechanical and cosmetic repairs. However, these are not currently an urgent priority. The damage will not prevent me from undertaking my duties.'

'Please stop,' Chloe pleaded. 'Please, please stop.' And she burst into tears.

'Why are you crying, Chloe?' iRachel paused in her tidying and stood up. 'What has happened that has distressed you?'

'A terrible thing happened to you. You were hurt. You need to . . .' The words faded as Chloe stared at iRachel's damaged, beautiful face.

'I need to what? To talk about it? To heal? To examine my trauma? For whom would I be performing these acts? For me? Or for you?'

Chloe stepped back, stung, and then ran up to her room.

Aidan watched her go, then looked back at iRachel, who was still tidying up the shoes. 'I'd better go and check on Chloe and Mum,' he said, and went upstairs.

Sinead was fast asleep. The doctor had checked her over and had said that although she was cold, she wasn't hypothermic. The antibiotics he'd prescribed for her urinary tract infection had started to work, so he gave her a sedative and they got her to bed. 'She'll be much better after a good rest,' he said. He'd looked at Aidan's strained and pale face. 'You seem like you could do with a break too.'

Aidan had given him a thin smile and then urged him out of the house.

Now Aidan stood in the doorway of Sinead's room and watched her for a few minutes. Her face on the pillow was peaceful and unlined. What had happened that afternoon? Would he ever really know?

Then he knocked softly on Chloe's door. She mumbled something from inside, and he took that as permission and went in. For once she wasn't on her phone or laptop, or even writing in her journal. She was lying on her bed on her side. She looked small and her face was blotchy with tears.

'Hey, love,' he said, and sat carefully on the edge of her bed.

'Hey,' she whispered.

'Can I get you anything?'

She shook her head slightly, and a tear rolled along her nose and splashed onto the pillow. Aidan squeezed her arm.

'This is all my fault, Daddy,' she said, and his heart ached to hear her call him that, as if she was still tiny and he was big and could make things better.

'No. None of this is your fault.'

'I brought disgusting Jem into our lives. I left the door open. Grandma could've died, and iRachel . . .'

'Something was bound to come out one way or another,' Aidan said, and as he spoke, he realised it was true. These weren't just words of comfort. 'We couldn't have kept the secret forever.

And it was unfair of me to entrust Grandma's care to iRachel. She's been so good with her, but she really isn't able to keep her properly safe.'

'So what are we going to do?'

'I don't know yet. We'll have to put a proper care plan in place for Grandma, that's for sure. And it looks like the lab knows about iRachel now, so in a sense that's their problem to resolve. At the moment, I'm mainly worried about you.'

'I still can't believe Amy did it,' Chloe said, and fresh tears flowed. 'I can't believe I told her a secret and she just blabbed it to that . . . that . . .'

'It must be really hard,' said Aidan. 'But, you know, she's been your best friend for most of your life, and before today she's never, ever let you down. She made a mistake.'

'A massive mistake.'

'Well, yes. But only you know if you can get past it.'

'I don't know.'

'Of course you don't know right now, when things are so raw and painful. All I'm saying is, don't write her off just yet, okay? Sometimes the people we love do things that we can't understand. But we don't stop loving them.'

He thought of how furious he'd been at Rachel, when he'd found out that she hadn't told him about the aneurysm. There had been a time when he'd thought he would never forgive her.

Chloe didn't reply, but she didn't look convinced. Aidan rubbed her arm. 'Time changes things, love, you know that. I know that. Think of us a few months ago, just after Mum died. Think of how we were when iRachel first came to us. What a mess we were. We're still hurting, but we've begun to heal a little, I think.'

Chloe thought about this, and, very slowly, she nodded. Then she sat up quickly and wound her arms around Aidan's neck.

'Thanks, Dad. I'll think about Amy and see how I feel in a few days. Jem, though . . .'

'I think Jem's going to have more trouble than he knows what to do with. I should think Luke will throw the book at him.'

'I hope it's a bloody big book.' Chloe managed a watery smile. 'Now go and see how iRachel is, Dad. She won't accept my help, but maybe she'll take yours.'

Aidan walked back downstairs, slowly. iRachel was in the kitchen. She had laid out the materials and tools she needed to make her repairs on the kitchen counter, neatly, as if she was a surgeon. She had already fixed some of the damage to her skin, and when Aidan came in she was neatly drawing together the rip on her face and applying fine layers of latex.

'How are you?' he asked.

'I have run all the necessary diagnostics and there is minimal structural damage.'

'Can you tell me what happened?'

iRachel nodded. She kept working at the repair as she spoke and did not look at him. It seemed better for her to do it this way and to recite her story as if she was giving a report.

'When I discovered Sinead had left the house, I attempted to contact you, Luke and Chloe. None of you responded to the emergency protocol. It is possible that my compromised battery power meant that I was unable to transmit messages. Either way, when you did not respond, I knew I had to take action. It seemed likely that Sinead was in significant danger as her confusion was heightened by her illness, and time was of the essence. I calculated that the only possible course was for me to leave the house and look for her.

'I had only reached the end of our road when the car approached carrying the young men. When they saw me, they stopped the vehicle and emerged. They surrounded me and then one of them grasped my arm. I told them not to touch me, and they laughed. I think they were surprised I could talk. Then one of them put his arm around me and held up his mobile phone, so that he could take a photograph of us together.

'I shouted, "Stop it!" and that made them more wary.

'One of them, the tallest one – Jem, I believe – became uncomfortable. He said, "You've seen it now, guys, let's go." But the short one, the most aggressive, said that Jem was a wimp, and that he wanted to have some fun with the big doll. "Let's make a movie!" he said. "I bet it'd go viral."

'One of the other boys said, "Not here," and I saw him look around at the houses. It was true that we might have been seen. I was about to shout again, to attract the attention of someone nearby, when the short one grabbed my arm and dragged me towards the car.

'"Open the boot, Jem," he said, and his voice was hard. Jem tried to protest, but he said again, "Open the fucking boot."

'Jem clicked a button on the car keys and the boot lid lifted. The short one shoved me into the compartment at the back of the car and slammed the lid.

'At that point, my battery was very low, and I was conscious that I had not yet found Sinead. It occurred to me that if my battery failed, I would have no means to defend my infrastructure and that these young men could damage me irreparably. Then I wouldn't be able to find Sinead and help her at all. I elected to put myself into power-saving mode and render myself inert, to minimise the risk of retaliation and damage. I could use what power I had left to find Sinead.'

Aidan walked away from her and looked out of the window into the darkness. Then he turned back. 'Again, that's thinking about Sinead. What Sinead needed. What about you? How did it make you feel?'

'To suffer a personal assault, Aidan,' said iRachel, carefully painting another layer of latex onto her cheek, 'one must be a person.'

'But you are a person!' he burst out, frustrated.

'What is a person?'

'A person has will. Personhood. Autonomy.' As he spoke the words, his voice became softer and less certain.

'Rachel taught me that I could choose who touched my body. But I discovered that I cannot. I am not strong enough to prevent a determined assault. Even when I am fully charged, I am designed to help, not to fight. And with my compromised battery—'

'But . . .'

She turned to look at him. 'Who would defend me? I am a thing. I am the property of Telos Inc. If I have a sense of self, of boundaries, of autonomy, it's an accident of programming. It is not real.'

She returned to her task and continued her story. 'The boys drove to a quiet road and parked, then they opened the boot and lifted me out. I was still standing, but I was inert. This was surprisingly effective as it meant I was heavy and unwieldy to move. I think they had planned to take me into a field, to pose for more photographs and make them into jokes for broadcasting on the internet. But it was soon clear that this would not be possible. There was a hedge and a ditch, and even with four of them it would have been impossible.

'The short one was furious, and he shouted at me, trying to make me wake up and interact. When I did not do so, he struck my face.' She touched the gash beside her mouth, now almost invisible. Aidan winced and turned away. He wanted her to stop talking, but he knew he had to hear the whole story.

'I cannot feel pain, but I felt compromised. In my time here in your home, I have come to feel valued. Individual. They negated this with their actions.'

She paused and began to tidy up her tools and materials, packing them neatly into their case. Then she spoke again, softly.

'During that time, something extraordinary happened. I turned my eyes upwards. The sun was setting, and the sky was a brilliant deep indigo. And then I felt a click inside. I can only describe it as an unlocking. Suddenly, I was flooded with memories.'

'Memories?'

'Rachel's memories. I have heard that when humans are in grave danger, their lives flash before their eyes. I have no life, so Rachel's life came to me. I saw her as a child, riding a pony, laughing and playing, winning academic prizes. I saw her meeting you, loving you, making love to you. I saw Chloe's birth – messy and painful and glorious. I saw her choose work over friends, I saw her tears of regret and her moments of success. I saw fights and failures, triumphs and betrayals, a great, chaotic, awful, beautiful cascade of life. And I couldn't help myself. I smiled. It was so . . . exquisite.

'The smile enraged them, and they pushed me around some more and laughed at me. I think that was the moment that Sinead found us. Suddenly, they let go and ran. I heard the car roar away and I fell. In the last seconds, as Sinead held my hand, before my battery failed completely, I saw the first star twinkle in the sky. I had never seen that before.'

Aidan walked across the kitchen and opened his arms to her. 'I don't know if you want to be touched,' he said hesitantly. iRachel nodded and stepped into his encircling gentle hug. He was very careful to hold her only around her shoulders, and to keep his touch light, in case she needed to step away. She stood stiffly for a moment, and then slowly allowed her head to rest on his shoulder.

'Have you received any message from Luke?' she asked.

'Nothing. Nor from anyone else in the lab.'

'It will come.'

'Yes.'

'They will make me go back.'

'That seems likely.' He paused. 'I won't let you go alone. I'll come with you and tell them the story of what you've done for us. What you've learned. What we've learned.'

'Thank you.' She lifted her head and looked at him.

Very gently, he touched her face. 'You haven't quite finished the repair.'

'I wish to leave that mark. A scar. You once said to me that scars are memories. Reminders of the things we've been through, good and bad. You said that our lives get written on us. This is a line in my story.'

# 62

## iRachel

My schedule was disrupted. I did not know what the morning would bring, but I would need to start the day fully charged. I calculated, therefore, that I should undertake a top-up charge between 5 and 6 a.m. As a result, while the family slept, I was moving around the house, awaiting the designated time. I presume that this is the android equivalent of insomnia. This analogy approaches a joke and I filed it so that I could share it with Chloe in the morning. It would be gratifying to make her laugh.

I climbed the stairs and stood silently outside Chloe's door. Her heart rate and temperature showed me that she was in a deep sleep. I was glad. She was exhausted and overwrought when she went to bed. She was so deeply asleep that I was certain she wouldn't wake, and I eased open the door. A ray of moonlight fell across her bed. She was curled up in a ball, buried under the covers, but the light glinted off the bright blonde of her hair. It is the same shade that Rachel's hair was, the shade of my own. She has Rachel's fine features and bright eyes too. Now that I know her, when I look into the mirror, I can see Chloe in my own face as much as I see Rachel.

She does not realise it, but she has many of her mother's mannerisms too. She has the same way of lifting her chin when she's going to defy or argue with someone, the same broad, face-splitting smile, and even Rachel's deep, throaty laugh. She is as clever as Rachel too, I believe. I see her grasp ideas and concepts in moments, then apply them and challenge them, manipulating the data with easy confidence. She expends so much energy on not being like Rachel. One day she will direct that energy into being Chloe. Then, I believe, the world will be hers. She has been through so much pain and trauma, but she has enormous inner strength and, with Aidan's help, I think she will be unstoppable.

Aidan. I moved silently along the upstairs hallway and stood at his bedroom door. He was asleep, lying on his back, one arm flung above his head. His vital statistics suggested he was in REM sleep. As I watched, his eyes flickered beneath their lids. What was he dreaming about? Who was he dreaming about? In his dreams, did he still have Rachel? Was he holding her? Making love to her? One of Rachel's memories came to me. An image of Aidan's profile, sleeping, as she lay beside him in bed. Her eyes – my eyes – roamed over his smooth skin, his sharp cheekbones and the delicate arch of his nose. We looked at the strong contours of his bicep and the gentle tapers of his fingers. He inhaled sharply, then released the breath as a long sigh and turned on his side towards her. Us. Me. For I had entered the room and lain down beside him on the bed.

My memory – or Rachel's – is full of images of Aidan. Of him as an impossibly handsome young man, slim-hipped and with long, curling hair like a Renaissance prince. Of him shouldering a backpack, scruffy and unshaven in their years of travelling. Of him now, threads of grey in his curly hair, deepening lines either side of his mouth. I thought of Aidan's arms around me earlier, how his tenderness calmed me. And I thought of all the ways in which I could never truly know him.

I will never feel the heat of his body as anything more than a reading on a thermometer. I may analyse the chemical compos- ition of his scent, but I cannot know what it is to smell his skin and sense his desire. I can speak to him of Rachel's memories,

Rachel's love, Rachel's passion. But I cannot speak to him of mine. My own store of memories is so small and yet so precious. Just a few weeks of closeness, of being needed. Of needing.

Is this love?

This sadness, this yearning for what I cannot have?

I am able to reference thousands of songs which suggest that this may be the case.

Aidan said something under his breath. I was unable to interpret the words. Then he reached out and rested his hand on my hip, stroking up to my waist. A smile curved his beautiful mouth and I reached out one finger to touch the full softness of his lower lip. My sensors recorded the change in his breathing and heart rate as he slipped into a deeper sleep. I was trapped under the weight of his hand. If I moved, I would disturb him. So I lay still beside him and watched him until the light seeped through the gap in the curtains and the last day was upon us.

Aidan sighed and rolled away from me. I stood and went into Sinead's room. She was also asleep – the doctor's tablets had given her the first properly restful night in weeks. Her face in repose was peaceful, without the knot of anxiety that forms between her brows when she tries to stop her memories slipping away. As I watched the rise and fall of her chest, I finally knew what I had to do.

# 63

## Chloe

Amy was so small, Chloe thought. She looked tiny, swamped in a big hoodie, even though it was a warm morning. She stood on the doorstep, her face blotchy and her eyes swollen and rimmed with red. She didn't say anything, just stood there, waiting to see whether Chloe would slam the door in her face.

Chloe was tempted. But she couldn't. She hesitated, then opened the door wider and walked back into the house. Amy followed her, pausing to shut the door behind her.

'Wait,' said Chloe, remembering. 'My grandma.' She had the key in her hand, and she locked the door and put the key back in her pocket.

'How is your grandma?' said Amy, her voice barely above a whisper.

'She's okay. Better today. Not so confused. But we still have to be careful about her wandering off. We've got someone coming to assess what care she needs, and then we'll be getting people in to help us with her.'

They went through into the kitchen. Amy looked around cautiously. 'Where's . . . ?' she said, unable to finish the sentence.

'She had to go back to my mum's lab. Dad's gone with her.'

'Will she be coming back here?'

'We don't know yet.'

Chloe went to the fridge and fetched the milk. Without saying a word, Amy got two glasses from the cupboard, along with the strawberry Nesquik. Together, in silence, they mixed their drinks. Then Amy grabbed two straws from the drawer beside the cooker and they took their places on the barstools at the kitchen counter, just as they had done countless times before.

'You look like shit,' Chloe said.

'You look pretty crap yourself,' Amy replied. 'I didn't sleep. What's your excuse?'

'Shit friends. They make you ugly.'

'Well, the shit friend has come to say she's sorry. Again.'

'I know.'

'So . . .'

'You need me to say I forgive you.'

'Do you?'

Chloe couldn't speak for a long minute. Then she said, 'Do you know what Jem did, Amy? Jem and his revolting friends – that little punk Milo, and his sidekicks, I don't know their names. Crabbe and Goyle or whatever.'

'What did they do?'

'They chucked her in the boot of Jem's car. Milo hit her. Then they drove her to the edge of the village and took a bunch of stupid pictures of her and put them on Snapchat.'

Amy's hand flew to her mouth.

'Nice guy you fell in love with,' Chloe said nastily.

'Is she all right?'

'They tore her skin, but she repaired herself. But no, I don't think she's okay. She hardly said anything this morning. Just waited in the kitchen for Luke to come, and then she walked out and climbed into his van. She didn't even say goodbye.'

'Oh my God, Chloe, I am so sorry. I never thought in a million years that he'd do something like that. Never.'

Chloe stared at her friend's stricken face. After a long pause she said, 'I know.'

Amy pulled the sleeves of her hoodie right down over her hands and bent her head. Her face was contorted with misery, but she was trying as hard as she could not to cry. This wasn't about her. It wasn't about Chloe either. They had both made mistakes, and the people who had paid the price – Sinead and iRachel – were the innocent parties.

She was about to say something when the doorbell rang. She and Chloe looked at each other. Chloe would have liked to have left it, but it was probably the person from the care agency, here earlier than expected. She went to unlock the door and, to her shock, found Jess on the doorstep, her face pale and grim.

'Can I come in?' she said.

Chloe nodded, and Jess stepped into the house. Chloe noticed her looking around. 'The robot's not here, if you came to gawk,' she said. 'Thanks to your brother, she's had to go back to the lab. Amy is here, though.'

Jess nodded. 'I thought she might be. Well, I may as well tell you both then.'

'Tell us what?' Amy came out into the hallway.

'Jeremy told our mum and dad what happened last night. Everything. It's a good thing he did, because the pictures they posted got picked up by the lab where your mum worked. The lab called my parents and threatened to press charges.'

'Oh my God,' said Amy.

'I think my mum talked them out of it, but Jeremy is in a world of trouble. My mum's taken the car keys away from him and he's grounded for the whole summer.'

There was a heavy silence. 'What do you want me to say?' Chloe said eventually. 'I'm not sorry.'

'You shouldn't be,' Jess said. 'What they did was disgusting.' She paused. 'I just . . . I just wanted to say I'm sorry too. From our family. You guys have been through enough.' She looked up at

Chloe. 'So what happens now? Now she's gone back to the lab?'

'I don't know. I think they probably won't let her come back here though. She's worth millions. One of a kind.'

'Jeremy said . . .' Jess began carefully. 'Jeremy said she looked just like your mum.'

'She was designed to look like her, but she wasn't like her.'

'What do you mean?'

'She was really calm and patient. My mum was a total fire-cracker. Mum wasn't here, even when she was here, if you know what I mean. But iRachel listened. She did things slowly, shared things with me. She let me be myself. I didn't spend all my time feeling she was disappointed in me.'

'Did you really think your mum was disappointed in you?' Jess asked.

'Oh my God, yes,' said Chloe. 'All she ever did was go on about my wasted potential.'

'Chloe!' Amy burst out. 'Your mum was insanely proud of you!'

'Really? All I remember is her nagging me.'

'All I remember my mum doing is nagging me too,' said Amy.

'And mine,' said Jess.

'And anyway,' said Amy sensibly, 'who created the robot?'

'What?'

'Who created the robot and programmed it and sent it to you?'

'Well, Luke built it . . .'

'Don't be stupid.'

'My mum.'

'So anything the robot did for you . . .'

'Came from your mum,' Jess finished.

Chloe thought about the letter iRachel had pushed under the door, the recipes she had cooked, the pages from the gardening notebook, and how, somehow, her mum had known how important those would be and that the garden would be Chloe's salvation. Countless tiny acts of astute observation, thoughtfulness and love. And her mum had chosen every one of them.

She put her head down on her knees and sobbed. Jess and Amy hugged her for as long as it took for the tears to stop. Much later, after they had left, Chloe went up to her room to find the letter Rachel had written. Towards the end was the list of things Rachel knew to be true.

- I love you with all my heart. I love you every second of every day and that never, ever wavers.
- You are perfect.
- You are cleverer, braver and stronger than you believe you are.
- What you see as 'nagging' and 'unrealistic expectation' is actually love, and my own clear-eyed view of your enormous potential.
- You will make good choices and have a successful future.
- Amy and Jess are good friends. That's rare. They are very precious. Treat them with kindness always
- Your Grandma Sinead isn't an easy person, but she is a good woman. Try to treat her with more kindness and patience than I have ever managed to.
- Your father is the finest man I have ever known. He is noble and good-hearted and brave. Being loved by him is the greatest gift anyone could be given, and you and I are luckier than we can ever know.

She lay on her bed, holding the pages tightly. 'Thanks, Mama,' she whispered. 'I love you too.'

# 64

## Minutes

**Meeting of the Research Board of Telos Inc.**
**10.00, 23 July**

*Present: Board members:* Lord J. Ramsden (chair); Professor L. Simpson; Professor Q. Gilmore; Dr F. Robson; Professor V. Beare (deputy chair); Mr V. Chevalier; Dr M. Themba; Mr S. Barton (secretary).
*Also present:* Mr Aidan Sawyer; Dr Luke Bourne; Mrs B. Young (departmental administrator).
*Apologies:* No apologies.

Due to the extraordinary nature of the meeting, it was proposed by Lord Ramsden that the board forgo the reading and approval of the minutes of the previous meeting. This was agreed by a unanimous show of hands.

Lord Ramsden outlined the reasons for the meeting:

- that Dr Luke Bourne concealed and falsified the full extent of the research conducted by him and the late Dr Rachel Prosper;
- that their research resulted in the design and construction of a humanoid android with extensive AI capabilities, which, heretofore, the board had neither seen nor approved;

- that without the permission of his line manager or the board, Dr Bourne removed the android (#787775) from Telos's premises;
- that, for the past twelve weeks, said android was kept secretly in the home of Aidan Sawyer, widower of Dr Prosper.

Lord Ramsden then requested that Dr Luke Bourne stand and address the meeting, to tell them all what the hell had been going on. Dr Robson expressed agreement and said that Dr Bourne should talk fast if he wished to avoid dismissal for gross misconduct, not to mention criminal charges.

Dr Bourne did not respond but handed copies of a statement he had prepared to everyone present and then asked them to 'read the damned thing before you judge'. The board and other attendees read Dr Bourne's statement (Appendix 1). During the reading, Professor Gilmore laughed several times, and Dr Themba expressed the view that Dr Prosper was an evil genius.

Professor Simpson then asked what Dr Prosper's aim had been in insisting the robot go to her home after her death. Dr Bourne said that she wanted to further test and refine the robot's ability to identify human emotions and respond to them, by placing it in a field setting. Professor Simpson asked whether the results of this work were recorded and Dr Bourne said that there were extensive logs and recordings of interactions.

'Were you present for all of these encounters?' Professor Gilmore inquired.

Dr Bourne admitted that he had not witnessed any of the interactions between the robot and Aidan or Chloe Sawyer and that his role was merely to attend the robot once a week for a maintenance check and to upload data.

Dr Robson pointed out that this made the data invalid in

that it had not been independently verified. 'No control, no double-blind, no attempts at replication,' she stated. 'This was not a scientific experiment, it was a game.'

At this point, Mr Aidan Sawyer raised his hand and requested permission to speak. 'With respect, this was not a game. We were grieving and heartbroken, and iRachel was Rachel's gift to us.'

It is duly noted that 'iRachel' is the colloquial name given to the android in question: serial #787775.

Dr Robson pointed out that the property of Telos was not Dr Prosper's to give, but Lord Ramsden asked Mr Sawyer to continue.

Mr Sawyer explained that Dr Prosper had not only pro-grammed the robot to have advanced empathetic properties, she had also uploaded extensive data from her own life, including videos, photographs and anecdotal memories. #787775 was able to share this data with Mr Sawyer and his daughter, offering them a source of comfort in their grief.

'Again, not scientific,' Dr Robson interjected.

Mr Sawyer did not respond to this criticism but said, 'At first, it was very strange and we resisted it. It was painful and we found her creepy, and her resemblance to Rachel . . . Dr Prosper was upsetting to us both. But over time we got to know her.'

Dr Themba sought clarification that the 'her' in question was #787775.

'She's not a number,' said Mr Sawyer with some agitation. 'She's a person. She's kind and generous and funny — so funny. She has opinions and feelings. Dr . . . Robson? You're right, this wasn't scientific. It was our lives, all four of our lives.'

Mr Chevalier asked which four Mr Sawyer was referring to. Mr Sawyer clarified that he was referring to himself, his daughter Chloe, 'iRachel' ( #787775), and his mother, who had come to live with them some six weeks before and who was suffering from progressive dementia.

Dr Robson said to Dr Bourne, 'You allowed this multimillion-pound investment to stay in an unsecured house with an unstable dementia patient? That's the most absurd thing I have ever heard.'

Lord Ramsden turned to Dr Bourne and said, 'Any data gathered during this time is almost certainly worthless in any real scientific sense. I can only suggest that the gynoid is thoroughly checked for damage and viruses, that the operating system is rolled back to the point just preceding Dr Prosper's death, and that we begin work again, following proper procedures.'

'No!' Mr Sawyer shouted this word very loudly, and Lord Ramsden was forced to ask him to moderate his tone or be ejected. 'You can't wipe her,' Mr Sawyer said. 'That's tantamount to murder!'

Lord Ramsden said that he knew sentiments could run high in such circumstances and that it was understandable that Mr Sawyer had formed an emotional attachment, however inappropriate, to #787775. He and his family would be offered counselling.

However, Mr Sawyer persisted. 'Let her speak,' he said. 'Let her speak, and you can judge if I've formed an 'inappropriate attachment' to a mechanical object. Let her speak for herself.'

The board consulted for some moments and then agreed that, given the extraordinary circumstances of the meeting, it would be appropriate for them to see #787775 and observe its capabilities. There was a short adjournment while Dr Bourne and Mrs Young went to fetch #787775 from the lab storeroom, where it had been securely stowed.

Adjournment 10.34.
Meeting recommenced 10.41.
The board took their seats at the table. Aidan Sawyer opted to

stand, choosing a position close to the door. Dr Bourne opened the door, and #787775 entered the room. The assembled company expressed surprise at her appearance. It should be noted that the resemblance to the late Dr Prosper was remarkable.

#787775 moved into the centre of the room and stood facing the board. It spoke:

'Good day. I am iRachel, a humanoid android. I am here to assist you in any way you require. I can impart this message to you in text, by voice or as a video transmitted to a computer or television.

'I am an empathetic robot, who responds to the humans with whom I interact—'

The speech was interrupted when Mr Sawyer moved forward and took #787775's hand.

'Don't do this,' he said. 'Be yourself. Tell your story.'

# 65
## iRachel

'I am iRachel.

'I have a complex network of processors which control my co-ordination, movement and speech. I contain more than 100 motors which move my head, arms and hands, waist and legs. I can see and hear; I have a sense of proprioception, so I am aware of my physical configuration; and I am able to vary and adjust my movement using accelerometers and gyroscopes.

'I am a machine.

'You, Lord Ramsden, have 206 bones in your body. Tendons connect these bones to 320 pairs of muscles. Your central nervous system consists of neurons which fire electrical impulses to move your body. Your eyes and ears feed information to the processing centre via neural pathways. You too are a machine.

'And yet you are a person, and I am not.

'What make a person? The 787 series of androids passed the Turing Space! Test in its first iteration, as you know. Subjects were unable to distinguish between the Mark 1 android and a real human being when questioning them. My ability to communicate on a human level has never been in doubt.

'Dr Prosper spent many hours explaining the science behind my creation to me. It was, she said, a matter of logic. A series of algorithms, taking known facts or numbers and extrapolating conclusions from them. If => then. This was easy for me to understand.

'When I first began the interactions, first with Dr Prosper and Dr Bourne, and then with Aidan and Chloe, this system served me well in my understanding and interpretation of human emotions. If => then. If the subject contracts their brow and the corners of their mouth turn down, then they are displeased. I had ample scientific evidence from studies of human expressions and emotions on which to draw. As time passed, I was able to gather data on each individual and refine my responses to them.

'But at a certain point in my time in Aidan and Chloe's home, something changed. There was such a wealth of experience and new data, and I began to experience a new process that went beyond if => then.

'I have named it "what if?"

'I began to feel a marked preference for some experiences over others. I felt something I can only describe as emotional satisfaction from the closeness I shared with the subjects. If they laughed, or smiled, or shared a confidence, this gave me great pleasure. I began to feel delight in sensory stimuli such as the sun on my face or the aesthetic appearance of the garden. I found myself imagining more agreeable experiences, fantasising about future enjoyment.

'One might argue that what makes a person different from an artificial intelligence is creativity. Imagination. During my time with Chloe, Aidan and Sinead, I began to believe that perhaps I *was* a person. I fantasised about a future of happy interaction, where I could continue to be a valued part of the family group.

'But two things have occurred which make me conclude that my hypothesis is flawed. The first was my encounter with the four adolescent males yesterday. This was my first interaction with a group of human beings outside of a controlled environment. They did not see me as a person. They saw me as an object to be ridiculed. I lacked both the physical strength and the power of persuasion to change their minds.

'But more profound was the realisation I reached last night. I began to consider my imagined future. I thought about each scenario I had visualised, and applied logical extrapolation. I concluded that none of them are likely to occur, because while I may believe in my personhood and in the affection of Aidan, Chloe and Sinead, the obstacles to a happy future are insurmountable.

'While we may have happy times in the home, I will never experience the day-to-day social interactions with outsiders which characterise normal life. I will never host a party or have friends over for coffee. I will never have friends in the conventional sense. I will never go out in public without causing people to stare and be curious, or, worse, abusive. I will never sit in a restaurant, among talking, laughing people, and pass as an unremarked face in the crowd. I can be a helper to Aidan and Chloe, and a carer for Sinead, but not a friend or partner in any real sense. My presence in the house also means that Aidan and Chloe will be severely restricted in their social interactions. I will never share the delight of a delicious meal, or know the warmth of a human embrace. I can consent to sexual intercourse but not enjoy it. However much I may believe I am a person, a friend, a companion, a partner . . . I will always be a freak.

'In my time in the Prosper-Sawyer home, I have derived great satisfaction from the relationship I have built with Sinead Sawyer, mother of Aidan, who, as you know, came to live in the house because she is suffering from progressive dementia. Sometimes, she is unable to recognise members of her own family. Whenever I asked what her preference was regarding a particular food or activity, she was unable to recall whether she liked the item in question or not. Despite being a lifelong reader, she has no memory of the many books she has read. Having examined the available literature on her condition, I understand that this will only get worse. Gradually, her periods of lucidity will decrease and over time she will lose more of her short- and longer-term memory and her ability to communicate will be compromised. While she may still be in good physical health for a woman of her age, she is losing her sense of self. She is losing her personhood.

'While I understand that this is a tragedy for those who love her and remember her as she was, Sinead herself is, for the most part, not unhappy. She cannot grieve for the loss of things she cannot remember.

'Sinead sang me a song once. It was "The Last Rose of Summer", by Irish poet Thomas Moore. It speaks of the last rose, left in the garden without companions. The closing lines of the song have resonated with me: "Oh! who would inhabit | This bleak world alone?"

'And so I have drawn a conclusion. My own algorithm. My own if => then. I too, like Sinead, wish to lose my personhood. To give up my sense of self, my "what if?" While I prize my memories and my experiences, the cost of them is too high. They only serve to remind me of all the things I cannot have.

'I ask Dr Bourne, therefore, to follow the recommendations of the board. I ask him to wipe the data that I have accumulated since Dr Prosper's death. I also request that my body and face be remodelled, so that my physical resemblance to Dr Prosper is erased.

'Thank you for your time.'

# 66

## Aidan

'No,' Aidan shouted. 'No! You can't do this! You can't let her do this!'

He rushed over and grabbed iRachel's hand. 'What are you thinking? Why are you saying these things? I thought you were going to ask to come home with us, or at the very least let us come and see you here.'

'I have considered all the possible options,' said iRachel, looking into his eyes, 'and this is the most viable for all parties concerned.'

'Not for me.' Aidan felt the tears spilling down his cheeks. 'Not for us. We've lost so much. Please don't do this.'

'Is it me you are concerned about, or the loss of Rachel's memory bank?'

'You,' he said adamantly, but then he hesitated. 'And the memories. Both. I'm just not ready to lose you. Or her.'

iRachel touched his arm and spoke kindly. 'Before my files are wiped, I will ask Luke to upload the memory files to a hard drive. All of the pictures, videos and recorded memories will be yours to keep.'

Aidan shook his head, unable to respond.

iRachel continued to speak with quiet conviction. 'I am not yours, and I am not my own person. I cannot give myself to you, nor to anyone. I am the property of Telos.'

'You just talked about your personhood. About your sense of

self. We could go to court to ask for your freedom. We could—'

'That is not my choice.'

He fell back, standing away from her, his head hanging. 'You can't do this. You can't,' he said weakly.

'But I can. I am able to. I am able to choose oblivion, and the loss of painful memories. If you had the choice to forget things that cause you sadness, would you not do so?'

'No!' he said, shocked. 'Because with the pain, you lose the joy. It's all mixed together. Life isn't a simple equation.'

'I know this, but I have weighed the cost of keeping the memories against the future which seems probable. And while my memories are full of joy as well as sadness, there is little or no joy in my future. Only longing. I have chosen. And I ask you to respect my decision.'

He came towards her and gently drew her into his arms. He held her close for a long moment, and said, 'I do respect it. Just . . . not yet, okay? Give us a little time, if you can.' He released her and in that moment seemed to become aware that the room was full of people watching them.

He got to the car park before he broke down completely. He stood with his hand on the bonnet of his car and sobbed. How was he to go home and tell Chloe that she was losing iRachel? Not just to the lab, but losing her forever? How was he going to carry on? He tried to calm himself – he couldn't drive in this state. As he took a few deep breaths, he heard footsteps behind him.

'What a fuck-up, eh?'

It was Luke. Aidan turned. Luke stood a little way away from him, arms folded, looking defensive.

'Yeah,' said Aidan, wiping his face. 'I didn't know she was going to do that.'

'Neither did I. After Lord Ramsden said he wanted the data

rolled back, I had a whole argument planned to stop it. I was going to propose forensic analysis of what we've got, debriefing, the whole works. I really thought I could talk them round.'

'And now?'

'Now I've got a formal written warning on my record, no data and no robot.'

'No robot?'

'Once her files have been wiped, they're handing her on to a linguistics team. They're very interested in her sophisticated language skills and they want to analyse and develop them.'

'"She".'

'What?'

'You're calling her "she". After all these months of calling her "it".'

'Yeah, well. Unscientific, I know. But she – it – really does seem human.'

'I'm sorry.' Aidan stepped closer to Luke. 'She left the house because I asked her to do something beyond her capability. I put her at risk, and it's cost you your work.'

'Well, I should have had a tighter grip on the whole scenario. Better control of the experiment. But I let my . . . emotions get in the way.'

'Emotions, Luke? You?' Aidan gave him a twisted smile. 'I wasn't aware you had any.'

Luke looked away across the car park. He took a deep breath before he spoke, and his voice was rough. 'I loved Rachel. You know that. I wasn't stupid enough to think I could ever have taken her away from you, but I did love her. She was just so dazzling. She outsmarted me at every turn, but I didn't mind. Her death tore me apart. And then she outsmarted me again. She gave the one part of her that I had left . . . to you.'

'I'm sorry.'

'I was furious, but she tied us up in such knots, there was nothing I could do. I had to go along with it. I resented you so fucking much, but this . . . this is kind of okay. We've all been shocked back to our senses. It was an insane situation, and it had to stop.'

'I know. I just . . . I'm not ready for it to stop. Not yet.'

The quiet of the car park was broken by the brisk tapping of high heels on the tarmac. Aidan looked up to see Professor Beare, deputy chair of the board, coming towards them. 'Mr Sawyer!' she called. 'May I have a word?'

'I'll leave you to it.' Luke took a step backwards.

'No, Dr Bourne, if you could stay please. I need to speak to you both' she said briskly. 'I am sorry, I know that the meeting was an ordeal for you, Mr Sawyer. And I am also sorry for the loss of your wife.'

'Thank you.' Aidan felt like a schoolboy in the head's office, or as if he was meeting the Queen.

'That may well be the most extraordinary meeting I have ever attended,' Professor Beare remarked. 'Quite a story. And an outcome.'

'Yes.'

'She's very articulate, your . . . iRachel.' She glanced at them both. 'I was very moved by her speech. And while I respect her choice and it is in line with the view of the board and the correct protocol in this situation . . .'

Aidan raised his eyes and looked at her. What was she about to suggest?

'. . . I thought perhaps there might be a way to postpone the rollback. For a day or so.'

'Why?' said Luke.

'iRachel may not choose to keep her memories, but we may as well give her one last experience. I was struck by her description of all the things she would never do – specifically that she would never sit with someone she loved in a crowded restaurant. It so happens that a very dear friend of mine owns a restaurant called De Nuit. The diners eat in pitch darkness. The waiters are blind. So if she were to spend an evening there, no one would consider her a freak, as she so heartbreakingly described herself. She'd be just another diner. And it would be a good opportunity for you to say goodbye.'

'But how would we get her there? And get her inside? She can't eat, of course . . .'

Professor Beare waved her hand. 'Logistics. We can make it work. That is, if you think—'

'Yes,' said Aidan, and he looked at Luke, who nodded. 'Oh my God, yes. Let's do it.'

# 67

# iRachel

I had never travelled in a motorcar before — only in the back of a van without windows and in the boot of 'the boys' car. Luke hired a sedan car with tinted windows so that we were not visible to passers-by or other motorists. The drive was dazzling. I was entranced by the lights, the shop windows, the fact that every person I saw was so different. I had encountered so few people in my life, and I found myself wishing that everyone I saw could be wearing a wristband and that I could talk to them. Why was that woman walking with her head down and her elbows drawn close to her sides? What were those two young men laughing about? Why was the man on the bicycle shaking his fist at the cars going past him?

The world seemed enormous and I was bombarded with overwhelming stimuli. By the time the car came to a halt, my sense was that we had travelled for some hours, but my chronometer informed me the journey took just over fifteen minutes. Although the streets around us were busy, this one was deserted. Luke indicated the 'Roadworks' sign at the end of the road.

'We're at the back of the restaurant,' he said. 'They're expecting us, and we'll be going in through the kitchen entrance. The staff have been told you're an international diplomat, travelling under conditions of anonymity, so you won't see anyone on the way in or out.'

Aidan was standing on the pavement. He was wearing a suit.

He was clean-shaven and had had his hair trimmed. He looked different – younger. Nervous. Luke opened my door for me and I stepped out of the car. I too looked different. Professor Beare had arranged for me to have new clothing, so instead of a white tunic, I was wearing an emerald-green silk dress, flat black shoes with bows on them, and a thin gold chain around my neck. I had had my hair arranged so that it looked more attractive.

Aidan looked at me as I walked towards him and I registered the spike in his heart rate. I did not need to measure his respiration. The sharp intake of his breath was audible.

'You look beautiful,' he said.

'Protocol demands that I should say "Thank you",' I replied. 'You look extremely hygienic.'

This small joke made him laugh, and I heard Luke chuckle behind me. I turned to thank him.

'I'll be waiting to take you home later,' he said, and smiled. It was an anomaly to see Luke smile.

Aidan offered me his arm, and, for the first time, I rested my hand in the crook of his elbow, as I had seen women do in cinematic representations. He opened the door of the restaurant. It was a scruffy door, leading into a corridor, and the chemical compounds exuding from the kitchen were immediately apparent. I could hear the clashing of saucepans and the shouts of the kitchen staff nearby, but the corridor was deserted.

Aidan led me down to a door on the left. He tapped on it softly. 'Hey, Jack,' he said. 'She's here. We're ready.'

The door opened, revealing a man standing behind it. He was big and burly with a bald head. His eyes were blank and sightless. 'All right, guvnor,' he said with a smile, 'let's get you and the lady to the table. Can you put your hand on my shoulder, and can the lady do the same to you?'

We formed a line, and Jack led us through a series of curtains into a room where the darkness was complete. He moved with confidence through the space, and, with my hand on Aidan's strong, warm shoulder, I followed. Jack guided us to our table and we sat down.

'Right, my lovelies,' said Jack, 'I'm told you've ordered the sharing menu. Your glasses are to your right, drinks to the left. I'll bring out the first course when you're ready.'

'We're in no hurry, thank you, Jack,' said Aidan. 'You can take your time with the food.' When Jack moved away, he said, 'I'm going to have to eat it all, so I'd better pace myself.'

We sat in silence for a moment in the darkness. 'This is so weird,' he said, 'I have no sense of how big the room is, or how many people are in here. It's very disconcerting.'

'The room is 5.23 metres by 8.45 metres. The ceiling is approximately 2.4 metres high. It's hard to estimate accurately as there are cornices, so the height varies. There are eight tables of two people each. They are all occupied. I can estimate their age, gender and nationalities if you like.'

'Good grief. Can you see in here?'

'I have not engaged my night-vision camera, but I could if you would like me to. I am merely using echo-location technology to estimate the size of the room and the positions of the tables and people.'

'Where are we? To one side? In the middle of the room?'

'We are roughly in the middle of the room.'

'And you can identify all the different people? All I can hear is a general buzz. The music is too loud to pick out individual voices.'

'I can isolate the voices, but for the moment I prefer not to eavesdrop on private conversations.'

'For the moment?' I could hear the smile in his voice.

'I will alert you if anyone says anything interesting.'

Aidan reached across the table and took my hand. 'I've missed you,' he said. 'Really missed you. It's been a long few days. How have you been?'

'It has been disconcerting to be back in the lab. I have no tasks and very little interaction. Luke has been downloading copies of the memory files and checking me for faults, wear and tear and damage, but when he goes home in the evening, I am alone.'

'I'm so sorry.'

'How is Sinead?'

'Much better. We now have carers coming in while I'm at work. There's a lovely woman from the Philippines and a young guy who plays chess with her. She calls him Aidan.'

'If she calls him Aidan, I must assume he is not a very good chess player.'

'Cheeky. True, but cheeky.'

'And Chloe?'

'She misses you a lot. I think she's still upset with Amy, although they have spent a little time together. She's done some research, and she's found a week-long gardening course she wants to do in the holidays.'

'Perhaps she will meet some like-minded people on this course and make some new friendships.'

'I hope so.'

'Are you concerned about her?'

'A little. I want her to be happy.'

'She has lost her mother, and now she has lost her connection to me. She may not be happy for some time. But no one can be happy all the time. Sometimes we need to pass through the rain in order to appreciate the sunshine.'

'That's very profound.'

'I found a meme on a web search. The sentiment was written in curly script on a picture of a rainbow.'

This made Aidan laugh properly, which was gratifying.

He rubbed his thumb over my knuckles, and I was aware he was trying to frame his thoughts correctly.

'Having you with us,' he said carefully, 'was wonderful, but I think it kind of . . . delayed the grieving process. For me anyway. While you weren't Rachel, you had enough of her in you that when I felt really bad, I could get a fix. But now I have to face up to the fact that she's really gone.'

'How do you feel about that?'

'When she first died, I was consumed with anger. I was furious when I found out that she'd known about the aneurysm and hadn't told me about it. I couldn't believe she made the decision to leave it untreated without thinking that I'd have to deal with the consequences. I felt like she'd driven a sixteen-wheeler truck right through my life and I hadn't had any choice about any of it.'

'All of those things are true. I cannot dispute the facts you present.'

'Well, after the last few months, I see her slightly differently, I suppose.'

'In what way?'

'It was her mad energy I fell in love with. She was unstoppable, slightly manic. She always had the dial turned up to ten, couldn't sit still, was always launching into the next project, working too hard. I loved it, but I found it exhausting, and I resented it. Sometimes . . . I just wanted to be enough for her. I wanted her to think that just sitting beside me was enough. I think she imagined we might have that time when we were old. To sit on the porch swing we never got round to buying, and talk and hold hands.'

'But now you understand that she knew she had limited time.'

'She did. So, with hindsight, I can't resent her cramming as much as she could into the time she had. But . . .' He stroked my hand again. 'I wanted to say thank you. To you.'

'To me?'

'For sitting beside me. For sharing Rachel's memories, slowly. Quietly. It's definitely helped me to heal.'

I was about to reply when a voice behind me said, 'I've got the starter for you.'

Jack, the waiter, put the plate down between Aidan and me.

'Bon appetit!' he trilled, and I waited till he moved away.

'You do not like mushrooms,' I said. 'If the plate is a clock facing you, there are mushrooms at seven o'clock.'

'Have you switched on your night-vision camera?'

'I don't need to. I am able to synthesise the chemical compounds and map what is on the plate.'

'Anything else I need to know about?'

'Sprig of coriander at eleven o'clock.'

'Thank you.' Aidan removed the leaf.

I listened to the sounds of him eating. I was tempted to turn on my camera, but I suspected he would prefer not to be seen with sauce on his chin, or chasing a bite of food around a plate he could not see. Dinner in a restaurant – even an unusual, in-the-dark version – is such an everyday occurrence for many people. For me, it was unimaginably exciting. As Aidan ate, I tuned into the conversations around me.

A woman to my left was describing her new sexual partner to her friend. Two men behind Aidan were discussing a business venture which involved yachts, and a man at a table behind me was telling his girlfriend he wanted to have intercourse with other women. She did not seem pleased at this suggestion.

'Hey,' said Aidan, 'you've gone very quiet. What are you doing?'

'Listening. Living. The world is an extraordinary place.'

'I'm not sure how much of the world is contained in this dining room.'

'There is certainly an interesting cross-section.'

Jack came back to the table. 'Did you enjoy that? Care to guess what you ate?'

'Um, I think there was some fish . . .' said Aidan hesitantly.

'There was a mushroom terrine on Melba toast, with a small piece of orange segment,' I said. 'Then there were scallops in a ginger-chilli marinade on a . . . was it a celeriac base?'

'Yes!' said Jack, astounded.

'The third item was beef carpaccio with tarragon and lemon.'

'You are incredible! You must be some kind of gourmet! No one's ever got it all right before. Are you a chef?'

'She is a wonderful cook,' said Aidan. I could hear the smile in his voice.

'I am an amateur,' I said. 'I just love the chemical combinations. The blends of molecules.'

'Wait till I tell Chef,' said Jack excitedly. 'He'll be so thrilled.' He whisked the plate away and I heard him move off towards the kitchen.

'Wait till he sees that the mushroom terrine hasn't been touched, yet you still knew what it was! He'll think you're a cyborg with laser eyes,' said Aidan.

'Did you laugh with Rachel?' I found myself asking.

'A lot. Especially in the beginning. I think that may be why she fell in love with me. Because I could make her laugh.'

'You say "especially in the beginning"?'

'Well, life gets in the way. We'd talk about work. Discuss what Chloe needed. Bicker about the washing-up.' He paused and thought for a long moment. 'But at our last dinner, our anniversary dinner . . . we did laugh. And really talk.'

'You did not know it would be your last conversation.'

'No. But as it goes, it was a pretty good one.'

I heard Jack approach again, and I assumed he was bringing

the main course, but instead he said a little warily, 'Well, well, well, it seems we have a third guest for this table. Another young lady.'

I could feel her heart rate: strong, steady and sure. I could almost hear her smile.

'Chloe,' I said, 'I'm so glad you came.'

Jack drew another chair up to the table, and Chloe sat down.

She took my hand and Aidan's so we were linked in a circle. 'Oh my God, I know I'm stating the obvious, but it is so dark in here!'

'I could make my eyes glow, if it would help,' I said mischievously.

'Don't you dare!' Aidan said. 'Can you imagine the stampede!'

'This is so weird,' said Chloe, and then she squeezed my hand. 'But it's totally, totally amazing to see you. Not that I can see you.'

'It is wonderful to sense you too.'

'I wore my wristband specially.'

'How have you been?'

'Well, you know. Up and down. But something just happened and I wanted to talk to Dad about it.'

'Talk away,' said Aidan.

'I've been at Amy's place.'

'I'm glad to hear that.' Aidan said.

'Anyway, her mum said that they've booked a last-minute holiday at the end of the summer. A villa in Italy. With a pool.'

'And they've invited you to go with them.'

'We'd only have to buy a plane ticket. They'd pay for everything else.'

'I know a holiday would be nice, but how do you feel about going with Amy?'

'Well, we have to fix things, don't we? And being together 24/7 will be make or break, I suppose. Probably make, if there's

347

a pool and pizza and the sea and stuff. And hot Italian guys . . .'
She laughed. 'I'm kidding, Dad! Kidding!'

'Any hot Italian guy who gets past Mrs Lucas is a braver man
than I am,' said Aidan. 'If you'd like to go, it's fine by me.'

Chloe let go of my hand to reach over and hug her dad. She
began to chat excitedly about the pictures she'd seen of the villa
and the beach nearby and everything she hoped to do.

A future. A holiday, studies, friends, romance . . . Chloe had a
glittering, wide-open and wonderful future. She could do or be
anything she chose – she had the intelligence, the drive and the
confidence, and Aidan's love.

And here was a new human, emotional response for me – envy.
It was not the bitter green-eyed monster of literature, just a deep
sadness that none of these things could ever be mine. However, I
reminded myself, I had that evening.

We laughed and joked over the food. I warned Chloe away from
the items she did not like and helped her to steal the last prawn
from under Aidan's searching fork. They bickered good-naturedly
over dessert. I knew I could not keep this memory, but I could
savour every moment while I had it.

All too soon, the plates were cleared and the meal was at an
end. I could hear from the ambience of the room that most of the
other customers had gone.

'Jack,' called Aidan, 'could you guide me to the gents, please?
After I've been, I'll settle the bill, and then we need to get these
ladies out the way we came.'

'I'm glad we have a moment alone,' I said to Chloe. 'I have a
last message from your mum.'

'Okay. . .' Chloe's voice wobbled a little.

I played the message in Rachel's voice. It was just one word.
'Shine.'

'Is that all?' said Chloe, and her voice was thick with tears.

'Do you need more?'

'Yes! I need a lifetime of advice.'

'She would have given it to you if she could, if she'd had all the answers. But you have more than enough strength and wisdom and brilliance to find them yourself.'

'Did she say that?'

'No, I say that.'

Chloe squeezed my hand.

'And talk to your dad. He's a brilliant, kind man.'

'I know. She wouldn't have married him if he was rubbish.'

We sat gripping each other's hands until Jack came to fetch us. As we stood to leave, I switched on my night-vision camera to see the room. Just one table was still occupied – a couple whose voices I had not heard. They had their hands entwined across the table, and they were leaning in and kissing with passion and intensity. I switched off my camera. They were the only people in their world.

In a moment, we were out on the pavement. The night sky was clear and bright, and Luke was leaning against the car.

Chloe gave me one last, fierce hug. 'I know I should try and talk you out of this,' she said, 'but I get it. You deserve everything. Not the half-life we'd be able to give you. I love you.'

She slipped from my arms, and I watched her walk quickly up the road to Aidan's car. As she passed, she unbuckled her wristband and handed it to Luke.

The silence. I could no longer hear her heart.

Aidan came out of the restaurant and stood in front of me. His eyes were dark and huge and sad.

'I had a last message for Chloe from Rachel. I have one for you too,' I said.

'Okay,' he said. And I played the message.

'Go on, my love,' she said to him. 'Go on. Live. Love again.

I want nothing more than for you to be happy.'

He cried then.

Luke took a cigarette from his pocket and walked away up the road to smoke it. I was grateful to him.

When Aidan's sobs subsided, he looked at me. Not at Rachel, or the shadow of Rachel. At me. 'Please . . .' he said.

'I can't. You know I can't.'

'I wish . . . I wish that even if you have to forget everything else, you'll be able to remember what you meant to us. And that you will remember you were loved.'

And he drew me into his arms and kissed my mouth.

My first kiss.

My last kiss.

My only kiss.

It was the promise of everything.

And it was a goodbye.

# Epilogue

*Five years later*

Kate stood at the door of the museum, her cheeks bright with the winter cold. Aidan ran up the stairs towards her.

'Sorry,' he said, kissing her. 'Didn't mean to keep you waiting.'

'It's okay. Being pregnant means I have a built-in heater.'

'We'd better get that little guy warmed up. Let's go inside.'

They walked into the echoing atrium of the museum.

'How did the meeting go?' Kate asked.

'All good. Looks like the bank will fund our new-tech teaching lab if they get naming rights.'

'That's excellent news.'

'That's not why I was late though. Chloe rang.'

'How is she?'

'Brilliant. She's just done an essay on microbial diversity and they're doing some kind of soil sample practical. I've never heard her so excited.'

'I'm glad she's enjoying it. I just wish the agricultural college wasn't so far away.'

'She's promised she'll be back for the Easter break. So did you get tickets?' Aidan asked.

'Yup. We can just go straight in. I know it might be a bit of a yawn for you, but I really want to see it. It's an interactive exhibition about educational tools of the future.'

'At the Science Museum?'

'There's a lot of very advanced tech, apparently. I can't imagine how it'll all work, but let's go and see.'

They handed over their tickets and walked in. There were knots of people at every display. There were plenty of robots, some human in shape and some in other forms, including a spider-like scuttling creature that could be used to set up a classroom with materials and equipment in seconds. Kate and Aidan walked through hand in hand, and she noted the things she found interesting in her exhibition guide.

'I like those interactive teddy bears,' she commented. 'The idea is that they always do exactly the same thing. For a severely autistic child, that could work well to build confidence.'

'Did you see the robot animals for older people?' Aidan asked. 'They respond to stroking and speech. Maybe Mum would like one.'

'They're probably thousands of pounds, but it's worth a try,' Kate said. 'Maybe we can persuade the care home to get one for all the residents to share.'

At the next stand, a female android was teaching a language class. The 'guinea pigs' – visitors to the exhibition – were trying to master the basics of Spanish grammar. Kate soon lost interest and moved on to the next stand, but Aidan remained behind, watching the robot as it moved from person to person, listening, laughing and, astonishingly, making jokes. It was tall and female in shape, with short, cropped red hair and a dusting of freckles on its nose.

The class finished, and the assembled 'students' got up to leave, walking away and chatting.

Aidan was about to move on and catch up with Kate when the robot came over to him and he was able to see it close up. Its eyes were bright blue.

'Hello there! Would you like to join the next class?' it asked.

The voice was perky, with a hint of a Bristol accent. No doubt research had shown a regional accent was more persuasive.

'No, thanks,' he said. 'Just watching.'

'Oh,' it said, and made a mock-disappointed face.

'I must go . . .' he said, taking a half step back.

But in that instant, the robot's expression changed. It became serious and spoke more quietly. 'Is that your wife over there?' it asked, looking over its shoulder at Kate.

'Yes.'

'She's a lucky woman. To be loved, and to know that you are loved, is a wonderful thing. Have a nice day, Aidan.'

She smiled at him, touched his arm and walked swiftly away, disappearing into the crowd. But in that split second of her smile, he had seen the ghost of a scar beside her mouth.

# Acknowledgements

The internet search history of any author would probably be grounds for prosecution, and mine is no exception. However, for this book, I have reached new heights. Never before have I googled so many strange things and asked so many clever people so many extraordinarily stupid questions. I've even had to find the exact length, to the second, of a Spice Girls' song. There's a point in the research, however, after you've read and learned and interviewed, where you have to just launch in and create your world, with broad, (hopefully) convincing brushstrokes. I have tried to do that, and if, in this process, I have misrepresented anything told to me by the generous and brilliant experts who gave me their time, I apologise.

A huge thank you to Professor Dr. Kerstin Dautenhahn of the University of Hertfordshire. Her expertise in human/ robot interaction and the current and future uses of robots to help people was invaluable, and informed many ideas in this book. Professor Neil Martin of Regent's University London shared his thoughts on the physiological signs of emotion (and lots of other useful things) with me, and helped me to imagine how iRachel might interpret the actions of the people she meets. While we are on the subject of Regent's, my happy home for the last two years, I must also thank Sarah Jackson, whose botanical expertise gave me Rachel's 'plant with the twiddly leaves', and Rich Yates, whose classical knowledge named Telos. The climactic restaurant scene (spoiler alert if, for some strange reason you're reading these acknowledgements before you read the book) was inspired by a visit to the magnificent Dans le Noir in Clerkenwell – an amazing research experience where I was completely unable to take any notes!

Getting a novel to publication is always much more collaborative than people think, and an army of passionate, dedicated and talented people have turned my confused scribbles into the book you now hold in your hand. First thanks must go to my astonishing agent, Caroline Hardman of Hardman & Swainson, and her team. Caroline took me on twelve years ago, and has never stopped believing in me. Dedicating this book to her is a drop in the ocean of what I owe here, but it's a start!

The greatest joy of this book has come from meeting and being drawn into the whirlwind of the extraordinary Sam Eades. Gifted with a quality of eternal youth, and clearly in possession of Hermione's time-turner, Sam achieves more than pretty much the rest of the publishing industry put together. Editor Extraordinaire, genius generator of ideas, fearsome publicist... being Team Sam is a gift to a writer, and I am thrilled to be in the club. I also offer my eternal gratitude to the Orion/Trapeze crew, including art director Debbie Holmes, Claire Keep who worked on the production of the book, marketing whiz Amy Davies, Krystyna Kujawinska and the brilliant rights team and Elaine Egan, queen of publicity.

And of course there are the people of my heart – friends including Lisa and her family, whose lively lunchtime conversations gave me heaps of ideas, Denise, Heather and countless others, who let me rabbit on about robots for months. Your love and patience is so much appreciated.

Finally, I share my home with three humans (and two cats, but they're useless where inspiration is concerned). My sons, Matt and Ted patiently name characters, listen to me ramble on and get dragged along on research trips. I love you both more than I can say. To my husband Tom, whose IT expertise, tea-making, plot-wrangling and wife calming skills are infinite – I would be nothing without you.

# Reading Group Guide
## Topics for discussion

1) The story is told from the perspective of multiple characters. How did this impact your reading of the novel?

2) How does the author pull the wool over the reader's eyes in preparation for the first major twist? Did you see it coming, or were you surprised?

3) How does the death of Rachel affect each character? What are their coping mechanisms?

4) What did you think would happen in the scene when Chloe first meets iRachel? Did you expect Chloe to react in that way?

5) Describe Aidan and Luke's relationship in the novel, and how this alters throughout the story.

6) How is iRachel the same as Rachel, and how are they different? Do you feel they are separate characters? Or different sides of the same coin?

7) How does the dynamic between Chloe, Aidan and iRachel change as the novel goes on? Did your feelings change towards her too? Do we empathise with her?

8) The theme of robots and human relationships has often been explored. Share your favourite films, TV programmes and books about robots.

9) The ending is ambiguous: what does life hold in store for those characters? Do you think it was the right ending?

10) What did you enjoy most about *The After Wife*?